THE HEART OF EVERTON INN

BETWIXT THE SEA AND SHORE
BOOK 2

The Heart of Everton Inn

Betwixt the Sea and Shore Book 2

CLAIRE KOHLER

ISBN: 979-8-9855674-1-0

To Dawn:
The greatest fan and grandmother-in-law I could ever ask for.
Thank you for your love and support. You are a blessing and a
treasure.

Acknowledgments

Thank You, Lord, for the strength, inspiration, and time that was needed to complete this novel.

Thank you also to all the people who made this book possible. My family and friends were such a great support throughout this challenging endeavor.

Thank you to my launch team for the time they put into reading and sharing this story with the people around them. Thank you to Meghan Black, Becky Briggs, Ava Brown, Lydia Brown, Janice Broyles, Patsy Case, Sydney Castro, Lois Corrigan, Carrie Joiner Cotton, Bethany Cox, Isa Deal, Tricia Dehler, Kendall Draughn, Norma Draughn, Missy Durham, Slavka Edelmayer, Sarah Everest-Jindrich, Leslie Fitzpatrick, Elizabeth Haber, Keri Hamilton, Charity Henico, Brooke Hickman, Karla Holdier, Kristi Horton, Kylie Hunt, Heather Isales, Shirley Kale, Amanda Keller, Dorcas Krug, Renee Lewis, Beth Ann Marlowe, Laura Marlowe, Sherry Marlowe, Pat Martin, Felipe Marulanda, Ashleigh Mays, Kim Moore, Jordan Moore, Darleen Nelson, Carmen Post, Dorislynn Quiñones, Sheri Small, Danielle Smith, Aimee St. Amand, Maxie Sue, Julia Sweet, Dianne Vanhoy, Margie Vanhoy, and Hannah Waldo.

And special thanks go to Donald Morrison, my critique partner, and Shea McIntosh Ford, my sprinting partner.

Prologue

John Burgess had almost finished sowing the bere[1] for his field when a slight, brown-haired boy darted up to him. It was mid-afternoon, and the two of them had both been hard at work since they finished lunch a few hours before.

"Da', may I go see my friends?" William asked, trying not to squirm as he awaited his father's decision.

John always insisted on completing chores before doing leisure activities, and today was no exception. "Have you finished yer chores, son?"

The young lad nodded enthusiastically. "Please, Da'. Blaine and Christopher said they had something important to tell me."

"Is everything in the right place in yer room?"

"Aye," he said, clenching his hands together.

"Did you finish washing the clothes?"

"Aye," he repeated, his volume rising.

"Did you sweep all the rooms?"

"A—" William grimaced and shifted his gaze to the dirt.

"Well?" John pressed, raising his eyebrow.

The boy fidgeted a bit with his hands before mumbling, "Na exactly . . ."

"And what does that mean?"

"I did all the rooms except the kitchen." William looked

---

[1] A type of barley grown in Orkney.

up and gave his father his best smile as if this would help his chances.

But the redheaded farmer shook his head. "Then I suppose you can' 'exactly' go play with yer friends."

"But, Da'—"

"How about I take care o' it?" offered a new voice.

The two of them turned to see Henry Milligan just outside the gate. The young man's bright green coat stood in stark contrast to John's worn shirt and vest. Most of Hollandstoun's residents were too poor to afford luxurious clothing, but Henry had found much success since moving here and becoming an apprentice to the local coppersmith.

"Henry, hello," John greeted with a tight smile, trying to hide his impatience with his son.

"Hi, Mr. Henry," William squealed, waving to him. "Did you really mean it when you said you'd sweep the kitchen fer me?"

The man ruffled William's hair and nodded. "Aye, so why don' you go ahead and go see yer friends?"

The boy glanced at his father to make sure it was all right and then scurried down the road.

"Just make sure yer back in time fer dinner!" John called to the disappearing figure.

"You really shouldn' be so hard on him. The lad has been through a lot. You both have. Have you even talked about her since she died?" Henry asked gently.

"What are you doing here, Henry?" the farmer asked, ignoring his friend's comment as he swiped some sweat from his brow. The days were growing warmer, and coats such as Henry's would soon be too heavy to wear.

The younger man grinned. "I just wanted to let you know I'll be leaving soon. I received word that my sister's babe has been born, and I'd like to attend the christening."

"That's exciting news, Henry. I'm surprised yer planning to go back though. Didn' you swear you'd never go back there? Something about it being too dull fer you?"

The man flushed and put a hand on his neck. "Aye, I did say that. But that was two years ago, and this would be a great time to tell my sister about Sonneta."

"You haven' told her yer getting married?"

Henry shrugged.

Has he learned nothing since he got here? John wondered. *I was hoping a bit more responsibility would have rubbed off on him by now.*

"When do you leave?"

"First thing in the morneen[2]. I've already told Sonneta my plans, and she was elated. She has been dying fer me to tell my sister about our betrothal ever since I proposed."

John frowned. "It almost sounds like yer na taking her with you."

"That would be right," Henry replied.

"Why na?"

"Sonneta has a lot to do right now, planning the wedding and all. . . ." Henry trailed off, his eyes sliding back and forth. "Anyway, I just wanted to let you know. I'm na sure how long I'll be gone. I hope 'twill just be a few days since Sonneta will be missing me, but my sister will probably try to keep me there as long as she can."

The man chuckled, but John saw through his ruse in an instant. *Why wouldn' he want to bring his intended to meet his relatives? I know he said he left on bad terms, but were they that bad?*

Henry hadn't shared much about his life in Everton, and John had been kind enough not to pry. Unfortunately, that meant the farmer knew almost nothing about the small village north of them. *Perhaps his sister will be angry when she sees him? But Henry said she'd want him to extend his stay. Hmm.*

"Well, I hope you have a pleasant time," John said. "Be sure to stop by in the morneen before you go. William will want to say goodbye. He's very fond o' you, you know."

Henry's smile stretched over his entire face, something it often did when William was around. "And I'm very fond o' him, too. He has been a good friend to me since I arrived here."

Henry's expression turned more solemn as he clapped John on the shoulder. "And you've been a good friend, too."

John grinned in return. "Likewise."

"I just wish you could forgive yerself fer what happened.

----

[2] Morning.

'Twas na yer fault."

When the farmer's mouth hardened, Henry turned up his hands. "Anyway, I'll see you in the morneen."

John said nothing as his friend turned and made his way back up the road, for the farmer knew without a shadow of a doubt that Henry couldn't be more wrong. By the time evening came, John fully expected William to come charging through the door with a rumbling belly. The boy was small for his age, but John liked to say he had the appetite of a starving horse.

When John opened the door and didn't spot him, though, he started to get concerned. It wasn't like William to be late, and he knew better than to make John worry over him.

John waited for a long while, his anxiety and agitation growing with every passing minute. But, as the sky darkened, William still didn't return.

When the mantel clock struck seven, John decided he'd waited long enough and went to the door, but as he opened it, the boy stumbled inside, his chin suspiciously tucked into his neck.

"William? What's wrong?"

"Nothing, Da'," William said, trying to slide past his father and go inside.

But John grabbed the lad's shoulders and said, "Look at me, William."

When the boy looked up, John spotted what he'd been trying to hide: a large bruise on William's cheek.

"What's this?" John took hold of the boy's chin to examine him.

William pulled away and moved his gaze to the ground.

"William?"

"I fell, that's all."

"That doesn' look like it came from falling. Did one o' the other lads hit you?"

William's shoulders sagged, and he nodded, still keeping his eyes on the ground.

"What happened? Did you get into a fight?"

William slid his shoe around in the dirt. "James was saying all these awful things about Mum. That she didn' really die and had just run off and left us because she didn' want to be with us anymore."

John seethed. "The nerve o' that lad. Why, I'll—"

"Da', don'," William said, grabbing his father's arm. "Please don' do anything. 'Twill just make it worse."

"Has this been going on fer a while?"

William nodded.

"Why haven' you said anything?"

"I . . . I knew you'd be upset. Usually, I can handle it when everyone's talking like that," he said with a shrug.

"Everyone? What do you mean, everyone?"

William flinched. "Did I say everyone? Nay, I just meant . . . um . . ."

He licked his lips as he searched for something to say, but John just crossed his arms and waited.

After a few seconds, William sighed in resignation. "All the other bairns make fun o' me now."

"What about yer friends? Christopher and Blaine?"

"That's what they wanted to tell me today. That we couldn' be friends anymore."

John pinched his nose and took a deep breath as he tried to rein in his anger. It wouldn't do any good at this point. What he needed to focus on right then was how best to help William.

Then an idea came to him. It wouldn't solve everything, but John was sure it would put a smile on his son's face.

"William, would you like to take a trip?"

Proper Greetings

Orkney Islands,[3] 1759

Adaira Stubbins drew in a hearty breath of morning air, swinging the basket in her hand as she practically skipped through the market. Most people weren't in such good spirits at seven o' clock in the morning, but the innkeeper's daughter was almost perpetually cheerful. At least, that was what her neighbors thought.

Today, though, the woman had a special reason for being so upbeat: she was preparing for a christening feast[4].

Gregor and Elspet Martin's first child, a tiny, sweet-tempered girl, had been born two weeks ago, and they had asked Adaira if she would be in charge of the christening feast since she was the best cook in town. These celebrations always took place right after the child's baptism, and that was supposed to be tomorrow, so Adaira had a lot of work to do.

She'd already talked to all the other women who would be cooking, and she'd bought most of the food she needed, but Adaira had realized the night before that she didn't have enough carrots and onions.

Good thing Mr. Buchanan had what I needed, she thought as she glanced at the lovely vegetables in her basket.

---

[3] An archipelago in the Northern Isles of Scotland.
[4] The last of three feasts to celebrate the birth of a child. This was celebrated directly after the child's christening (baptism).

Cooking was one of Adaira's greatest joys in life, for it reminded her of her times in the kitchen with her mother, Valerie. Today, she was also hoping it would afford her with a good distraction from the argument she'd had the day before with her father.

Adaira exhaled a long breath, making her light-brown hair fly about her face. *I thought time would make things better, but it almost seems like he's getting worse.*

Ever since Adaira had lost both her mom and brother when Valerie Stubbins had gone into labor too early, her father, Terrence, had become someone Adaira barely recognized. His drinking habits had spiraled out of control, and even when he was sober, he was so unpleasant that most people avoided him as much as they could.

"Need any fish, lass?" Vincent McLaren asked as Adaira passed his stall. The smelly, middle-aged fisherman pointed to an impressive display of fish, all freshly-caught, from the looks of them.

Adaira gave the man a half-smile to be friendly, but she didn't dare step closer. Mr. McLaren had always made her uncomfortable with the strange things he would say. And she still remembered those scary stories he'd shared when she was a bairn[5]. His tales of monsters and death had been so vivid she'd had nightmares for weeks anytime she heard one.

"Can' say as I do, Mr. McLaren, but if that changes, I'll be sure to let you know. I just needed some carrots and onions this morneen[6], and Mr. Buchanan gave me plenty," she explained, showing him her basket.

"Ah, in that case, have a nice day, Mistress Stubbins. I'll be seeing you morn[7] then," the almost-toothless fisherman said with a grin.

Adaira inclined her head in thanks before continuing her trek back toward the inn. Not many people were out yet since it was so early in the day, and she was especially surprised when she spotted a familiar head of blond hair perusing the jewelry at Mr. Kennedy's stall.

---

[5] A child.

[6] Morning.

[7] Tomorrow.

"Good morneen, Elspet!"

The second woman turned around quickly, her mouth curving upward at the sight of Adaira. "And good morneen to you!"

The innkeeper's daughter looked her friend over, noting the bags under her eyes. She put a hand on Elspet's arm. "Should you be out and about yet? You only just had yer babe two weeks ago!"

The other woman rolled her eyes. "Don' you go fussing over me, too. Gregor's doing enough o' that as 'tis. We already had the fittin' feast[8] three days ago, and you know that means 'tis time I get back to my duties as a wife. Besides, Briony said I was completely healthy."

"Oh, that makes me feel a lot better."

Briony Fairborn was not only Everton's sole midwife, but she was also Adaira's dearest friend. If Briony thought it was safe for Elspet to resume her everyday responsibilities, then that was good enough for Adaira.

Elspet nodded, but Adaira didn't miss how her face dimmed. Even though Briony's skills were well-respected, her illegitimate status made her an outsider in the town. The fact that Adaira was so fond of the midwife was something no one could understand, and had Adaira not been such a kind, likable soul, she probably would have been shunned for even associating with Briony.

"Do you think you'll be able to come to the christening itself, or will you be too busy with all the food?"

"O' course I'll be there! I daresay the whole town will be. . . . Well, except my father, that is. I'm sorry about that," Adaira said, breaking eye contact with her friend.

That had actually been the reason for Adaira's argument with him the day before. No matter how much Adaira had pleaded with the man, she hadn't been able to convince him to attend. Instead, Terrence was planning to stay home for both the christening and the feast afterward since he didn't see any reason to celebrate bringing another mouth into the world.

---

[8] The second of three feasts to celebrate the birth of a child. This was an intimate dinner for the immediate family. It also marked when a mother was to return to her normal household tasks.

"Don' feel bad, Adaira. I don' hold it against you in the slightest. Yer doing so much fer us already. Gregor and I can' thank you enough."

Adaira brushed off her friend's words. "You know how much I love cooking, and when 'tis fer such a happy occasion as this, that just makes it even better."

Elspet's eyes shot past Adaira, and her expression became sheepish. "Actually, do you think there will be enough food fer a few extra people?"

"A few? Who else is supposed to be—"

"Adaira! Is that you?"

The young woman twisted around at the familiar voice, only to find herself face to face with none other than Elspet's brother: Henry Milligan.

The man who'd broken her heart two years ago.

He's here? When he didn' come to the blide-mael[9] last week, I thought that meant I wouldn' have to see him again. He made it very clear he wanted nothing more to do with Everton when he left. And nothing more to do with me . . .

A cascade of memories swept through her as she stared, and it was all she could do to keep her feet planted on the ground when her heart was screaming for her to run the other direction.

He looks almost exactly the way I remember him. . . .

He was as handsome as ever, with his strong jaw, dimples, and dark eyes that seemed to pierce her very soul. His skin was tanner than the last time she'd seen him, and Adaira wondered if he'd had to work many long days out in the sun.

"I must say 'tis very heartening to see you this morneen. How have you been?" Henry asked with a charming grin.

But Adaira didn't miss the distance, the propriety of his demeanor. As if he was talking to an acquaintance he hadn't seen in a long time.

Adaira bit her lip to keep it from trembling, but she couldn't stop moisture from gathering in her eyes. *Is that how yer going to treat me? As if we're na important to each other? You once told me you loved me. . . .*

---

[9] The first of three feasts to celebrate the birth of a child, given to visiting relatives and friends.

When she didn't answer, Henry's smile faded, and he turned to the man beside him that Adaira hadn't noticed before then.

"This is my friend, Mr. John Burgess."

The innkeeper's daughter flushed, embarrassed at how out of sorts she was, especially in the presence of a stranger. She put on a welcoming expression and extended a hand of greeting. "A pleasure to meet you, Mr. Burgess. I'm Adaira Stubbins."

Mr. Burgess, a redheaded gentleman with a thick beard, took Adaira's hand tenderly in his own. "And you as well, Mistress Stubbins. I've heard a lot about you."

Adaira's blood went cold as she stared into the man's friendly face. *How much has Henry told him? Could he know about—*

Mr. Burgess's eyes widened, and he dropped her hand. "All good things! No need to look so concerned. Mostly about yer incredible cooking, which I'm very eager to try."

"They just got here last night. Mr. Burgess wanted a change o' scenery, so Henry brought him along. *Without* asking me first," Elspet said, raising her eyebrows at her brother.

Henry put his hand on the back of his neck and laughed. "Ah, I figured you'd be so happy to see me that you wouldn' mind if I brought some friends."

Elspet's reprimanding gaze shifted in the blink of an eye, and soon, she was patting her brother on the arm. "You know I'm just teasing. I'm glad you've been doing well in Hollandstoun, and 'tis good to meet yer friends. The only thing is, there's na enough room in our house. Adaira, would you mind if Mr. Burgess and his son stayed at the inn?"

Adaira started to nod her assent, but then her brain picked up on one of the last things Elspet had said. ". . . Son?"

Mr. Burgess stepped around Henry and replied, "Aye, he's—"

"—Here, I am!" shouted a voice behind her.

Adaira jumped and spun around, her stomach colliding with the voice's owner in the process.

"Ow!" cried a brown-haired boy, no older than eight, as he toppled to the ground.

"Oh, my! I'm so sorry! Are you all right?" Adaira quickly

squatted and held out her hand.

The boy grumbled under his breath as he took her hand and rose to his feet. When he first looked up, his face held a scowl, but almost instantly upon meeting her gaze, his mouth lifted into a shy smile. "Aye, 'twas nothing, mistress! You'd have to be the size o' a whale to hurt me!"

Adaira raised an amused eyebrow. "A whale, huh? I did na think I was quite *that* large."

The boy's dark eyes widened as he realized how offensive his words sounded. "Um, I-I . . ."

A chuckle drew everyone's attention back to Mr. Burgess. "I've told you that big mouth o' yers is going to get you into trouble, son. Apologize to Mistress Stubbins before she decides na to give us a room."

The lad gasped, clearly taking his father's joke seriously. "Sorry, mistress!"

"My son was so busy trying to see everything that he didn' stay still long enough fer me to introduce him." Mr. Burgess gestured for the boy to come over.

The lad hung his head and shuffled to his father's side while Adaira tried not to giggle at how adorable he was.

"Let's try again. This is William." Mr. Burgess clapped a hand on the boy's shoulder.

"How do you do, William? You can call me 'Adaira,'" the innkeeper's daughter said, smiling as she held out her hand.

"How do you do, A—"

"—*Mistress* Stubbins," Mr. Burgess interrupted with a pointed glance at his son.

Adaira's cheeks heated, for she hated getting others into trouble.

"My apologies, Mistress Stubbins, but we'd never presume to be so familiar with you when we've only just met," Mr. Burgess said with a polite nod.

Adaira bent down to William's level and whispered at a volume she knew the adults could still hear, "Then we'll just have to get to know each other fast, won' we?"

Guilt and Shame

Adaira led the Burgesses up the hill toward Everton Inn, glad that Elspet and Henry had stayed behind in the market to buy a few items. It was much easier to put on a smile and be lighthearted without her former sweetheart nearby.

How sad that I'm more at ease with strangers than I am around the man I thought I was going to marry.

She took a covert peek at her companions as they walked, noting how different their appearances were. Mr. Burgess was of average height but broad-shouldered and muscular, with eyes bluer than a summer sky. William, on the other hand, was short and slim, with eyes so dark they seemed black.

William must take more after his mum. I wonder why she didn' come, too.

"Mistress Martin told me you do most o' the work running the inn now. Are yer parents just na up fer it anymore?" Mr. Burgess asked.

"Actually, my mum died ten years ago, and my father . . . he hasn' been the same since she passed."

Mr. Burgess winced, guilt coming over his face.

Adaira waved her hand back and forth. "Don' feel bad fer asking."

But the man seemed just as uncomfortable, so Adaira quickly changed the subject. "What do you do fer a living, Mr. Burgess?"

"I'm a farmer. I have a—"

"—What's that?" William interrupted, pointing toward a large building as it came into view.

A beautiful, two-story house stood a few feet off from their path. The building's features were mostly the same as its neighbors'—it, too, had a thatched roof and stone slabs—but there was something about the house that just made it more vibrant than the rest of town. Perhaps it was the thick green ivy making its way up the walls. Or perhaps it was the lovely view of the horizon on either side of it.

But Adaira liked to think it was the hospitality she showed everyone who entered its gate, for this building was none other than Everton Inn, her pride and joy.

The woman grinned as she answered, "That's my home."

"Wow . . . I've never seen a house that tall before," William said, craning his neck to glimpse the very top of the chimney.

His father, too, was peering at her home with wide eyes.

Adaira snickered. "Well, 'tis na just a house. 'Tis also the town inn."

The boy stumbled backward a bit. "You mean that's where we get to sleep?"

Mr. Burgess rolled his eyes, but the corners of his mouth were turned up in amusement. "Weren' you listening earlier?"

William shrugged.

"If you think that's impressive, you should see where the tacksmen[10] live. And Laird[11] Oliver's mansion!" Adaira told the boy.

"There's a mansion in Everton?" he asked, slack-jawed.

"Well, it pretty much is, but make sure you don' call it that in front o' the laird, otherwise you'll hear all about how many bays and stories a house has to have to be a 'mansion.'"

She bent down and whispered, "Most o' the people here don' particularly care about those details."

William smiled. "Thanks fer the warning!"

---

[10] Scottish landholders whose rank was just below lairds and just above the farmers they would sublet land to.

[11] Scottish equivalent of a lord who owned a large piece of land in the community.

"Anytime you want to know something about Everton, you just come to me." Adaira winked and stood back up. "Perhaps I can take you to see the laird's home while yer here. Would you like that?"

The boy nodded so enthusiastically his head looked like it might fall off. "Aye, please!"

Adaira glanced at Mr. Burgess, who said, "If it doesn' inconvenience you too much."

The woman shook her head and started walking again. "Nay, I'd be happy to take you there. I can introduce you to Laird and Lady Oliver at the christening feast morn, and we can ask them about seeing it. I'm sure they won' mind."

"Well, as long as 'tis no trouble, that would be great," the farmer said warmly.

At this point, they were coming up to the inn's front door, and Mr. Burgess jumped in front of Adaira to open it for her. "Let me get that fer you."

"Thank you," Adaira said, feeling mildly flattered.

Did Henry ever open doors fer me? I can' recall.

Briony Fairborn was standing in the foyer when they entered, and her face instantly lit up upon seeing her friend. "Finally! I was wondering when you'd arrive! Would you mind if I helped you get ready fer the feast? I'm sure you have everything under control, but I need something to take my mind off—oh, you have guests."

Briony let out a self-conscious chuckle as Mr. Burgess came in, William following close behind him.

Adaira smirked, enjoying her friend's embarrassment. "Mr. Burgess and William, let me introduce you to Briony Fairborn, my greatest friend in all the world and Everton's midwife. And, Briony, meet Mr. Burgess and his son, William."

"How do you do," Mr. Burgess said with a grin. "I suppose congratulations are in order fer you also."

Briony cocked her head to the side. "What fer?"

"Fer a wonderful job delivering the Martins' wee lass. Mistress Martin told us the babe wasn' breathing when she was first born and 'twas only yer quick thinking that saved her life."

"Briony comes from a long line o' midwives, some o' the best Orkney has ever seen," Adaira said, only too eager to brag on her talented friend.

Briony flushed at the compliment and said, "'Tis just lucky I remembered what my mum did when that happened to the McGuffs' lass. . . . Oh, you know the Martins then? Are you here fer the christening?"

Mr. Burgess shifted a bit before answering. "In a way. I really just wanted to give William a chance to go somewhere new since he has only ever seen Hollandstoun. Say hello, William."

Everyone looked to the boy, but he was just gawking at Briony as if he'd seen something shocking.

Mr. Burgess nudged him. "William, what are you doing? 'Tis rude to stare."

After another second, William rubbed his eyes as though waking from a dream and said, "There's something funny about you, mistre—"

William turned to his father, who had just swatted the boy's back. "I didn' mean it badly, Da'. Honest!"

The boy gaped at Briony once more. "'Tis just that you remind me o' my mum."

Briony's black eyebrows squished together. "Oh, really? Does she look like me?"

"A wee bit, but yer eyes are too yellow. Hers were dark like mine."

"Were?" Briony asked before she and Adaira both turned to Mr. Burgess for clarification.

Mr. Burgess's gaze flickered to the floor. "She . . . died six months ago."

Briony gasped. "I'm so sorry." But then she fixed her attention on William in much the same way he'd been staring at her. "Actually, you remind me o' my mum, too."

What's she talking about? Adaira wondered as she looked from Briony to the boy. *Bethany Fairborn didn' look like him at all—*

From the corner of her eye, she saw Mr. Burgess's mouth harden. *He must be offended. I better say something fast.*

"Well, let me go ahead and show you two yer room. Briony, would you take these vegetables to the kitchen?" Adaira said, practically shoving her basket into the midwife's hand before ushering the Burgesses down the hall. The two of them followed behind her without a word, and Adaira was grateful Mr. Burgess didn't say anything about Briony's strange comment.

Once she'd left her new guests in their room, though, a trace of bitterness ran through her. *There I go again, always smoothing things over. One o' these days I'm just na going to say anything and Briony will have to deal with it herself.*

But when Adaira reached the kitchen and saw her friend already hard at work on a pie for the christening feast, she leaned against the doorway and sighed. *Poor, sweet Briony. You may be terrible at people skills, but yer still the best person I know. And now that yer mum's gone, I'm the closest thing you have to family. That means 'tis up to me to protect you.*

And yer secret.

"You did want this one to be a chocolate pie, right? I certainly hope so since that's what I'm making," Briony said without looking up.

Adaira pushed herself off the doorway and strolled over to the midwife. "Aye, that's right. But, Briony, there's something you should know."

"What is it?" Briony asked, her focus on the bowl of batter in her hands.

"Those new guests, the Burgesses? They came here from Hollandstoun." Adaira looked at her friend pointedly.

"So what?" The midwife dipped a finger into the batter and put it in her mouth. "Hmm, needs more sugar."

"Don' put yer fingers in the food!"

After Briony reluctantly complied, Adaira came back to what she'd been about to say. "Anyway, Hollandstoun . . . I guess you don' remember, do you?"

"Remember what?"

Adaira gulped. "The other person who lives in Hollandstoun."

"Who?" Briony asked, this time giving Adaira her full attention.

Adaira braced herself and mumbled, "H-Henry Milligan."

"Henry Milligan?!" The spoon in Briony's hand flew across the room, and the entire bowl of batter spilled on the floor.

Out of all the people in the village, Briony was the only one Adaira had confided in about her ill-fated romance with Henry. Briony had taken the blame many times when Adaira came home late after secretly meeting up with her former sweetheart. She'd also been the one who comforted Adaira after Henry left.

But today, as Adaira glanced at the brown mess all over her kitchen, she couldn't say she was exactly thrilled about Briony's awareness. She raised her eyebrows at the midwife. "Aye, Henry Milligan. The Burgesses came with him fer the christening."

"Henry's *here?*" Briony's voice rose another octave.

"Can you calm down long enough to help me clean this up?" Adaira snapped.

The midwife glanced around, only now noticing what she'd done. "Oh. I'm sorry, Adaira. You just sit down, and I'll . . ." Briony's eyes flicked to the specks of batter on the chairs, and she cringed.

"I'll be right back," she said before disappearing out the doorway.

Adaira groaned. *If she's this upset just knowing Henry's in town, how will she be when she sees him?* Her thoughts strayed to Henry himself . . . and how good he'd looked. *I do believe that smile o' his was even more attractive than I remember.*

She squeezed her eyes shut as a sharp voice came into her head. *Forget about his smile! That doesn' matter! What matters is that he left you.*

She could still hear his final words to her: ". . . There's nothing fer me here. Na anymore."

How could he say that?

Adaira swallowed thickly, her chest strangely tight as a question she'd promised not to ask herself came to her mind: *If he had known everything, would he have stayed?*

Another memory started clawing its way to the surface of her mind, so painful Adaira had to grip the side of the counter to keep herself upright—

Nay, I can'. I can' relive tha—

But then Briony walked in with some towels, and the memory lost its grip, falling to the back of Adaira's mind like a beast returning to its cage.

"Thank you," Adaira said as Briony placed a towel in her hand.

Briony nodded, her face still apologetic, and the two of them began wiping the floor.

After a few minutes of cleaning, though, Adaira felt her friend's eyes on her. "What? Why are you looking at me like that?"

"I feel like I'm about to explode right now, but yer still as put together as always. Are you sure yer human?" Briony jokingly poked the woman in the shoulder.

Adaira scoffed. "It barely takes anything fer you to explode. You should be glad I have more self-control. And that I'm yer friend."

"Oh, really? And why's that?"

"Because I'm the one who keeps you from splitting open the heavens every time you have a fit."

The midwife crossed her arms and pouted. "They're na fits."

"If you say so," Adaira said before continuing to clean.

But then a thought came to her, and the innkeeper's daughter shot to her feet. "I better let my father know about the Burgesses. Can you finish up in here?"

Briony looked up at the woman and smiled. "O' course. And then I'll go get some ingredients from Drulea Cottage to replace what was lost."

Adaira nodded before making her way to her father's room, glad she'd remembered to tell him they had new guests before he found out on his own. The last time that had happened, her father had been so furious he hadn't spoken to her for two days.

I wonder what state he'll be in today. He's na overly fond o' receiving visitors anymore, regardless o' the fact that they're our main source o' income.

When she arrived at the door, she gave it two sharp raps. "Father? Are you awake?"

A growl erupted from the bedroom, making Adaira instantly regret coming here.

"I certainly am now! Ungrateful lass, why are you bothering me this early?"

Adaira flinched, the man's harsh words weighing her down like stones. "I'm sorry, Father. I should have waited. . . ."

Terrence wrenched the door open.

Adaira tried not to grimace as she took in the sight of him, for the man's appearance was even more wretched than she'd expected. His full head of gray hair was a rat's nest atop his head, and he was wearing the same shirt he'd worn the day before, except now it was on backwards. He would have looked utterly ridiculous if not for the terrifying indignation on his face.

Indignation that was not to be ignored.

"What was so urgent?" Terrence snapped, blowing rancid breath in her face.

Adaira coughed and stepped back. "I just wanted to let you know we have guests: Mr. Burgess and his young son. They came fer the christening."

Terrence's eyes narrowed. "*More* people here fer that? Ugh, what a waste o' time."

The man waited for Adaira to respond, clearly trying to bait her into another argument.

"They seem very nice, Father. I've put them in the room below yers—"

"Now, why would you do something so stupid? I don' want to hear them when I'm trying to sleep!"

"I put them there because 'tis the only room with two beds. Besides, you probably won' hear them at all. I never hear guests when I'm trying to sleep, and my room is right next to yers."

More likely, they'll hear you coming in at all hours o' the night, she thought, though she didn't dare say that to the man's face.

Terrence pointed a finger at her and said, "If I do end up hearing them, I'm holding you responsible. *And* they'll have to move somewhere else."

Adaira looked deeply at her father, trying to find even an inkling of the man he'd been prior to her mum's death. A man everyone had respected and admired as an upstanding member of the community.

But the longer she stared, the sadder she felt, for all she could see was a bitter shell, someone most people now viewed with a mixture of pity and disgust.

Maybe he's still in there somewhere though. Maybe, if I keep trying, I'll be able to bring him back.

"Well, what are you still standing there fer?" Terrence snarled.

Adaira gave him a hopeful smile. "Would you like to come out and have a cup o' tea with me? Briony is cleaning up in the kitchen, but it should na take her long."

Terrence's eyes bulged as if the very suggestion was horrifying. "I don' want to have tea with that strumpet[12] and risk her reputation rubbing off on me!"

"She's na like that, Father. . . ." Adaira said weakly.

"Maybe na *yet*, but 'tis only a matter o' time before she ends up like the rest o' her family. And if you had any sense, you'd stay away from her, too."

With those words, Terrence slammed the door in his daughter's face.

Adaira stood there for a few seconds, wilting like a flower that hadn't seen the sun in weeks. *No matter what I do, I always seem to disappoint him.*

She turned on her heel and trudged down the stairs, her mind so unaware of her surroundings that she barely stopped herself from walking into the Burgesses' door as it opened in front of her.

"Hello, Mistress Stubbins! Yer da' sure was loud. Why was he so mad?" William asked as he popped out from behind it.

Adaira blanched. "You heard that?"

Before he could respond, though, Mr. Burgess stepped out into the corridor as well and grabbed his son by the shoulders. When he looked over to Adaira, his face was full of remorse.

"I'm so sorry, mistress. We were just finishing unpacking our things and—"

---

[12] A promiscuous woman.

"Nay, 'tis fine," Adaira said, turning away and slipping past them as quickly as she could without breaking into a run.

They heard. They both heard. What must they think?

When she got back to the kitchen and saw that Briony had already left, she placed a relieved hand on her heart. Adaira was great at hiding her true emotions from most people, but Briony would have taken one look at her and known something was wrong.

I'll go up to Loch Isla fer a bit and clear my head, she decided. She still had a lot of chores to do, but they could wait for an hour or so.

Adaira went to the closet, grabbed her fishing rod, and headed for the front door.

But just as she opened it, she heard, "Wait, mistress!"

"Aye, Mr. Burgess?" Adaira asked over her shoulder, trying to seem as if she was too busy to turn and face him.

"Mistress, I . . . please, don' be embarrassed about earlier. Na when you've done nothing wrong."

Adaira frowned in confusion, unsure if she'd heard him correctly. She spun around and asked, "What did you say?"

The redheaded farmer was standing a few feet from her, staring at the floor as though he was the one who had done something to be sorry for. "I just wanted to say that my son and I deeply appreciate yer hospitality."

He looked up then, locking eyes with her. "If there's anything we can do to help you while we're here, please say so."

Adaira blinked a few times, for that wasn't even close to what she thought he'd said. "T-Thank you. I'll be sure to do that."

Instead, she just stammered, "T-Thank you. I'll be sure to do that."

As soon as he nodded, she turned away and stepped outside, closing the door behind herself. She took a few steadying breaths, leaning her back against the door as she tried to process what had just happened.

But the more she thought about it, the more she was certain Mr. Burgess had said she hadn't done anything wrong.

You don' know me, Mr. Burgess. Don' assume I've done nothing wrong.

A few minutes later, Adaira was on her way to Loch Isla, Everton's largest source of fresh water. The shallow loch sat in a dip between Mary's Hill and Cramer's Field, its waters both calmer and gentler than the tumultuous ocean waves Adaira often watched from the inn.

And after seeing Henry again and her embarrassing encounter with the new guests, some peace and quiet was exactly what she needed. *I'll catch a few fish fer tonight's dinner and just forget about everything else fer a little while.*

Unfortunately for her, though, her plans for relaxation didn't come to fruition, for as soon as she'd cast her line, a rustle caught her attention.

"Oh, Matthew! Hello, there!" Adaira said when she realized where the sound had come from.

Young Mr. Levins stood nearby with his flock of sheep. He seemed self-conscious as he glanced back at his animals. As if it was beneath him to take care of them like any common farmer would.

Matthew Levins was one of only two tacksmen in Everton, the other being Donal McGuff. This meant Matthew was just below Laird Oliver in terms of social status, a fact the tacksman made sure everyone remembered. However, since Laird Oliver had pushed several of Matthew's tenants to turn to fishing and kelping[13] instead of farming in recent months, Matthew could no longer live off of just what he collected from the farmers. He was now forced to work the land himself, and that left him in a perpetually sour mood.

With light-blond hair and an impressive physique, Matthew was one of the most attractive men in town. Were it not for his general unpleasantness, Adaira was certain he would be married by now.

"I was just bringing the sheep up fer some water before I take them back to the beach. Don' mind us. We'll be gone soon so that the sheep don' eat too much grass. Better fer

---

[13] An Orcadian practice of burning seaweed carried out from the early eighteenth century until the early nineteenth century.

them to stick with seaweed and leave the pasture fer more important things."

"But won' they be in the way o' everyone kelping down there?"

A sinister gleam came into Matthew's brown eyes, canceling out his naturally handsome features. "Aye, that's the idea."

Adaira frowned. It was no secret that Matthew resented Laird Oliver for forcing him to take up farming, but letting the sheep eat the seaweed meant there was less for people to gather.

Is he so eager to get back at Laird Oliver that he's willing to hurt others' livelihood in the process? Burning kelp is the Calhouns' only source o' income, and Freda is going to have a baby soon.

The woman huffed and turned back to her fishing, assuming Matthew would get the idea that she didn't want to talk anymore.

But the man either didn't notice or didn't care about her wishes, for he soon said, "I haven' seen you out here in a while. Has it been very busy at the inn?"

Adaira plastered a fake smile onto her face as she faced the man again. "Actually, I have two guests who just arrived in town last night—Mr. Burgess and his son, William."

"More guests already? I hope you don' work yerself too hard."

Adaira's grin slowly became real as she replied, "Don' worry, Matthew. I'm fine."

The man raised an eyebrow at her. "Are you? It seems like yer doing something all the time. I know you feel bad because o' yer father's . . . condition, but you could slow down occasionally. You don' have anything to make up fer."

"*I'm fine*," she said through her teeth.

Matthew folded his arms in such a way that Adaira could tell he didn't believe her. "So why did yer guests come to Everton?"

"They came fer the christening feast," she said, trying not to look too pleased that he'd moved to a different topic.

"Are they friends with the Martins?"

"Nay, Mr. Burgess is actually a friend o' Henry Milligan," Adaira admitted, her stomach dropping at the mention of the man's name. Especially since she knew Matthew wasn't fond of the fellow.

And, indeed, the tacksman's face started to darken, so Adaira quickly added, "I know you've always disliked him. He's only here fer his niece's christening celebration, and then he'll be leaving."

At least, I hope so. She broke eye contact and tightened her grip on her fishing rod, trying to stifle her guilt over the lie.

"He came, too," Matthew said, his voice deepening to a rumble. "That man creates nothing but trouble. He's a curse on everything he touches."

Adaira felt Matthew's gaze boring into her, and a shudder went through her as she made a mental note never to come to the loch for solitude again. *'Tis na worth the risk o' another conversation like this.*

"I best be going, then. Have a good day, Adaira." Matthew's eyes were bright as he bid her farewell, but his jaw was still clenched as though he was barely containing his anger.

Adaira watched him and his sheep wander off, glad not to be on the receiving end of such blatant hatred.

But if people knew everything I'm hiding, 'twould na be just Matthew's hatred I'd have to contend with—'twould be the entire town's. She sighed and rose to her feet, for she knew there was no hope of enjoying herself now.

A Joyous Celebration . . .

The following day came far too quickly, and before Adaira knew it, the babe's christening was over, and it was time for the christening feast.

She hastened from the church to the inn as fast as was proper, anxiously hoping all would turn out as planned. There were just so many things that could go wrong.

The day had gotten off to a good start so far: the sun was shining, a slight breeze was blowing through the air, and not a cloud stood in the sky. Adaira sent up a prayer of thanks and asked for the weather to hold out long enough to get through the feast. Orcadian storms could rise up at a moment's notice, and Everton was particularly infamous for them.

Adaira began taking food outside to the tables she and Briony had set up the day before. Though she usually served meals indoors, there was no way she was going to fit the entire town in her dining room.

There was so much food that it took a little longer to put out everything than Adaira had expected, and by the time she'd grabbed the last of the dishes, her neighbors were arriving, some with their designated food and others just with hungry bellies.

"Here. Let me give you a hand," said a familiar voice.

Adaira turned with a tense smile even as her heart leaped in her chest.

"Thank you, H—" she broke off, unable to say the man's name as he stood only a few inches away from her.

"Yer welcome. So, which dishes did you make? I have to make sure I taste all o' yer cooking. 'Tis one o' the things I've missed most since leaving Everton," he said with a wink.

Adaira blushed. "Um . . . I . . . everything over there," she said, pointing at one of the tables.

Henry took the dishes from her hands, but rather than moving, he just watched her curiously, his eyes boring into hers as though he was searching for something.

For her part, Adaira tried to say something else, anything else, but she found herself completely tongue-tied, frozen beneath his piercing gaze.

But then, without warning, Henry looked away and said, "I'll just put these with the rest o' yer food."

With the spell broken, Adaira retreated to the safety of the kitchen without a word, all the while wondering what was wrong with her.

I can' still have feelings fer Henry. I can'! Na after how much he hurt me.

But what if he came back to make amends?

Adaira shook her head. *He didn'. He came back fer his niece's christening, and that's all. I can' let myself start to dream again, start to believe again. Otherwise, I'll just end up getting my heart broken a second time.*

The sound of the front door opening jerked her from her train of thought, and she looked over as Briony stomped in with two plates full of food.

"What's the matter?" Adaira asked, grateful for the distraction.

"I claimed two seats fer us, but the Martins insisted on sitting next to you."

"What's so bad about that?"

Briony raised her eyebrows at her like Adaira should already know the answer. "That means someone I absolutely hate will also be sitting with us, so he can be near his sister."

Adaira grimaced as she realized whom Briony was talking about. *Perfect. That's the exact opposite o' what I need right now.*

I'll just tell Briony I'll be so busy with the food that I won' be able to sit down and eat.

Adaira opened her mouth to voice her excuse, but then another potential problem rose up in her mind, one far more important than dealing with a little discomfort.

If Briony loses her temper, what will happen to Henry? Will she hurt him?

Almost as soon as the thought came to her, Adaira tried to dismiss it. *Nay, o' course na! She wouldn' do something like that.*

But Adaira couldn't quite make herself believe that, for she knew what Briony was capable of. Adaira's mind flew back to twelve years ago, to the day Adaira had realized Briony wasn't human. She tried not to think about that day, for not only had it been terrifying but it had also been a day when Adaira had done things she deeply regretted. Things that harmed both Briony and someone else. She could still hear his screams in her ears:

"Stop, please!"

A plate full of food was inches away from Adaira's nose, jogging her out of the memory.

"Adaira, are you all right?" Briony asked.

The woman jumped in surprise, but once she remembered where she was, she tried to act as if everything was normal.

"O' course, Briony. Other than you shoving food in my face," Adaira said as she took the plate from her friend's hand.

The midwife rolled her eyes. "I only did that because you weren' answering me. I called yer name three times. What on earth were you thinking about?"

Adaira's eyes moved past her friend, and a sad expression came over her face. "Nothing important. What were you trying to tell me?"

"I was asking if you were ready to go sit down. *Despite* who will be sitting with us," Briony said with gritted teeth.

Adaira slowly nodded. "I suppose so as long as you try to be civil with Henry."

Briony glared. "Fine, Adaira, but only fer yer sake. And if you change yer mind at some point, just give me some sort o' signal, and I'll happily murder him."

A shiver ran down Adaira's spine. "Let's just go."

As they came up to their table, they found Gregor Martin sitting at one end, Elspet in the chair beside him, and their babe in Elspet's arms. The Burgesses sat directly across from them. Henry Milligan was next to his sister, leaving only three empty seats at the table: one on the man's other side, one across from him, and the other—

Adaira moved toward the third chair since it was the farthest from Henry, but just as she grabbed hold of it, Briony slipped into the seat and looked back at her with a mischievous grin.

Adaira narrowed her eyes at her friend before sitting in the chair next to her, which, unfortunately, put Henry directly in front of her. Rather than looking at him, though, she quickly turned her attention to William Burgess on her right side.

"Are we waiting fer anyone else?" Adaira whispered with a nod toward the empty chair beside Henry.

"Nay, just you two," William whispered back.

"Henry Milligan, how good 'tis to see you," Briony blurted, her voice so syrupy sweet that Adaira cringed.

The air seemed to drop a few degrees, and Gregor Martin, who had been talking to Mr. Burgess, instantly went quiet.

"Thank you fer the kind greeting, Briony," Henry replied, his teeth clenched together into a grin that was anything but pleasant. "When Elspet said we would be eating with Adaira, I did na realize you would be joining us."

"You didn'? I guess Elspet forgot to mention that. Still, you should na be surprised since I usually like to sit with my best friend," Briony said as she put an arm around Adaira's shoulders. "Has it really been that long since you were here? I do hope you have na forgotten everything. *I certainly haven'.*"

Henry gawked at her, seemingly speechless at her implications. Briony smirked, but then her lips parted like she was about to speak again —

"—I'll say grace so we can get started," Mr. Burgess spoke up.

Adaira put her hand on Briony's arm, and the woman gave her an apologetic nod before everyone closed their eyes.

"Dear Father in Heaven," Mr. Burgess started, "we thank You fer this meal and ask You to bless the Martins' sweet babe, Elinor. I also ask that You bless Mistress Stubbins fer graciously providing our food today. Amen."

"Amen," everyone echoed.

As soon as that was done, the innkeeper's daughter thanked Mr. Burgess for his kind blessing and opened up a new conversation about the weather, one which the Martins eagerly participated in; they, too, seemed eager to keep the previous hostility from returning.

For the next several minutes, everyone chewed and chatted together quite amicably, other than Briony, who seemed content to stew silently in her seat.

Adaira took a moment to observe the expanse of people. She really admired how the whole town had come together to celebrate this happy occasion.

All except my father, she thought sourly, glancing at the empty seat next to Henry.

"Everything tastes delicious, Adaira," Gregor called down the table.

"Aye, we couldn' have asked fer a better christening feast fer our wee Elinor," Elspet agreed, looking down at the baby and kissing her cheek.

"I'm glad to hear that," Adaira said, her spirits rising at the praise.

Briony leaned over and whispered, "They're absolutely right. Look, even Lady Oliver seems impressed."

Adaira's gaze zoomed over to the older woman, who was currently scrunching up her nose at the carrots on her plate.

Adaira turned back to the midwife with lifted eyebrows. "She doesn' look very impressed to me."

"Oh, she is. Trust me. Remember, her face is just very difficult to read," Briony said, obviously trying to not to laugh.

Adaira snorted. Lady Oliver had one of the most expressive faces of anyone in town. And it almost always displayed one of two emotions: anger or disgust.

But then Adaira remembered something and leaned back in her chair to look Mr. Burgess in the eye. "I still need to introduce you to the Olivers, don' I?"

"Ah, that's right," the farmer said, quickly wiping his mouth and rising from his seat. "William, let's go say hello."

Adaira rose and led the Burgesses to the Olivers' table, nodding respectfully as they approached. Laird Joseph and

Lady Laura sat across from each other while their eighteen-year-old daughter, Muireall, sat next to her mother. The Levins and McGuff families filled in the other seats at the table.

"Laird Oliver, Lady Oliver, Muireall, I wanted to introduce my newest guests to you. Mr. Burgess, William, this is The Much Honored Joseph Oliver, Laird o' Harray, Lady Laura Oliver, and their daughter, Muireall. Mr. Burgess is a farmer in Hollandstoun."

Mr. Burgess smiled politely. "'Tis a pleasure to meet you."

Laird Oliver and Lady Oliver nodded in return, but Muireall curled her lip like she couldn't believe a common farmer was talking to them.

Adaira rolled her eyes. *Just because she's the laird's daughter, she thinks she's better than everyone else. 'Tis hard to believe we're related.*

Mr. Burgess didn't seem to notice, though, and he gave his son an encouraging smile.

It took him a second, but William soon realized his father was waiting for him to speak, so he turned to the Olivers and said, "Aye, we've heard a lot about you! Do you really have a mansion?"

Adaira winced and opened her mouth to correct him, but it was too late. The laird instantly launched into a long speech about how his home, while grand and luxurious, didn't meet the criteria to be called a "mansion."

When he started telling them about his plans for expansion, though, Adaira was quick to jump in with, "That's something we were hoping to talk to you about."

The laird's eyes narrowed at her interruption, but she plowed on and said, "The Burgesses would love to see yer house. If I brought them over later, would you be willing to give them a tour?"

Laird Oliver's face cleared. "Why, o' course! I have a very busy schedule, but I think I can find time to show you Rigmore House. Come over this evening after dinner."

"We will, thank you," Adaira said.

"Adaira is my great-niece, you know," the laird explained to Mr. Burgess. "Her mother, the poor dear, was my brother's daughter."

"Aye, that's right," Adaira agreed, trying to take control of the conversation, so she could steer it toward a different topic. "Anyway—"

"Nasty business, dying like she did. Went into labor too early, and our no-good midwife couldn' do a thing to save her or the bairn," Laird Oliver continued. "Have you met her yet? The Fairborn wench?"

"Yer thinking o' Briony's mum, Bethany," Adaira said. "Bethany's the one who tried to save my mum and brother. She simply didn' get to them in time."

"Bah. If she'd known what she was doing, they'd be here celebrating with us today. 'Tis just lucky her daughter hasn' killed anyone yet; otherwise, I'd have gotten rid o' her by now."

Adaira clasped her hands together, forcing herself to hold back the angry tears threatening to burst forth at the man's callous words. *Bethany delivered yer own bairns, you old fool! And if Briony wasn' such a kind person, who knows what she would have done to you by now.*

Meanwhile, Mr. Burgess's face seemed to have lost a good bit of color, and his eyes kept nervously cutting over to Adaira.

"Must have been a decade since it all happened now. I bet you barely even remember her, do you, Adaira?" the man said, turning his attention to the innkeeper's daughter.

"I was eight, Great-Uncle. I remember a lot."

"Yer father seems to remember far too much. Stuck in the past, he is. And in his bottle, right?" Laird Oliver laughed, turning to the other people at the table for support.

The McGuffs and the Levinses awkwardly nodded their heads, but then Matthew Levins bolted up from his chair.

"If you'll excuse me, I need to go speak to the Martins. I haven' told them congratulations yet."

But there was a dangerous glint in the man's eye, one that made Adaira suspect his intentions were far from friendly. Mr. Martin was a tenant farmer for Matthew, and Adaira was well aware Mr. Martin had been behind on his payments for a few months now.

"We better get back to our seats, so young William can finish his food," Adaira said, herding the Burgesses to their table and sitting down just as Matthew started talking to the Martins.

"Mr. Levins! How nice to see you," Elspet sputtered, unconsciously tightening her grip on her baby.

"Aye," Gregor said with a hard swallow. "To what do we owe the . . . pleasure?"

"I realized I've been terribly remiss in my duties as yer tacksman, fer I hadn' yet congratulated you on yer new addition," Matthew explained before eying the babe. "She looks very much like you, Elspet. I'm sure she'll be quite the beauty when she's grown."

Elspet laughed. "Yer too kind, Mr. Levins."

"Matthew, hello!" Henry said cheerfully, reaching for the man's hand. "I must say, yer looking quite well. I've missed seeing you."

Matthew stiffened, and any trace of civility on his face vanished. He turned to Henry and, in a voice as cold as the dead of winter, said, "'Tis Mr. Levins now. *And I haven' missed you.*"

Then Matthew looked away, effectively ending their conversation.

Henry's smile fell flat, and he slowly withdrew his hand.

"Now that you have another mouth to feed, I wonder when I can expect you to pay me all you owe," Matthew remarked to Mr. Martin.

Adaira could almost see the sweat dripping down Gregor's brow as the man struggled to respond. "W-Well, this won' put me behind any farther. You don' need to worry!"

Matthew took a step closer to the farmer. "That doesn' mean yer going to pay me back though. You have quite a lot o' catching up to do if yer going to keep yer house."

Gregor gasped. "Our house? You wouldn' take that from us!"

But the stern look on Matthew's face made it very clear he wasn't jesting.

"Like I said before, you don' need to worry. The crops are looking great this year, and the oats will be ready fer harvest before Johnsmas[14]. I'll have all I owe you and then some!"

"You've said as much before. Why should I believe this time will be any different?" Matthew sneered, poking Gregor in the chest.

"Because he won' be doing it alone," said an unexpected voice.

---

[14] Orkney's Midsummer celebration.

An Accidental Offense

Everyone turned as Mr. Burgess rose and walked over to Matthew. He met the tacksman's eye and declared, "*I'll* make sure it gets done. You have my word."

Matthew didn't say anything at first, for he seemed too shocked. Then he cleared his throat and looked the man over. "And how am I to know yer word is good?"

"I can vouch fer him," Henry piped in. "He was a godsend when I first got to Hollandstoun. And he's an excellent farmer."

Matthew's eyes were menacing as they cut over to Henry's. "I wasn' asking you."

Henry slumped in his chair and went back to eating as Matthew returned his attention to Mr. Burgess. "The company you keep is . . . questionable at best, but I'll give you a chance. I hope fer yer sake you follow through."

With that said, Matthew tromped off to his house without even bothering to tell his family he was leaving.

The entire table seemed to heave a long sigh once the man—and all the tension he'd brought with him—was gone. Mr. Burgess didn't say anything as he started moving back to his seat, but Gregor grabbed his arm. "Mr. Burgess, you don' need to—"

The redhead shook his head. "I insist, Mr. Martin. I can' stand the thought o' you losing yer home when I'm more than able to help you keep it."

Gregor slowly released the man's arm, his eyes wet and appreciative. "I . . . I don' know what to say."

Mr. Burgess just smiled and returned to his seat.

Henry, though, had his own opinions to share. "It really shouldn' be you, John. If Gregor and Elspet need the extra help, I should be the one doing it."

Elspet perked up and said, "Oh, that's a splendid idea! I'd love fer you to stay longer."

Henry's confident smirk went slack for a moment, making Adaira doubt his offer was sincere.

"I've seen you with a heuk[15], Henry. You'd be lucky na to lose yer hand," Mr. Burgess said as he picked up a slice of bread. "Nay, I'm fine with staying."

"Well, I suppose if yer really sure," Henry answered. His voice had a pretense of reluctance, but Adaira didn't miss the relief in his eyes.

Adaira gaped at him in disbelief. *Are you serious, Henry? You'd rather let yer friend give up his time and money than help yer own sister keep her home?*

"I'm sure," Mr. Burgess confirmed. "What about you, William? Would you like to stay and help Mr. Martin with his crops?"

The young boy beamed. "If it means we get to stay longer, aye!"

"But what about yer own crops?" Adaira asked.

"I appreciate yer concern," Mr. Burgess said with an earnest smile, "but I have a cousin in Hollandstoun who can take care o' them fer me. As long as you don' mind William and me staying at the inn a while longer."

"O' course I don' mind," Adaira said, looking away as her face turned cherry-red.

"Great. Then 'tis settled," the man replied before shifting his focus to Mr. Martin and asking him about farming tools.

"I've never seen anyone stand up to Mr. Levins like that," Briony whispered to Adaira.

---

[15] A sickle.

"Neither have I . . ." she answered, but her mind was somewhere else. She was still trying to figure out why Mr. Burgess would volunteer to help the Martins in the first place.

Just who are you, John Burgess?

Almost as if he'd heard her question, the man's sky-blue eyes strayed to hers—

"Adaira, did you hear me?" Henry asked.

She and Mr. Burgess immediately broke eye contact, and Adaira turned to her former sweetheart. "Hmm?"

Henry raised an eyebrow. "I was saying I heard Hamish Dunnet and Bridget Calhoun got married."

"Aye, the ceremony was a couple months ago," Adaira said with a nod, unsure why he was bringing this up. He'd never been close with Hamish or Bridget.

"It seems I've missed a lot more than I thought. I was so sure Hamish was going to finally win you over one o' these days. I can' recall a time when he wasn' sweet on you."

Adaira's mouth dropped open. *You thought I was going to marry Hamish? How am I supposed to respond to that?*

Elspet saved her from having to answer though. "Hamish works fer the Olivers now." She gestured to the young man in question as he brought Lady Oliver a drink.

"Is that so?" Henry said, but he sounded only mildly interested and didn't bother glancing Hamish's way. "Adaira, have you—"

"Mr. Burgess, I'd love to hear a bit from you," Briony interrupted, leaning back so she could see the redhead at the other end of the table. "How did you and Henry become friends?"

Mr. Burgess smiled genially at the midwife. "That's a funny story, actually. When Henry first came to Hollandstoun, he didn' realize his horse had injured its foot. As he was passing my farm, the horse collapsed, dropping Henry right onto my cornstalks. My wife and I were inside the house, and when we heard the commotion, we ran out to see what was going on—"

"—John, you don' need to tell them *everything* that happened," Henry cut in, stabbing his chicken with a little more force than necessary.

But Mr. Burgess continued as if his friend hadn't spoken. "When we got to Henry, he was so confused that he looked up at my wife and said, 'Yer face shines like the light o' the sun. Will you marry me?'"

Everyone at the table burst into laughter, their great guffaws so loud that people sitting nearby turned to see.

Everyone at the table except two. Adaira's eyes zoomed to Henry as he gripped his fork and slowly brought his meat to his lips. She knew he could feel her staring, but he refused to look anywhere but at his food.

And as the rest of the table calmed down, Gregor asked, "And what did you and yer wife do?"

"My wife was so surprised she didn' know what to say, but I immediately told him she was already married."

Mr. Burgess's answer spawned another round of chuckles, but this time, William noticed that Adaira wasn't laughing.

"Mistress Stubbins, are you all right?" the boy asked.

Just as he put a tender hand on Adaira's arm, Mr. Burgess said, "And what makes it even funnier is that my wife's name means 'shining light.'"

The farmer then turned to Henry with a grin. "You never did tell me if you used that line when you proposed to Mistress Wood."

All the breath left Adaira's lungs. *Proposed? What?*

Before she knew what she was doing, Adaira had shot to her feet. She glared down at Henry through the tears pooling in her eyes, waiting for him to say something. Anything.

But the man just kept eating, and if not for his clenched jaw, he appeared as though all was well.

Adaira turned and ran off, ignoring her neighbors' whispers as they watched her from their seats. She knew everyone was wondering what was going on and that racing away like this would lead to terrible gossip, but she simply couldn't stay there a minute longer.

She fled to the inn, wrenching the door open and flying up the stairs toward her room. Just as she reached the upper floor, though, her father appeared.

"Daughter? What are you doing here? Why aren' you down at the—" Terrence's grumpy expression dissolved when he realized she was crying, and something Adaira hadn't seen for years came over the man's face: concern.

"What happened?"

But Adaira couldn't tell him, so she just whimpered and fell into the man's arms.

Terrence was tense as she hugged him, but after a few seconds, he awkwardly returned the embrace.

Only for a moment though.

All too soon, he was pushing her away with the words, "If 'tis na something worth talking about, then 'tis na worth blubbering about either. Calm yerself down. There's a lot that needs to be done, so get going."

But it was Terrence who stepped away and started going down the stairs, leaving Adaira to cry the rest of her tears alone.

That's what Henry used to call me. His shining light. But he never asked me to marry him. Na even after I gave him everything.

***

John watched in confusion as Mistress Stubbins leaped from her seat and dashed to the inn without a word.

"Is she all right?" he asked, looking to his table companions.

"Adaira has a weak stomach. The stress o' preparing fer the feast must have been too much fer her," Mistress Fairborn quickly explained, but the worry dancing in her eyes told a different story. In fact, the midwife looked as if she was about to run after her friend, herself, but then she said, "I'm sure she's fine."

No one said anything more about it and went back to eating their food, but John noticed how Henry kept glancing toward the inn every few minutes.

There's something else going on here. Mistress Stubbins didn' look like she was ill when she left. She looked upset.

And when the woman didn't return by the time everyone had finished eating, John started getting anxious.

"Well, we better take this wee babe home fer a nap, otherwise she's na going to be happy fer much longer," Elspet said as she stood from her seat, her daughter squirming in her arms.

Gregor also rose and turned to Mistress Fairborn. "Please tell Adaira everything was excellent and that we hope she's feeling better soon."

The midwife nodded and began collecting the dishes and silverware to take back to the inn. "I'll tell her. She'll be glad to hear it."

Mistress Fairborn looked to the Burgesses. "'Twas nice talking to you, Mr. Burgess. You, too, William."

After that, she shot Henry a quick glare and took the dishes she'd gathered into the inn.

I wonder what he did to warrant that, John thought to himself. *Mistress Fairborn did seem to be implying something about their past earlier. Maybe Henry did something that hurt her or Mistress Stubbins?*

"Henry, why don' you come along, too? Gregor has been meaning to move our bed closer to the window, so there's more room fer the cradle, but I haven' the strength to help him," Elspet said with an expectant grin.

"O' course," Henry answered and got up from his chair to follow them. He winked at William. "Be glad you don' have an older sister to tell you what to do all the time."

Henry then nodded at John. "Come over to the house after dinner, and we can play a game o' cards."

"So you can lose again?"

Henry placed a hand on his chest as though he was offended. "I? Lose? You must be thinking o' someone else."

William giggled, but then his mouth widened into an 'o.' "Mistress Stubbins is supposed to take us to the laird's house tonight though."

"Oh, she is?" The man's playful smile flattened as he looked toward the inn. "She may na be well enough fer that. 'Twould probably be best to do it another time."

The little boy's face fell. "I was really looking forward to seeing it today."

John put a hand on his son's shoulder. "I'll go talk to her, and see how she's doing."

Henry's brow furrowed for a split second before his face smoothed into a more neutral expression. "All right, then. I better get going."

He turned and hurried after the Martins as though he hadn't a care in the world, but for some reason, John got the distinct impression he was hiding something.

The farmer bent down and pointed to a group of children playing tag nearby. "William, why don' you go play with the bairns over there while I talk to Mistress Stubbins?"

When his son looked over and saw the other children, a spark of his characteristic joy came back into his eyes. It was just one of the many things John loved about him; it was also something that had been sorely lacking in the last few months.

"All right, Da'!" William said, starting to scurry off.

Before he'd gone five feet, though, he paused and turned back. "You should make sure you apologize. I think 'twill make her feel better."

John scratched at his chin. "Apologize? What fer?"

"I don' rightly know, but something you said when you were telling that story about Mr. Henry made her really sad. When everyone else was laughing, she just looked like she was about to cry."

William scampered away before John could ask anything else, but the boy had told him enough.

Could it be . . . Mistress Stubbins was in love with Henry before he moved to Hollandstoun? Is that what Henry was trying to hide?

John thought back to the way the woman had stiffened when she first saw them in the market. At the time, John had just chalked it up to surprise, but now it seemed like something else entirely.

And what about the way Mistress Fairborn has been so cool toward Henry? She and Mistress Stubbins are close friends, so Mistress Stubbins probably confided in her—

Henry never said anything about it, but could he and Mistress Stubbins have been sweethearts? Or maybe even betrothed . . .

But just as all these thoughts came to him, another revelation hit John's mind, one that left him staggering. *If I'm right about all this, then 'tis thanks to me she found out he's betrothed to Mistress Wood. That would mean 'tis my fault she ran off.*

And if she's crying now, then that's my fault, too.

The farmer marched toward Everton Inn with purpose, only narrowly avoiding Mistress Fairborn as she came back out to clean the rest of the tables. He went to the kitchen first, but when he didn't find Mistress Stubbins there, he moved on to the sitting room.

An old man was snoring in one of the chairs when he arrived, but once John stepped into the room, the man woke with a start.

"Who are you?" he asked suspiciously.

"I'm John Burgess, sir," the farmer replied with an amicable smile. "Are you Mr. Stubbins?"

"I suppose I am. Why are you in here?"

"I'm looking fer—"

John cut himself off, realizing how awkward it would be to say he wanted to make sure he hadn't made the man's daughter cry.

"What are you looking fer?" Mr. Stubbins pressed, his voice more impatient.

Maybe there's another way to find out where she is.

"I wanted to ask about dinner tonight," John lied. "Do you know—"

"—That's a question fer my daughter, so you better ask her. She's upstairs."

"Thank you, sir."

John hurried to the staircase, but as he started climbing, Mr. Stubbins called out: "If she's still up there fussing, you tell her she needs to get back to work. She doesn' have time fer such nonsense."

The farmer didn't know how to respond to the inconsiderate remark, especially when it was about the man's own child, so he just bounded up the rest of the way to the second floor.

He hardly gotten there before he heard what the man had been referring to: soft weeping coming from one of the rooms.

John moved toward the sound, but he stopped before he knocked on the closed door. *What am I doing? I barely know this woman, and I'm about to bother her when she's crying? She probably wants to be alone right now.*

John turned to leave, but then the woman's sobs grew louder. There was such pain in them, such sorrow, that John's heart couldn't take it.

Especially when he suspected he was the cause of her tears.

And so, without any idea what he was going to say, John spun around and knocked on the door.

Nerves and Apologies

KNOCK!

Adaira's eyes widened. *Did Father come back?* She rose and went to the door, wiping her cheeks before she opened it.

"Mr. Burgess!" Adaira exclaimed when she saw the redheaded man standing there. She dabbed at her face again, hoping it wasn't all puffy.

"Can I help you?" she asked, completely baffled as to why he was there.

The farmer started fidgeting with his hands as though he was nervous. *What does he have to be nervous about? I'm the one who was just bawling my eyes out. . . .*

"Mistress Stubbins, I need to ask you something personal. Are you . . ." Mr. Burgess let out a heavy breath and glanced away.

After a moment, he turned back, no longer giving off the same nervous energy but instead looking fiercely determined. "May I ask why yer crying?"

The woman paled, her heart racing, for, unlike most people when they saw someone emotional, Mr. Burgess wasn't pretending everything was fine. Instead, he was acknowledging her pain directly, and that made Adaira feel much more vulnerable than she liked.

She was used to being noticed—everyone in town knew exactly who she was. But she was the one people went to for help, not the one who needed it. Her friends didn't ask her about her own problems, for she usually kept them so well-guarded no one knew about them, not even Briony.

And I wish that was the case now as well. This is the second time in two days that Mr. Burgess has caught me unaware. I hope this doesn' become a habit.

"What makes you think I was crying? I was just . . ." Adaira trailed off, for Mr. Burgess's expression told her she wasn't going to fool him.

"I guess my face gives it away, doesn' it?" Adaira laughed sheepishly. "I really do look terrible when I cry. Some women manage to just look more beautiful. My mother was like that. She didn' cry often, but when she did, she looked like . . . like a woman from a tragic tale, so breathtaking it makes you cry, too. But me? I just turn into a giant mess."

Adaira sniffled, feeling more moisture building in her eyes.

"Yer far from a mess," Mr. Burgess whispered.

The woman's eyes shot to his, for there was something in the farmer's words beyond simple courtesy. She tried to discern what it was, but when she realized she was staring, she dropped her gaze.

"A-Anyway, I came because I wanted to apologize," the man said.

"Apologize? What fer?"

"Lest I was the one who made you cry. Believe me, 'twas na my intent at all."

Adaira drew in a sharp breath, her head starting to go dizzy. *If he knows he's the one who made me cry, then does he know 'tis because o' Henry's betrothal? Do Elspet and Gregor know? Did anyone else hear? What if the whole town knows we were sweethearts now? What about my father?*

"What did Henry say after I left?!" she screeched.

Mr. Burgess's expression went slack. "He didn' say anything. . . . 'Twas my son who told me I'd upset you."

"Oh . . . that's good to hear—" Adaira broke off with a wince, for she realized she'd just made a terrible blunder.

Why did I mention Henry? If he didn' know it before, now Mr. Burgess is sure to figure out I was crying because o' the betrothal!

Adaira grabbed the farmer's hand and whispered, "Forget everything I just said. Please!"

Mr. Burgess didn't say anything for such a long time Adaira began to question if he'd heard her, but then his ears turned red.

What in the—What's he looking at? Adaira followed his line of sight, which trailed downward to their joined hands—

Adaira lurched backward, sputtering, "I'm so sorry!"

She clasped her hands behind her back as if hiding them would somehow help. She couldn't believe she'd done that; Mr. Burgess was practically a stranger.

"Nay, you don' need to apologize," the farmer said, but the way he wasn't looking her in the eye made it obvious that he was uncomfortable.

"I-I . . ."

"Adaira?" asked a new voice.

The two of them turned as Briony came up beside Mr. Burgess. The midwife peered at the farmer curiously for a second before her eyes flicked to her friend. "Adaira, I wanted to let you know the tables are all clear. The Martins were very grateful, and they hoped yer stomach feels better soon."

"My stomach?"

Briony nodded at Adaira like she was trying to tell her something. "Aye, how is yer *stomach*? Na unsettled from the food anymore?"

Adaira's gaze drifted to Mr. Burgess, who seemed to be attempting to blend in with the wall. "I'm all right, Briony. You don' need to worry."

"Good. I'll just be going, then. I need to check in on Freda Calhoun, but if you need anything, let me know," the midwife said as she placed a gentle hand on Adaira's shoulder.

Adaira nodded, and once the other woman was gone, she turned to her guest. "Well, I'm sure there's a mountain o' dishes fer me to wash, so I better get started. Excuse me."

She turned and walked toward the stairs, berating herself for letting her emotions get in the way of her responsibilities. *I knew this would be a busy day, and now I've let myself get behind.*

When she heard Mr. Burgess follow her into the kitchen, she looked back at him in puzzlement. "Did you need something else?"

The man shoved his hands in his pockets and cleared his throat. "'Tis just that William was really wanting to see the laird's house, and I was going to ask when you think you'll have time—*I don' mean today!*" He threw this last part in quickly with a strong shake of his head. "I don' want to add to what yer already doing. I just wanted to be able to tell him a specific day to look forward to."

Adaira shut her eyes and drew her lips together. "Oh, I completely forgot!" She looked up at the farmer, resolve coming over her face. "Nay, I told the Olivers we would be there today, so today it must be."

"Surely we can just go a different day. Won' Laird Oliver understand that yer too busy?"

"You don' know my great-uncle like I do," she said with a wry smile. "He'll be quite put out if we don' come today. Please let William know we'll go as soon as dinner is over."

***

That evening, John and William ambled along beside Mistress Stubbins as she led them to Laird Oliver's home.

"Is it close? When will we be able to see it? Just how big is the laird's house?" William shot question after question to their hostess so fast the lad barely had enough time to breathe, let alone hear the answers.

"Have patience, William," John urged, though he suspected the boy was too excited for his words to have much effect.

And if the way William kept scurrying back and forth was any indication, there was a strong chance the lad would have left them entirely had he known how to get there.

'Tis a good thing William has such an awful sense o' direction. 'Twould na be appropriate fer him to just barge into the laird's house by himself.

Mistress Stubbins pointed out several places as they went, explaining who lived there and what their livelihood was. She had many funny stories to tell and got John laughing more than once. The farmer also couldn't help but notice how she seemed to have something kind to say about everyone.

And from what he'd seen, all her neighbors thought well of her, too. John felt himself relax as the tension he'd been feeling about traveling to a new place started to disappear.

"I'm glad we came here," he blurted.

Mistress Stubbins stopped mid-stride. "You are? Even though now yer visit is going to be much longer?"

John nodded firmly. "I came to give William a change o' pace, but I'm starting to think this trip is helping me, too."

The woman's gaze clouded. "How so?"

"Well, the cooking, fer one thing," he said with a wink. "But more than that, there's an atmosphere in this place that's so different from our home back in Hollandstoun. 'Tis like a breath o' fresh air that I didn' even realize I needed. Thank you fer all you've done. William and I couldn' have asked fer a better hostess."

Mistress Stubbins peered down at her hands, making John fear he'd somehow said the wrong thing again.

But after a moment, she beamed at him and said, "Ah, where are my manners? I should have asked sooner, but is there anything else you'd like in yer room? I have thinner blankets if yers were too warm last night."

John smiled and shook his head. "Nay, they were perfect. You've done an amazing job taking care o' us. Above and beyond what you need to."

Mistress Stubbins waved aside the compliment as if it was unwarranted.

"Nay, I'm serious," the farmer insisted. "You don' need to go out o' yer way fer William and me. Especially when you have so many things to do."

The woman thrust up her chin and crossed her arms. "You mean, you don' think I can handle it on my own?"

John threw his hands up. "Nay, that's na it at all. I just wondered when you have time fer yerself."

Mistress Stubbins's face softened. "You don' need to worry. I still find time to enjoy myself."

When John didn't say anything, she added, "Truly, I do. For instance, I . . ." she trailed off, staring off to the side and biting her lip as she tried to think of something.

The expression was so endearing John had to hold back a chuckle.

"Ah!" She snapped her fingers. "Yesterday, when I left the inn, I went up to Loch Isla to go fishing," she said, smirking triumphantly.

John put a hand over his mouth to hide his smile. "Indeed?" he asked.

Mistress Stubbins nodded, but then her brow furrowed in comprehension. "Are you laughing at me?"

John cleared his throat and broke eye contact, but he could feel his lips twitching under her piercing gaze. "Nay, o' course na."

"You *are* laughing."

John tugged at his collar. "Only a bit."

He glanced at her to see her reaction, but rather than the annoyance he'd expected, there was a trace of amusement in the woman's eyes.

He let the rest of his grin show forth on his face, and slowly but surely, Mistress Stubbins smiled back.

"I suppose I don' do as much fer myself as I should, but 'tis na fer lack o' desire," she said, pointing a finger at him as if he better not say anything more about it.

"Are you two coming? Which way do we go now?" William called from a ways ahead of them on the road.

"Keep going straight fer now," Mistress Stubbins replied as she and John started walking again.

An awkward silence fell over them for a few minutes, the previous tension from their conversation playing back through John's mind.

"About the fishing though—how did you start doing that?" John ventured, trying to transition to a topic she wouldn't get defensive about.

"Well, my father was a fisherman. Everton Inn actually belonged to my mum's family, but as my grandparents' only bairn, my mum inherited it when they died. My father kept fishing fer a while after they started running the inn, but once Laird Oliver decided he wanted more o' his tenants fishing and kelping instead o' farming, my father had a lot more competition. . . ." The woman peeked up at him with a blush as if she didn't expect him to be listening anymore.

But she didn't need to worry about that, for John was still fully engaged. He wasn't sure exactly what it was, but something about this Adaira Stubbins intrigued him, and the more he listened to her, the more fascinated he became.

"What about you?" she asked. "Have you always been a farmer?"

John nodded. "Aye, my family has been farming fer many generations now. 'Tis a good living. I enjoy working with my hands and providing food fer my table."

They reached William just as a small cottage appeared up ahead.

"Hey, that's the Martins' farm! I thought we were going to Rigmore House," William said, turning to Mistress Stubbins with pursed lips.

"We are going there," the innkeeper explained. "The Martins' house is just on the way."

The woman turned back to John, seemingly to ask a question, but before she could, William shouted, "Oh, hi, Mr. Henry!"

John looked over, and indeed, there stood Henry, waving at them from the Martins' doorway. He made his way over to them and said, "So you decided to come fer cards, after all. Adaira, I'm surprised you came."

Something unsaid passed between them, and Mistress Stubbins lowered her eyes.

What was that? John thought to himself. He didn't like how Mistress Stubbins's shoulders curled forward. She was already several inches shorter than him, but now she just looked far too fragile. As if the slightest word would break her.

"We're na here to see you!" William stated in his naturally brazen tone.

Henry pursed his lips and bent down to William's level. "Yer na? That wounds me deeply."

"You'll get over it," William sneered.

Henry gasped and looked over to John. "John, do you hear this lad? How did you ever raise such an inconsiderate son?"

John shrugged. "I keep asking myself that very same question."

"Hey!" William shouted, turning to his father with a scowl.

John and Henry laughed at the boy's indignation, and John was happy to hear a giggle from Mistress Stubbins as well.

William glared at the adults, but once he realized they weren't being serious, his frown turned into a small smile.

"Well, if yer na here to see me, then what are you doing here?" Henry asked the boy.

"Mistress Stubbins is taking us to see Rigmore House, o' course!"

"In that case, mind if I come along? Elspet tells me the Olivers have done quite a lot to the place since I last saw it."

"Race you there?" William asked, wiggling his eyebrows.

"If yer prepared fer the consequences," Henry replied.

William's smile widened, and he took off running in what John hoped was the right direction. Henry soon chased after him, crying out that the boy was cheating.

John chuckled at their antics and looked over to Mistress Stubbins to see if she found them entertaining, too, but his laughter died away as he took in her body language: back hunched even more than before, mouth trembling, arms clutched over her chest.

She isn' just nervous around Henry; she's hurting. And based on how she ran off after finding out he's betrothed, there can be only one reason fer it.

John had considered the possibility earlier when he'd found her crying, but now he was certain of it: Mistress Stubbins didn't just have a romantic past with Henry. She'd been in love with him.

And maybe she still is.

"Mr. Burgess? Aren' you coming?" Mistress Stubbins asked from a few feet ahead, drawing him out of his thoughts.

"Hmm? Oh, aye. Sorry about that," he said, rubbing his jaw as he hurried to catch up with her.

"Have you hurt yerself?" she asked, gesturing to his mouth.

John shook his head and let out a weak laugh. "I must have been clenching my teeth together without realizing it."

"Ah. Is something bothering you? I hope I'm na to blame fer it."

"Nay, 'tis nothing . . . nothing at all."

A Sanguine Invitation

As John came up to Rigmore House, he had to stop himself from gaping in astonishment. To say it was impressive was an understatement. It didn't even look like a house; it was really more like four houses arranged in a rectangular formation with the largest building at the back. The three smaller buildings were all one-story, but the tallest one contained three rows of windows and a chimney on each end. A walled courtyard surrounded the buildings, making the home seem even larger. The laird may claim it wasn't a mansion, but to a common farmer like John, it might as well have been a palace.

He glanced at his son, whose eyes looked like they were about to pop out of his head. Henry, on the other hand, didn't seem affected in the slightest. *I suppose one would get used to seeing it after a while. . . .*

John eyed the house again and shook his head. *Nay, I'm na sure I could ever get used to something that grand.*

"Did you get lost back there?" Henry asked haughtily.

Mistress Stubbins ducked her head and didn't respond, so John said, "Some o' us have a wee bit more decorum and don' run everywhere we go."

Henry rolled his eyes at the slight, but then his expression turned playful. "Are you sure 'tis na because yer getting old?"

John folded his arms. "I'm na old."

"Really? William, what do you think?"

"Who, me?" William's gaze darted from Henry to John. "I don' really . . ."

John stared pointedly at the boy, trying to will him to give the right answer.

But then a smirk came over William's face. "Da', Mr. Henry's right! You are pretty old."

John huffed. "What? William, you can' be serious!"

William shrugged and ducked behind Henry with a cheeky smile. Henry chuckled and shrugged at John as if the matter was decided.

Mistress Stubbins leaned over to John and whispered, "You don' look old to me."

Her words sent a flurry of warmth through him, but he said, "Thanks, but I'm sure I'm a great deal older than you are."

When the woman's forehead wrinkled, he continued, "I'm thirty."

Mistress Stubbins flinched, but then she caught herself and shook her head. "That's na so bad."

"'Tis old when yer only eighteen, though, right, Adaira?" Henry countered.

The woman blushed. "W-Well, I still don' think 'tis old, and you look more able-bodied than most o' the men in town anyway." Her eyes widened, and she threw a hand over her mouth.

The warmth in John's chest grew, and he started to reply, "That's very—"

"Ah, it looks like Hamish is coming out to meet us," Henry cut in.

John's eyes flew to the front gate as a young servant came out to them with a cordial grin.

"Hamish, hello!" Mistress Stubbins greeted.

"I was wondering when you were going to arrive," the man grumbled. "I've had to keep watch at the window."

"I'm sorry we couldn' get here sooner," the woman said with a warm smile. "There was a lot to do after the feast. I hope you understand?"

Hamish's posture relaxed a bit, and he nodded. "Aye, that I do." His eyes shot toward the house for a moment. "I just hope Laird Oliver does, too."

Mistress Stubbins laughed. "Don' worry, Hamish. My great-uncle will be so excited to show off his house that he won' be upset fer long."

"Perhaps. We better go," the servant said before leading them through the gate.

At first, John thought Hamish was going to take them into the main building, but just as they reached the stairs, Hamish stepped to the side and turned to them. "I was told to keep you here, so Laird Oliver could personally escort you inside."

William's eyes lit up at the grandeur of such a thing, but John caught Mistress Stubbins scoffing out of the corner of his eye.

They didn't have to wait long; within a couple of minutes, the door burst open and the laird waltzed out. This was the first time John had seen the man standing up, and he was much larger both vertically and horizontally than John had realized.

"Ah, Adaira! I got so caught up in my duties that I completely forgot you were coming."

Henry let out a cough that sounded suspiciously like a snort.

Laird Oliver didn't notice, though, and he turned to the Burgesses with an arrogant grin. "So, what do you think o' it? Mighty beautiful, is she na?"

"She? Who's he talking about?" William whispered.

Henry laughed. "He's talking about the house, my lad."

Understanding came over the boy's face. "Oh! Aye, 'tis the biggest house I've ever seen! Do you really live here?"

"I really do," Laird Oliver said, nodding his head as if living there was somehow a burden.

Is he serious? John glanced over at Henry, and when his friend saw the incredulous look on John's face, he mouthed, *What?*

John scowled and raised his eyebrows as if to say, *You know exactly what.*

Henry looked away, but John thought he spotted the man's lips curling up at the corners.

"And you! I don' recall inviting you, Mr. Milligan," the laird said, waggling his finger.

"Aye, I know, but I heard about all the improvements you've made to yer home since I was last here, and I was too curious na to see fer myself," Henry explained, turning on the charm.

And the laird ate it right up; John could see it in the way the annoyance faded from the man's eyes and a proud gleam took its place.

"How old is it?" William asked, shamelessly butting into the conversation.

The laird didn't seem to mind, though, for he said, "Well, Rigmore House was built in 1697, but like Mr. Milligan was saying, I've made several adjustments to keep up with the styles they use on Mainland." He turned to admire the building for a moment before continuing with, "Aye, I daresay she looks just as good as any you'd see there. Maybe even better!"

"Great-Uncle, I'm sure they'd love to see yer chandelier," Mistress Stubbins said.

"Oh, good idea, Adaira! Come along, then." He strutted back into the house, jabbering away as he went without even checking if anyone was following him.

William and Henry went first, and John and Mistress Stubbins brought up the rear. John didn't know where Hamish had gotten off to; he'd managed to slip away unnoticed after the laird had arrived.

"What about Lady Oliver and their daughter?" John asked. "Are they too busy to come out and greet us?"

Mistress Stubbins pinched her lips together like she'd just tasted something awful. "Too busy fer the likes o' us," she said under her breath. "If you hear a clarsach[16] at any point, that's Muireall playing."

"A clarsach?" John echoed. "I've never gotten the chance to hear someone play that before."

"I'm sure you will at some point while yer here. She's very talented," the woman said in a neutral tone.

"But you don' think I'd like it?"

---

[16] A small Scottish harp.

Mistress Stubbins frowned. "I didn' say that. Muireall is just . . . how should I say this? She's . . . difficult to like, I suppose. She's na—"

"Did one o' you have a question?" Laird Oliver called.

Mistress Stubbins's face bloomed a brilliant rosy-red, and she slammed her mouth shut as the rest of the group turned to them.

"I was just marveling at the architecture," John said.

The laird's scowl morphed back into a boastful smirk. "Ah, well, do please make sure you say yer compliments loudly enough fer all o' us to hear them. We're just about to move on to the ballroom, which I believe you'll like very much."

John nodded as the laird turned away and continued with his tour. This time, John tried to pay more attention as he learned about each and every room. All of it was quite stately, and while John enjoyed seeing the beautiful home, the farther they went, the more displeased he became with his host.

"I'm sure you both are far too poor to have seen something like this before," Laird Oliver said for the fourth time as he showed them the large table in his dining room.

John gritted his teeth. While the statement was true, John wasn't exactly thrilled that the laird kept rubbing their noses in it. *Maybe I should have declined when Mistress Stubbins offered to bring us here. . . .*

He glanced over at the innkeeper's daughter, and she didn't seem very enthused about the tour either.

"Mistress Stubbins," John whispered.

The woman turned to him. "Hmm?"

"I'd like to get some air, but I'm all turned around. Do you think you could help me find my way outside?"

She raised her eyebrows at first, but then a look of sympathy came over her. "I can do that. I doubt Laird Oliver will even notice." She inclined her head toward a long hallway. "This way."

The two of them wandered through the corridor silently, passing several more rooms as they went, each far lovelier than anything John could ever dream of possessing. But there was something else about them that gave him pause, some strange sense of grief that seemed to hang over them.

They went through a back door and came out behind the main part of the house. A large garden sprawled out to their left, and there was a gorgeous field of wild heather directly in front of them. Mistress Stubbins led John over to some chairs, and the two of them sat down.

John asked, "Mistress Stubbins, I know this is a bizarre question, but . . . did someone die recently in Laird Oliver's family?"

Mistress Stubbins tilted her head to the side. "How did you know?"

"There's just something in the house that seems . . . sad. I don' really know." John shook his head. "May I ask who 'twas?"

"Laird Oliver's firstborn, Alastair," she replied, staring dully back at Rigmore House.

"Were you very close to him?"

The woman's eyes snapped over to his. "Nay, I wouldn' say so. Why do you ask?"

"You just seem very affected by it."

She gave him a quivery smile. "Oh, nay, na at all. . . ." Again, the woman looked away, blinking a few times as if she was holding back tears.

John let the silence stretch on for a few minutes, not sure what to say next and not wanting to intrude if the woman needed time to herself. He let his eyes fall away from her, and before he knew it, he found himself peering at the ocean beyond the heather field.

O' all places . . . John grimaced and moved his gaze to his hands. He didn't want to look at the ocean for too long; otherwise, he was bound to start thinking about things better left in the past.

But he wasn't fast enough, for a dark-haired beauty rose up in his mind's eye, reaching out her hand in a silent invitation. Longing swelled in his heart, but then he saw the blood staining her dress—

"Nay, stop!" John shouted, squeezing his eyes shut and putting his hands on his temples.

Mistress Stubbins gasped. "Mr. Burgess?"

John didn't answer, though, for he was still trying to force his wife's image from his mind. His head was throbbing with pain, and the more he tried to alter his thoughts, the stronger it became—

"John?"

The farmer opened his eyes in surprise. Mistress Stubbins was no longer in the chair next to him; she now stood before him with one hand outstretched—so much like his vision from before—

But then the woman's face flushed, and she dropped her hand. "I'm sorry, that was inappropriate o' me. You just seemed so distressed. . . . Are you all right?"

"You truly want to know?"

Mistress Stubbins nodded, her face dripping with concern.

John blew out a heavy sigh. "I'm na quite sure."

Before the woman could respond, footsteps caught their attention.

"There you are," Henry said, grinning as he strolled over. William and Laird Oliver were close behind him, the first of whom was still looking at everything in awe, but the second had a very pronounced glare on his face.

"You left us," the laird accused as he reached them. "I was just about to head to my favorite part o' the house when William asked where you two had gone off to. Took us a terribly long time to find you. What are you doing out here?"

Mistress Stubbins quickly said, "Mr. Burgess wasn' feeling well, so we stepped out fer a bit o' fresh air. I didn' want to interrupt yer tour, so I thought we'd just slip out fer a few minutes before coming ba—"

"Well, you *did* interrupt it! We barely got through any o' the house, and now I'm na sure I'm up fer finishing," Laird Oliver pouted.

The woman's lips twisted as she seemed to consider his words. "How about you show us the garden?"

"'Tis far too late fer that. 'Tis more pleasant to see the flowers in the mornee—"

"Great! Let's do that, then!" Mistress Stubbins proclaimed. "That's a wonderful idea. I'm sure Mr. Burgess will be better in the morneen. Would you mind, Great-Uncle Joseph?" She smiled sweetly and batted her eyes.

"W-Well," the man blustered. "I've got many things I need to do morn. I'm na sure I'll be able to fit it into my schedule. . ."

Mistress Stubbins gently elbowed John, who soon realized she wanted help in the convincing.

"'Twould be quite appreciated," the farmer said. "I'm terribly sorry fer the inconvenience. We'd love to come back morn and see the rest o' it."

"Please, sir!" William added.

"Oh, all right," Laird Oliver grunted. "If you insist."

John thought he saw a tiny smile on the man's face as he turned his back to them and started walking back to the house. "But you best be here at ten o' clock sharp, or you'll miss yer opportunity!"

Mistress Stubbins leaned over and whispered, "Thank you fer going along with me. It may seem silly, but you don' want to get on his bad side if you can avoid it. And that man is very easily offended."

"She's right," Henry said, coming up on John's left. "I remember one time I thought 'twould be funny to plant some corn in his flower garden and see how he reacted." The man's face turned into a pained grimace. "Let's just say 'twas na pretty. I think he's still angry with me about it, too."

Mistress Stubbins chuckled. "How did I forget about that?"

"You forgot? But yer the one who told me I shouldn' do it. 'Tis too bad I didn' listen," Henry said, laughing along with her.

The two of them smiled at each other for a split second before their eyes widened and they turned away.

"Well," Henry coughed, "if we're all done here, I guess 'tis time to head back."

"I suppose yer right," John said, glancing at his son. "I'm sure William could use some rest."

The boy groaned. "I guess. Goodnight, Mr. Henry."

"Goodnight," the man said, looking each of them in the eye.

Mistress Stubbins nodded before turning to William with a grin. "Let's see how well you remember the way back, hmm?"

"I know the way. Follow me!" William declared, dashing up the road without hesitation.

John started to follow him, but then he realized Mistress Stubbins wasn't walking beside him. He turned around, only to find Henry grasping the woman's arm.

Rumors and Truths

Adaira stood there, completely stunned. There had been no warning, nothing to suggest he was going to reach out and touch her in such an improper manner. Shivers went up her arm at the contact. *What is he thinking? He's betrothed to someone else.*

"Henry, what are you doing?"

The man dropped her arm like it was on fire. "I apologize. I . . ." He looked away for a second, rubbing the back of his neck. "I just wanted to ask, may I take a stroll with you before you head back to the inn?"

Adaira's fell open, and she immediately glanced at the Burgesses, who had stopped to check if she was coming. William was a ways ahead, but Mr. Burgess was still close enough that he'd undoubtedly heard Henry's question.

And he was currently watching her with a look of . . .

Is that concern? Adaira peered at the man in confusion. *He doesn' have a reason to be concerned about me. Perhaps he's just anxious to get back to the inn.*

She turned to Henry. "The Burgesses probably still need a guide to get ba—"

"Nonsense. John knows the way," Henry interrupted. "Right, John?"

The redhead's brow furrowed, but he said evenly, "Aye, I can get us back on our own. That is, if you want to go with him."

Adaira looked between them helplessly, not wanting to go with Henry but also unable to think of another excuse to decline.

Better just accept it, then, she told herself.

She peeled back her lips into a smile and said, "All right, Henry. I'll see you in the morneen, then, Mr. Burgess."

Rather than answering, though, Mr. Burgess glowered and marched off.

Well, that was a bit rude. Adaira stared after the farmer in bewilderment, unsure what she'd done to deserve that kind of behavior.

"Are you ready?" Henry asked after a moment.

"Oh, aye, o' course," Adaira said cheerily, despite the dread coursing through her heart.

Henry held out his arm, and soon, the two of them were meandering along in the direction of the docks. Adaira tried her best not to think about the warmth of Henry's arm against hers, but then she found herself speculating about what had happened at Rigmore House with Mr. Burgess.

He seemed really upset when he cried out fer someone to stop. . . . What could he have been thinking o'?

"Adaira, is something troubling you?"

The woman jumped and turned to Henry with an apologetic look. "Nay, everything is fine. I just have a lot on my mind right now."

The man's face turned grim. "I hope taking care o' the Burgesses isn' too much o' a burden fer you. Would you like me to see if my sister can house them once I'm gone?"

"You don' need to do that. She has more than enough to handle right now."

"But—"

Adaira shook her head. "Really, 'tis no problem, Henry. They're lovely guests."

"Indeed . . ." he said vaguely, pulling her farther down the path.

They came up to the docks, but instead of walking onto them, Henry veered toward the beach. Adaira wasn't paying much attention to the change in direction, but as soon as her feet hit the sand, a memory hit her like a giant wave:

It was late September, and Henry and Adaira were sitting together on the beach. The hour was late, far past midnight, and the only ones out besides them were the stars.

They'd met up like this so many times, but tonight, it felt different somehow. A gnawing dread had been growing in Adaira's stomach, and Henry's clammy grip on her hand was only making the feeling worse.

"Henry, is something wrong?" the sixteen-year-old asked.

The young man beside her winced ever so slightly before looking down at her with a lazy smile. "Why do you ask?"

Adaira's heart always did flips when Henry turned that charming grin on her, but this time, it wasn't desire that made her pulse quicken. It was fear. Something was off about this. Very off.

"You just don' seem like yerself tonight," she replied, looking away so he wouldn't notice how anxious she was.

Henry let out a heavy breath and released her hand. He rose to his feet and stared out at the black sea. "I . . . I've been trying to think o' how to tell you this fer days now."

"Tell me what?" Adaira asked. She tried to will herself to stand and grab his hand again, but for some reason, she found she couldn't move.

"I'm leaving fer Hollandstoun in the morneen."

All the air whooshed out of Adaira's lungs. This wasn't even close to what she'd been imagining. This was something she could barely even process. "Yer what?"

Henry turned and faced her, his boyish features still just on the cusp of manhood, for he, too, was only just sixteen. "You know I've always wanted to get out o' here, and now that Da's gone, I finally can. I'll make a fresh start in Hollandstoun where no one knows me or my family."

Adaira knew Henry was never going to be a farmer like his father, and he had talked about getting away from Everton plenty of times, but she hadn't thought he'd really do it.

"What about Elspet? Are you just going to leave her here all alone?"

"My sister can take care o' herself. Always has. But I know I can never be the man I'm meant to be if I stay here all my life."

When Adaira didn't answer, Henry added, "Besides, Da' left plenty o' money fer us. She'll be fine."

Anger rose in Adaira's chest, an emotion she usually put aside and did her best to ignore. But not this time. This time, it flared up so explosively she had no hope of containing it. "So, that's it? Now that yer da's dead, yer just going to take yer inheritance and leave?"

Henry seemed surprised by her outburst, but then his nostrils flared. "When you say it like that, you make me sound like some horrible person."

"Well, maybe you are. Yer da's barely been gone a week!" she said, throwing her hands in the air. "How could you even think o' going now? Elspet will be so hurt. Na to mention the rest o' the town . . ."

Her eyes fell from his as she trailed off, knowing he would understand what she wasn't saying: *What about me? How could you hurt me like this?*

Henry's hand came to rest on her shoulder, and with his other hand, he gently turned his face toward his. He stared deeply into her eyes, making Adaira's knees quiver as he said, "Come with me."

The girl's breath caught. "You want me to come?"

Henry nodded earnestly and grasped her hands in his. "Say you will."

For half a second, Adaira considered his offer. They'd have enough money to get started, to get married and raise a family, to have the beautiful life she'd always dreamed of—

But then she thought of the way Briony's expression hardened whenever Adaira mentioned Henry's name or asked her to cover for her, so she could sneak out to see him. "He's na the one fer you," she'd told Adaira once.

Could she be right? Adaira searched Henry's face, easily finding the love he claimed was only for her. *Nay, she's wrong. He does love me.*

But can I leave everything else behind fer that love?

The question sent a jolt of fear through her, too powerful for Adaira to dismiss.

And before long, Henry saw it in her face, for his eyes grew sad, and his grip on her hands loosened.

"I . . . I'm sorry, Henry," Adaira choked out, trying to ignore the colossal lump in her throat. "I want to be with you, but na like this."

The lad looked away, his chin trembling with emotion.

"That's all there is to it, then," he muttered, releasing her fingers.

"All there is to it? Nay, that can' be. You must stay."

Henry shook his head, growing impatient with her. "I've already told you why I can' do that. Don' you understand?!"

"Stay with me," Adaira whispered, desperate not to let their relationship end like this.

The lad's face smoothed, and he tucked a strand of hair behind her ear. "Oh, Adaira. I wish you loved me as much as you think you do."

"But I do love you!" she screamed, water spilling down her cheeks.

Henry wiped at her face, his lips curled up in a sad, resigned smile.

Adaira closed her eyes, focusing on the warmth of his touch.

"If you did, you would come with me," he said. "I'm sorry to have hurt you, but I thought yer love would go farther. Now I know the truth: there's nothing fer me here. Na anymore."

Adaira's eyes shot open. *Nay, that's na true at all! I will go with you if it means na losing you!*

But something clawed at her throat, effectively locking her words inside her. She tried to overcome it, but it was no use.

And when Henry left the next day, Adaira was certain it would be the last time she ever saw him.

Tears sprang to the innkeeper's eyes as the heartbreak flooded over her afresh. *Nay, I have to be strong. I'm past this; I really am!*

Adaira blinked her tears away and planted her feet, not wanting to continue this walk any longer than she had to. "So, what was it you wanted to say to me?"

"Why did you stop all o' a sudden? There's still a lot o' beach left. . . ." Henry trailed off as understanding came over him. "Oh, Adaira, I'm sorry. I wasn' even paying attention to where we were going."

The woman crossed her arms. "Well?"

"What makes you think I had something I—" he tried to say, but he broke off when he saw her glare.

"Fine, yer right," he groaned. "You already know I'm getting married."

Henry hesitated, eying her warily. Almost as if he was waiting in case Adaira had some sort of reaction.

But hearing it this time didn't birth the same jumble of emotions as it had before. There was still the pain of regret, but rather than feeling like a knife to her gut, the sensation was more like tiny needles—acute but short-lived. Much less painful than she would have anticipated.

I . . . I don' love him anymore, do I?

Maybe I did once, and when Mr. Burgess revealed that he's betrothed, it did hurt, but perhaps na fer the reason I thought it did. Perhaps . . . 'twas just my pride in knowing I'd been passed over.

The realization was jarring, for loving Henry had been such a big part of her identity ever since she'd first fancied him as an eleven-year-old. And when he'd abandoned her two years ago, she'd shut the door of her heart and locked it away without daring to examine it again since.

But now she took a good, long look at the man beside her as he nervously awaited her response. He was still just as handsome as he had been two years ago, and she knew she still had some physical attraction to him, but—

That's all 'tis now. I feel like I'm seeing him clearly fer the very first time. And when I look beyond those intriguing, dark eyes and that strong physique, there's na much left, is there?

Maybe I was just in love with the idea o' him and na with Henry himself. The lad I knew two years ago was arrogant, irresponsible, and unkind to those he deemed lesser than himself, like Briony. That's na the kind o' person I want to be in love with.

And from what I've seen o' him since he has been back, na much has changed. He still looks down on Briony fer being illegitimate, and he's still quick to let others take on burdens they shouldn' have to bear. Otherwise, he would be the one staying behind instead o' Mr. Burgess.

It was embarrassing to think she'd wasted so much time longing for a man not even worth her affection. But breaking out of her infatuation, one she now recognized as childish, was so incredibly freeing that she couldn't help but smile.

"Aye, I'm glad fer you," she said.

"Yer . . . glad fer me? But earlier, I thought—"

"I've moved on, Henry. It sounds like you have a bright future ahead o' you, and I wish you all the best."

And to Adaira's surprise, she truly did. She hoped the woman he married would be good for him. Maybe being a husband would help him mature and let go of some of his selfishness.

Henry scrutinized her for a moment, but when her grin stayed in place, he frowned. "Well, thank you. I've been wanting to tell Elspet and Gregor, and the christening seemed like a good opportunity to come back to Everton after being away fer so long."

Adaira's expression didn't change, but his words just confirmed her previous conclusions about his character. *And here I thought he'd actually returned fer an unselfish reason. But 'twas still about him, after all.*

"I'm trying to save up some money to build a big enough place fer the two o' us," he continued, "so 'twill be a while before Sonneta and I can get married, but my sister has insisted on meeting her before the wedding. I'm going to head back first thing in the morneen to tell her how excited Elspet is. But Sonneta does have a sickly mum, so it may be difficult to find time to come back. Maybe later this summer—"

"Why are you telling me this?"

Henry kicked at a bit of sand, not making eye contact with her. "I just thought you might be . . . hurt to see me with another woman." He looked up then with a weak smile. "But, like you said, you've moved on, and that's great. I hope you find love, too. Just . . . be careful whom you choose to find it with."

This time, Adaira couldn't hold back a snort. "What's that supposed to mean?"

Her companion lifted his eyebrows as if it was obvious. "Maybe you've moved on from me because you have someone else in yer heart now. My friend John, perhaps?"

Adaira's eyes bulged. "What? I don' know what yer talking about." *He thinks I have feelings fer Mr. Burgess??*

"He's a great man. If he hadn' befriended me, I doubt Sonneta would have given me a chance." Henry sighed and gazed out at the ocean as if his mind was far away.

"Henry?"

The man flushed as he seemed to remember where he was. "I'll have to tell you how Sonneta and I met another time. My point is, John Burgess isn' someone you want to get involved with. There have been a lot o' rumors going around Hollandstoun about his late wife. Specifically about how she died."

A sense of foreboding gathered in Adaira's stomach. "How she died?"

Henry nodded, his expression grave. "I think that's why he wanted to come with me—to get away fer a bit so William didn' hear them."

Adaira didn't want to know more, but something inside her compelled her to ask, "What do the rumors say?"

"They say he killed her."

Adaira's chest tightened even as she tried to dismiss the outrageous claim. At least, it should have been outrageous.

"You don' believe that, do you?" she asked in as nonchalant a tone as she could. As if they were discussing something as unimportant as the weather.

Henry looked at her earnestly, his brown eyes unwavering. "Na fer a second. That man would never, never, harm his wife. She was the moon and stars to him. And to William. She was a quiet, odd woman but a rare beauty—"

"How did she die, then?" Adaira interrupted, not wanting to hear how beautiful the late Mrs. Burgess had been. Or how much Mr. Burgess had loved her.

"That's the problem," Henry explained, starting to walk again. "No one actually knows. She just vanished one night. John told everyone he found her shoes on the beach, so she must have drowned, but how many people swim at night? And to make matters worse, there was no body."

Adaira shivered. "How sad fer Mr. Burgess. He couldn' even bury her."

"Aye, 'tis very sad indeed. And dealing with whispering neighbors on top o' that just makes it so much worse. He's na the same man he was before she died."

Henry turned to her and placed his hands on her shoulders. "I know I said some things I shouldn' have before I left, but the truth is, I still care about you. Please trust me on this, and don' get too close to John. You know how dangerous rumors can be. I don' want you to get hurt."

Adaira opened her mouth to tell him he didn't need to worry, but the man turned from her and started talking about something trivial before she could answer.

And so, she let the topic drift away, filling the rest of their walk with lighter conversation that was much easier to discuss.

But all the while, his warning resounded in her head, and she couldn't help but wonder how he'd come to the conclusion that she fancied Mr. Burgess.

"Have a lovely rest o' yer night, Adaira. I'll be back in the morneen to say goodbye," Henry told her once they'd gotten to Everton Inn.

Adaira nodded, shutting the door as soon as he'd stepped back over the threshold.

That wasn' even close to how I imagined that conversation would go, she thought to herself with a sigh. *Poor Mr. Burgess. What a terrible thing to go through. To lose yer wife and then have yer neighbors talking behind yer back like that? I'm glad he's enjoying his stay in Everton so far. Maybe his neighbors will have moved on by the time he goes back to Hollandstoun. . . .*

"Did you have a nice walk?" asked a voice.

***

The woman yelped before a spark of recognition lit her eyes. "Mr. Burgess! I didn' realize you were there."

John held back a smirk; he hadn't expected Mistress Stubbins to be so jumpy. *She didn' answer my question though. Was that intentional?*

"You looked like you were thinking hard about something," John said, hoping she'd tell him about her walk with Henry.

"Oh, na really," Mistress Stubbins replied with a laugh. "Just . . . Henry said he was going to come by in the morneen to bid us farewell, and then he's going straight back to Hollandstoun."

"Ah, I figured he wouldn' stay very long. He's pretty attached to—" John winced.

"Mr. Burgess, you don' have to do that."

John blinked. "Do what?"

The woman put her hands on her hips. "Try na to mention Henry's fiancée."

"Oh . . . that. I . . . I just didn' want to upset you," John explained, moving his gaze to the floor.

"Thank you fer trying to be thoughtful, but at this point, 'tis na necessary. What I'd prefer is fer you to be honest about how much you know. And who else knows."

John shook his head, still not looking at her. "No one else! I haven' spoken to anyone about it, I assure you. I would never share something so personal, especially when all I have are suspicions."

"And what do you suspect?"

"Well, I . . ." John gulped as he lifted his eyes to hers. "Were you in love with him?"

The woman took in a sharp breath, no doubt surprised at how direct his question was. She didn't say anything for a long time, but eventually, she murmured, "Aye, I was."

Something about the way she said "was" stuck out in John's mind. "But na any longer?"

He wasn't sure what made him ask that; this conversation was already going into territory that was far from appropriate. That became even more apparent when the woman's cheeks flushed and she started fidgeting with her hands.

What's the matter with me? Did I really just ask her if she was still in love with Henry?

He opened his mouth to apologize and take back what he'd said when he heard, "Nay, I . . . I'm na."

John tilted his head to the side. Her body language wasn't very convincing, but her tone was so final, so assured, that John had to believe her.

"That's a relief to hear," he said. The words bubbled from his lips like lava, burning his tongue with regret the instant they came out.

What am I saying? She's going to take that the wrong way!

And what's the right way, John? What did you mean by that? asked an annoying voice in his head.

I just don' want her to be hurting, he replied, as if that would rationalize his behavior. *Henry's very much in love with Sonneta, and if Mistress Stubbins is holding onto feelings fer him, 'tis just going make it worse fer her.*

Somewhere inside himself, though, John knew that wasn't the whole truth.

Meanwhile, Mistress Stubbins was watching him strangely, no doubt trying to figure out what he'd intended.

John's eyes darted away, and he cleared his throat. "I just know he's planning to bring Mistress Wood here, and I didn' want you to have a hard time when he does."

"So, he hasn' told you anything?"

The farmer shook his head, chancing another look at the beautiful innkeeper. She was smiling a bit, apparently glad Henry hadn't said anything. When she caught him staring, though, she grimaced.

"I guess I should just tell you, then. Henry and I . . . were sweethearts before he left. I really thought I was going to marry him."

Even her ears were red with embarrassment now, and there was so much fear flickering in her eyes. Clearly, it had taken a lot for her to share this with him, and it hurt John's heart to think she was worried about what he would do with this information.

"Thank you fer trusting me, mistress. Like I said before, I would never share something this personal with anyone."

The woman peered at him closely as though searching to see if he was telling the truth. Soon, a tiny grin brightened her face, one which John hoped meant she believed him.

And that was when something unexpected happened. A strange energy began coursing between them, making it impossible for John to look away. There was something in

Mistress Stubbins's brown eyes, something hidden beneath the surface that was drawing him in. Like a moth to a flame.

What is this? the farmer wondered, but he didn't have time to find an answer before Mistress Stubbins looked away, ending the bizarre phenomenon.

"I better get to bed. I have a lot o' chores to do in the morneen. Have a good night, Mr. Burgess."

John barely heard her as she slipped away, for another sound was pounding in his ears that dampened all others. A sound that both terrified and excited him at the same time.

It was the sound of his heart beating in his chest. Faster than it had in a long time.

John took a few deep breaths, trying to calm himself down. He wasn't sure what had just happened, but he didn't like it.

Not one bit.

At least, he hoped not.

The Trouble with Eavesdropping

Henry's departure the following morning held far less turmoil than Adaira had anticipated. In fact, she barely felt anything as the man smiled and told them he hoped to be back in late summer with his intended.

But then Henry gave Adaira a sharp nod, reminding her of what he'd told her the night before: *"John Burgess isn' someone you want to get involved with."*

Adaira smiled in return, wishing she could tell him what she was thinking. *Yer wrong, Henry. Mr. Burgess is barely even a friend.*

But instead, she held her tongue and kept her opinion to herself. Just as she had all her life.

The next several days passed quickly, falling into a rhythm much more pleasant than normal because of the Burgesses' presence. Mr. Burgess continued to be kind to everyone around him, even Briony, which was a nice change since Adaira was sure he knew the midwife was illegitimate by that point. The farmer was also quite skilled at home repairs, something Adaira greatly appreciated when he fixed the inn's roof.

William, too, was growing on her in a way she wouldn't have expected. She had always loved children, but there was something special about this boy that she couldn't quite put her finger on.

As for Henry's claim about a connection between Adaira and Mr. Burgess, though, the longer the farmer stayed, the more Adaira fought the very idea of it.

She could admit that Mr. Burgess was physically attractive in a rugged, unassuming sort of way, but Adaira knew better than to be taken in by handsome looks. Plenty of men were handsome, but that didn't mean they had much substance underneath that. That was what had gotten her in trouble with Henry.

Mr. Burgess's strength of character, on the other hand, was something Adaira took much more notice of. The way he loved his son, the way he showed respect to everyone, the way he never minded giving up his time to help someone. These were traits Adaira knew held so far greater value when it came to finding a husband.

But Adaira also knew none of those great qualities mattered as far as she was concerned. She and Mr. Burgess were destined to be friends, nothing more.

So why can' I stop thinking about him? Adaira groaned as she pressed her forehead against the wall one evening. She'd just put an apple pie in the oven, and her first thought had been that she hoped Mr. Burgess would like it.

Maybe if I list the reasons why we can' be together, that will help.

She lifted her head and started to pace the floor. *First, it hasn' even been a year since the man lost his wife, so he must still be in mourning over her. Second, I may be one o' the prettiest women in Everton, but Henry said Mistress Burgess was a rare beauty.*

Adaira glanced at her reflection in one of the windows. *My curly hair and brown eyes are nice, but they're definitely na "rare."*

She sighed sadly, for she'd never cared so much about her appearance before.

Then a third reason blazed through her mind, one that outdid all the others: *I don' deserve to be happy with someone.*

Adaira's blood froze in her veins, as it did every time she thought about her past. It was an unwelcome thought, but she wondered if she should force herself to think about it more often. *Maybe that will be enough to make all my foolish wishes fer romance die away. After all, Mr. Burgess could never want someone who—*

"But, Da', I'm just going down to play with my friends!" someone yelled.

Adaira spun around. *That's William. It sounds like he's in the foyer. What could he be so angry about?*

"I don' care what the reason is. I already told you yer na to go anywhere near the water!" Mr. Burgess shouted back.

Many people would have tried to secretly leave, or at least not have listened in, but Adaira was really bad about eavesdropping. Especially when the topic of conversation was this interesting.

She tiptoed forward and peeked around the corner. The father and son were facing each other in the foyer, with Mr. Burgess's back to her. William looked like he was on the verge of tears.

"You don' let me do anything I want to do!"

"That is na true, and you know it," Mr. Burgess argued. "'Tis far too late to go out anyway even if you didn' want to go to the beach."

William huffed, but then he asked softly, "Why don' you come with me, Da'?"

The farmer shook his head. "You know that's na an option."

"But—"

"Just trust me. I'm doing this to protect you."

The boy's expression turned to contempt. "I don' need you to protect me. That's what Mum needed. Why didn' you protect her?"

Adaira gasped and, without thinking about the implications of what she was doing, strode up to William.

"Stop," she said, reaching out to the lad—

But before her fingers brushed William's shoulder, Mr. Burgess yanked her back. "Don' touch him!"

Adaira trembled under the man's terrifying gaze. *What's happening?*

"Don' be mean to her," William cried, jumping forward and grabbing his father's arm.

Mr. Burgess winced and immediately pulled himself away from them both before tucking his arm behind his back. The man took a deep breath, and when he exhaled, it almost seemed like he was hissing in pain.

"Mistress Stubbins," he said calmly, "I apologize fer disturbing you at this time o' night. Unfortunately, my son gets too excited sometimes and—"

"—Too excited? Da', that's na right at all!" William stamped his foot.

Mr. Burgess ignored him and said, "And perhaps 'twould be best if he and I continued our conversation in our room."

The man looked to his son expectantly, but William was seething with rage.

"You always treat me like this!"

Then, before Adaira or Mr. Burgess could predict it, William darted past them both and—

The front door flew open and smacked the inner wall as William raced out of the inn.

"William! Come back here!" the farmer called.

But the boy swerved to the right and started going up the hill that led away from town.

The adults moved to follow him, but then Mr. Burgess turned to Adaira. "*Please*, mistress. This is between me and my son."

Adaira froze, for there was something desperate about the way he'd said *please*.

Almost as if there was more going on than she realized.

Almost as if I'm the one he's trying to protect.

And as much as that made no sense, Adaira found she couldn't argue with it.

She nodded to Mr. Burgess and watched as he charged out the door after his son, who was quickly disappearing from view.

It took a lot of willpower, but somehow, Adaira forced herself to shut the door and not follow them, so the Burgesses could settle their affairs privately. Instead, she wandered back to the kitchen and started pacing once more.

A faint rumble of thunder hit her ears, and she dashed to the nearest window. Several dark clouds loomed a few miles out over the water, sparking with lightning and dumping rain into an already churning ocean.

I hope that doesn' come inland, especially with the Burgesses outside—

"Adaira, why are you gawking out the window?"

The woman turned to her father, who was standing in the kitchen just behind her.

"Oh, Father, I didn' know you were there," she replied. "There's a storm brewing over the ocean. Did you hear that thunder just a bit ago?"

"Nay, I didn'. Must have been in yer head; otherwise, I'm sure I would have heard it, too. There's nothing wrong with my hearing, after all!" Terrence grumbled, but Adaira caught how he tried to subtly tap at his right ear.

She'd suspected his hearing was getting worse for months now, but the man was too obstinate to admit it.

"Did you get dinner at the Dunnets' house?" she asked, trying to distract herself from worrying over the Burgesses.

"Aye, but Angus was so greedy with the bread that I'm still hungry."

"Well, I'm baking an apple pie right now. Would you like a slice when 'tis ready?"

A hint of a smile passed over the man's lips, something seldom seen nowadays, but then it vanished under the heavy frown lines Terrence wore most often.

"I suppose that wouldn' be so bad. I'll just be upstairs until then," he said before turning and hobbling out of sight.

Adaira shook her head with a chuckle. For all the man's faults, he was still her father, and she couldn't help but love him.

A few minutes later, the scent of apples hit her nose, and she realized she'd lost track of how long the pie had been baking. She jerked the oven door open and sighed.

Just in time, she thought, taking out the precious pie. *Any longer and it probably would have burned—*

"Hello, Adaira!"

The woman leaped into the air, making the pie in her hands tip. With reflexes as fast as the lightning outside, Adaira steadied herself and just barely managed to keep the food from becoming a delicious mess at her feet.

She whirled around with a scowl, prepared to give whoever had startled her a good scolding.

But her irritation fizzled when she realized who it was.

There stood her friend Briony, looking a little anxious herself.

"Briony, you gave me such a fright! What are you doing here at this time o' night?"

"I'm sorry to trouble you, but there are newcomers at the dock, and I thought I'd give you some time to prepare lodging fer them."

"Newcomers? How many?" Adaira's mind sprang into action, and she hurried to the linen closet to get some towels.

"I only saw the ship from my cottage, so I could na tell you," the midwife replied.

"There better na be very many. Otherwise, I won' be able to accommodate them all."

"Would you like some help?"

"Aye, please," she said as she handed Briony some towels. "I may need quite a bit if there are a lot o' newcomers. Especially if my current guests remain much longer. Mr. Burgess and his son, William, have been here fer twelve days, and they seem to like it so much that I would na be surprised if they decide to build themselves a house."

Adaira internally winced at her own words, for she hadn't meant to say that much. *That's just what I've been wishing they would do.*

"Do you truly think so? William would certainly like that, given how attached he is to you."

Adaira shrugged and looked away, so Briony wouldn't see the smile on her face.

I've gotten pretty attached to him, too. . . . 'Twill be incredibly sad when they leave.

But what about what happened just a bit ago? The way Mr. Burgess grabbed me was frightening. I never would have thought he was the kind o' person who would do that.

And then why did it seem like he was trying to protect me? What would he be protecting me from? Did I misunderstand?

A man's voice interrupted her thoughts. Adaira and Briony rushed to the foyer and found a soaked Gareth Peterson standing at the front door.

"Adaira! Do you have any rooms?" the man asked, gasping for breath as if he'd just run a race.

"Aye, Gareth, what is it?"

"There are some strangers who just came in! One o' them is seriously hurt! Doctor Sherwin is with him, but they have to move him inside. I had to see if you had anywhere to put him up!"

"How many—" Adaira broke off when she realized Gareth was already rushing back outside.

She turned to Briony in confusion, and then they both raced to the door. Three townsfolk were carrying a young man on a stretcher while Dr. Sherwin walked ahead of them. The group was a good distance away, slowed down by the steep incline. The rain was still falling heavily, making it difficult to see.

The poor man! Adaira whirled around and returned inside, determined to have everything ready by the time her new guest reached her doorstep.

Soon, the inn was full of noise, and Adaira was running from room to room like a madwoman. Only two people from the ship ended up needing a room: the injured man, whose name was Santiago Mendes, and Mr. Mendes's younger sister, a beautiful blonde woman named Lucia.

Adaira's heart went out to them when Lucia explained how they'd gotten caught up in a storm that had damaged their ship and injured Mr. Mendes's leg. The ship's first mate had even been swept overboard, and now Lucia worried that her brother wouldn't survive either.

"Dr. Sherwin is a very skilled doctor. Yer brother is in good hands," Adaira said in her most reassuring voice as she gave the young woman a cup of tea.

Lucia's hands shook, but she smiled and thanked Adaira for accommodating them on such short notice.

Adaira could tell her new guest was doing her best not to cry, so Adaira excused herself in order to give the woman some privacy. Besides, there were plenty of other things Adaira needed to attend to.

I hope her brother's all right. She seems very young. If Dr. Sherwin can' save Mr. Mendes—

Let's na think like that, Adaira. Let's focus on what you can control.

With that in mind, Adaira spent the next few hours going out of her way to make her new guests' stay as comfortable as possible. That way, maybe they'd have at least a few good memories of their time in Orkney.

When Adaira finished for the night, she was exhausted. So exhausted she almost didn't notice the light shining under the Burgesses' door.

I didn' realize they'd gotten back. I hope they were able to settle everything.

I wonder how Mr. Burgess will act in the morneen. Will he be the kind gentleman I've known fer most o' his time here, or will he be the confusing, dangerous man I saw tonight?

But Adaira lacked the energy to consider it further, and by the time she'd climbed into bed, the man's strange behavior had completely drifted from her thoughts.

She didn't know Mr. Burgess had come in through the back door. She didn't know he'd sneaked into his room so quietly that no one had seen him. And she definitely didn't know he'd been carrying his unconscious son in his arms.

The Lies We Keep

John tenderly laid William on the bed, still out cold from earlier. He quickly changed the boy into his nightclothes, wondering when he would wake. *Should I get Dr. Sherwin?*

The farmer dismissed the thought almost immediately, though, for he knew that wasn't an option. *He'll be all right. He has to be.*

John's gaze went to his bag, tucked almost out of sight beside the dresser. He snatched it up in his fist. *At least, he will be after I follow through on my promise to Ellie.*

He took a deep breath before slipping out into the hallway, determined to do what was necessary despite how hard it would be—

But then a series of whispers tickled his ears. The voices were too low to make out, but he recognized one as Dr. Sherwin's. They were coming from the room across the hall.

The farmer was well aware that a large ship had arrived at the docks only hours before. He'd also seen the fellow who'd been brought up to the inn on a stretcher. *Dr. Sherwin must be in there with the injured man. I hope he'll be able to help him.*

John thought he heard approaching footsteps from the other end of the hall, so he darted to the back door and ducked out. It wouldn't do for anyone to see him moving around at this time of night. People might ask questions John couldn't answer.

He scanned the area and was pleased when he saw no one around. It was close to midnight now, and most of Everton tended to be both early to bed and early to rise. As a farmer, John was typically like this, too, but tonight, he had a mission too important to delay.

He sneaked around the outside of the inn, through the gate, and up the path, the very same path he'd just walked only a little while ago.

And though last time John had been carrying William in his arms, it hadn't felt nearly as difficult as it did now.

John knew what he had to do. It was what he'd promised his wife he would do if this ever happened.

But guilt still squeezed his heart, and each step he took felt heavier than the last.

This is the only way, he tried to tell himself. *Ellie would never have made me promise this if there was another option.*

John groaned, gripping his bag tighter. *Then why does it feel like I'm letting them both down? Why does it feel like I'm about to make the greatest mistake o' my life?*

Despite these doubts, he forced himself to march onward until he reached his destination: the cliffs past Drulea Cottage. The clouds had all drifted away, leaving no sign of the storm which had rent it in two. The waves, too, were deceptively calm, giving the impression of safety and rest.

But John wasn't fooled. He knew exactly what had happened in this very spot. And he had to make sure it never happened again.

This is wrong, John, and you know it, whispered a voice in his mind.

And as he slowly removed the contents of his bag, John did know it. He knew it with every fiber of his being.

***

A long time passed before John returned to the inn, dragging his feet like dead weight. It wasn't that he wanted to be seen, but he lacked the strength to move any faster. Indeed, his limbs had become as heavy as lead, and it was all he could do just to get himself back to his room. Such sluggishness would normally spawn from physical exhaustion, but such wasn't the case this time. Instead, John's ailment came purely from the emotional toll of the decision he'd just made—perhaps the hardest decision of his life. And as he opened his door with his head hung low, he feared he'd condemned them all.

"Da', yer back!"

John's head shot up, for William wasn't asleep as he'd expected—instead, he was sitting in bed with a smile.

The farmer was in front of his son in an instant, his bag tossed to the side without a care.

"William! Are you all right? How are you feeling?" John asked, placing his hands on the boy's shoulders.

William frowned and touched his temple. "My head is pounding something awful! Why does it hurt so much?"

John leaned away. "I'm so sorry, son. I didn' want to—wait." He turned back to the boy, his brow furrowed. "Don' you remember what happened?"

William grimaced and shook his head. "I just remember getting angry and running out o' the inn when you told me I couldn' go to the beach. What happened after that?"

John's eyes widened, and an idea came to him. A spark of hope.

But it was a risk, a terrible risk that could have grave consequences if William was to ever remember the truth.

Is it worth it?

John stared into the night-black eyes of his son, so innocent, so eager to hear his father's next words. There was no doubt in them. Only complete trust.

And so, John opened his mouth, letting the lie tumble out: "It started raining while we were outside. You slipped in the mud and hit yer head."

"I did? How did I end up back here?"

"I carried you," John explained, trying his best to look sincere.

Will he believe me? He has to!

A grateful smile came over William's face, and the boy said, "Thank you, Da'."

But when John smiled in turn, the emotion rising in his chest wasn't relief. It was more guilt. Guilt for lying to his son. Again.

And guilt for breaking his promise to his wife.

Involuntarily, John's eyes strayed to his bag. *I know you made me swear to do it when the time came, Ellie, but I just couldn'. I'm sorry.*

John threw a smirk onto his face and ruffled the boy's hair. "How many times have I told you yer na careful enough?"

William winced and pulled away from his father's touch. "Da', that hurts! And you don' have to keep telling me the same thing over and over."

John laughed. "Perhaps I do since you don' listen! I hope that bump on yer head will help you remember better."

The boy grimaced, but there was a crinkle of mirth in the corners of his eyes.

"You better go back to sleep," John said after a moment. "We have a lot o' work to do on the Martins' farm in the morneen."

William started to do as he was told, but then he paused.

"What is it, William?" John asked, trying to sound impatient. As if it was just an ordinary night and William had stayed up past his bedtime. As if they were an ordinary family with ordinary problems.

"Da', where were you just now?"

"I stepped out fer a bit o' fresh air."

"Did you see any o' the visitors?"

"Visitors?" he asked casually. But inside, John's heart was hammering in his chest. *Is William's memory returning?*

"Aye," the lad confirmed. "Mistress Fairborn told me they came in late last night."

A crease appeared in the farmer's forehead. "You talked to Mistress Fairborn?"

"Just fer a minute. She and Dr. Sherwin were arguing about something in the hallway and woke me up."

"Dr. Sherwin? You didn' talk to him about yer head, did you?" The man's knees were buckling now, but he tried to hide them by leaning against the bed.

"I wanted to, but he looked like he was in a hurry, so I didn' say anything," William answered, not noticing his father's odd behavior. "Do you think Mistress Stubbins has enough rooms?"

John let out a quick breath and smiled. *Dr. Sherwin doesn' know. William is still safe.*

"Let's think about that another time," the farmer urged, his pulse starting to slow as his strength returned. "Fer now, we both need some sleep."

William huffed in disappointment, but he didn't argue when his father tucked the blankets around him. After a few minutes, the boy drifted off once more.

John, on the other hand, stayed awake for a long while replaying everything that had taken place. *If only I could just go back and do it over. . . .*

He groaned. *But what if that wouldn' change anything? What if this has been inevitable from the beginning?*

His mind turned to the visitors then, and apprehension surged through him. For if even one of them had seen what had really happened that night, all his efforts to hide the truth were for naught.

Dismal Conditions

When the Burgesses woke, John insisted on he and William taking a walk before going to breakfast. He told his son it was because Mistress Stubbins must be busy from having new guests. That was only partially true though.

The main reason John delayed going to the kitchen was because his stomach was in knots at the thought of facing the beautiful innkeeper again. During the hours he'd lain awake the night before, he'd spent a long time thinking about how incorrigible his behavior must have seemed. And while he knew grabbing the woman's arm and keeping her away from William had been the only rational thing to do at the time, there was no way he could explain that to Mistress Stubbins.

Na unless I tell her the truth, and I couldn' possibly do that. If only she hadn' been eavesdropping, then this could all have been avoid— John cut off the thought with a sigh; she wasn't to blame for what had happened. He was.

The farmer's gaze darted to his son, strolling beside him without any idea of the worries swirling around John's head. *And 'tis going to stay that way if I can help it.*

"Da', look!" William shouted, pointing to the large ship down at the docks.

The farmer viewed the vessel spitefully, for it was a painful reminder of his own failures. One of the masts had collapsed, its top half lying in useless pieces on the ship's deck.

"Hello!"

The farmer jumped as a middle-aged man appeared in front of him. It was the fisherman, Mr. McLaren. *How did I na notice him before? Was I so focused on the ship that I didn' even hear him?*

"Good morneen, Mr. McLaren!" William called with a friendly wave.

"Same to you, young Mr. Burgess. And you, older Mr. Burgess," the fisherman replied with a chuckle.

John nodded politely, but he definitely wasn't happy to see the man. John had noticed that many of the villagers found Mr. McLaren annoying, calling him the "mad fisherman" behind his back. But there was something else about the man that made John uncomfortable. The farmer wasn't sure exactly what it was, but his gut told him Mr. McLaren was hiding something.

William, on the other hand, loved talking to the fisherman. The man was a wonderful storyteller, weaving yarns that seemed to transport listeners directly into them. He had an odd way of talking, too, almost like he knew all the answers to life's deepest questions.

"The weather sure was frightening last night," Mr. McLaren remarked.

It was an innocent statement, just an observation that anyone might make in passing.

If not for the suspicious twinkle in the man's eye as he said it.

John immediately froze, his palms starting to sweat. "Aye, I suppose. . . ."

"And those clouds . . ." Mr. McLaren continued, glancing up at the sky with a smirk. "They looked mighty angry."

"Were you out when the storm happened?" John asked.

"Nay, I was at my brother's tavern, but everyone in there heard the thunder rumbling and had to take a peek. That was when we saw the ship coming into port."

William's eyes widened. "Did you get to talk to the newcomers?"

The fisherman turned his attention to the boy with a warm smile. "That I did. Strange folks. Talked real funny like nothing I've ever heard."

"They don' speak English?" the lad asked, appearing both slightly disappointed and more intrigued at the same time.

"I don' know about all o' them, but when we went down to the ship, the captain was calling fer a doctor. Saying something about how he'd lost his first mate and wasn' about to lose the ship's owner, too."

John blanched and looked away. "Someone died last night in the storm?"

"Aye," Mr. McLaren said solemnly. "Such a shame, losing control like that."

John's head whipped back to the fisherman. "What? *Lost control?*"

The man smirked as if he hadn't said anything peculiar. "The sea, o' course. She's such a violent, temperamental thing." Mr. McLaren turned and gazed out at the waves. "And yet, she's so generous in what she provides . . . so beautiful. . . ."

William followed the man's lead and peered at the ocean, too. "Aye, beautiful . . ."

John cleared his throat and said, "The ocean is a danger to us all. I don' see anything 'generous' or 'beautiful' about it."

Mr. McLaren seemed to come out of a daze and turned to the redhead. "Ah, but that's because yer only looking at one aspect o' her. She has so many faces, yet some people only see the ugly ones. I wouldn' have a living without the fish she gives."

John pursed his lips. "I suppose that's true fer *you.*"

"But yer also right that she's dangerous!" the fisherman said with a cackle. "Especially in Everton, where her powers can be swayed . . . in the proper hands."

"What are you implying?" the farmer growled.

Mr. McLaren held up his hands. "Nothing! In fact, I better be going. Lots to do today. I'll see you later, William."

The fisherman winked at the boy and scurried out of sight, leaving John to wonder what he'd been talking about.

"Da', may we go back to the inn now?" William asked.

John was about to decline, but then his son's stomach rumbled.

I can' put it off forever. I'll have to face Mistress Stubbins eventually.

"I suppose since yer stomach can' wait much longer," he said, gently elbowing the boy.

"Da'!" William jumped away, covering his stomach with his arms.

"I'm getting hungry as well. We should get our coats before we eat though. There's more o' a chill in the air than I expected."

William nodded, and the two of them headed back to their room. They didn't glimpse the innkeeper's daughter as they entered the inn and passed by the kitchen, a fact John was very grateful for.

Perhaps we won' see her this morneen at all, and I can think o' a good way to apologi—

But then John's hopes were dashed, for she and Mistress Fairborn were in the hallway.

"Agreeable? Hmm, that's good. Even if he was na, I might overlook it since he's such a handsome fellow. Perhaps he may need to stay longer than Dr. Sherwin initially thought. Broken bones do take a long time to heal," Mistress Stubbins was saying with a sneer.

"Nay, Adaira, you can' be thinking that!" Mistress Fairborn shouted.

Who are they talking about? John wondered.

But that was when the two women noticed the Burgesses and clammed up, spots of color appearing on their cheeks.

Now I'm the one eavesdropping, John realized with embarrassment. He looked away and tried to shuffle past them, but then he became aware that William wasn't following him.

The farmer spun around and frowned when he saw the boy staring at the women shamelessly. John grabbed his son's shoulder and said, "William, come along. Yer being impolite. My apologies, mistresses."

Mistress Stubbins nodded at John, but the movement was stiff and cold.

"Sorry!" William added before giving his father a nervous smile. He mouthed another "sorry" to John, but the farmer didn't say anything else as he and the boy went to their room.

John tried to be nonchalant as they retrieved their coats, but an uneasy feeling had taken hold of his heart.

The expression on Mistress Stubbins's face when she'd looked at him replayed in his mind over and over again, and the longer he thought about it, the more certain he was that his actions last night had deeply hurt her.

More deeply than they should have for acquaintances.

Which only made John's guilt intensify.

William and John made their way back out into the corridor—now empty—before entering the dining room. There they found bread and muffins sitting on the table, along with some plates and silverware. Cups had also been set out next to a large pitcher of milk.

Mistress Stubbins takes such good care o' us. How ungrateful I must seem. . . .

"Are you angry at me, Da'?" William asked once they'd sat down and blessed the meal.

John turned to his son. "What? Why do you ask?"

"You've been frowning ever since we saw Mistress Stubbins in the hallway. Is it because I was rude?" the boy asked, picking at his food and not meeting his father's eyes.

John smiled and shook his head. "Nay, I'm na angry at you."

"That's good!"

Just angry at myself, he thought, biting into a muffin.

A minute later, William asked, "Who was Mistress Stubbins saying was handsome?"

John almost choked. "What?"

"When she and Mistress Fairborn were talking, she said someone was really handsome. Who was she talking about?"

"Oh, that . . . she was probably talking about one o' the guests who arrived last night," John explained before drinking some milk.

I guess Dr. Sherwin was able to help that injured fellow, after all.

He kept his lips curled up as he put the cup down, but an unpleasant emotion was sliding through the farmer's veins.

It was a feeling John hadn't experienced in a long time, but once he focused in on it, it was easy to identify: jealousy.

Jealousy at hearing Mistress Stubbins compliment another man.

And almost as soon as John recognized the emotion, shame slithered into its place.

How could I be feeling this way after what happened to Ellie? 'Twas only six months ago that she passed, and I'm already thinking about another woman? Nay, I'm na thinking o' another woman! I just . . .

An image of Adaira Stubbins flooded his mind. From the moment he'd first seen her, John had been struck by her sweet, unassuming beauty. He thought of the way her hair cascaded over her shoulders. The way her brown eyes sparkled. The way her nose crinkled when she smiled.

John gulped, heat spreading down his neck. *Control yerself, man.*

"Da'? Are you sure yer all right?"

The man blinked a few times, returning to the present. He looked down and saw he'd crushed the rest of the muffin in his hand.

John turned to his son with a light laugh. "Oops. I'm fine, son. I'm fine."

Another lie, he groaned inwardly. *This is becoming a habit.*

∗∗∗

Adaira stood in the kitchen brewing tea as she tried to sift through the conversation she'd had with her friend. Briony had just left to go to the market, but not before revealing something startling.

When Briony said she wanted to check on Mr. Mendes this morneen, I didn' think anything o' it. After all, she helped Dr. Sherwin take care o' the man's leg last night, so why shouldn' she want to see how he's doing?

What Adaira hadn't expected was for Briony to come out of the man's room five shades of red. Then she'd admitted to Adaira that Mr. Mendes had tried to flirt with her.

Adaira giggled, enjoying the incredible turn of events. *No one has ever shown interest in Briony before. How I wish I could have watched that scene unfold. Mr. Mendes must have been very obvious fer her to realize he was flirting. That man has no idea what he's getting himself into!*

But then Adaira's spirits fell. *He really doesn' know, does he? Maybe I shouldn' have encouraged Briony. What if she gets angry, and*

I'm na there to keep her from flying off the handle? I can' hold her hand all the time.

Adaira sighed, wishing she could just tell Briony she was a selkie. *That would solve so many problems. Then she would know to be careful o' her temper, and she might even figure out how to control her powers. Besides, doesn' she have the right to know what she is?*

You know why you can' tell her, said a voice in her head. *You promised.*

Another voice came into the woman's mind, the voice of someone who had been both an enemy and a friend. Adaira tried to ignore it, but her thoughts still pulled her back to that terrifying moment when she'd stumbled upon the Fairborn secret.

Adaira had only been a small lass at the time, hardly old enough to even understand what a selkie was. But after she'd thought she saw Briony talking to a seal, she'd made the mistake of going directly to Drulea Cottage and telling Briony's mother about it.

"And you thought talking to me was a good idea?" Bethany said with raised eyebrows. There was something frightening about the woman's tone, and Adaira immediately took a step back.

"W-Well, I thought you'd want to know."

Bethany motioned for Adaira to lean closer, and once she had, Bethany whispered, "The thing is, though, I'm a selkie, too."

"What? You?"

Bethany nodded. "And yer na going to tell a soul, na even Briony. Right?"

The girl opened and closed her mouth like a fish, too shocked to respond.

"Because if you do, I'll summon so many seals they'll drag all o' Everton to the bottom o' the sea. You don' want to be responsible fer that, do you, Adaira?"

"Nay, I-I won' tell!"

"You must swear it."

"I . . . I swear."

Adaira ran her hand down her face. That threat had haunted her for years, and even now that it had lost its power, she still felt a shudder anytime she thought about it.

A ray of sunshine streamed into the kitchen, breaking through the dark cloud hanging over Adaira's head.

Since when did I become so gloomy? I'm Adaira Stubbins, the town optimist, she told herself, putting her hands on her hips. *I'm na supposed to be melancholy. I'm supposed to build everyone up.*

Adaira lifted her lips into a smile, and as she did, she felt her mood lift as well. *That's better. Now, let's try to be more positive about Briony and Mr. Mendes, too. Hmm. . .*

Well, Briony is a wonderful person, and she hasn' had an incident in over a decade. If something else was going to happen, it probably would have by now.

I don' know anything about Mr. Mendes, though, since I haven' spoken to him yet. His sister seems nice enough, but I need to find out more about the man himself—

Adaira's stomach gurgled, reminding her she hadn't eaten yet.

I'll have to talk to Mr. Mendes after breakfast. Adaira marched to the dining room, her head held high.

Until she saw who was at the table, and all her confidence flew out the window.

Assumptions and Judgment

Adaira swallowed, but her mouth was bone-dry as she stared at Mr. Burgess and his son. She pinched her lips into a smile, but that did nothing to curb the anxiety in her heart. She'd felt it earlier when she'd seen the farmer in the hallway, but this time, she recognized its cause.

Why am I still upset about what happened last night? Mr. Burgess already apologized fer "disturbing" me. Isn' that enough?

Somewhere deep down, though, she knew it wasn't enough. An apology like that might have been sufficient coming from someone else but not from Mr. Burgess. *Why? Why is it different fer him? Do I have some expectation o' him that goes beyond—*

She could sense a headache building in her temples, so she took a cleansing breath and shoved those thoughts aside.

"I'm glad to see you two," Adaira greeted. "I was getting a wee bit worried."

"What fer?" William asked, his mouth full of bread.

"Don' talk with food in yer mouth," Mr. Burgess nagged, his face unreadable.

"I hope you got everything resolved," she continued, looking to William.

But the boy just cocked his head to the side like he had no idea what she was talking about.

"With yer argument, I mean."

"What argument?"

Adaira glanced at Mr. Burgess in alarm, and the man said, "William slipped in the mud last night and hit his head, so he doesn' remember what happened all that well."

She gasped and turned back to the boy. Her hands instantly went to his face as she inspected him for bruises. "You did? Are you all right? Does it still hurt?"

"I'm all right, mistress. 'Tis just a wee bit sore today, and—" The boy broke off with a wince, and Adaira realized she'd grazed a lump on the back of his head.

"Oh, forgive me!" She yanked her hands back.

"You don' need to feel bad, mistress. I'm pretty tough."

"There was a lot o' commotion last night. Some late-night guests came in?" Mr. Burgess asked.

"Aye, their ship got wrecked in the storm, and the ship's owner broke his leg, so they had to bring him up on a stretcher. Dr. Sherwin and Briony must have been in there with him fer hours," Adaira said. "And their first mate went over—"

"Were there any other injuries?" Mr. Burgess interrupted.

"Na that I know o'," Adaira said, caught off guard by the man's gruff tone.

She sneaked a glance at him, curious about the dark expression he wore. It was sad, but it also seemed strangely guilty.

Maybe he's still feeling bad because o' how he grabbed me last night?

Almost as soon as she thought that, though, she scolded herself for being ridiculous. *He wouldn' still be thinking about that.*

"Were there any bairns on the ship?" William asked.

Adaira chuckled. "Nay, I don' think so."

The boy's lips stuck out. "Aw, that would have been fun!"

"But they're definitely na from around here. Maybe they can tell you some stories about where they're from."

William's eyes lit up at the thought.

"Do you have enough room fer everyone to stay?" Mr. Burgess said.

"The man with the broken leg and his sister are staying here, but the crew is still on the ship, so there's enough space."

"That's good."

"I did notice the door isn' in good shape after all the ruckus last night. Mr. Burgess, do you think you could look at it fer me before you lea—"

"I fear na," the man said, cutting her off. "We have quite a lot o' work to do at Mr. Martin's farm today, and I want to make sure all the crops are doing fine after that storm."

"O' course," Adaira said, ducking her head so he wouldn't see her disappointment.

"In fact, we better get going now," Mr. Burgess said, rising to his feet. "Come along, William."

"But, Da', I'm na finished!"

"You've eaten enough. Thank you fer the great breakfast, mistress," he said with a quick nod.

William opened his mouth like he wanted to protest, but Mr. Burgess was already marching out.

"Bye, mistress," William said before dashing after his father.

Adaira watched them leave, getting the distinct sense the farmer was trying to avoid her.

Nay, he's just busy. Why would he be avoiding me?

But a hint of doubt remained clinging to her like a barnacle, despite how illogical it seemed.

The woman's shoulders drooped. She didn't like the idea that he didn't want to spend time with her. *I know I overstepped last night; Mr. Burgess made that very clear, but I didn' think that would create a rift between us.*

The clock in the sitting room chimed, telling Adaira it was nine o' clock. She glanced at the food and dishes on the table. *Time to get back to work.*

***

By lunchtime, Adaira had almost managed to forget about the redheaded farmer. The tightness in her chest had faded, and the anxiety had slipped from her mind.

She went to Mr. Mendes's door and softly knocked. She'd seen the man's sister that morning, but she'd yet to speak to Mr. Mendes himself. Lunch seemed like the perfect opportunity to get to know the man better.

And to see if he's worthy o' Briony's attention.

"Come in!" called a cheery voice.

Mr. Mendes was sitting on his bed with a bright grin as she entered, and his sister, Lucia, was in a chair beside him. Lucia didn't look nearly as pleased to see her, but she gave Adaira a courteous nod.

"Hello! I'm sorry I didn't introduce myself earlier. I'm Adaira Stubbins," the innkeeper's daughter said. "Yer sister explained yer situation to me. I'm very sorry fer yer misfortune."

"Thank you," Mr. Mendes replied, his face clouding over for a brief moment before he smiled once more. "It's good to meet you, Senhorita[17] Stubbins. You are the . . ."

"She runs the inn," Lucia whispered out of the side of her mouth.

"Ah. Then I owe you even more thanks for your generous hospitality. You probably don't get many visitors with my particular . . . complications." The man eyed his cast with a frown.

"I'm happy to have you here, Mr. Mendes," Adaira said, hoping he could see her sincerity. "I just wish you and Mistress Mendes were coming to Everton under better circumstances."

"Oh," the other woman cut in, waving her hand. "Please call me 'Lucia.' I can't stand such formality."

Adaira's eyebrows rose, for her request seemed to conflict the rest of her uppity behavior. Not that she was downright rude, but Adaira had definitely gotten the impression this woman liked having boundaries between herself and the common folk.

Kind o' like Muireall Oliver . . . But maybe I judged Lucia too quickly?

The blond woman was still waiting for a response, so Adaira quickly said, "Aye, that sounds nice. Almost everyone around here calls me 'Adaira,' and I'd be happy fer you to do that, too."

She turned to Mr. Mendes. "Please don' misunderstand when I say I don' intend to call you by yer first name. As nice

---

[17] Portuguese title for an unmarried woman.

as my neighbors are, I don' want them to make any assumptions about you."

"Nor do I want them to say anything about you, Senhorita Stubbins," the man said with a nod.

Aye, I definitely don' want that. I've seen how brutal they can be. Adaira suppressed a shiver as an image of a much-younger Briony came to her mind.

"A-Anyway, I was just about to have lunch, and I wanted to see if you two would like to eat with me." She looked to her guests expectantly.

Lucia cringed ever so slightly. "It's still very difficult for my brother to move around, so I'd prefer we stay here. Perhaps you could—"

"Join us," Mr. Mendes finished, gesturing to the second chair in the room.

Lucia glared at her brother, but he blatantly ignored her and kept his attention on their hostess.

Adaira held back a smirk. *I guess Mr. Mendes enjoys getting on his sister's nerves. I'll have to keep that in mind. Briony could do with someone who has a good sense o' humor.*

"Thank you, sir," Adaira said, her eyes sparkling. "I'll go get lunch, then."

"What are we having?" Lucia asked.

"Bannock[18]!" she answered, knowing the woman would have no idea what that was.

And before she could ask, Adaira strolled out, laughing to herself at Lucia's confused and slightly nervous expression. The fact that Mr. Mendes had looked like he wanted to laugh, too, had made it even better.

Adaira went in and out of the room a few times until she'd brought in all the food, dishes, and drinks they'd need. As she was finishing up, she also went to the sitting room and grabbed an interesting novel by an Irishman named Jonathan Swift[19].

"I thought this might help you pass the time," Adaira explained, setting the book on Mr. Mendes's bedside table before she sat down with her food.

---

[18] A traditional Scottish bread made from oatmeal or barley flour.

[19] Jonathan Swift's book *Gulliver's Travels* was originally published in 1726.

"Oh, thank you," the man said. "That's very thoughtful of you. My sister has been trying to keep me company, but I know she'd like to see the town." He turned to Lucia. "Now you can do so without worrying that I'll have nothing to do."

Lucia blushed before looking to Adaira. "I didn't know you people could—I mean . . ."

The woman clamped her mouth shut, but Adaira knew exactly what she'd been about to say.

Rather than getting angry, though, Adaira smiled and said, "Yer right in yer assumption. Most o' Everton doesn' know how to read. My grandparents insisted on teaching my mum when she was a bairn, and she taught me when I was a lass. I grew to enjoy it so much that I've collected several books over the years. They're all on the bookcase in the sitting room. Yer welcome to read any that you'd like."

Lucia seemed surprised at her calm response, making Adaira wonder what kind of social circles she must be used to. *If they're the kind where people can' speak civilly to each other, I'm glad I'm na part o' them.*

"This is very good," Mr. Mendes remarked as he brought a large piece of bannock to his lips.

"Thank you. I hope the muffins I had my friend bring down earlier were just as good," Adaira said, intentionally mentioning Briony to see how Mr. Mendes would react.

"Ah, yer friend . . ." he said, his green eyes trailing away from hers. "Is she always so . . ."

The man seemed to be struggling to think of the word he wanted.

Adaira's mind went back to her conversation with the midwife after she'd gone in to see Mr. Mendes.

"I may have been a wee bit rude to him earlier. I'm sure his opinion o' me is na good," Briony admitted.

"Why were you rude? Did he say something that made you angry? You know you let that temper get the better o' you all too often."

The midwife shook her head, her cheeks pink. "Nay. He was—I think he was . . . flirting with me."

Adaira winced as she came back to the present, for she was well aware of how impolite Briony could be. *And that's just when she loses her temper. If she was being rude on purpose, who knows what* she might have said! Ooh, if she messed up her chances with Mr. Mendes, I'm going to be so angry with her—

"Reserved?" Mr. Mendes finished.

Adaira leaned back in surprise. "That's a generous way o' putting it, sir. Briony Fairborn has . . . been through a lot. She's a wee bit wary o' people sometimes."

"Isso parece você[20]," Lucia told her brother with a pointed glance.

Mr. Mendes looked down at his food. "So, what are the ingredients in bannock?"

Adaira blinked. "Um . . . well . . . I use flour, salt, lard, water, and a few special ingredients that I keep to myself."

"Well, this is very tasty. My sister and I have never gotten to try anything like it, and I've been to many places. . . ."

Mr. Mendes continued talking, sharing many intriguing details about his life as a Portuguese merchant as he not-so-subtly shifted their conversation away from Briony. Adaira noted the change, but since she didn't know what Lucia had whispered to her brother, she wasn't sure if the change was a good thing or a bad thing.

Adaira discovered a lot about the Mendes siblings as they ate. Mr. Mendes was a merchant from a place called Aveiro. He and Lucia had been on their way to Norway when their ship went off course. And Lucia had just celebrated her seventeenth birthday.

But the most interesting thing she learned was that Santiago Mendes seemed like a good man.

And that maybe, just maybe, he could be the right fit for a certain lovable, short-tempered selkie.

And what about Mr. Burgess? Could he be the right fit fer you?

Adaira gasped, startling her guests.

"Are you all right, senhorita?" Mr. Mendes asked.

She held up her hand. "I'm sorry. Yer . . . story frightened me a bit."

"Oh." The man's brow furrowed, and Adaira could tell he didn't believe her.

---

[20] That sounds like you.

"Brother, you do tell some pretty gruesome tales," Lucia said. "Actually, we've been talking for quite some time. Adaira, I'm sure you have things you need to do."

Adaira would have bristled at the woman's attempt to get rid of her, but right then she was eager to get away. "She's right. Let me take yer plates."

She grabbed their empty dishes and rose to her feet. "I'll be seeing you later, then. Let me know if you need anything."

Lucia and Mr. Mendes smiled and thanked her for the meal, but Adaira barely heard them as she went out. She was too busy worrying about the mad thought that had entered her mind a moment before.

'Tis completely mad . . . right?

Attraction and Repulsion

For the next couple of days, John did his best to spend as little time at the inn as possible. "We need to help Mr. Martin," was the excuse he gave William one morning. They were just finishing getting dressed, and John had told William they needed to grab their food and eat as quickly as possible.

"But I want to eat breakfast with Mistress Stubbins," William whined. "I've barely gotten to talk to her lately."

John held back a wince, for that was exactly what he was trying to prevent.

Talking to Adaira Stubbins wasn't safe anymore. She'd seen John's argument with William. And if she asked them about it again, William might remember what had actually happened.

Besides, John was becoming a little too attached to her, and it wasn't like they were going to stay there forever.

John opened his mouth to tell the lad that wasn't an option, but then William grimaced and put a hand on his forehead.

"Dizzy again?" the farmer asked.

The boy nodded. William had complained that his head was spinning yesterday, too, and he'd had to take a break from working for a while. John hadn't expected the boy would be feeling that way again today.

"Perhaps we've been working too hard. Why don' you go back to sleep, and I'll come check on you in a bit?"

"All right, Da'," William said weakly. John helped him back into bed, and within seconds, the boy was fast asleep.

I hope rest is all he needs, the farmer thought as he made his way to the dining room.

No one else was there, but Mistress Stubbins had set out some porridge on the table. John thought he heard her working in the kitchen, so he slurped down a bowl of food as quickly as he could. He'd noticed that she often ate breakfast with her father, and Terrence Stubbins was a late riser. If she heard someone moving around in the dining room, she might assume it was Terrence and come in.

John had told Mr. Martin they'd be at his house by eight o' clock, so when he was done, he got up to check the time. Everton Inn's sole clock was on the fireplace mantel in the sitting room, but as he neared the room, he heard a pair of voices.

One belonged to Mistress Fairborn, but the other was an unfamiliar woman's voice with a strange accent.

It must be one o' the foreigners. I'll just peek in to see the time and then be on my way, so I don' interrupt them—

"Speaking o' that, why is yer ship here?" Mistress Fairborn asked.

John froze, beads of sweat appearing on his brow. *How could I forget? I never did find out if the foreigners saw anything that night.*

Surely they were too far away, he tried to tell himself. *Aye, I don' need to worry.*

But John's hands were shaking.

The foreign woman started to speak, and John leaned closer.

"We were on our way to Norway from our home in Portugal when the storm hit us. It was a business trip for my brother but a pleasure trip for me since I've never been there before. I must say, it was the strangest storm I've ever seen. It appeared out of nowhere; there hadn't been a cloud in sight. Then, suddenly, everyone was fighting to keep the ship from flipping over, and I was trying not to be swept away. I've never been more terrified in my life."

"And was that how yer brother broke his leg?" the midwife asked.

"Aye, one of the masts broke, and he was right underneath it. After all that happened, I'm honestly surprised he wasn't hurt worse."

The last part of what the woman said hit John like a ton of bricks. *Surprised he wasn' hurt worse? She doesn' mean . . .*

Mistress Fairborn asked about the ship's destination, but that didn't matter to John. What he needed to know now was if this woman recognized him. Because, if she recognized him, she would also recognize William.

The farmer stepped into the room and strolled toward the two women with a smile. He took in the stranger's features as he approached them, for he'd only seen her from a distance up until now.

She was a young woman, perhaps sixteen or seventeen years old, with long blond hair and full lips. She was very pretty, but the thing that struck John the most upon seeing her was how sad she seemed.

To be in a place so far from home must be hard, John thought, his heart swelling with compassion.

But then the woman's eyes met his.

John's pulse quickened with anxiety. *Does she know?*

The farmer waited for her expression to turn fearful, but to his surprise, the woman's mouth curved into a smirk, and rather than recognition in her eyes, John saw only . . . interest. Blatant interest.

"Good morneen, ladies," John said as he reached them. "I don' think we've been properly introduced. Mistress Fairborn, would you do the honors?"

John turned to the midwife, who looked startled to see him. "O' course, Mr. Burgess. Mistress Mendes, may I present Mr. John Burgess. And Mr. Burgess, this is Mistress—"

"Lucia, please. The pleasure is all mine," the other woman interrupted, batting her eyelashes.

She's . . . she's flirting with me. There was no hesitation, no nervousness in her voice as she gazed at him in a way that bordered on predatory. She wore her beauty confidently, and

John got the distinct impression she knew how to use that beauty to get what she wanted.

The only problem was she wasn't anywhere close to the type of woman he wanted. Or rather, *the* woman he wanted.

"Charmed," John lied. "I hope yer stay here is very restful and relaxing, fer both you and yer brother. My apologies fer his accident."

"Thank you, sir," Lucia said, continuing to watch him in a manner she probably thought was flattering.

But all John felt was mildly repulsed.

"I'll let you get back to yer discussion now. Excuse me," John said, eager to get away from this woman as quickly as possible.

Surprise and disappointment came over Lucia's face, but John was quick to nod and escape to the hallway before she could say more.

Only once he could no longer feel the woman's eyes on him was he able to shake off the chill running down his spine. *That's definitely na what I need right now.*

The farmer ambled toward his room and had just reached the door when a new sound hit his ears.

It was a soft, sweet sound that reminded John of the lovely birdsong he'd heard outside his window that morning. And yet, the sound sent such a shock of adrenaline through him that his first instinct was to scoot into his room and lock the door.

For the sound he heard was a voice saying, "Mr. Burgess?"

John reluctantly turned. "Hello, Mistress Stubbins."

The innkeeper's daughter stood before him, fidgeting with her hands.

"Did you need something?" John asked when she didn't say anything more.

"I-I wanted to see how you were doing this morneen."

John grimaced and looked away. *Has she picked up on the fact that I've been avoiding her?*

"A-And talk to William!" she added.

John swallowed thickly and braved another look at her, but this time, the power of her big brown eyes was too strong, and he felt himself fall into her gaze like quicksand.

"I'm doing perfectly well. William, on the other hand, wasn' feeling his best, so I told him to sleep in a bit."

Adaira's fingers touched her lips. "William isn' feeling well? What's wrong?"

"He has been getting dizzy sometimes, and I wanted to make sure he—" John broke off. *Why did I say that? I should have told her he had a stomachache or some other inconsequential thing—*

"Dizzy? Is it because he hit his head the other night? Have you taken him to see Dr. Sherwin?"

"I'm sure he'll be better soon. No need to worry. Now, *if you don' mind,* I need to cut our conversation short, so I can check on him."

The words tumbled out more harshly than John had intended, and when he saw the flash of hurt in Adaira's eyes, he opened his mouth to apologize—

But then a thought came to him: *Maybe being rude is the best way to keep space between us.*

It was an awful idea, but it might just work. And if she didn't like him, perhaps it would be easier to fight his feelings for her.

Feelings that grew stronger every time John laid eyes on her.

The color drained from Adaira's face. "O' course . . . don' let me trap you in unwanted conversation."

John didn't miss the bite to her tone, but he said nothing more and simply turned away. He reached out to open his door, but then she muttered, "You weren' in nearly such a hurry when you were talking to Lucia."

The farmer whirled around, only to find her giving him a spiteful glare that dared him to refute her statement.

Is that how 'tis going to be? Yer na going to let this go without it turning into an argument?

"What are you trying to say?" John asked.

The woman crossed her arms. "Perhaps yer na that concerned about William at all. Perhaps you just don' want to talk to me."

John fixed an equally unpleasant scowl on his own face. *Fine. Have it yer way, then.* "That could be true. Or maybe you just have poor judgment."

Adaira broke eye contact, her mouth a thin, angry line. John expected her to shout back at him; in fact, he hoped she would, for it would give him the opportunity to push her away farther.

Instead, a long, tense silence settled over them. One that made John's guilt increase tenfold.

And when the woman finally did look back up at him and speak, her voice wasn't filled with anger. It was filled with regret.

"You might be right. I was under the impression you were a good man."

She spun on her heel and stomped off, leaving John without a second glance.

***

When Adaira reached her room, she slammed the door behind her and collapsed onto the bed.

Why did I react like that? I'm the calm one. The peacemaker. I don' lose my temper in front o' people.

She groaned and pushed herself up onto her elbows. *Seeing him with Lucia like that just . . .*

The foreign woman's sultry expression as she'd introduced herself to Mr. Burgess ran through Adaira's mind once more.

She shook her head in disgust. *Ugh. Is that the kind o' woman Mr. Burgess likes? If that's so, I'll be happy to stay far away from him, too. Na that I care what sort o' woman he likes. I do hope William is all right though. . . .*

"Adaira! Are you in there?" called an angry voice.

The young woman jumped to her feet and patted down her hair before opening the door. "Father? What is it?"

Terrence took in her slightly rumpled appearance and frowned. "Are you just going to be lazy and stay in yer room all morneen? What about my breakfast?"

Adaira held back a sigh. She wasn't in the mood for this right now. "I already made it."

The man scoffed. "I don' know if I should believe you."

Adaira rolled her eyes. "I'll show you."

She marched down the stairs and into the lower hall, her gaze instinctively going to the Burgess' door. That is, until she realized what she was doing and tore her eyes away.

I don' want anything to do with that man. He's na worth my time.

When they reached the dining room, Adaira gestured toward the table. "See? I made porridge fer you."

Her father's brown eyes narrowed. "Looks like there's a lot here. You haven' eaten yet, have you?"

Adaira clutched her stomach. "Nay, I haven'."

"Might as well do it now, then," Terrence said, plopping into a chair. "Hurry up."

She nodded and did as she was told, though inside she was bristling.

"Are you keeping up with all the housework?" her father asked a few minutes later.

"Aye, Father," Adaira said, not glancing up from her porridge.

He constantly asked her this question, whether they had guests or not. And no matter how much she cleaned, he always seemed to find something in the inn that wasn't quite clean enough.

"I saw a lot o' dirt and leaves at the front entrance. You better get to that soon."

Adaira's shoulders slumped. *Why can' he tell me something good I did, just this once? That would be really nice right now, so I could stop thinking about—*

Wait. That's it!

She turned to her father with bright eyes.

"What?" Terrence snarled. "Don' like me noticing all the things you've neglected? That's too bad. Especially since there are *a lot* more things that could use tidying up around here."

"Father, what else needs to be done? Tell me everything you can think o'."

Safety and Danger

Over the next few days, Adaira happily filled her time completing every chore her father gave her, careful never to slow down long enough to think about more than her current task.

She liked doing chores. They were methodical. Predictable. Safe. And with four guests to take care of, Adaira had more than her fair share of things to do.

By the time Sunday arrived, she'd convinced herself she'd been wrong about having feelings for Mr. Burgess at all and that it had just been her mind playing tricks on her. Even so, she still sat far away from the Burgesses at church.

Just to be safe.

Briony came in a few minutes before they started, asking her where Terrence was.

"He claimed he was 'ill.' He usually is after a night at the tavern," Adaira huffed. She didn't expect the man to come to church with her anymore; he stayed home about half the time now.

Soon, Vicar Peterson started his sermon, but it wasn't long before Adaira got the distinct sense she was being watched. She peeked at the pew two rows behind her, for that was where the Burgesses were sitting. But, to her surprise, the farmer didn't seem to be looking her direction at all.

There was, however, someone else who was definitely peering at her.

Or, more accurately, at Briony.

Adaira held back a smile as she turned around in her seat. *How interesting . . .*

The prickly sensation at the back of her neck remained as the sermon progressed, and anytime she happened to glance backward again, the same person was still staring right at Briony.

Eventually, Adaira couldn't hold back her excitement any longer and leaned over to the midwife. "You must tell me what's going on between you and our favorite merchant. I declare, he has been looking at you this entire time!"

Briony blushed crimson and put her head down.

Adaira waited a few seconds, wondering if the woman was too embarrassed to answer.

"I honestly don' know," the midwife finally mumbled. "Fer one moment, we were friends. The next, we were arguing. And now . . ." Briony looked up at Adaira helplessly.

The innkeeper's daughter smirked. "Even a blind person could see there's more than friendship on that man's mind."

"Adaira, be quiet!" Briony pleaded.

"Shh!" said Mrs. McGuff from the pew in front of them.

Adaira almost laughed as she watched the midwife slouch in her seat like she wanted to disappear. And the way she kept trying not to look back at the merchant was just too endearing.

This is really happening, isn' it? Briony and Mr. Mendes are actually falling fer each other. . . .

Once the sermon was over, Adaira tried to reassure her friend that Mrs. McGuff couldn't have overheard their conversation because the woman's hearing was too poor, but Briony wandered off before Adaira finished talking.

Hey! Where did she . . . Adaira's head swiveled around until she spotted Briony just outside the church with a man Adaira had never seen before. He was very pale with black hair almost touching his shoulders. His expression was bright as he spoke with the young midwife.

Who could that be?

"Lass, is something wrong?" asked a voice.

The woman turned to see Vincent McLaren standing beside her, his face full of concern.

"Oh, nay!" Adaira jumped up from her pew. "I'm perfectly well, thank you."

She tried to smile, but the fisherman's forehead wrinkled like he didn't believe her. "If you say so."

When he started to leave, though, Adaira cried, "Mr. McLaren, wait!"

"Aye?"

Adaira pointed to the stranger with Briony. "Do you happen to know who that man is there?"

Mr. McLaren observed the man for a long minute before shaking his head. "I fear I don'. Must be someone visiting town."

"I suppose so . . ." Adaira muttered, peering at the dark-haired man again as he and Briony started walking off together. She glanced toward Mr. Mendes, who had also noticed the midwife and the stranger leaving.

And he didn't look happy about it at all.

"I think Donal McGuff spoke to him earlier. You should ask him," Mr. McLaren remarked, reminding Adaira that he was still there.

"Thank you, Mr. McLaren. I'll do that." Adaira strolled out, biting her lip to keep a giggle from escaping as she passed Mr. Mendes. The man was still glaring in the direction Briony and the stranger had gone, a fact that made Adaira absolutely giddy.

But she needed to know who this newcomer was, and whether or not Briony was safe in his company.

"Mr. McGuff!" Adaira called, slowly approaching the tacksman.

"Mistress Stubbins, hello!" the man replied, smiling kindly. Donal McGuff was a good sort, always offering to help when someone was in need. His wife, Penelope, and their two children stood next to him in the grass at the church entrance.

"I'm sorry to bother you, but I wanted to ask if you knew anything about that man who was talking with Briony just now."

Mrs. McGuff's eyes narrowed at the mere mention of Briony, and not just because she'd been too loud during the sermon. Penelope McGuff had made it no secret how much she disliked the illegitimate midwife.

But Mr. McGuff was a bit more agreeable, and he said, "Oh, I didn' catch the man's name. He was asking fer Mistress Fairborn, and she came over before I could introduce myself. Something about him seemed . . . odd though."

The man shuddered as though the air had grown cold. "We better get back to the house fer now. We'll see you soon, mistress."

Adaira nodded, her thoughts still on the stranger. *If he's here to see Briony, he must know her somehow. Or maybe he just knows o' her? He didn' seem familiar to me. Hmm.*

Then she spotted the Burgesses heading toward the inn and realized she needed to go, too. *I'll just ask Briony who he is later.*

***

That evening, Adaira was just putting the finishing touches on her soup when a friendly voice said, "Hello, Mistress Stubbins?"

She spun around, only to find herself face to face with the pale stranger from before. This time, though, she was immediately struck by how handsome he was. His mouth was turned upward into a pleasant grin, and he had this aura about him that made Adaira immediately feel at ease.

As soon as they made eye contact, though, the man frowned. "Have we met before?"

Adaira shook her head. *I would remember someone as beautiful as you. . . .* "I don' think so, but I *am* Adaira Stubbins. Who might you be?" she said warmly, hoping to bring the smile back to the stranger's face.

But the man's brow furrowed as though he was in deep thought. "I'm an old friend o' Briony Fairborn. We met as bairns—" he broke off abruptly, the expression freezing on his face.

"Are you all right?" Adaira took a step forward, her hand reaching toward the man's shoulder.

Then his eyes narrowed, drawing her attention to how dark they were. Much like someone else's she knew.

"Liar. We've *definitely* met before," the man said through bared teeth.

Adaira's hand dropped to her side. "I'm sure yer mistaken—"

The man cut her off with a low growl. "Do you think I'm a fool?! I know exactly who you are, and *I remember what you did.*"

He took a step toward her. Slowly. Deliberately. Like a predator cornering its prey.

What's he doing? Is he going to hurt me? Adaira's eyes scanned the room, searching for anything she could use as a weapon.

But then a third person entered the kitchen. "What's going on here?"

Adaira looked over, gasping in relief when she saw her friend.

Briony! Thank goodness!

The man's ominous gaze cut to the midwife. "Briony, how could you befriend her?! After she tried to—"

"Niall, calm down," Briony interrupted with a raised hand. Her voice didn't waver; she didn't even seem the slightest bit frightened of this man.

Adaira, on the other hand, was trying not to faint. "Briony, what's he talking about? I don' know what I did to upset him so! He's talking like a madman!"

The stranger whirled around to her and snapped, "Don' tell me you've forgotten! Or was it *normal* fer you to abuse strangers as a child?"

Adaira trembled, her breath escaping in short bursts as she tried to figure out what he could be talking about. But her mind couldn't come up with anything, not with this monstrous man's gaze on her.

Then Briony stepped in between them, shielding Adaira from the stranger. "Adaira, this is Niall. He's the boy from the beach that day. The boy—"

"The boy you threw rocks at and laughed at till he cried!" the man sneered.

What? Adaira's heart, which before had been beating like a drum, came to a screeching halt.

She peered at the intimidating man. *It can' be. It can' be him!*

But her heart was telling her something different. *The boy on the beach—The one Briony rescued twelve years ago?*

Adaira felt tears forming even as her heart tried to pry open the door of her memory.

Nay, I don' want to remember!

But the truth was there in the stranger's night-black eyes. And try as she might, Adaira couldn't help but relive the shameful day she'd seen him for the first time.

A Shameful Day

Twelve years ago

One bright spring morning, six-year-old Adaira stood in the market with some other bairns as they listened to Mr. McLaren's latest tale. The fisherman was a master storyteller, weaving together adventures of peril and magic that kept everyone eager to hear more.

Today's story was about something new: a magical creature that looked human but could call down storms, charm people with a song, and transform into a seal. It sounded so intriguing that when Mr. McLaren finished and people started dispersing, Adaira stayed behind to talk to him about it.

"Mr. McLaren, sir?"

"Aye, lass? Did you like the selkie story?"

The small girl grinned. "Very much, but there's something about it that's bothering me."

"What's that?"

"From what I can tell, the selkie-woman did na do anything wrong, and 'twas actually the man who stole her sealskin and forced her to be his wife."

The fisherman raised his eyebrows, but then a smile slowly came over his face. "I'd have to say I agree with you there. Why does it bother you?"

"I thought humans were good, and fairies were evil. Are selkies na like that?"

"Selkies are one o' the most powerful beings in the ocean. Na evil, but na to be trifled with either. Be sure to remember that."

The fisherman turned to leave, but Adaira grabbed his arm. "But, Mr. McLaren, if they look human when they're on the land, how can you tell they're selkies?"

Mr. McLaren bit his lip as if he was considering how to answer. "Well, that is a fine question. It can be very difficult to know, but there are a few signs to look fer. If a person has all o' them, yer probably looking at a selkie."

"What are the signs?"

The fisherman glanced about as if he was worried someone would overhear them. "I should really get going. Maybe next time I'll tell you."

"Please, Mr. McLaren, tell me now."

The man looked hard at her for a long moment, and then he sighed. "How old are you, lass?"

"I'm six!" Adaira declared proudly.

Mr. McLaren's face brightened, and he bent down until they were at eye level. "I suppose 'twould be all right to tell you. Here are some things to look fer when yer wondering if someone is a selkie: one, the person must be very beautiful, as all selkies are. Two, the person must have a bond to the ocean. Three—"

"Adaira, are you coming?" Elspet asked as she appeared next to her.

Adaira turned to the older girl in surprise. "You want me to come with you?"

Elspet held out her hand. "Like you said, yer six now. I'd say that's old enough to play with the rest o' us at the beach."

Adaira giggled as she took the girl's hand, and the two of them scurried down to the beach, Mr. McLaren and his story forgotten.

When the girls arrived, St. John and Gareth Peterson, Ewan Sherwin, and Alastair Oliver were already there. The four boys were trying to see who could throw rocks and sticks the farthest into the ocean, a competition that was quite tame for the likes of them. They often got into trouble when they were together, but all the other bairns wanted to be just like them because they were fearless.

Who else was bold enough to touch the well where the trows[21] liked to play? Who else would dare walk on the haugr[22] on the edge of Laird Oliver's estate and risk upsetting the hogboon[23]? Who else had the spine to leave dead toads on Drulea Cottage's doorstep for the Fairborns?

According to Elspet, only Alastair had been brave enough to leave the toads though. Adaira didn't know why everyone hated the Fairborns, just that the adults were always whispering about them with words she didn't understand.

"Watch this," Elspet whispered in Adaira's ear. Then she ran up to Ewan and splashed water on his feet.

"Hey! Stop that!" The boy glared and jumped away before she could get him again.

"Yer so boring, Ewan! Have a bit o' fun, why don' you?" Elspet said, sticking out her tongue at the older boy.

Alastair turned away from the water, a rock still in his hand. "She's right, Ewan. You need to lighten up. Life is na as serious as you think 'tis."

Ewan pouted, but he didn't argue with Alastair. No one ever did. He was too scary. Not just because his father was the laird but also because he'd beat people up if they tried to say he was wrong about something.

"Hey, what's that?" Gareth asked, pointing farther down the beach.

Adaira squinted. A small figure was peeking out from behind some stones that went out a little ways out into the ocean.

"Is it a seal?" St. John wondered, dropping his stick and standing up to get a better look.

"Let's go see," Alastair said and started running toward the figure.

All the other bairns slowly followed, their curiosity overriding their caution. As it usually did.

---

[21] An Orcadian troll.

[22] An Orcadian burial mound.

[23] The spirit of a deceased ancestor who lived in the haugr and watched over its family's land.

"Where did it go?" Elspet asked when the small face went out of sight.

Adaira stayed right behind her, nervous about what it might be. But when she got closer and the face reappeared, she realized it wasn't a seal at all. It was a boy.

A pale, thin, practically nak—

Adaira gasped and averted her gaze. *Where are his clothes? What's that around his waist?* She chanced another look.

The boy held a strange spotted material at his waist as he studied each child in turn. When his black eyes landed on Adaira, she flinched.

"Who are you? And why do you look like that?" Alastair asked with a guarded tone.

The boy cocked his head to the side, eying Alastair from top to bottom. His stare gave Adaira cold shivers all over, and she ducked behind Elspet completely.

Alastair tried again: "What's the matter with you? Can' talk?"

The boy was completely silent. Adaira sneaked a few more glances, wondering why the boy wasn't answering. He was definitely old enough to talk. Adaira would guess he was six or seven years old, though he was hunched over so much it was hard to tell.

But there was something eerie about him. His movements were wary, as if he didn't know what to make of them, but there was more to it than that. Something felt off about him.

And dangerous.

Adaira tugged on Elspet's sleeve and whispered, "We should go."

Elspet's head turned toward her, but then Alastair shot forward until he was right in the other boy's face. He leaned down and shouted, "Did you na hear me, whalp[24]?"

The pale boy jerked away, which made him lose his balance and tumble into the water with a splash.

Alastair threw back his head and laughed, a chilling, heartless sound. "Yer so ugly and clumsy that I don' think yer a

---

[24] Devil.

whalp, after all. You must be a sea-trow[25]. And the best way to get rid o' one o' them is to beat it."

Gareth and St. John snickered and stepped up behind Alastair with wicked gleams in their eyes.

The boy scrambled to his feet, his expression equal parts alarmed and enraged.

"Let's go," Adaira whispered again, more urgently this time. If this boy really was a sea-trow, she didn't want him to come after her and Elspet. *Better fer the boys to take care o' him.*

Then the stranger hissed, crouching as if he was about to pounce at Alastair.

"Don' even try it," Alastair snarled, taking a few steps back.

When the boy's eyes narrowed in defiance, Alastair glanced back to make sure St. John and Gareth were right behind him. Then he hurled his rock into the boy's face.

The stranger yelped in pain, and before Adaira realized it, St. John and Gareth were wielding rocks of their own as Alastair picked up another one.

"What are you doing?" Ewan screamed, watching the other boys in horror.

But before the doctor's son could say more, the black-eyed boy snarled at the group like an animal. He charged forward and rammed straight into Alastair, trying to knock the taller boy over.

Alastair screamed and threw the boy off himself before giving him a swift kick in the stomach.

"St. John, Gareth, what are you waiting fer? Throw the rocks! Ewan, Elspet, help!"

Ewan and Elspet immediately did as he said, grabbing stones to defend themselves. Adaira trembled when her human shield left her, not knowing what she should do.

"Adaira, come here!" Elspet called, handing her a rock once Adaira reached her.

As more stones hit the boy, the angry look slipped off his face and was replaced by sheer terror. He wailed and tried to flee into the water, but Alastair was just getting started.

---

[25] A type of Orcadian troll that lived in the sea and was known for being ugly, clumsy, and stupid.

"Where do you think yer going? You can' get away from us!" he sneered.

"Stop, please!" the pale boy yelled.

Adaira's mouth fell open. *He can talk! Maybe he's na a monster, after all. But he tried to hurt Alastair—will he hurt me, too?*

Adaira's eyes swept over to her friends. Alastair, St. John, and Gareth were clearly enjoying tormenting the lad, laughing and yelling insults as they pelted him mercilessly. Ewan and Elspeth just seemed so scared that they were following along.

Adaira stared at the rock in her hand, shame filling her heart. *Should I just ru—*

But then a girl appeared from the edge of Adaira's vision, racing toward them like her life depended on it. Alastair stuck out his leg just as she reached them, making her fall forward into the sand.

The other children laughed, and as the girl rose to her feet, Adaira recognized her: Briony Fairborn.

Adaira drew back. *I'm na supposed to talk to her. Mum and Da' will be so mad if they find out!*

"Leave him alone," Briony shouted.

"Make us!" Alastair roared.

Adaira watched in shock as Briony pushed him, giving him a taste of his own medicine as his head collided with the ground.

I've never seen anyone stand up to Alastair before. . . .

Quick as a flash, Briony grabbed the strange boy and led him up the beach—

"Don' let them get away!" Alastair glared at his friends as he stood up and brushed the sand off his hands. "Or 'twill be one o' you getting the beating instead!"

St. John and Gareth took off after the two children without hesitation, more like hungry wolves than boys. Ewan and Elspet followed behind, reluctant but unwilling to be on the receiving end of Alastair's threat.

"Well? Are you one o' us?" Alastair asked, turning a hateful eye on Adaira. Then he pointed to Briony and the stranger, who had stopped a little ways off and turned back. "Or one o' them?"

Adaira gulped and shook her head, her feet moving beneath her and pulling her after the other bairns.

"Stop it, all o' you! This is wrong!" the Fairborn girl shouted, planting her feet and narrowing her eyes at Adaira and her friends.

"He's a trow! He deserves it!" Alastair argued.

"He's no trow! He's just as human as I am!"

Then Elspet opened her mouth and, in a cruel voice that Adaira had never heard before, snapped, "What do you know? You don' even have a da'!"

Adaira's eyes widened. *Is that why the grownups don' like the Fairborns?*

But before she could consider it further, Alastair gave her a sharp look. And all she could think of was what he'd said before: *"Are you one o' us? Or one o' them?"*

Adaira glanced around, trying to think of what to say. *What if he turns on me and then I get picked on, too? I don' want to lose all my friends!*

That was when her eyes caught something strange, something she hadn't seen before.

What's wrong with that girl's toes? Is there skin between them?

A horrible thought formed in Adaira's mind. Something that would protect her from Alastair for sure.

"And she's na human, anyway! Just look at her feet!" Adaira cried, pointing at Briony's toes.

The Fairborn girl scoffed. "O' course I'm human! My feet are just a wee bit different. They're special—"

But Adaira wasn't about to let it go, not when it was her best chance of getting Alastair's approval. "They're na special—they're ugly! There's something wrong with you, and I know what 'tis!"

Adaira took a deep breath then, wondering if she shouldn't say the next part. But she'd already started, and before she knew it, the words spilled out: "Yer a changeling!"

Tears bubbled up in Briony's eyes, and Adaira instantly knew she'd made the wrong choice.

How could I say that? I better—

Before she could take it back, though, Briony punched her in the chin, sending the smaller girl to the ground.

"She hit me!" Adaira whimpered.

The rest of the bairns were quick to react, picking up more rocks and throwing them at Briony.

The Fairborn girl tried to run away, but she didn't account for Alastair, and before anyone knew what was happening, the boy had slapped her in the face.

Serves her right fer hitting me, Adaira thought as Briony fell down.

Adaira took another look at the girl's funny feet, and a sliver of fear shot through her. *Could she really be a changeling? What if she casts a spell on us?*

The other children continued their assault with the rocks for a few seconds until Gareth decided it would be more fun to just start kicking the Fairborn girl.

"Changeling! Changeling! Briony the changeling!" St. John and Alastair cackled.

Briony covered her head with her hands, tears springing to her eyes.

Ewan and Elspet joined in the chant, completing the circle around Briony and blocking all means of escape.

But Adaira was too frightened to participate any further, too frightened even to move, for she was staring at what no one else had noticed yet: three grey seals coming up out of the water.

And they were angry.

They continued moving closer, but only when they were about twenty feet from the group did the other children finally hear the growling.

Adaira's eyes slid to her friends; she hoped one of them would know what to do. But she saw her own terror mirrored in their faces; they seemed just as dumbfounded by the animals' arrival as she was.

Only Alastair didn't seem scared, though how that was possible Adaira didn't know. She shifted her eyes over to Briony, who was—

Adaira's breath caught. Briony didn't look worried at all. In fact, she was locking eyes with one of the seals as if she was somehow communicating with it.

And at that moment, Adaira's worst fears were confirmed. *I knew it. I knew it. She called them here.*

But Alastair, for all his maturity as the eldest of the group, didn't seem to realize that. And Adaira was sure it was about to get them all killed.

"Are you talking to it, Fairborn? Does it understand you since neither o' you is human?" the boy asked.

Ewan, the most sensible of the group tried to stop him by saying, "Let's go, Alastair. I don' like the looks they're giving us."

But the laird's son balked. "If yer too much o' a coward, go on ahead. And the same goes fer the rest o' you. I'll just catch up with you later."

Adaira raced off, not waiting to see if any of the others came, too. *I have to get help!*

She'd almost reached Everton Inn when she spotted her father coming out the door with Laird Oliver. "Da'! Da'! Come quickly!"

Terrence's eyes widened when he saw her. "What's going on, Adaira?"

"The beach! You have to help! My friends and I were playing down there, and some seals showed up. They're really mad, and they might hurt Alastair!"

"My son? Show us, lass," Laird Oliver ordered. "Don' waste any time!"

Adaira nodded. "This way!"

As the three of them hurried toward the beach, a few other villagers noticed their panic and rushed over.

"What is it? Where are you going?" they asked.

A piercing scream hit everyone's ears.

"That was Alastair!" Laird Oliver cried.

The townsfolk sprinted toward the sound, and when the beach came into view, they saw a terrible sight: two of the seals had Alastair's legs in their mouths and were dragging him into the water.

The men charged forward, knives in their hands. Adaira slowed to a stop, her hands against her knees as she tried to catch her breath.

The Milligans came up on either side of her; Elspet must have gone to her parents for help, too.

Then Adaira heard more shrieks, so she turned and watched as the villagers attacked the seals. The animals released Alastair, and two managed to escape beneath a wave, but the largest one, the one Briony had been staring at, got caught between Laird Oliver and Adaira's father.

"Briony!" called a new voice. Bethany Fairborn came into view, dashing down to the beach toward her daughter.

Just as she arrived, though, a flash of light caught Adaira's eye. Mr. McLaren, the mad fisherman, now stood in front of the remaining seal, his knife raised high—

He struck without hesitation, stabbing the beast in the back as the seal loosed a bloodcurdling howl.

The hairs on the back of Adaira's neck stood up. That wasn't just the sound of an animal dying; it was far more than that. It was the sound of suffering, of fear, and of longing. And as its life passed from its body, something that looked suspiciously like a tear fell from its eye.

That's na just an animal, is it? That's—that's—

Adaira didn't know, but there was one thing she knew now for sure: Briony Fairborn wasn't human.

***

"That was you?!" Adaira said. Her voice was a pathetic cry as disbelief, terror, and soul-crushing guilt pressed in on her from all sides.

"Aye, that was me, you evil witch! I'm na such a wee bairn anymore though," the man spat.

"I-I'm so sorry fer what we did to you! 'Twas so wrong—"

"Are you *truly* sorry? Do you have any idea how traumatizing that was?" He slunk forward, and this time, even Briony seemed to shrink back a bit.

This is all my fault. I can' let him hurt Briony!

Resemblance

"Truly, 'twas a horrible mistake! I've regretted it ever since," cried a voice from the kitchen.

Mistress Stubbins!

John rushed forward without a second thought, William close behind him.

When the two of them arrived at the kitchen, John quickly took stock of the situation:

Mistress Stubbins was cowering behind Mistress Fairborn as a man slowly walked toward them. John had noticed him lurking around the church this morning, but he had no idea who he was. Mistress Fairborn seemed alarmed but otherwise all right as she stood between the stranger and the innkeeper's daughter. Mistress Stubbins, on the other hand, looked terrified.

What's he doing? Is he threatening them? I need to calm everyone down as fast as possible.

"Stay behind me, William," John whispered before clearing his throat.

The two women and the stranger turned to him, but when John caught sight of the man's face, he had to hold back a gasp. He hadn't gotten a good look at the stranger before, but now that John was seeing him at close range, there was something incredibly familiar about him.

Who does he remind me o'?

But then he noticed the tears shining on Mistress Stubbins's cheeks, and the man's familiarity became irrelevant.

How dare he make her cry! He has no right, and I'm going to make sure he knows—

Settle down, John, said his more rational side. *Yer trying to get everyone calm, remember?*

John forced himself to act oblivious and said, "Pardon me, but has dinner already been served? My son and I were taking a walk and lost track o' the time. I hope we're na too late."

Mistress Stubbins smiled at him, the relief in her eyes just making it even more difficult for John to keep his anger in check. "Nay, yer just in time. Please have a seat. I'll bring it out shortly."

He turned his gaze to the stranger, sticking his hand out with a scowl. "I don' believe I've had the . . . *pleasure* . . . o' meeting you yet. My name is John Burgess."

No one bothers Mistress Stubbins without dealing with me. John didn't say these words aloud, but he hoped his expression made that very clear.

And just in case this stranger wasn't very bright, John squeezed his hand extra tightly when he shook it.

"Niall Moreland," the man said stiffly, eying the farmer up and down as if to determine whether or not he could beat him in a fight. "I've just arrived in town."

"Ah, yer here fer dinner, then?"

Mr. Moreland narrowed his eyes at John's aggressive tone. "Aye, Briony was—"

Mistress Fairborn jumped in. "He was just on his way out, and I was about to see him off. Go ahead and start without me, Adaira." The midwife grasped Mr. Moreland's arm and pulled him toward the foyer before any more could be said.

John went to Mistress Stubbins's side and took her hands in his. "Are you all right?"

The farmer could feel her shaking as she struggled to answer. She slowly tugged her hands away. "I'm f-fine. Thank you fer asking."

"You don' seem fine. You look like you've seen a ghost," William said, coming out from behind his father.

John couldn't agree more, and he glanced over his shoulder in the direction the stranger had gone. *Just who is Niall Moreland?*

He turned back to Mistress Stubbins. "Do you know that man?"

She stared off into the distance as if she was pondering something. "I . . . I knew him once. A long time ago."

But then a guarded expression came over the woman's face. Like she was putting her walls back up. As she'd done many times. "'Tis na something I want to talk about right now."

"Oh," John said, trying to hide his disappointment.

"I need to know exactly why that man made you cry," he wanted to say. So many questions were weaving through his mind: *Are you in danger? Are you going to see him again? Do you want me to tell him to stay away?*

Yet he couldn't voice any of those things. He couldn't tell her what was on his mind and in his heart. *She's na mine. I shouldn' be feeling this way.*

But as much as he told himself it was wrong, John couldn't help himself. He had to protect Adaira Stubbins. No matter what.

And if she wasn't going open up to him about her connection to Niall Moreland, John would simply have to find another source.

***

As soon as dinner was over, John told William he needed to go out for a bit.

"Where are you going?" the boy asked.

"Just need to talk to someone."

When William's face wrinkled with concern, John ruffled the boy's hair and added, "Nothing to worry about. I'll be back soon. Just stay here at the inn, all right?"

William nodded, and John went off to find this "Niall Moreland."

It didn't take him long, for the first person he asked about the strange visitor pointed him toward the beach. The last place John wanted to go.

But this was important. Too important to allow his personal feelings to stand in the way of his goal. And so, John marched down to the beach, praying he wouldn't have to stay there long.

I'll just find out how the man knows Mistress Stubbins, make sure he's na going to hurt her, and then I'll leave. As simple as that.

When John had almost reached the docks, he took a left turn and walked out onto the beach. And there, about fifty feet away from him, the man sat, peering at the waves as they broke over the sand.

John padded toward Mr. Moreland, his footsteps so soft the man didn't notice him until he was only a short distance away.

As soon as he did, though, the man turned and stood, his mouth twisting into a smile.

"Ah. Mr. . . . Burgess, was it?" he said, brushing some sand off his clothes.

Clothes that were strangely large on him, almost as if they weren't his own.

"Aye, that's right," John said as he crossed his arms.

"And what can I do fer you?" The man's voice carried a slight accent John couldn't place. Orcadian still, but there was something off about it.

"I want to know what yer connection is to Mistress Stubbins," he stated plainly. Normally John wouldn't be so direct, but this man seemed to be bringing out the worst in him.

"The innkeeper's daughter? Ah, now I understand. Don' think I didn' notice yer grip on my hand," Mr. Moreland replied, stretching out his fingers a few times.

"How do you know her?" John said more forcefully.

"Wouldn' you like to know," he sneered.

John's temper flared, and before he knew it, he was in the man's face. "How do you know her?"

Mr. Moreland held up his hands. "Easy there. Easy. We can be civil, can' we?"

John stepped back a bit, but he stayed vigilant in case the man did anything unexpected.

Mr. Moreland chuckled. "She's a childhood . . . enemy. Met her here, actually," he said, gesturing to the sand. "I just wanted to play with the other bairns. Just fer a bit o' fun. But they took one look at me and decided I wasn' good enough fer them—threw rocks at me—called me names. Might have done worse if Briony hadn' stepped in and taken the punishment fer me."

"Yer saying Mistress Stubbins attacked you?" John asked, raising an eyebrow. "That doesn' sound like the woman I know."

"That's what I've been hearing. Briony tells me Mistress Stubbins has 'changed,' and I need to give her a chance." He shrugged. "I suppose I can go along with that. Any ideas on how I should make amends?"

"I don' know that you can make amends if you don' truly mean it," John snapped, but his mind wasn't fully on their conversation anymore. He was also trying to process how Adaira—sweet, kind Adaira—could have done what this man claimed.

He's lying. He has to be.

"Perhaps yer right," Mr. Moreland said, turning away from the farmer and picking up a small stone at his feet. "But 'tis very important that I at least try fer Briony's sake."

"Why do you care so much what she thinks?" John asked.

The man tossed his stone into the water, saying nothing for a long time.

Just when John was certain he wasn't going to answer, though, he glanced over his shoulder and said, "Because she's everything to me."

The farmer blinked a few times. The rest of Mr. Moreland's words hadn't seemed genuine, but there could be no denying his sincerity now.

But something else was bothering John. What Mr. Moreland had just said—John had heard something similar once before.

"You and William, yer everything to me. . . ."

John froze. That was the last thing his wife had said before she'd died. And now, after hearing Niall Moreland say it again and seeing the look in his black eyes, John realized who this man reminded him of.

He reminds me o' Ellie.

The farmer's gaze fell to the man's feet. He was wearing shoes. An uncommon thing this time of year, at least for Orcadians. *Unless he's trying to hide something.*

"Looking fer anything in particular?" the stranger asked.

John glanced up, slightly embarrassed at having been caught staring. "What did you say yer name was?"

"Niall Moreland," the man said carefully.

"And where do you come from?"

"Why so many questions? Yer na trying to befriend me, that much is clear."

"No reason. Just trying to be welcoming," John said.

The man scoffed. "Do you want to know my favorite food, too?" An antagonistic smile came over the man's face. Except, it wasn't really a smile, per se; it was more like an animal showing its teeth.

"Nay, th-that's all right. I'll talk to you later," John stuttered before hurrying off.

Fear pooled in the farmer's gut as he headed back to the inn with a single thought in his mind: *I must be imagining things.*

Tumbling Walls

When Adaira woke the following morning, her heart was racing and she was covered in sweat.

Where is he? was her first thought, and it took several seconds before she remembered she was at home and that she was safe.

She heaved a sigh as she realized the danger that had felt very real only moments ago was just a nightmare. She couldn't recall the details of it, but she knew whom she'd been afraid of.

She'd gone to bed early last night, partially because she was worn out but mainly to avoid Niall Moreland. The woman shivered, not wanting to get out of bed and face the day when it meant seeing him again.

For she knew she would. After all, he was her guest now— her father had told her shortly after dinner that the man had paid for a room.

That means he's sleeping here in the inn right now. . . .

Adaira gulped as fear rained down upon her, locking her body in place.

The sounds of others moving around jerked her out of her paralysis. *Everyone else must be waking up, too. I better prepare breakfast.*

Adaira pulled herself from the bed and put on her favorite green dress. If there was one thing Adaira wasn't going to slack on, it was keeping her guests fed.

She started cooking some eggs and porridge as quickly as she could, nodding to the Burgesses as they came into the kitchen. "I'm just finishing up! I'm sorry—I had a slow start this morneen."

She expected Mr. Burgess to wait in the dining room since he'd been doing such a good job at avoiding her lately. To her surprise, though, he told William to go ahead before turning back and walking over to her.

"Um, can I help you?" she said awkwardly. She hadn't been alone with the farmer in a while, and she felt her cheeks heat up as he drew near.

Mr. Burgess gave her a searching look, his sky-blue eyes swirling with worry. "I wanted to ask how yer doing this morneen."

Adaira broke eye contact, his scrutiny making her uncomfortable. "I'm very well. Why do you ask?"

"Well, Mr. Moreland seemed to upset you quite a lot yesterday and . . ." He leaned a little closer to her. "You look a bit flushed. Yer na getting sick, are you?" He reached out and put his palm on her forehead.

Adaira's temperature leaped at the man's touch, and she was sure her cheeks were even redder now. *Yer the reason my face is warm right now! But it feels so nice. . . .*

She took a sharp breath and stepped back. "I'm fine. Thank you fer yer concern though."

Mr. Burgess gave her a weak smile. "As long as yer sure."

Adaira turned back to the eggs to escape the man's gaze. "Ah, they're finished. The porridge is all done, too, so we can go ahead and eat."

"Great. Why don' you sit down then, and I'll bring everything out?"

Adaira pressed her lips into a fine line. "I haven' gotten the silverware or drinks ye—"

"I'll take care o' it."

The woman was tempted to protest, but the thought of someone waiting on her for a change was rather nice, so she nodded and waltzed out of the room.

When she entered the dining room, she did a double take. Her father was sitting next to William. *'Tis early fer him to be up. I don' think he was at the tavern last night.*

She internally shrugged. *Maybe he'll be more pleasant today.*

"Good morneen," Adaira chirped and took a seat.

Terrence frowned when he saw the lack of food in her hands. "Where's breakfast?"

"Mr. Burgess offered to serve us this morneen."

William's eyes bulged. "He's na cooking it, is he?"

"What was that, son?" Mr. Burgess growled as he popped into the room set the food down on the table.

The lad grimaced and stared at his hands. "Um . . . sorry, Da'."

Silence followed, and Adaira could feel the tension stretching like a bowstring—

But then a sound hit everyone's ears, blasting through the silence like a cannonball: a laugh!

The Burgesses and Adaira spun toward the sound in disbelief, for Terrence Stubbins was the one laughing.

And it wasn't a little chuckle either; this was a full belly laugh that grew louder and louder until the man almost fell out of his chair—

William giggled once before he threw a hand over his mouth and pretended to cough. He looked to his father, flinching as if he expected the man to reprimand him.

But a smile was spreading over Mr. Burgess's face, and—

The farmer snorted.

Adaira and William simultaneously burst into laughter, and Mr. Burgess, blushing in embarrassment, soon joined them.

"Quiet! What's the matter with all o' you? Yer hurting my ears with all this racket," Terrence shouted, throwing his hands over his ears.

The change in attitude was so abrupt that the Burgesses didn't seem to realize the man was being serious, for they didn't stop their howling. But Adaira knew to clamp her mouth shut.

"Didn' you hear me?" Terrence bellowed, glowering at the guests. "That's no way to treat yer host. I should just throw the two o' you out right now!"

Mr. Burgess instantly stopped laughing and cleared his throat to get his son to do the same. The boy looked from his father to the grouchy innkeeper in confusion.

But then his body crumpled as understanding dawned on him, and a second silence, more unpleasant than the first, settled over the group.

Mr. Burgess slipped into the chair beside Adaira, but as soon as he did so, Terrence groaned.

"What is it, Father?" Adaira asked, regretting her question as soon as she voiced it. *What if he says something awkward about Mr. Burgess sitting next to me?*

"I do believe you forgot something, Mr. Burgess," the man said, staring at the farmer.

Mr. Burgess glanced around; then his mouth dropped open. "Oh! The silverware!"

He jumped up and went back to the kitchen as Terrence barked, "And the drinks!"

Adaira winced, so humiliated that she tried not to meet the farmer's eye when he came back. He made a few trips to get everything, but just as he was about to sit down, Lucia Mendes poked her head into the room.

"Oh, hello! I thought you'd be long gone by now, Mr. Burgess. Yer always so eager to get to work in the mornings. I was going to ask Adaira to bring two plates to my brother's room, but I'd love the chance to talk to you more and hear about yer home."

The woman batted her eyelashes at the farmer, but before he could reply, Terrence snarled, "Yer keeping us from eating our food, lass. Get a couple o' plates, and leave already."

Lucia drew back at the man's harsh tone. "Well, I . . . I never . . ." She blinked several times, apparently at a loss for words.

"Here, take these," Adaira said, handing over her plate and Mr. Burgess's. She leaned close to the other woman and whispered, "My father's na in a good mood. 'Tis probably best if you and yer brother eat on yer own this morneen."

Lucia slowly took the plates, her eyes sparkling with understanding. "Thank you."

She peeked over at Mr. Burgess and smiled. "I'll see you later on, then, Mr. Burgess."

The redhead nodded. "O' course."

Lucia gave Terrence a nasty scowl when he wasn't looking, and then she sashayed off.

"Why don' you say the blessing, Father, and then I'll go get two more plates fer Mr. Burgess and me?" Adaira suggested.

Terrence grumbled under his breath, but he did as she asked, and soon enough, the tense atmosphere subsided.

After a few minutes of eating, Mr. Burgess said, "So, Mr. Stubbins, yer daughter told me you used to be a fisherman."

Terrence's eyes narrowed. "Aye, what o' it?"

"Well, William has been wanting to learn how to fish fer a while now. I'm no good at it, but I wondered if you might have time to . . ." Mr. Burgess trailed off, for the old man's glare had become so hostile there was no need to finish the sentence. Not when it was so obvious what Terrence's response would be.

The farmer coughed before turning to Adaira, his expression a clear cry for help.

Sympathy rose up within her. She'd been in the very same place as Mr. Burgess far too many times.

I gave up trying to get my father to go fishing years ago. I don' think he has gone once since Mum died. And I doubt that's ever going to change.

"What he means to say is, he wonders if 'twould be all right fer *me* to teach William how to fish. If you think you can . . . *handle* taking care o' the inn on yer own while I do that," Adaira said, careful to enunciate the right words as she spoke.

For she knew her father, and if there was one thing he couldn't stand, it was when people thought he couldn't handle something on his own.

True to form, Terrence's eyes flashed with fury. "Well, o' course, I can take care o' the inn by myself. I'm the innkeeper! Do you think I'm too old to do it or something? I ran this place before my daughter could even walk. And I could still run it without her help if I wanted to . . . but the lass needs something to do if she's going to stay out o' trouble."

Adaira kept her mouth in a neutral line, trying to disregard Terrence's words as he continued his tirade.

I'm doing this fer the Burgesses, na me, she reminded herself.

The man shakily stood and announced that he was going down to the tavern for a drink. He turned to Adaira expectantly, probably to see if she was going to object.

But the woman was only barely keeping herself from breaking into tears, so instead of saying anything, she picked up a spoonful of porridge and crammed it into her mouth.

"Bah!" Terrence scoffed, shaking his head like Adaira was the biggest disappointment of his life. He grabbed his cane and waddled off, muttering to himself about what a disgrace she was.

Adaira slowly chewed, smiling at the Burgesses as if nothing was wrong even after her father was out of the room. Mr. Burgess and William's faces, though, were frozen in shock.

But as soon as Terrence shut the front door, Mr. Burgess's expression hardened.

Adaira swallowed. "A-Anyway, let's talk about when you'd like to go fishing—"

Mr. Burgess jumped to his feet so fast he knocked over his chair. "Does he always talk about you like that?"

"Like . . . that?" Adaira repeated, stunned by his sudden mood swing.

"Like if he wasn' yer father, he'd have thrown you out on the street by now," the farmer snapped. "I know I haven' been here long, and I've barely spent any time with the man, but he always seems to have something hateful to say about you. And the things he says—they're na even close to true. You do most if na *all* the work around here, and I doubt yer father could take care o' the inn half as well as you do."

Adaira gaped at the farmer's passionate display. *He's . . . defending me?*

"You misunderstand," she tried to explain. "My father's just . . . I-I need to do a better job o' . . ."

But Mr. Burgess's expression was so indignant that Adaira lost her train of thought.

Why is he so angry? Is he angry at me?

"William, I want you to go back to our room fer a bit," Mr. Burgess said, keeping his focus on Adaira.

The boy got up without a word, pausing to give Adaira a sweet smile before scurrying out.

And as soon as William was gone, Mr. Burgess stepped around the table and marched toward her.

On some level, Adaira knew she should be frightened right then, for this wasn't the composed farmer she normally saw. This was the man she'd seen the night the foreigners had arrived. The mysterious, dangerous, unpredictable one.

But this time, she wasn't afraid.

Not even as Mr. Burgess grabbed her chair, turned her toward him, and knelt before her.

What is he doing?

The farmer's eyes pierced hers, and in a calm voice, he said, "Don' try to justify him. Yer father is wrong about you."

And that was when the final wall holding back Adaira's tears came tumbling down.

Unforgivable

The woman looked up at John as water slid down her cheeks. This was pain, raw and exposed. Without pretense. Without excuse. Completely vulnerable.

And it was altogether too much for him to take.

John grasped her hands in his own and lifted her to her feet. He rubbed his thumbs against her knuckles in what he hoped was a soothing gesture as he said, "Mistress Stubbins, I know 'tis na my place to say anything, but I can' stand the thought o' you believing you deserved any o' that. I don' know how yer father can' see how blessed he is. Why, yer the heart and soul o' this town!"

Mistress Stubbins sniffled, and John closed his mouth, fearing he'd somehow made her feel worse. But then she leaned against him, placing her head on his chest and wrapping her arms around his back.

John's body went stock-still, but inside, his heart was pounding so loudly he was sure she could hear it.

After a moment, he returned the embrace, trying not to get caught up in the feel of her body against his. "Mistress, are you all right?"

The woman whispered something too soft for him to make out.

"What?" John asked as he pulled back and looked down at her, trying not to wince at how hoarse his voice had become.

She turned her face up to his, her cheeks beet-red. "Adaira," she squeaked. "Please, call me 'Adaira.'"

Desire blazed within him, and he tested the name on his tongue. *"Adaira."*

The woman's gaze darted to his mouth, and it almost looked like she was leaning in—or maybe he was the one doing the leaning—closer, closer, until their lips were just inches apart and he could feel her breath—

John stopped, and with more strength than he knew he had, he pulled back.

The movement seemed to jar Adaira to her senses, for she jumped halfway across the room, her eyes filling with revulsion. "I'm so sorry! I . . . I don' know what came over me."

The farmer shook his head. "Don' be sorry. 'Tis my fault."

He reached out to her without thinking, but when he realized what he was doing, he drew back his wayward hand and closed it into a fist.

"I'll just be going now." He spun on his heel and tramped off, feeling like a complete boor.

What am I doing? I can' lose control like that!

But she wanted that kiss, too, another part of him argued. *I could see it in her eyes.*

It doesn' matter. We're na courting; we're na engaged; we're nothing to each other.

John tried to ignore the twinge in his heart, for he knew that last part wasn't true. Adaira had become important to him in the time he'd been here.

Too important.

That can' happen again. 'Tis unfair to her when we can' possibly be together. I don' want to lead her on like that. These burdens I'm carrying . . . I can' ask her to carry them, too.

***

After the farmer was gone, Adaira fell back into her chair, for her knees had become like jelly. She took several long breaths, ordering her heart to slow down as her mind replayed all that had just happened.

What was that? How could I—I almost kissed him!

Adaira put her hands over her burning cheeks, wishing this could all be a dream she was about to wake up from.

She shook her head at the silly thought. *'Tis too real to be a dream. It definitely happened. And if Mr. Burgess hadn't stopped me, I would have followed through with it. I would have kissed him.*

She was so ashamed of herself. Mr. Burgess was her friend, and she had just ruined everything. *He must think I'm such a strumpet now.*

"And he would be right, wouldn' he?" Adaira whispered, her voice full of venom.

But . . . I wouldn' have done that with just anyone. Mr. Burgess is diff—

Nay, John is different, she corrected herself with a tiny smile. Her given name had sounded so wonderful on his lips; she wondered if he would enjoy hearing her use his given name, too.

Adaira took a sharp swallow and replaced her grin with a scowl, for that brief moment of happiness was simply further proof of something she hadn't wanted to face. And as she sat alone in the dining room, her heart still racing despite her best efforts to calm it, Adaira finally admitted the truth to herself:

What she'd thought was just a foolish interest in the redheaded farmer had grown into something far worse. She'd fallen in love with him.

Adaira sensed another headache forming, and she shut her eyes as if that would also shut out her feelings.

But Adaira couldn't escape herself, no matter how much she wanted to. And she knew she had no one to blame for her predicament but her own weak, sentimental heart.

Adaira groaned and slapped the table, sending a jolt of pain through her palm.

This won' do. There's only one way to fix this.

Adaira bolted to the foyer and out the door, not slowing until she'd reached her destination.

Her headache was practically unbearable now, but she forced herself to look. To remember.

There, just beyond Everton Inn's gate, where the cries of birds hit her ears and the sea breeze filled her lungs. There, where she could watch storm clouds roll in at a moment's notice, eager to douse the town's residents with rain.

The place Adaira hated most.

While it was indeed a feast for the senses, the spot also contained something so insignificant that few people noticed it, and fewer still made mention of it. There, at the base of the inn's main wall, sat the reason why Adaira had come—a small pile of weathered stones.

Sometimes Adaira feared them; sometimes she loved them. Sometimes she stared at the stones with eyes like knives, wishing she could rid herself of them for good and be free to find the love she longed for.

But she knew she never could.

For as much as Adaira loathed the stones, she also couldn't bear to part with them. They were her shame and punishment, the very evidence of her sins.

And, unlike the rest of Everton, she knew all about them. She knew their secrets, and she guarded those secrets more closely than anything else, even the truth about Briony.

For the secrets of these stones belonged to her and her alone.

How could I let myself fall in love when I know how unworthy I am?

Self-loathing pressed upon her shoulders, choking the breath from her lungs—

Until a series of footsteps sounded behind her.

Adaira looked over her shoulder, only to see Matthew Levins frowning at her.

"Adaira? What are you doing out here?"

The woman turned her back on the stones, removing them from her sight but not from her thoughts.

She pressed her mouth into a smile, blinking several times to clear the moisture from her eyes. "Hello, Matthew. I just . . . came out fer a bit o' fresh air."

Really? She scolded herself. *That's the best you can come up with?*

And, indeed, the man was pursing his lips like he didn't believe her.

Please don' ask me any more, she silently begged. *I don' think I can handle it right now.*

Matthew took a few steps until they were side by side. But, rather than calling her out for her lie, he gazed out at the horizon and said, "It looks truly lovely this morneen, doesn' it?"

Adaira followed his line of sight, taking the time to really study the view—the fluffy clouds blowing through the air, the waves breaking along the shore, the birds flying across the sky.

It was surprisingly refreshing, and she found that the longer she stood there, the better she felt. The shame and anxiety that had all but consumed her only minutes before didn't seem nearly as powerful anymore.

Adaira didn't know how long they stood there, but once she felt in control of her emotions again, she turned to Matthew with a grin. "Was there a particular reason you came by? Did you need my help?"

The tacksman opened his mouth like he wanted to say something, but then he seemed to change his mind and slowly shook his head. "Nay, I . . . I was just passing by and wanted to see if you were all right."

"That's kind o' you. I'm fine."

First, John and now, Matthew? Do I really look like I'm na all right?

"Well, good. Lady Oliver is actually waiting fer me right now, so I need to go over to Rigmore House. I'll talk to you later."

The woman nodded, watching as he started to walk away. "Have a good afternoon, Matthew."

He beamed at her. "Thank you, Adaira. You, too."

Adaira smiled back, feeling strong and self-assured as she watched him depart.

But once the man was gone and Adaira was alone again, a question blazed through her mind: *I know I told John and Matthew I was fine, but am I really?*

Without meaning to, her eyes strayed back to the pile of stones once more.

I used to think I was. What happened to my confidence?

Adaira sighed and tried to stop thinking about such things. Everyone else in Everton thought she was fine, so she would just have to keep working at it until she believed it again, too.

But in the back of her mind, a tiny sliver of anxiety lingered. Quietly. Patiently. Like a spider in the dark.

For some part of her knew she was only lying to herself. And the beautiful life she had built was in danger of collapsing.

Adaira went inside, but not before she'd sent up yet another prayer that her sins would stay buried beneath those rocks, never to see the light of day.

The next few hours proved much more normal. Penelope McGuff stopped by to talk about Johnsmas plans; her father came back from the tavern and hid in his room; Briony arrived and took Mr. Mendes for his daily walk.

Adaira liked normal.

But just as she started to relax while making dinner, a new person waltzed into the kitchen. Someone she really didn't want to see.

"Oh . . . Mr. Moreland, hello," Adaira greeted in a cheery voice.

If one had gone around to the other side of the counter, though, her shaking knees would have betrayed her terror. She propped herself up against the counter for support, hoping the man wouldn't notice.

Why did he have to come now? Everyone else is gone. . . . I don' want to face him alone.

The dark-haired man's eyes homed in on her, and Adaira braced herself for the barrage of criticism he was about to spew at her—

But then he did something she never would have expected.

He smiled.

Adaira gaped, partially in disbelief, and partially because the action made him look even more handsome than he had before.

"Mistress Stubbins, yer just the person I was looking fer."

"I-I am?" Adaira swallowed.

"Aye, I wanted to give you these," he said, lifting his hands into view. Adaira hadn't realized it before, but he was holding a bouquet of red and yellow wildflowers.

He offered the bouquet to her, but she was too shocked to react.

"Please consider them the start o' my apology fer the other day. Briony told me how you've been a true friend to her in the time since we met, yet I behaved like a beast. Perhaps you can find it in yer heart to forgive me?"

The man flashed another brilliant smile at her, and Adaira felt so foolish for being frightened of him before. Now, he seemed entirely harmless, even charming.

She set down the dish she'd been working on and took the flowers. She returned the man's grin. "Aye, I think I can do that. After all, you didn' know things were different fer Briony and me now. What I did to you both was awful, and I understand why you were so upset."

"I'm so glad to hear that."

Adaira took a deep sniff of the bouquet. "Thank you fer these. Let me just get something to put them in."

She went and found a vase that would suit them nicely before turning back to the pale gentleman.

"I thought they'd look lovely on yer dining room table," Mr. Moreland said, his voice light and bubbly. "But! They're na the only way I want to apologize."

Adaira raised her eyebrows. "You really don' need to do more. If anything, I should be the one trying to make amends."

Mr. Moreland waved his hand. "Nay, I insist. Any friend o' Briony deserves at least that much. Especially one who's still willing to let me stay here? I paid yer father fer a room yesterday, but if you want me to leave, I understand. Is that . . . what you want me to do?"

Adaira shook her head shyly. He seemed so different from the monster she'd met before. *I wonder what Briony thinks o' him. . . . Perhaps Mr. Mendes isn' her only option anymore.*

Mr. Moreland clapped his hands together. "Excellent. The second way I wanted to apologize was by cleaning up around here fer you, but everything already looks so perfect you'll have to help me find something to work on."

Adaira thought for a moment. "Ah, we'll be celebrating Johnsmas in a few days, and I'm about to be very busy. Why don' you lend me a hand preparing the food?"

Mr. Moreland nodded. "'Tis a deal. Why don' I put that vase on the table fer you?"

Adaira handed it to him, and just as the man disappeared into the dining room, the Burgesses approached from the foyer.

"Yer back," Adaira said. "What great timing—I'm almost done with dinner."

"Perfect," John said, hitting her with a smile so potent it sent her heart soaring . . . and her mouth running.

"And after we eat, perhaps we could all take a stroll together? I know a good place near the docks fer spotting dolphins and—"

"Nay, that's na happening," John cut in firmly, his face no longer warm and open. "William and I aren' going near the ocean."

Adaira internally kicked herself. *Right, I forgot. John doesn' want William down there. That's why they had that fight right before William hit his head.*

"That's a shame. The ocean is the most wonderful thing in the world," Mr. Moreland said, stepping back into the room.

Everyone started, even Adaira, for the man had been so quiet up until now.

"Are you bothering Mistress Stubbins?" John asked, his eyes watching the man like a hawk.

"Na at all. I just came to bring her some flowers," the man said, gesturing toward the bouquet in the other room. He smirked at the farmer, and from the way John glared back, it almost seemed like the two of them were having some private conversation.

Just as the silence started to get awkward, though, Mr. Moreland turned to William with a smile.

"I didn' get to properly introduce myself earlier. I'm—" He broke off with a sharp breath.

But before Adaira could figure out why he'd reacted like that, the man's smile returned, and he said, "I'm Niall Moreland. What's yer name?"

"William," the boy replied, angling away a bit. "You were mean to Mistress Stubbins before. Are you friends now?"

Mr. Moreland stood back up to his full height and glanced at Adaira. "Aye, I'd like to think we're friends."

Adaira nodded in support, earning a wink from the man before he turned back to William. "I try to make friends with as many people as I can. Do you think you'd be interested?"

The boy started to grin, but then he peeled the expression off his face and scanned the man closely. "Hmm, I don' know. . . ."

"Would it help if I told you I know some stories about the creatures in the ocean?"

William nodded, his earlier cynicism vanishing in an instant. "You do? What kind o' creatures?"

"Dangerous ones. Creatures o' mystery," Mr. Moreland said vaguely, but there was a twinkle in his eye. He lowered his voice. "And magic."

"Magic?" William turned to John. "Da', can we listen to his stories?"

The farmer crossed his arms but nodded. "I suppose so. Are you staying fer dinner?"

And for the next couple of hours, this strange Niall Moreland delighted everyone with tales of monsters, adventure, and romance. His stories held so much suspense that it was always a surprise if they ended happily. And quite a few of them didn't. That didn't seem to bother William very much though. The boy was perfectly enthralled, and every time Mr. Moreland finished one tale, he'd ask for another.

Even John seemed to enjoy listening, and by the time the evening came to a close, he was smiling and laughing along with everyone else.

How nice this is, Adaira thought to herself. *'Twill be a shame when the Burgesses have to go home.*

Who's to say they have to? whispered a voice in her head. *Why couldn' they just stay?*

They have a farm back in Hollandstoun, Adaira pointed out. *John can' leave that behind.*

Maybe he could if you asked him to.

At that moment, John turned to her as if he'd heard her thoughts. His striking blue eyes locked her in place, rendering her unable to look away. *Do you want to be with me as much as I want to be with you? Would you stay if I asked?*

After a few seconds, the farmer looked away, but not before Adaira was sure she saw love gleaming in his eyes.

I can' ask him. Na after what I've done.

A new thought flickered in her mind. *What if . . . what if John didn' find out? Then it wouldn' matter that I don' deserve to be with him because no one would know.*

The woman's conscience seized up at the notion. *Can I keep secrets from the man I love?*

The question lingered in Adaira's mind long after she and everyone else had gone to bed. And only once she'd tossed and turned for half the night did she finally reach a decision.

If it means na losing him, then aye. The truth will stay sealed up forever, and John will be none the wiser.

Rising Doubts

The following day, John's morning was going remarkably well. Almost too well, in fact, as he glanced at his son in the field beside him.

I was sure he'd ask about going to the ocean after Mr. Moreland told him all those stories yesterday. . . .

They'd been cutting oats since early morning with Mr. Martin, and now, the sun was high in the sky. The work was tiring, but John didn't mind. There was no way Mr. Martin would have been able to take care of all this on his own, especially since his daughter kept him pretty sleep-deprived most of the time.

You wouldn't have known it based on the man's perseverance and work ethic though. And he had the heart of a saint—in all the time John and William had been working with him, Mr. Martin hadn't complained once. In fact, the thing he'd spoken of most often was how blessed he was to have their help. And how his crops were going to help so many people in town.

He was yet another reason John hated that he had to leave.

Mr. Martin paused to wipe some sweat from his brow. "I do believe we're almost done," he said, turning to the Burgesses with a grin. "William, why don' you and yer father take a break and we'll get back to this after lunch? I'll go and tell Mr. Levins the good news."

The greedy tacksman had been coming by every few days to check on their progress, and despite Mr. Martin's assurance that everything was going well, Mr. Levins hadn't seemed convinced. John had heard him remind Mr. Martin many times about what would happen if the harvest wasn't as fruitful as Mr. Martin had promised.

"Actually, Mistress Adaira said she was going to take me fishing this afternoon," William piped up. "Da', may I still go?"

It warmed John's heart to see his son so eager to please him, even to the point that he seemed willing to forgo his fishing lesson if John said so. William and Adaira had grown so close in the time they'd been here.

Is it really fair o' me to take William away from her?

"Since when did you start calling her 'Mistress Adaira'?" John asked with a raised eyebrow.

William smiled sheepishly and kicked at a bit of dirt. "I . . . I don't know."

John chuckled. "Mhmm. Well, as fer yer question, I think Mr. Martin and I should be able to finish everything up on our own. Right, Mr. Martin?" he said, turning to the other farmer.

The tall gentleman nodded with an easy smile. "That's no problem at all. I hope you enjoy it, William. Adaira is a great teacher."

The boy's face brightened. "Thanks!"

"Well, I'm going to go tell Elspet I'm leaving fer Mr. Levins's house. I'll see you later," Mr. Martin said before walking off toward his house.

Once he was gone, John turned to his son. "What would you like to do before lunch? We've got some time."

William shuffled his feet a bit, but he didn't speak.

"What is it, son? We can do just about anything."

"Da', can I go play with Fergus?"

John deflated a bit at the fact that William didn't want to do something fun with him, but he tried not to let his disappointment show. "O' course you can. Just make sure yer at the inn in time fer lunch."

William nodded happily and started to scurry away.

"And, William?" John added. "Stay away from the ocean."

"I know, Da'. I promise I won' go near it."

"All right. Get going, then."

William grinned and sped up the road, vanishing from view in seconds.

Now what am I going to do? John asked himself. *As if I even need to think about it.* He chuckled, for his feet were already taking him where his heart longed to be.

Unfortunately, the first person he came across when he reached Everton Inn wasn't the one he was looking for.

"Mr. Burgess, hello!" said the beautiful blond woman, sidling up to him with a flirtatious grin.

"Ah, good morneen, Lucia," John returned with a weak smile.

"Briony went off with my brother for their walk before I could ask to go as well. It's too gorgeous of a day not to enjoy the sunshine, don't you agree?" She batted her eyelashes a few times, making it very obvious that she wanted John to volunteer to walk with her instead.

But that wasn't even close to what John wanted, so the farmer pretended to be clueless. "I guess you should go fer a stroll, then. I was trying to find Adaira. Do you know where she is?"

"Oh, she's very busy. I think she's in one o' the guest rooms."

John's eyes widened. "Whose room?"

Lucia frowned and tapped a finger against her lips. "Hmm, I'm na sure."

The farmer tried to move around her, but Lucia grabbed his arm.

"Why don' you go fer a stroll with me? She'll probably be finished by the time we get back."

"Um . . ." John tried to think of a way to decline, his skin crawling at the woman's touch. "Ah, I have a better idea. Since Adaira works so hard all the time, I'll ask her if she'd like to stop and go with us."

"W-With us? But I—" She broke off with a blush.

So she can *feel embarrassed?* John tried not to laugh at how the woman's mouth wriggled like a snake.

"But what?" John raised his eyebrow.

"Nothing," Lucia sputtered. "Nothing at all." She giggled.

"I'll be right back." John turned and sauntered to the hallway with a smirk.

But then he saw the door to his room was open. *Oh, no. What if she finds—*

"Adaira? Adaira, are you in here?" he asked as he hurried inside.

"John!" she exclaimed, almost dropping the sheet in her hands.

The farmer's gaze instantly went to his bag. To his relief, it appeared untouched.

"Yer awfully jumpy, aren' you?" John said, hoping she wouldn't notice where he'd been looking.

Adaira glared. "Are you making fun o' me? I know I'm a bit clumsy, but that's na very kind."

"The look on yer face was just so adorable I couldn' help my—" John cleared his throat. "I came to ask if you wanted to go fer that walk we never had yesterday."

The woman's countenance softened. "With you?"

"Well, with Lucia and me."

"Oh," she said, her shoulders slumping. But then she nodded and gave him a weak smile. "Aye, that sounds fun."

"Good. Lucia and I will wait fer you in the foyer."

Soon, the three of them were strolling down the road, chatting about all manner of things. Lucia was very interested in hearing about Johnsmas since it wasn't celebrated back in Portugal. It was one of John's favorite holidays, and he and Adaira got so focused on talking about it that he didn't realize they were walking straight toward the dock.

"Oh, I'd love to go out on the beach," Lucia squealed. She grabbed the farmer's arm and looked up into his eyes. "John, can we go?"

He stiffened, as much from the physical contact as from her use of his first name. He caught sight of Adaira from the corner of his eye—the hurt on her face was unmistakable.

"Lucia, I—"

But before he could ask her to let go, Lucia gasped and pointed. "What's that?"

John followed her line of sight, just barely spotting a figure in the water by the cliffs.

"'Tis Briony!" Adaira cried. "And she's pulling something—"

"Santiago!" Lucia shouted. "She's trying to save him. We have to get to them!"

The trio charged onto the beach, but they were so far away, and Mr. Mendes didn't look like he was breathing—

We might na make it in time! Anger burned in John's chest. *Nay, the ocean's na going to take anyone else. I won' let it!*

The farmer's feet flew faster, but as he drew near, he realized Mistress Fairborn was actually doing it—she was successfully pulling Mr. Mendes to shore. And by the time John and the others had gotten close, Mr. Mendes was sitting up.

"Santiago!" Lucia yelled once more.

The merchant and the midwife turned toward them, their eyes widening in surprise.

Lucia sank to her knees as soon as she reached them, putting her arm around her brother's shoulder. "Are you two hurt? What happened?"

Mr. Mendes smiled at her and shook his head. "Nay, I fell from the ledge up there," he said, inclining his head toward one of the cliffs.

John pursed his lips. *He fell from up there when his leg is still healing?*

"But Briony came in after me and saved me," added Mr. Mendes.

And that was when John's attention shifted. No longer was he just relieved that the two of them were all right; instead, suspicion was blooming in his mind.

He stared at the midwife with new eyes. "Mistress Fairborn, that's amazing! How did you do that?"

And when the woman just shrugged, John's curiosity only grew.

"Well, whatever it was, I'm eternally in your debt," Lucia said before turning back to Mr. Mendes. "We better still take you to Dr. Sherwin now, brother, to make sure nothing is amiss."

Mr. Mendes nodded, and Lucia helped him rise to his feet. The man was unsteady, though, and John jumped forward to give him more support.

"Eu não posso acreditar o quão perto eu cheguei de te perder[26]," Lucia whispered.

"I'm fine, sister. Truly," Mr. Mendes replied, seemingly speaking in English for John's sake.

But John could tell the merchant was only trying to comfort Lucia—from the way Mr. Mendes was moving, John wondered if he hadn't damaged his leg further.

A thought flooded the farmer's mind, one that made his heart seize up: *What if that had been Adaira?*

John peeked over his shoulder at the innkeeper's daughter, who'd stayed behind to talk to Mistress Fairborn. *She's so lovely. . . .*

But the reality of life's fragility was now in John's face, right here walking beside him. *How could I have forgotten when Ellie and I only got ten years? I've spent the last six months thinking about all the things I wish I could tell her, all the things I wish we could do. . . .*

John's mouth hardened, and at that moment, he made a promise to himself, a promise not to let fear run his life anymore. Not when life was far too short already. Instead, he was going to go after what he wanted and enjoy the time he had left.

And John already knew the first thing he needed to do to achieve that.

Unfortunately, it was something he really didn't want to do.

***

"Where's the whiskey?" Terrence asked. Dinner had only just started at Everton Inn, and John was already wishing it was over.

The farmer was at the end of the table next to his son, the Mendes siblings were across from William and Adaira, and

---

[26] I can't believe how close I came to losing you.

Terrence sat at the head. Niall would have joined them, except he had set up a picnic outside for himself and Briony Fairborn.

What no one else knew was that John had spent the last couple of hours trying to think of ways to impress the old innkeeper. Now that he was sitting across from Terrence, though, he knew all his efforts would be fruitless.

This man doesn' have a kind bone in his body. He's never going to give me a chance.

"Well, Adaira?" Terrence snarled, shooting his daughter a sharp look.

Adaira flinched, and the farmer quickly jumped to her defense.

"I asked her to put it away," he lied. "She was only trying to accommodate a guest."

Truth to be told, John figured Adaira had gotten so busy with everything else going on that she'd probably forgotten to put whiskey on the table.

She has been working so hard lately—

Terrence slammed his hand down. "And what gives you the right to decide what does and doesn' go on my dinner table?"

"'Twas my mistake," John said, gritting his teeth to hold back the vitriol he wanted to spew back. "I just try na to drink much during the week. Makes it harder to get to work the next morneen."

This was actually a true statement. John enjoyed whiskey as much as any other Scotsman, but he preferred to do most of his drinking on the weekends, so he didn't have to work with a pounding headache.

"That sounds very responsible," Lucia cooed. "Though I do love a good—"

"That's na responsible at all," Terrence bellowed. "A man can do whatever he pleases, and that includes drinking when he likes!"

John's eyes zoomed over to Adaira, who seemed to be holding back tears. Rather than making the situation better, it seemed like John had only made things worse.

"And I say a man should be able to drink as much as he wants, whenever he wants, regardless o' what day o' the week 'tis!" Terrence continued.

Adaira grabbed her father's hand. "Da', don' get so upset! Mr. Burgess was only—"

"I know what he was saying! Don' try to cover fer him just because he's been making eyes at you since dinner started!"

John felt his face heat up even as Lucia started choking on her water. He turned to see what everyone else was doing: Adaira was gaping in shock, William was looking around the table in confusion, Mr. Mendes seemed to be trying not to laugh—

"I'm so sorry to interrupt—"

John's eyes widened. *Another person heard that?* He reluctantly turned, watching as Briony Fairborn entered the room.

"Has anyone seen Niall? I'm supposed to be meeting him here."

Adaira jumped up from her seat with a smile. "Ah, o' course! Briony! Mr. Moreland said you'd be coming. He's waiting fer you out in the back. He said he has something *special* in mind."

John thought he saw Mr. Mendes stiffen, and now it was the farmer's turn to hold back a chuckle. *I guess he's na too happy about Mr. Moreland's interest in Mistress Fairborn.*

Adaira took the midwife's arm and led her outside, seemingly glad to escape the tense room.

Once she was gone, though, Terrence sent John a withering glare. "Don' think I don' know what yer playing at, lad."

The farmer shook his head. "I don' know what you mean, sir."

"Bah! You can tell Adaira I'll be in my room. If I stay here much longer, I'll lose my appetite." Terrence grabbed his plate and hobbled out, leaving the Burgesses and Mendes siblings to themselves.

John slumped in his seat. *What am I going to do now?* He'd wanted to go about this the right way, but Terrence wasn't making it easy.

Adaira returned a few minutes later, and the rest of dinner proceeded as if the previous conversation hadn't taken place, which John was very grateful for. Instead, they spoke of Johnsmas plans and how the holiday compared to Festa de São João, the Midsummer celebration Lucia and her brother were accustomed to. It was a very pleasant discussion, though John's mind wasn't fully engaged in it since he was still stewing over what to do about Terrence.

He decided to go for a walk after dinner, hoping a solution would present itself. It was about William's bedtime by the time John was ready to go, so he told the boy not to wait up for him and that he'd be back soon.

Just as he started to leave, though, William called from his bed, "Hey, Da'?"

"Aye, son?" John said, turning back to the boy.

"What did Mr. Stubbins mean when he said you were making eyes at Mistress Adaira tonight?"

John coughed. "Oh, um . . . nothing."

"Was he talking about how yer in love with her?"

The farmer's eyes almost fell out of his head. "What did you say?"

William shrugged before a tiny smirk came over his face. "'Tis pretty obvious, Da'. You don' need to pretend."

John sat down on the bed next to him. "Really? I didn' think you knew."

William scoffed. "I'm smart, Da'. O' course I knew."

"And how do you feel about it?" John slowly asked.

If he's uncomfortable with me falling fer another woman, perhaps I shouldn' move forward with my plans. . . .

The lad frowned. "I . . . I miss Mum. I miss her so much."

John's heart dropped, but he tried to hide his disappointment. "So do I, William. Don' think I—"

"But!" William interrupted. "I've seen how the two o' you are together—you and Mistress Adaira, I mean. And she's really good fer you, Da'. She makes you happy." The boy's mouth widened into a huge smile. "And she makes me happy, too."

"So yer na upset?" John asked, searching his son's expression for any sign of disapproval.

William shook his head, still smiling. His voice lowered to a whisper as he said, "Can I tell you a secret?"

"What?"

"She's in love with you, too."

John's lips turned up. "Oh, she is? And how do you know that?"

William covered his mouth with his hands.

"Yer na going to tell me?" John's grin spread, and he stretched out his fingers toward his son. "Well, I have ways to make you talk."

The boy squealed and threw his blanket over his head. "I'll never tell!"

"A blanket isn' going to stop me," John warned before tickling William through the covers.

The lad cried out for his father to stop between giggles, and after a few seconds, John was kind enough to listen.

"Had enough yet?" the farmer asked.

William pulled the blanket off his head and scowled. "I'm still na telling."

But John could see the smile hiding in the boy's eyes, even now creeping out despite William's best efforts to look sullen.

The farmer stood up. "I better go. Go on to sleep, son."

"All right. Goodnight, Da'," William said, making himself comfortable once more.

With a wave, John slipped out the door and padded down the hallway. He didn't intend to stay out long, especially after he checked the clock in the kitchen and saw it was already nine o'clock.

Did Mr. Moreland finish his dinner with Mistress Fairborn yet? He hadn't heard the man come in, so he peeked out one of the windows.

The farmer's eyes widened. Mr. Moreland and Mistress Fairborn were still outside. The two of them were standing very close to each other, the remnants of their meal on the quilt at their feet.

John frowned. He wasn't sure how he felt about Mr. Moreland, but it didn't seem wise for Mistress Fairborn to get involved with him. He hated the thought of Adaira's dear friend potentially getting hurt.

Still, 'tis na my concern, he reminded himself, *and I shouldn' be watching them.*

John moved back from the window just as Mistress Fairborn stepped away as though bidding Mr. Moreland goodnight. The farmer started to wander out of the room, but then he wondered if he should offer to help Mr. Moreland clean up. *It looked like there was quite a lot o' food still out there.*

The farmer turned around and went to the kitchen door, which led outside, but when he opened it, the other man was gone. *Where did he . . .*

John glanced about in all directions before a flash of movement caught his eye.

"Mr. Moreland?" the farmer called.

But the man didn't appear, so John hurried in the direction the person had gone. At least, he thought it was a person.

When John rounded the inn, he glimpsed whoever it was scurry up the hill and out of sight. The figure had gone past the fork in the road where most people turned left, for there was only one other house beyond that point—Drulea Cottage.

John's protective instincts took over, and he hustled forward. Soon, the figure came into view once more and veered off toward Torin Woods.

What's he doing? John thought as he tried to catch up. He was fairly certain he was following Niall Moreland at this point, but he couldn't fathom why the man would be going into the woods at this time of night. There was nothing out there except an old well.

John slipped into the forest, careful not to get too close and announce his presence. Not before he discovered why the man was out here anyway.

Eventually, the figure stopped walking and turned toward an opening between the trees. An opening that led right back out to the main road. *Did he change his mind and decide to go back to the inn?*

But the man didn't head out of the woods; instead, he just stared, almost like he was watching someone.

Is he . . . watching Mistress Fairborn?

John leaned closer until—

SNAP!

The farmer held back a gasp. He hadn't meant to, but the branch he'd stepped on had just made a very noticeable crunch.

John ducked behind a tree just as Mr. Moreland's head turned his way.

He didn' see me. He didn' see me. Maybe he'll just think the noise came from an animal, John told himself, but the fear in his veins didn't abate.

Especially after the woods went dead quiet.

John gulped and peeked out, praying the man had left—

Only for Mr. Moreland to be inches away from his face.

John stumbled backward, almost falling to the ground before catching himself at the last second.

"What are you doing here?" Mr. Moreland growled.

The farmer took a deep breath to calm himself. Now that he was looking at the man properly, Mr. Moreland didn't seem nearly as frightening.

Just immensely angry.

"Well?" the man said, crossing his arms.

John turned up his chin. "That's what I wanted to ask you."

Mr. Moreland took a step forward, his black eyes swirling with contempt. "That's none o' yer business."

John blinked a few times. *I'd be offended, too, if someone was following me around, but he looks like he wants to hurt me. . . . Maybe I shouldn' be out here with him alone. . . .*

When John didn't respond, the man smirked and turned to leave.

A spark filled John's heart—whether of courage or recklessness, he couldn't tell—and he called out, "Why do you always wear shoes?"

Mr. Moreland stopped in his tracks and then spun around. John had to hold back a smirk of his own at the nervousness in the man's eyes.

"Can' I wear them if that's what I like?"

"Oh, o' course you can, but most people in Orkney don' at this time o' year," John pointed out.

"What o' it?"

John shrugged, giving the man a condescending smile. "It just seems . . . odd."

"No odder than how yer son always wears shoes, too," he snarled.

The fear John had felt earlier returned, and he instantly clammed up. *What's he implying?*

Mr. Moreland raised an eyebrow. "Now you have nothing to say?"

John glared, but internally, his heart was pounding. "Just treat Mistress Fairborn well, all right?"

The man's face became as hard as a stone. "I hardly think *you* have any authority over what I do, but that's na something you need to worry about. Like I told you before, she's everything to me."

John nodded, trying not to let his nerves show. "I remember."

"Then also remember this: I don' take kindly to people sneaking up on me."

The Things We Pine For

The following morning, Adaira buzzed about Everton Inn like a bee, trying to complete as many chores as she could, so she'd be ready for all the cooking she'd have to do tomorrow for Johnsmas. And since Penelope McGuff had asked her to bake an extra three pies this year, Adaira doubted she'd have time for anything besides food.

Is that really why yer so frantic? asked a small voice in her heart.

Adaira frowned. *O' course, 'tis. I always get anxious right before a big celebration. This is normal. . . .*

'Tis na because yer trying to ignore what today is?

Adaira ignored the question, dusting the mantel a little more vigorously.

She paused when the door opened. *That better na be Briony. She shouldn' be here today.*

The woman went to the foyer to make sure, but her suspicion had been right. There stood the beautiful midwife, back hunched and hands trembling.

"Dearie, what are you doing here?" she asked, her tone harsher than she'd intended.

Briony lifted her mouth into a thin smile. "Adaira, g-good morneen."

"Nay, 'tis na a 'good morneen,' Briony, so don' pretend otherwise. Did you think I would forget what today is?"

"Don' worry about me, Adaira. I'll be fi—"

Adaira narrowed her eyes, cutting the other woman off. "Don' you dare say 'fine.'"

Briony's lip quivered like she was about to cry.

"You know I know you better than that. Yer na to walk Santiago today, and yer na to report to Dr. Sherwin. I'll take care o' it. You need to take a day to yerself. Visit yer mum's grave, and let yerself feel everything that needs to be felt. You did na let yerself truly mourn her passing when it happened. You closed yerself off so much that fer a while, I feared I'd never get my old friend back. Go to the churchyard, and be with yer mum."

For today marked exactly one year since Bethany Fairborn's death.

Adaira hugged her friend, feeling Briony relax against her as she stopped trying to be strong and pretend this wasn't a difficult day for her.

Tis a difficult day fer me, too. I just wish I could tell you how much yer mum meant to me.

Briony pulled back, and her eyes held a little more light than they had before. The woman nodded and walked off.

Well, so much fer pretending everything is normal.

Adaira heaved a sigh. *Who am I trying to fool? How could anything be normal on a day like this?*

Memories with Bethany played through Adaira's head. The tears, the laughs, the secrets. Bethany had been there for her in ways no one else had. She'd quite literally saved Adaira's life.

And how did I thank her? By breaking my promise to keep her daughter away from the ocean yesterday . . .

Adaira shook her head and went to wash some dishes. *Well, even if she did go into the water, she doesn' know she's a selkie. And she hasn' harmed anyone. I hope that would be enough fer Bethany.*

A little while later, Mr. Mendes came into the kitchen, his cane in hand. When he spotted her, his face lit up. "Senhorita Stubbins, have you seen Briony?"

The anxiety in his green eyes was so heartwarming Adaira's lips curled up into a smile. "I have, actually. She came a wee bit ago, but I told her to leave."

A shadow passed over the merchant's face. "Why did you do that? Is she all right?"

Mr. Moreland poked his head in the doorway. His face bore a matching expression of concern. "What's wrong with Briony?"

"Today isn' the best day fer her if you must know," the innkeeper explained. "She needs some time to herself today. I can take you fer yer walk if you'd like, Mr. Mendes."

The merchant shook his head. "Nay, I'm sure yer busy. That's quite all right. I'll just—"

"What's so bad about today?" Mr. Moreland asked, sliding into the room.

Adaira sighed. She hadn't wanted to talk about this; she was already struggling to deal with it herself. "If you must know, today is the anniversary o' her mum's death."

Understanding dawned on the men's faces.

"Ah, I see," Mr. Moreland said. "And how did she die?"

"Influenza," Adaira snapped. *Can' they see I don' want to talk about this?*

The woman lowered her gaze back to the dish she was working on, praying the men would get the hint.

"Thanks fer letting us know, Senhorita Stubbins. I'll just be going now," Mr. Mendes said softly.

Adaira raised her eyes to nod farewell, noting how the merchant didn't walk back to his room. Instead, he was hobbling toward the front door.

And based on the purposeful set to the man's jaw, Adaira had a feeling she knew exactly where he was going. *Maybe that will help Briony feel better. I certainly hope so.*

Mr. Moreland, on the other hand, was positively smirking.

"What are you so pleased about?" Adaira snarled.

The man's eyes widened for a moment, but then a lazy smile came onto his face. "Ah, nothing. Just thinking what a lovely day 'tis."

"You should hardly think 'tis a lovely day after what I just told you."

Mr. Moreland turned as if he was going to leave, but then he seemed to change his mind. "Bethany wasn' the person you believe she was."

Adaira frowned. *Is he trying to say he's glad she's dead??*

Once her shock had worn off, she asked, "You knew Bethany?"

The man shrugged.

"If you knew the woman at all, then you'd know losing her was a terrible thing fer this village."

The man's smile stretched wider, but it wasn't a warm smile. It reminded Adaira of the mad fisherman, except where Mr. McLaren seemed harmlessly mad, Mr. Moreland looked all too dangerous. "Perhaps people aren' as kind as they pretend to be. Or did she change her tune like you supposedly did?"

Adaira drew back, her mouth dropping open at the man's hostility. "I thought you wanted to make amends."

"Oh, I do," Mr. Moreland said, slinking toward her until their bodies were almost touching. "I'm just eager to find out if yer the changed person Briony says you are."

The man's dark eyes stared into hers, looking into her very soul.

But, rather than feeling outraged like she should have, Adaira's nerves were on fire at the man's proximity. *What's this? I should be wanting to get away from him right now and yet . . .*

Why do I want to get closer?

"Adaira?" a voice called.

Adaira and Mr. Moreland both turned—John stood in the kitchen doorway with a look of confusion. Adaira immediately came to her senses, stepping back until she and Mr. Moreland were an appropriate distance apart.

But what was that strange feeling? Why was my heart racing?

"John! Hello," she said with a nervous grin. "Mr. Moreland was just . . ."

She turned to the dark-haired man, not sure how to finish her sentence.

"Leaving," Mr. Moreland supplied. A self-satisfied smirk hung on his lips, one that made Adaira flush with embarrassment and anger.

He likes Briony, na me. Why would he—Did he do that on purpose to make me look bad?

Nonsense. 'Tis na like he could have known how I'd react. . . .

But it almost seemed like that was exactly the case, for he appeared to be enjoying her discomfort far too much.

"Have a good day, mistress," he said, throwing a glance John's way before sauntering out.

***

John didn't know what to make of what he'd just witnessed, for it made absolutely no sense. Adaira had been terrified of Niall Moreland only a few days ago, yet when he'd walked in just now, it had looked like she was about to kiss him.

Then what does that say about what happened between us? Does that mean she doesn't care fer me as much as I thought?

Was she just mocking me all this time?

Anger filled the farmer's belly, and before he'd fully thought through his words, he spewed, "What was that?!"

The woman jerked back in surprise and, if John wasn't mistaken, fear. He didn't want her to be afraid of him, but right then, he needed to know if he'd been wrong in what he thought about her. Maybe the Adaira Stubbins he'd fallen in love with didn't exist.

"Wh-What was what?" she stuttered.

"Don' be coy with me. Were you about to kiss him?"

Adaira's face turned ashen, and she instantly looked away. "Nay! I—That is, I—"

"Just who is Niall Moreland to you?"

"He's . . ." Her voice broke as though she was trying not to cry.

But John couldn't bring himself to care.

"He told me you met as bairns and that you and yer friends attacked him."

"He did?" the woman whispered, covering her mouth with her hand.

John waited for her to refute the accusation, for her to tell him she would never do something so cruel. For her to tell him he didn't need to worry about Niall because *he* was the one she loved.

But no such words came.

And the longer the silence between them grew, the farther John felt from her.

"I guess I was wrong about you, then," he spat.

Adaira looked up into his eyes, tears trailing down her cheeks. "Aye, you were."

There was something in her voice—something broken— that made John's rising anger come to a careening halt.

There has to be more to this. I know this woman. I've been living in the same house with her fer weeks. I've seen her good heart. What's she na telling me?

"What's the rest o' the story?" John asked, taking a step toward her.

Adaira's eyes shifted nervously, and the farmer almost expected her to draw back. "What are you asking me?"

"All I know about how you and Mr. Moreland met is what he told me. I want to hear it from you."

The woman shook her head, shifting her gaze to the floor. "There's nothing more to tell. 'Tis just like he said. I attacked him and Briony, too. I threw rocks at them and called them horrible names that they didn' deserve."

John took hold of her chin, lifting her face so she was looking at him once more. "But that's na who you are."

Adaira whimpered. "And how do you know who I am?"

The farmer's thumb traced a circle over her cheek. "I know from what I've seen. Yer kind and thoughtful and so generous. You give up yer time and yer skills to anyone who needs them. Yer friendly and funny, and you make everyone feel at home. Yer amazing, and I—"

But before he could say the rest of what was on his heart, the woman reached up and brought her lips to his.

***

Adaira pulled back almost immediately, fearing John would react as he had the last time she'd tried to kiss him.

She stopped a few inches from him, the man's warm breath fanning her lips in a way that made her want to continue where she'd left off.

But not until she knew how he felt about all this. *Did he want the kiss, too, or did I make a mistake?*

"John?" His blue eyes watched her, darker than she'd ever seen them. Regret washed over her. *I shouldn' have done tha—*

He leaned forward, bringing his mouth back to hers.

Adaira's lips moved against his fervently as all the tension that had been building between them ignited in a kiss that sent butterflies through her stomach and stole all thought from her brain. John's hands found their way to the small of her back as he pressed her closer against him—

Until someone cleared their throat.

Adaira gasped and drew back, her face flaming up when she saw Matthew behind them.

"Mr. Levins," John coughed, looking as embarrassed as Adaira felt.

Matthew glared at the farmer murderously, and for a second, Adaira thought he was going to grab John by the collar.

But then he turned his gaze on Adaira, and the look he gave her was far worse.

For it wasn't rage shining in his eyes anymore—it was pain.

"Adaira, I wanted to ask if you needed another set o' hands to prepare fer Johnsmas morn, but I can see you already have plenty o' *help*." Matthew whirled around and stomped out of the inn, slamming the door as he went.

"Matthew?" Adaira stared at the spot where he'd been, trying to understand why he'd reacted like that. "I've never seen him so upset before. . . ."

"Hmm . . ." John hummed cryptically.

"What?" Adaira said, turning back to the redhead.

As soon as she looked him in the eye, though, embarrassment overtook her at the reminder of what she'd just done. What they'd just done.

She stared down at her hands. "So, what happens now?"

"I . . . I need time to think."

Adaira's eyes shot back to his. *Time to think? Yer na sure you want to be with me?*

Hurt crashed over her, her heart tumbling in its wake.

But she couldn't let him see that, so she said, "That's . . . That's fine. I understand."

She swallowed the lump in her throat and smiled up at him.

John shook his head, his eyes full of anguish. "I know you deserve better than that, but I . . . There's a lot to process."

"Nay, don' feel bad. You've got yer son to think about and Hollandstoun. Take all the time you need."

Surprise came over the man's face before a grateful grin took its place. "Thank you, Adaira."

The woman's cheeks heated at her name on his lips. So many other people in town used it that she was more accustomed to hearing it than "Mistress Stubbins," but it just sounded so different when John said it.

"And about Niall Moreland—there's truly nothing going on between us. Nothing like *that*, anyway. I don' want to be with him. Na like—" Adaira slammed her mouth shut, but the implication was still as plain as day: "Na like I want to be with you."

"I'm glad to hear that," John replied, but he was starting to back away.

"And also!" Adaira blurted, trying to keep the man from leaving.

John stopped, waiting to hear what she had to say.

"The day I first met him, 'twas my friends' idea to throw rocks at him and Briony. I just went along with it because I didn' want them to stop liking me. . . ."

She flinched. *That sounds like I'm making excuses.*

"Na that what I did was right! I still knew better, and I should have gone to get an adult when it happened," she said, nodding a few times to be more convincing. "I've tried to make it up to Briony over the years. 'Tis na something I'm proud o'. . . ."

She broke eye contact with the man, for she realized she'd been babbling again. *I really need to stop doing that when I get nervous. I think I'm just making everything worse.*

"We've all done things we wish we hadn'. 'Tis honorable o' you to try to make things right with yer friend."

Adaira's gaze zoomed back to his, but the look he was giving her was so intense she forgot whatever she'd been about to say.

John smiled at her and said, "I'll have an answer fer you at the Johnsmas celebration, all right?"

The woman nodded, keeping her mouth shut, so it wouldn't run wild again *Just let him go, Adaira.*

And though it was difficult when she didn't know if she'd just wrecked her chances with him, that was exactly what she had to do.

A Fresh Start

After sleeping fitfully for half the night, Adaira woke even earlier than usual and got to work in the kitchen. The morning passed in a flurry of flour, eggs, water, and sugar. She was barely aware of whom she spoke to and how much time had passed, for she was so anxious to do everything she needed to for Johnsmas that her brain couldn't think about much else.

That was easier, anyway, for she wasn't overly eager to think about the conversation she and John were going to have that evening. If it didn't go the way she hoped it would, Adaira didn't know what she was going to do.

Tis good I have so many people to help me this year, or there's no way I could finish everything in time, Adaira thought as she stirred some batter.

The Burgesses, the Mendes siblings, Niall Moreland, and Briony had all been at Adaira's beck and call, ready to do each task as she assigned it.

The only person who hadn't been very kind that day was Matthew Levins. Adaira really didn't know what was going on with the tacksman lately, but he'd come by at some point during the morning sharing rumors about Briony being indecent with both Mr. Mendes and Mr. Moreland.

Adaira had immediately told him not to say such things, and Matthew had stormed off, grumbling that that was the last time he'd try to help her anymore.

He has never spoken to me like that before. I wonder what could be bothering him. . . .

"Anyway," she mumbled to herself. "I still need to bake those extra pies or Mistress McGuff is going to skin me alive. I hope John gets back soon with the flour—"

Someone cleared their throat behind her, startling Adaira so much she almost dropped the bowl in her hands. *What in the—*

Adaira spun around. "Briony! Don' do that!"

The midwife stood before her with a mischievous grin. "I was na trying to frighten you this time. Truly! I was just wondering, where are the Burgesses?"

Adaira was tempted to call the other woman out for lying about not trying to scare her, but she decided not to and said, "They went to the market fer me, and then they were going to go fishing fer our dinner. 'Twas too thoughtful o' them. I did na wish fer them to trouble themselves, but John insisted on getting more ingredients fer me since I'd be cooking so much today."

"Aye . . . that was so thoughtful o' *John*," Briony sneered.

Adaira's eyes widened at her slip. "Now, Briony, don' be coming to any conclusions—"

"What sort o' conclusions are you talking about? I merely agreed with you that *John* was being so *thoughtful*. What's there to conclude? He must just be a thoughtful person. I'm sure he would have done that fer just *anyone*."

Adaira sighed. "Briony, stop it. Yer imagining things."

She turned away in the hopes that her friend would get the hint and stop talking about it. She wasn't ready to discuss this with Briony yet. Not until she heard what John had to say tonight.

"O' course. I must be. Then I suppose it does na matter to you that a certain young, *beautiful* blond happens to be speaking to him right now?"

"What?" Adaira whirled back around, her eyes quickly following Briony's finger pointing toward the foyer as John came inside. The man's arms were full of bags, but that wasn't deterring Lucia Mendes from her goal.

A goal that seemed to be about far more than just talking to the farmer—in fact, she looked like she was purposefully starting to slip—

"Lucia!" Briony shouted, seeming to realize what was happening at the same time.

John looked up at the last second and tried to catch Lucia, but the woman collided with him in such a manner that it sent both of them tumbling to the floor. John's bags fell, too, scattering sugar, salt, and flour in all directions.

Mr. Mendes and Mr. Moreland hurried in from another room, the former quickly holding out his hand to help his sister.

Neither John nor Lucia seemed hurt, but the young blond was so worked up over the whole thing that she burst into tears and ran off to her room, her brother trailing close behind her.

Adaira held out her hand to John. "Here, let me help you."

The farmer wrapped his fingers around hers, sending sparks shooting up her arm just as William padded into the foyer. "Da', I just don' see why—what happened?"

The boy's eyes were wide as he set down his own bags and grabbed his father's other hand.

"Just an accident, son. Don' worry. *I'm fine*," John said as he got back on his feet. He stared right at Adaira as if to make sure she wasn't worried about him, but the combination of his eyes on her while their hands were still intertwined made Adaira so embarrassed she dropped the man's hand and looked away.

"But what about all the food?" William asked.

"'Twill be all right, William. I do believe I'll have enough fer tonight, and I can buy some more morn," Adaira said, rubbing the boy's shoulder.

At least I hope 'twill be enough, she thought, biting her lip as anxiety started bearing down on her.

Briony must have noticed Adaira's worry, for she turned to her friend and said, "I've got some extra things at home. 'Twill be enough fer morn's breakfast, at least."

Adaira smiled and thanked her, for she already had plenty of things to think about today. Her eyes slid back to the redheaded farmer without meaning to, and when she found him still watching her intently, the pressure on her chest only increased.

She gulped. *Am I ready fer what he's going to tell me?*

***

That evening, Adaira took a deep breath as she looked around Mary's Hill. Everyone had just finished eating, and as far as she could tell, the food had been enjoyed by all. Now it was almost time for the second part of the night: lighting the bonfires and dancing until dawn.

The young woman stood amongst the crowd next to Briony and William, watching as Laird Oliver approached one of six woodpiles scattered across the hill. He always insisted on being the first person to light a bonfire; then, the village boys would take sticks to light the remaining woodpiles and make Mary's Hill shine like the sun.

Adaira's eyes went to John, who was standing on William's other side. Her stomach tightened when she realized his gaze was on her, too.

She'd been expecting him to talk to her during the meal, but there hadn't been much opportunity for a private conversation. Now that the dancing was about to start, though, it would be much easier to break off from the crowd long enough to hear John's decision.

Whatever that decision might be.

She studied the farmer's face for some hint of what he was going to say, but William broke her concentration before she could determine anything. "Can I go now?"

Adaira looked down at the boy, who was pointing at the laird's glowing bonfire. "Oh! Aye, go, go!" She lightly pushed William forward, smiling as she watched him scurry up to the fire with the other village boys. He giggled and whispered something to Fergus as he waited for his stick to catch flame.

He really has become a part o' the town, Adaira thought, her heart warming at the lad's squeal of delight when his stick lit up. Soon, all the boys' sticks were ready, and they dashed to the unlit woodpiles as the adults looked on.

A few of Adaira's neighbors had brought their instruments; Everton had some very fine musicians, and it was always a treat to hear them play. Dr. Sherwin, Donal McGuff, and Nathaniel Levins all had their fiddles, Gregor Martin had his flute, and Muireall Oliver had her clarsach.

Laird Oliver nodded to them once all the bonfires were lit, and in no time, a merry jig rose into the air.

The effect was like magic as people all over broke into dancing. Adaira looked over the gathering with a grin. This was what she loved to see the most: her friends and neighbors in harmony, laughing and smiling together without a care in the world. Even her father had come out this time; he wasn't happy, per se, and appeared to be complaining about the noise, but at least he was there.

Briony was dancing with one of the Portuguese sailors—a handsome, young fellow that many of the unwed women in town liked to ogle. *I think his name sounded a lot like mine . . . Adriano, maybe?*

But then the young woman smirked as her mind went to two people who might not appreciate seeing Briony dance with another man. *Where did Mr. Moreland and Mr. Mendes run off to?*

Adaira scanned the crowd and soon spotted Mr. Mendes sitting off to the side with his sister. Pity swelled in her heart, for the poor fellow's leg still hadn't healed enough for him to join the dancing.

She waltzed over to him and said, "What do you think o' all this?"

"'Tis quite a fun night. The people o' Everton certainly know how to throw a party," he said politely, but his smile didn't reach his eyes.

"And yet you don' look like yer having fun. Why is that?" Adaira remarked, raising her eyebrow suspiciously.

The man glanced toward the village midwife as she twirled with the sailor. "I'm just disappointed I can't join in on the dancing," he said before shifting his gaze back to Adaira. "The music is so lively."

"Ah. 'Twould be nice to be able to dance with certain people, too, wouldn' it?" she said, a wicked gleam in her eye.

"I'm quite sure we don't know what you mean," Lucia cut in, her upper lip curled in disgust.

Adaira tensed, for she'd forgotten the other woman was there, too, and she wasn't in the mood to talk to her. But she still forced a smile onto her face and said, "And how does this party compare to the balls yer used to?"

Lucia frowned as she examined her nails. "It's very . . . *different*, that's for sure."

Adaira rolled her eyes. She hadn't known "different" could sound so much like "pathetic." She opened her mouth to say something complimentary about her neighbors, but then she heard her name.

The woman turned, her heart in her throat. "Aye, John?"

"John!" Lucia said, her face immediately brightening. "I've been waiting for you to come over! Do you—"

But the farmer's attention was fixed on Adaira, to the point that it was like he couldn't hear Lucia at all. A light smile brushed his face, one Adaira hoped was a sign of good things to come.

He held out his hand, still ignoring the blond woman at Adaira's side. "Would you like to dance?"

Adaira couldn't help but smile back as she lifted her hand and placed it in his. "I'd be delighted."

With that, he swept her away, his touch sending shivers through her as the two of them spun to the music. They wove around the other dancers, leaping like the flaming bonfires, their bodies drawing ever closer—

Until Adaira smashed John's foot.

"Eek! I'm so sorry!" Adaira cried as the farmer came to a lurching halt.

John didn't say anything, but the discomfort on his face was very obvious. Adaira leaped off the man's foot and took a few steps back. *How humiliating. My clumsiness ruins everything!*

"I'm sorry," she repeated, squeezing her eyes shut with a grimace.

"'Tis all right. Don' worry about it," John said, though his voice sounded a bit pained.

The woman groaned. *I'm so stupid. So stupid . . .*

She was tempted to run away, but the farmer was still holding her hands. "Adaira?"

"So, what was it you were wanting to tell me?" she asked, opening her eyes but keeping her head down.

"How about you look at me first?" John said with a chuckle.

The woman's face heated, but she slowly did as he asked. The look on John's face was so deep, though, that the urge to flee almost overwhelmed her once more.

"Adaira, I've been thinking about you a lot since coming here," the farmer started. "From the moment we met, I could tell there was something special about you. You have this light inside you that's unlike anything I've ever seen. And now that I have seen it, I can' bear the thought o' losing it. O' losing you. That's why . . . I need to ask you something."

Perspiration gathered on the woman's palms. *He's going to feel all this sweat on my hands, isn' he? I better let go before—*

"Will you marry me?"

Adaira's breath caught in her throat, her sweaty hands forgotten. "Are you . . . what did you say?"

The farmer beamed at her, creating tiny crinkles around his eyes. "Adaira Stubbins, will you marry me?"

"B-B-But what about Hollandstoun? What about yer home?" she stuttered, not sure she was processing all this correctly. She glanced at the other dancers, wondering if they'd heard what the man just said.

"I want to make Everton a fresh start," John replied. "Fer me. And fer William."

Adaira's mouth fell open with a gasp. "William! What about him? I didn' even think about him! What did he say when you told him?"

The farmer smirked. "I haven' told him anything yet because you haven' given me an answer."

"Oh . . ." Adaira trailed off, her stomach doing nervous flips. "Did I na say it yet?"

John shook his head.

A smile appeared at the corners of her lips, and she ducked her head shyly. "I . . . that is, I . . ."

She leaned forward and pecked him on the mouth. "Aye, I'll marry you," she whispered, her voice not nearly as quiet as a whisper should be.

But she couldn't help it. Not when the joy was building up inside her so fast she could barely stand it. Not when everything in her was urging her to spin and shout and kiss the man until he was the one who couldn't breathe.

She lifted her head to do the thing that sounded most fun right then, but just before her lips met John's, the smile froze on her face.

For something was pressing up against her mind. *What is—*

A vision filled her thoughts, a memory of the night Bethany had saved her.

She trembled and shut her eyes, trying to ignore it. There had been so much pain that night, so much fear, but that wasn't the worst of it. That wasn't what she was trying not to remember.

"Adaira . . . are you all right?"

"Aye," she squeaked. "I'm great!"

She beamed brilliantly, trying to showcase her excitement, but John didn't seem so sure.

"Is there something wrong?"

"Nay! O' course na!" Adaira laughed as if he was being ridiculous. "There's nothing. I'm just *so* happy," she said, wrapping her arms around him in an embrace.

But the tears on her cheeks weren't tears of joy. They were tears of guilt.

He doesn' need to know, she reminded herself. *This is what I wanted, isn' it? He loves me just like I hoped!*

But a soft question knocked at the door of her heart, and Adaira was stupid enough to allow it entrance: *If this is what I wanted, why doesn' it feel the way I thought 'twould?*

Recognition

"I need to tell my father!" the young woman exclaimed, turning to go find him.

"I already told him when I asked fer his blessing," John said with a tight smile.

"You did?" She spun back to him, her mouth wrinkling with fear. "What did he say?"

"He said . . . Well, he wasn't exactly excited about the idea, but he said that if that was what you wanted, then he'd give his blessing."

Adaira's brown eyes widened in surprise, making John's guilt even worse.

For, in truth, their conversation a few minutes ago had gone quite differently, so differently that John wished he could forget it had even happened:

The farmer marched forward as soon as the music started, his stomach a bundle of nerves.

"Mr. Stubbins!"

The man didn't hear him over the musicians playing a few feet from them, though, so John called him again, louder this time.

"What?!" the man barked, turning the farmer's way. He scowled when he saw who it was. "Oh. What do you want now? Something wrong with yer room?"

John shook his head. "Nay, sir. I wanted to talk to you about something more personal. About . . . About yer daughter?"

Terrence's face darkened even further. "What about her?"

The farmer steeled himself and said, "Sir, I'd like to ask permission fer her hand."

John braced himself for the angry tirade he knew was coming, but instead, the older man burst into laughter.

John didn't know how to react, so he stood there stiffly as Terrence chortled for several seconds as if he'd just heard the funniest joke in all the world.

When Terrence caught John's eye, though, his scowl returned. "Nay."

John gaped. "What?"

"You heard me. Nay. You can' marry my daughter."

"But, sir, why—"

Terrence's brow wrinkled with scorn. "As if you could possibly be there fer her."

"Sir, I love her. What makes you think I couldn' be there fer her?"

"Love is one thing, but can you protect her?"

"Aye, I can. I will!" John promised, hoping to assuage the man's doubts with his sincerity.

But Terrence scoffed. "And here I thought you were honest. I'll na have my daughter marry a liar, that's fer sure."

"I'm na lying, sir," John argued, his patience growing thin. "I've done a fine job keeping my son safe, and I know I can—"

"Ah, but what about yer wife?"

Red appeared at the edges of John's vision. "My wife?"

Terrence nodded, his eyes dripping with condescension. "Thank you fer coming to me, but I'll na put Adaira in the same position yer wife was in. I'd like her to outlive me, you know."

John's temper snapped, and he jabbed his finger in the man's face. "Now, listen here, old fool. If you had any idea what really happened to my wife, you wouldn' be saying that."

But Terrence wasn't intimidated; in fact, he seemed to be enjoying John's anger. "Then why don' you tell me what happened, and fix the misunderstanding?"

"I . . ." John sighed. "I can' do that."

Terrence shrugged. "In that case, you can forget about getting my blessing."

The man turned as if he was going to leave, but then he seemed to remember something. "Oh, and one more thing. Just know that if you choose to disrespect me and ask Adaira anyway, I'll do everything in my *power to keep the two o' you apart. And, unlike you, I don' make promises I can' keep."*

"I wish I could have been there to hear that," Adaira said, pulling John out of the memory. She giggled, all the worry lines around her mouth disappearing as if she hadn't a care in the world.

John smiled, wishing she could always be so happy as she was right then. *She has been carrying so many burdens fer such a long time. Now I can help lift the weight off o' her, so she can breathe again.*

"There is someone else who needs to know."

"Oh?" Adaira cocked her head to the side.

John pointed at a small group of boys racing each other around one of the bonfires.

"You didn' tell him yet?" the woman asked.

"Na yet. I wanted to make sure you said aye first."

"Well, what are we waiting fer then? Let's go tell him!"

They made their way over to the group hand in hand, waving at William to get his attention.

"Why are you so out o' breath?" John asked when the boy came over huffing and puffing.

"We had . . . a race . . . to see who was the . . . fastest."

John twisted his lips. "And who was?"

William patted his chest. "Me, o' course!"

"I'm na surprised a bit!" The farmer chuckled. "But, William, there's something we need to talk to you about."

"You and Mistress Adaira? What is it?"

"We . . ." John looked to Adaira as if he couldn't bring himself to say the words.

"We'd like to get married," Adaira said, "but na without talking to you about it first."

William gasped, looking from one adult to the other without speaking for several seconds.

He finally settled his attention on Adaira and said, "You want to marry my da'?"

Adaira nodded. "I'm sure 'tis probably a bit shocking fer you, but I . . . I love yer father. Very much."

The tips of the boy's lips quirked up. "I knew it! I knew you were in love with each other!"

Adaira's face flushed. "You did?"

"I've known fer ages now."

"Then you knew before I did, I think. And you know what else?" Adaira asked.

William rolled back on his heels. "What?"

"I love you, too. Do you think . . . would you mind having me fer a stepmum?"

The boy's tiny grin spread over his cheeks. "I think I could tolerate it."

John snorted. "Tolerate it? What? Come here, you!"

The farmer opened his arms for a hug, and soon, the three of them were embracing. It was the start of a new family. One that came with its own unique challenges and—

CRACK!

A flash of lightning filled John's vision as it struck about twenty feet away from him, nearly hitting Laird Oliver. The portly man jumped in terror, and several people around him screamed.

Where did that come from? John lifted his head, noting the large clouds above him. Clouds that hadn't been there when the dancing started.

Soon, more lightning struck the ground around the revelers, and panic overtook everyone as they scrambled to find cover.

The sky swirled with darkness, and then another bolt appeared, setting fire to one of the trees.

Orkney was no stranger to tempests, but this was no ordinary storm. Of that, he was absolutely certain.

The farmer scanned the crowd, his eyes searching for the cause of the disturbance. That was when he saw someone who wasn't crying out in fear, who wasn't running away. Someone he should have recognized from the very beginning.

"Let's get out o' here!" John said to Adaira, who was eying the odd weather with an even odder expression.

He didn't have time to think on it, though, and grabbed her hand before reaching for his son.

"William, we have to go! Come on!"

The boy turned to his father, raindrops dotting his face— *or are those tears?*

John took his son's hand and led the three of them away, down toward Everton Inn. Toward safety.

But he also chanced one more look at Niall Moreland, wondering what had set the selkie off.

And when he did, Niall's eyes locked onto his.

Puzzlement crossed the man's face, but then a look of understanding came over him.

"Faster!" John shouted, turning away from Niall as they sped down the hill.

But a sinking feeling was growing in the man's stomach. For he knew the selkie wasn't going to leave him alone.

***

Once the three of them had gotten into the inn, Adaira let go of John's hand to focus on catching her breath. And on coming to grips with what had just happened.

That storm—Briony must have lost her temper. But why? Why now, o' all times? Is it because she went in the ocean the other day?

Or was it something Niall Moreland said? He and Briony were dancing at the same time John and I were. Maybe he told her something that upset her?

Thunder rolled overhead, reminding Adaira of how dangerous the night had become. What had been meant as a celebration of summer—of life itself—had somehow turned into something sinister.

I hope everyone found cover.

When the chaos had first ensued, Adaira had waved to Briony through the crowd, hoping the midwife would come down to the inn for safety, but Briony had headed the other direction toward Drulea Cottage with the Mendes siblings.

And now I have no idea what she's doing. Maybe I should go find her. What if it happens again?

Adaira's stomach dropped. *What if . . . What if she figured out she's a selkie?*

A figure burst into the foyer, scaring Adaira so much she almost leaped out of her skin.

"Dr. Sherwin!" she exclaimed once she recognized who it was. "Are you all right?"

The doctor peered at Adaira and the Burgesses with a crazed look in his eye. "I came to make sure no one is injured," he panted, water dripping from his brown hair.

"No one is hurt," Adaira confirmed, glancing at the Burgesses. "Na everyone is back though. I saw the Mendes siblings with Briony before, but I don' know about my father or Mr. Moreland. Have you seen them?"

Dr. Sherwin nodded. "Yer father is at Mr. Levins's house. I haven' seen Mr. Moreland—"

"Mr. Moreland is fine," John growled, speaking for the first time since they'd arrived. "And 'twould be better fer everyone if we never saw him again."

Adaira frowned and opened her mouth to ask what the farmer meant, but William spoke up first.

"Da's marrying Mistress Adaira!" he told Dr. Sherwin with a grin.

The doctor's eyebrows flew up to his forehead as though that was the most surprising thing he'd ever heard. He turned to Adaira with a hesitant nod. "I suppose congratulations are in order."

John put his arm around Adaira's shoulders. "Thank you."

The man's touch was soft, and, under normal circumstances, Adaira would have quite enjoyed it.

If not for the way his hand was trembling on her shoulder.

The storm must have frightened him even more than me. I wonder if it reminded him o' being out in the storm when William got hurt.

She leaned back and smiled up at John, trying to soothe his fears by showing him she was well. That everything would be all right.

He smiled back at her, but his hand continued to shake.

"I better go up to Drulea Cottage and see if Mistress Fairborn and the Mendeses are up there, then," Dr. Sherwin announced before turning and darting back out into the darkness.

"'Tis awfully strange," William mumbled, standing by the nearest window as rain continued to fall.

"What is?" Adaira asked, walking over to the boy's side.

"The storm. It doesn' feel right."

Something in the boy's voice snagged Adaira's attention. "What do you mea—"

William bent over and coughed several times, cutting off the rest of Adaira's question.

"Perhaps 'twould be best na to talk too much right now, William," John suggested. He looked to Adaira. "Maybe you could make him some tea?"

"O' course," the woman replied, ushering the lad toward the kitchen.

She couldn't help but notice, though, how John had ended any discussion about William's mysterious comment.

He said he felt the storm? You can' feel a storm, can you? Na unless yer . . . Adaira looked over at the lad as he sat at the counter, waiting patiently for a cup of tea. He looked perfectly normal.

Perfectly human.

I guess this storm is messing with me as well.

"Mistress Adaira?" William asked.

Adaira blinked a few times before she realized the boy was staring at her with a peculiar expression.

Why's he looking at me like tha—

"The tea!" she exclaimed, rushing to boil some water. "I'm sorry—I must have gotten distracted."

"Don' feel bad, mistress. I get distracted sometimes, too. Especially when there's a storm outside."

"Why's that?" she asked over her shoulder as poured water into a pot.

"They always just make me think about my mum."

"Yer mum?"

"Aye, she loved storms. Said they made her feel more alive than anything else."

Adaira nearly dropped the pot in her hand before setting it down.

She spun around and smiled at the boy like all was well, though, and said, "You know, I don' really know anything about yer mum. Would you tell me about her?"

William narrowed his eyes. "Yer na jealous, right, mistress?"

Adaira laughed as she got out three teacups. "Nay, that's na it. Just . . . curious, that's all. Was she a lot like you?"

"Nay, she wasn' like me at all. She was quiet and shy. Prettiest woman in all o' Hollandstou—oh, sorry, Mistress Adaira."

Adaira waved the apology away. "Don' worry about it. Did she . . . like the sea?"

William's countenance turned sad, and he moved his gaze to the floor. "She always told me 'twas dangerous and to stay away from it, just like Da' does, but . . ."

"But what?"

"There's just something I don' understand: If she hated it so much, why did she go swimming the night she died?"

"Did she like to go swimming?"

"Nay!" William said, his voice rising. "I just told you she thought the sea was dangerous. She never went near it as far as I know."

"Have you asked yer da' about it?"

The boy sighed heavily. "Aye, I did."

"And what did he say?"

"He said she just decided to that night. That she told him she was in the mood fer it," William said with a shrug before gesturing for Adaira to come closer.

And once she'd done so, the boy whispered, "I could tell he was lying."

"You don' think that's why she went?"

William shook his head. "I don' think she drowned at all."

Adaira pulled back in alarm. This conversation was starting to sound far too familiar. *What was it Henry told me about the rumors back in Hollandstoun?*

She shivered as the memory came to her: *"They say he killed her."*

"I'm sure yer wrong about that," she said to the boy, though the queasiness in her stomach suggested otherwise.

I'm being ridiculous. William is human, his mum was human, and John certainly didn' kill her!

"Would you like a muffin?" She pointed to the plate of muffins on the counter.

The boy grabbed one, but he didn't look like he was going to drop the subject so easily. "But, mistress, don' you—"

"Now, where did yer father end up? Let me see if he wants some tea, too." She padded toward the foyer, desperate to find John.

For her head had become a ship tipping back and forth in a storm of impossible thoughts.

A storm that might just capsize her if she didn't calm down soon.

But the relief Adaira was searching for never came, for as she approached the foyer, angry voices hit her ears.

She ducked into the dining room to avoid being seen, tilting her head to hear the conversation more clearly. But what she was about to overhear would steal the breath from her lungs and send her world spinning.

Unraveling

John stood motionless by the window as Adaira and William made their way to the kitchen. Thoughts and emotions whirled through him like the very lightning outside, zooming through this mind one after the other with no signs of slowing down.

He tried to convince himself it was all a misunderstanding, that his paranoia was making connections where none existed. *'Tis all in my head. Niall Moreland can' be a selkie. Just because he wasn' frightened o' the storm doesn' mean he was the one who caused it.*

But when the front door opened and someone stepped inside, he knew in his heart that he was absolutely right.

And that the man before him was no man at all.

"You . . ." John breathed, his eyes wide with both surprise and fear.

Niall smiled wickedly. "Were you expecting someone else?"

John glanced toward the kitchen, but Adaira and William must not have heard him come in.

Good. John didn't want them privy to this conversation anyway.

"What are you doing here?"

"Oh, I just came to get out o' the rain. 'Tis awfully frightening out there, don' you think?"

"Don' play coy with me," John snapped. "You could put a stop to it if you wished. Why are you really here?"

Niall leaned toward him with a curious look. "I wondered when you saw me earlier—there was this funny glint in yer eye.

Now yer blaming me fer the storm? Are you sure yer thinking straight?"

He held out his hands as if he was blameless, but the gesture only infuriated John further. "I'm quite sure. And I'm sure o' what you are, *selkie*."

Niall's mouth dropped open before an angry, suspicious frown came over his face. "How do you know that?"

"I know because . . ." John trailed off nervously, realizing he had no way to explain this without giving away a secret he'd sworn to keep.

But then, Niall's questioning gaze shifted, and his dark smile returned. "Ah, you don' need to tell me. I understand now."

"Understand what?" John growled, lifting his chin so the man wouldn't see his fear.

"'Tis William, isn' it? Now it makes sense why you've been keeping him away from the ocean. You didn' want him to know the truth, did you?"

The farmer's heart skipped a beat. "I don' know what yer talking about," he said firmly.

But the selkie laughed. "Who's playing coy now? You know, I thought there was something different about him. He just felt so *familiar*. . . . Now I know why."

John clenched his jaw. "*I'm warning you*, if you go near my son—"

"Yer warning me? If you know as much about selkies as you seem to, then you must know yer no match fer the likes o' me." Niall stepped closer.

John's instincts screamed for him to move back, to get away from the threat, but he wasn't about to retreat when his son's safety was at stake. "That may be so, but that doesn' mean I'm going to go down without a fight."

Niall raised his eyebrows skeptically. "If 'tis a fight you want, I'm more than happy to give it to a thief like you."

"A thief?" John asked. "And how did you reach that conclusion?"

"'Tis simple. Yer obviously na a selkie, so that means yer son got his selkie blood from his mother. Therefore, you must have stolen her skin and forced her to be yer wife."

John charged forward and grabbed a fistful of the man's shirt. "Never say that again!"

Niall put his hands on top of John's, scalding them with supernatural heat.

The farmer cried out and pulled his hands away. They were bright-red, but the pain was already fading.

The selkie was toying with him.

"I didn' force her to stay here," John continued. "She did so o' her own free will."

Niall snorted in disbelief. "What selkie would turn their back on their heritage?"

"My Ellie did. She *chose* to live as a human," John said through his teeth. "And I can' blame her if other selkies are anything like you. So, why did you make the storm? Did Mistress Fairborn decide you weren' worth her time?"

As soon as the words spilled out, John wished he could take them back, for he realized he was being reckless and that he was probably about to get himself hurt.

But John's insult didn't have the effect he thought it would. Rather than getting angry, Niall froze, his face turning ashen gray.

What in the world? Is he afraid o' me?

A creak in the floorboards nearby jostled Niall from his paralyzed state, and before John knew it, the selkie tore out the door like he'd seen a ghost.

What just happened?

After waiting a few minutes to see if the man would reappear, John tramped to the kitchen, his blood still cooling from the vicious encounter. He found William sitting at the counter with half a muffin in his hand.

"Where's Adaira?" John asked, glancing at the pot of water hanging over the fireplace. Three empty teacups sat on the counter, but the innkeeper was nowhere around.

"She went looking fer you a few minutes ago," the boy said. "Did you na see her?"

***

Adaira rose early the next morning, feeling like she'd barely gotten a wink of sleep. Which was most likely true since she'd spent most of the night thinking over John and Niall's conversation.

She'd fled to her room and locked the door because she hadn't known how to make sense of what she'd heard, but now it was a new day, and she was going to have to face this new reality whether she wanted to or not.

After a trip to Loch Isla, she told herself.

Adaira flew down the stairs, grabbed her fishing rod, and stole out the door. Her guests would just have to make breakfast on their own this morning while she tried to untangle the mess of feelings in her heart. She'd sort things out, and everything would be fine. Like it always was.

She darted up the hill toward the loch, keeping a brisk pace until she spotted the loch. The air felt cool on her skin, and the moist earth squished under her feet.

Na a good morneen to go fishing. Adaira looked down at her light-green dress. She hadn't thought to bring a blanket to sit on.

It can' be helped, she decided as she plopped onto the log she always sat on when she came here. She'd sat here with William not too long ago when she'd taught him how to fish.

Adaira chuckled as she cast her line. The poor lad had been utterly terrible at it, for he lacked the patience fishing required.

How could I na have known? How could I na have seen the signs?

She thought back to how William and Briony had reacted when they'd first met:

"'Tis just that you remind me o' my mum."

"Actually, you remind me o' my mum, too."

Adaira growled. *How could I be so stupid!* It seemed so obvious now.

And what about that argument I interrupted the night Mr. Mendes's ship arrived?

She gasped. *That's why John grabbed me! He didn' want me to touch William because he knew I'd get burned.*

I wonder how much it hurt then when William latched onto him. . . . I bet he got a pretty good burn on his arm that night.

What happened after that though? She wished now that she hadn't listened when John told her to stay at the inn. If she'd just followed them that night, maybe she would have figured everything out sooner.

And Niall Moreland . . . he's also a selkie?

"Why is this happening to me?" Adaira whispered to herself, blinking back a few tears.

For the woman was almost at her breaking point, and she was starting to suspect that even the magic of fishing wasn't going to be enough this time.

"Am I interrupting something?" asked a male voice.

Adaira didn't turn around, for she wasn't ready to interact with anyone yet today. Especially after how things had gone with him last time. "Aye, I'm quite busy fishing at the moment," she grumbled.

But she heard the owner of the voice come up behind her. "I'd say 'twas a wee bit more than that. What's wrong?"

"I don' know what yer talking about, Matthew," Adaira squeaked, trying to sound convincing but knowing that she wasn't even close.

"You tend to come fishing when yer anxious. Are you still shaken up from the storm last night? Or is it because I was avoiding you?"

Adaira frowned. "You were? I don' understand what I did to make you so angry."

She hadn't even noticed the tacksman was avoiding her last night. She'd been too caught up thinking about what John was going to say.

She looked up at Matthew, though, now, wishing she'd been more observant. She hated the thought of her friend being upset with her.

The man's dark eyes flickered with sadness, making Adaira wonder just how deeply she'd wounded him. She opened her mouth to apologize, but then he said, "I'm na angry anymore. I'm just concerned about you. Something's definitely wrong. What is it?"

The innkeeper sighed. "I-I'm na sure I can talk about it."

Matthew took a seat next to her. "Then just tell me what you *can* talk about. 'Tis na healthy to keep everything to yerself when yer obviously distressed."

Adaira pulled in her line and set the fishing rod down as she debated what to say, but when she looked into Matthew's eyes, words fell, unbidden, from her lips. "John Burgess proposed to me."

The man's jaw dropped for a second before he composed himself. "And what did you say?"

"I said aye. Nothing would make me happier. . . ."

Is that even true though? Adaira wasn't so sure anymore. She wasn't so sure of a lot of things this morning.

"Then what's the problem?"

"William is a selkie, and John didn' tell me!" was what she wished she could say. Instead, she mumbled something close to the truth: "I don' know if we can be good fer each other. And I don' know if I can be what William needs."

Matthew pursed his lips as he mulled over her words. "Well, I can' speak fer Mr. Burgess, but when it comes to you, there's no doubt in my mind that yer up fer whatever comes yer way."

"But what if—"

Matthew held up a hand to silence her before shaking his head. "No doubt in my mind."

He broke eye contact and turned his attention to her hands. He reached out and grasped them in his own before staring at her once more. "You'll be a great wife to whomever you decide to be with. And a wonderful mum. I know it."

Adaira was taken aback at the man's intensity; the sincerity in his brown eyes was undeniable. "How do you know? I've made so many mistakes. . . ."

"Because yer always thinking o' others. Yer always putting their needs first. What you should be thinking about is if Mr. Burgess is the right person fer you."

With that said, the tacksman stood and wandered off. Adaira watched him as he went, wondering why he hadn't brought his sheep up for a drink. *That's why he normally comes to the loch, isn' it?*

Perhaps he's right. Perhaps John isn' the person I'm meant to be with. It would certainly be easier to just walk away from all of this and go back to the way things were. Back to when she was just the friendly innkeeper's daughter, warming everyone's bellies with good food and kind conversation.

She was already carrying so many secrets. She wasn't sure she could handle more.

After spending a while longer deliberating over how to move forward and coming up empty-handed, Adaira stood and made her way back to the inn.

She slipped into the hallway through one of the back doors, hoping no one would be in there and see she'd been off fishing rather than attending to her duties. She just had to get the fishing rod back into the closet, and then she could—

A scuffle caught her attention. It seemed to be coming from the Burgesses' room.

Did Leah get stuck in there? Adaira's cat was notorious for sneaking into rooms, a trait which often led to her being stuck for hours before someone inevitably found her.

Adaira immediately went over and opened the door, but to her shock, it wasn't her elusive feline she locked eyes with.

It was Niall Moreland.

The man jumped when he saw her, quickly putting his hands behind his back in a guilty manner. He was standing between the two beds, both of which had unusually messy sheets.

"Mr. Moreland? What are you doing in the Burgesses' room?" Adaira asked, trying to sound casual despite the fear blazing through her heart. Now that she knew how dangerous this man—selkie—was, she didn't want to be anywhere near him. She knew all selkies weren't the same, but the way he'd acted toward John last night had told Adaira everything she needed to know about him.

"Oh, I was just . . . I was looking fer . . . I dropped my pen, and it slid under the door," he explained. "I must say yer looking especially radiant this morneen. Must be because o' the good news William told me about. Congratulations." He flashed his teeth at her.

A warm, fuzzy feeling came over Adaira, and she opened her mouth to thank him before warning bells blared through her mind.

This man is a selkie! Bethany told me they can weave their magic over humans.

She took in a sharp breath, remembering how she'd felt the urge to kiss him the other day. The feeling had been so potent she'd been powerless to resist it.

But that was before she'd known what he was.

"I don' know why you thought the pen would be in their beds, then, Mr. Moreland," she said stonily.

The selkie blinked a few times, clearly surprised at her cold response, but then he smiled wider. "Ah, how right you are. That was rather silly o' me. And please, call me 'Niall.'"

Adaira giggled despite herself. "I could help you . . . look fer the pen, I mean."

Niall tapped her nose and shook his head. "Thank you, but I already found it. 'Twas under the bed. I need to get going anyway, so I can help Mr. Calhoun."

He stepped around her toward the doorway, still not revealing what was behind his back.

"Niall?" Adaira asked, her voice slurring a bit. It would be so easy to believe his words, but she had to fight this. She had to remember . . . something. *What was it?*

"Aye?" the man said, his eyes gleaming with kindness.

And the only thing Adaira could think to ask was, "You have Briony's best intentions at heart, don' you?"

The man's brow furrowed just the slightest bit before smoothing out. "O' course. You know, Briony was right about you."

"How so?"

"You have changed." He winked, slid his hands around as he turned, and walked out into the hallway.

Only once he was gone was Adaira able to wipe the dazed grin off her face and really think through the man's last words. *What did he mean by that? It almost sounded like he was trying to say something else. . . .*

She groaned, reminding herself that she couldn't trust a thing that came out of the selkie's mouth.

I bet he didn' even have a pen in his hand! But if he didn' come in fer a pen, why did he come in here? Adaira thought, grabbing the wrinkled blankets at the foot of the nearest bed. That was when she caught sight of John's bag.

Adaira lifted the sack with the intention of moving it to the dresser, but when she did, she spotted something inside it. She reached her hand in, only to draw out a piece of long, gray material. It was soft and smooth and almost looked like—

Adaira gasped, dropping the sealskin to the floor.

She bent down and gingerly retrieved it, staring at the skin in fascination. She'd seen them in the market before, but never one this small. *This is William's.*

And to think Niall was just in here . . . was this what he was looking fer? A surge of protectiveness overtook her, and she quickly stashed the pelt under her clothes.

If he comes back in here, he's certainly na going to find it. She stepped back into the hallway and hurried up to her room, where she locked the pelt in her footlocker. *There. Now 'twill be safe.*

But I better tell John that Niall was in his room.

Adaira paused, her eyes homing in on a piece of paper on the floor. It looked like it had been slipped under the door.

What's this? Did John leave this fer me?

She picked up the note with a small smile, expecting something romantic and heartfelt.

What she read was anything but that.

Adaira's eyes widened, and she covered her mouth with her hand, aghast at the words on the page.

"This can' be happening. This can' be happening," she chanted to herself.

But right there in black and white were the words: "I know what you did. Cancel your betrothal immediately, or I'll make sure everyone knows your secret."

Tears sprang to Adaira's eyes. This was her nightmare coming to life. Her chest suddenly felt so tight she could barely breathe, and adrenaline raced through her veins.

But her mind felt sharper than ever. She'd been struggling to make a decision before, but now she knew exactly what she had to do.

Asunder

Adaira's stomach tightened when she heard the Burgesses come into the inn. It was about lunchtime, and she'd just put the finishing touches on the stew she'd been making.

Am I really going to do this? she asked herself.

The farmer strolled into the kitchen, his eyes lighting up when he spotted her.

"Hello, Adaira," John said with an adorable smile. "I missed seeing you at breakfast this morneen."

William appeared in the doorway, rolling his eyes. "Am I going to have to hear this kind o' thing all the time now?"

"Yer going to have to get used to a lot more than just that." John winked at the boy. Then he walked over and planted a kiss on Adaira's lips.

"Eww!" William cried, covering his eyes.

John chuckled before seeing that Adaira didn't look nearly as pleased. Her face was a complete mask, hiding the turmoil lurking just below the surface.

"Is something wrong?"

Adaira gulped. "I need to talk to you."

The farmer frowned before turning to William. "Son, would you go ahead to the dining room, so I can have a word with Adaira?"

The lad scurried off, his cheeks reddening in such a way that it was clear what he thought a "word" truly meant.

Once the two of them were alone, John took Adaira's hands in his. "I'm sorry if that was too forward o' me. Would you prefer I na kiss you in front o' other people?"

Adaira tilted her head down. *I can' look at him right now, na when he's being so sweet.*

"'Tis na that."

"What is it, then, love?"

The way he said the term of endearment as if it was as natural as breathing made Adaira wonder just how long he'd wanted to call her that. And how long he'd felt that way toward her.

But I can' ask. Na when I'm about to break his heart.

"I . . . I spoke too hastily before," Adaira whispered. "I'm na sure I can marry you."

The words hung in the air for several seconds before John replied, and when he did, she could tell he was trying to hold back his hurt. "Is this because o' William?"

Adaira's head snapped up in surprise. The man's eyes were shifting back and forth nervously.

"Nay, o' course na. I love William dearly."

Relief flooded John's face, but then he pinched his lips together. "Is it because o' yer father?"

"My father?"

John nodded, his brow furrowing with frustration. "Don' believe anything he says. He just can' stand the thought o' losing you, so he's filling yer head with lies."

What? What are you talking about?

Adaira narrowed her eyes. "You told me he gave you his blessing. You lied to me?"

John scoffed and shook his head. "O' course he didn' give me his blessing! He hates everything and everyone. Are you really that naive?"

"I guess I must be since I thought I could trust you! Now I'm sure I can' marry you!" Adaira shouted, her eyes filling with tears.

The anger on John's face faded to regret. "Adaira, I . . ."

"Don'," she snarled. "Don' say anything else. I've heard all I need to." She whirled around and stomped out of the room.

But when she reached the stairs, she paused, her ears straining for the slightest sound. For her heart was hoping he'd follow her. That he wouldn't let things end this way.

But there were no footsteps behind her.

He wasn't coming.

Adaira went up to her room, slamming the door so loudly she was certain John would hear it. Once she'd done so, though, she sat on the edge of her bed, her tears falling freely.

I had to do it, she reminded herself. *Someone was going to give up my secret if I didn'.*

Is it really worth losing John just to keep it though? asked a soft voice in her heart.

O' course 'tis! If he knew the truth, he'd never stay with me. And if the rest o' Everton found out, I'd lose everything. . . . John will be all right. He'll get through it.

***

Meanwhile, John was reeling from what had just happened. He wanted to race up the stairs, pound Adaira's door in, and beg her to take him back.

But the memory of Niall's words held the farmer's feet in place. The selkie was already a threat to both him and William. *Maybe this is better. I don' want to put Adaira in harm's way, too.*

Besides, I can' let her find out William is a selkie. John had been worried that she'd overheard his conversation with Niall last night and that that had been what she'd wanted to talk to him about.

But she said 'twas na because o' William. And she seemed surprised when I mentioned her father. . . . Maybe he hasn' spoken to her, after all.

John sighed. *Then why did she break things off?*

Before he could come up with an answer, the front door opened. The farmer went to see who it was and found three Portuguese sailors standing in the foyer.

"Umm, can I help you?"

Based on their confused expressions, John didn't think they understood his question.

"They're here because I invited them," said Lucia as she appeared next to him.

"You invited them?"

The woman smiled. "They've been wanting to try Adaira's cooking for a while now. You don' think she'll mind, do you?"

She didn' tell Adaira before she invited them?

There was a snide twist to the corner of Lucia's mouth, giving John the sense she wasn't actually trying to be kind. *Maybe she's upset about my betrothal and is trying to get back at Adaira.*

"Well . . ." John grimaced, wondering what he should do.

"I'll just go ahead and lead them to the dining room," she said before turning to the sailors. "Venham[27]!"

The sailors followed Lucia out of the room, but John stood there for a moment. After the conversation he and Adaira had just had, he was sure this wasn't going to go well.

The door opened again, and Santiago Mendes flew in. "Where's my sister?" he asked, his tone frantic.

"What's wrong?"

"I need to find her. Is she in the dining room?"

John nodded. "You—"

He broke off, for the man was already limping in that direction. *He shouldn' be going that fast when his leg isn' healed yet. What could be the problem?*

Lucia and Mr. Mendes's voices soon emerged from the dining room, and though they spoke solely in Portuguese, their rising volume indicated they were arguing.

Then a new shout caught John's attention. It had come from outside, but the farmer didn't recognize who'd yelled.

The Mendes siblings, the sailors, and William crept out of the dining room, their eyes wide with curiosity.

Except for Mr. Mendes. His countenance was pale, and he'd curled his arms over his head.

That was when Adaira came out of the hallway, her head darting about in confusion. "Is someone outside?"

She looked to John for a response, but it wasn't the farmer who spoke next.

"They've found us, sister," Mr. Mendes said solemnly.

---

[27] Come along.

Everyone turned to him; John, Adaira, and William with questions, but Lucia and the sailors with looks of defeat. *Whatever this is, they're all in on it*, John realized.

"Santiago, don't go out there. We can go out the back and escape on the *São Nicolau*," Lucia urged, grabbing her brother's hands.

But Mr. Mendes pulled away. "I left Briony out there."

And when he marched out the door, John couldn't help but feel like he was watching a man walking toward his own execution.

The people inside trailed after the merchant to see what would happen next. John, too, squeezed through the door just as William did, only to watch a bizarre scene unfold.

Just outside stood a group of men in uniforms, one of whom was squeezing Briony Fairborn's wrist. All but one held guns against their shoulders.

The oldest man in the group, the one not bearing a weapon, said with a foreign accent, "Now, senhorita, let's try again. Where is Senhor Mendes?"

"*Right here*. And why does that matter?" shouted Mr. Mendes as he stepped out.

Lucia was quick to follow him, as were the sailors.

"What's happening, Da'?" William whispered.

John turned to him, feeling just as bewildered as the boy was. "I don' know, son. I wish I did."

"I bet Mr. Mendes owes someone a lot o' money, and . . ."

The farmer ignored the rest of William's imaginative theory, leaning in to hear what Mr. Mendes and the man who seemed to be in charge were saying.

". . . I am Comodoro Cardoso of the king's navy, and on behalf of His Majesty, King Joseph, and the Royal Navy, I hereby arrest you for high treason."

John gaped at the wild accusation, but then he caught sight of the guilty expression on Mr. Mendes's face. *He . . . he isn' denying it. Could it be true?*

The farmer's gaze went to Adaira to see how she was handling all this. He wished he could be standing beside her right now, his arm wrapped around her shoulder.

The woman's attention wasn't on the men in uniform or even on the merchant himself—her eyes were fixed on someone else entirely.

Briony Fairborn.

John's heart went out to her when he saw how pallid her face was. *She looks like she's going to be sick.*

But then the midwife did something completely unexpected.

"What are you talking about? That's the most ridiculous thing I've ever heard!" she shouted, stepping between Mr. Mendes and Cardoso.

"Is it? Then you must not know Senhor Mendes very well, senhorita. *I* happen to know that Senhor Mendes was one of the conspirators in an assassination attempt last year."

"Nay, yer lying!"

The commodore sneered. "Oh, how noble of you, trying to defend him. What are you, his lover?"

The comment seemed to fluster Mistress Fairborn, so the man continued, "And not just any assassination attempt either. Senhor Mendes was part of a group trying to murder His Majesty the King."

"What!" William squealed, drawing the attention of a couple of the uniformed men.

John immediately positioned his arm in front of his son's body. "Let's go back inside, William."

"But I want to hear the rest!"

The farmer glared down at the lad. "Just listen to me."

William looked like he wanted to protest, but then he saw the hard look in his father's eyes and nodded.

The two of them slipped back into the inn, though William insisted on at least watching the affair from the window.

"Where's Adaira?" asked an ornery voice.

Rage boiled in John's stomach as Terrence Stubbins waddled into the sitting room.

The older man's eyes narrowed when he spotted John. *"You."*

John scowled back at him. "Spare me the venom today, you hateful snake."

"What did you just call me?!"

"What's the matter? Is the truth too painful fer you? You better brace yerself, then." The farmer took a deep breath, feeling like a dragon about to spew fire—

"Da'! They're taking Mr. Mendes away!" William called.

John didn't care about that right at the moment, and he took a step toward Mr. Stubbins, still ready to tell the old innkeeper exactly what he thought of him.

But then William screamed, "Mistress Fairborn just fell! I think she's hurt!"

John forgot his anger and raced outside. He found Adaira shaking her friend's shoulder while Mistress Fairborn lay unconscious in the dirt.

The farmer ran over and knelt at the midwife's other side. She didn't appear injured, but she wasn't stirring either.

"What happened?" John asked.

Adaira sniffed. "I don' know! She just collapsed. . . ."

"William!" John cried.

The boy, who had been peeking out the door, was at his father's side in an instant. "Aye, Da'?"

"Go find Dr. Sherwin. Quickly!"

As William darted off, John's eyes went back to Adaira's. He smiled at her in a way he hoped was encouraging, but Adaira's lip started to tremble.

"'Tis going to be all right," John said, putting a hand on the woman's arm before he knew what he was doing.

Adaira's eyes filled with tears as she stared at him, and for a second, John felt her lean into his touch.

But then her gaze skittered away, and she pulled out of his grasp. The movement only separated her from his hand by a few inches, but to John, the distance might as well have been a chasm.

The Battles We Choose

"I suspect 'twas just the surprise o' it all," Dr. Sherwin explained once he'd examined the midwife. It hadn't taken William long to find him, and it had taken even less time for the doctor to reach the same conclusion John had: Briony Fairborn had simply fainted from shock.

'Tis completely understandable under the circumstances. Would I be faring much better in her shoes?

John glanced over at Adaira for what felt like the millionth time, but the woman was completely focused on the doctor. William stood next to his father, rocking back and forth as his eyes darted from the doctor to the midwife and back. Terrence had disappeared shortly after John and Adaira had gotten Mistress Fairborn inside, muttering something about how the woman wasn't worth so much fuss.

There was a low groan, and everyone turned as the midwife began stirring. The young woman opened her eyes, tears dotting her cheeks and fingers clenched in her cushion.

"Oh, yer awake!" Adaira exclaimed, hurrying over and wrapping her arms around her friend.

The midwife pulled out of the embrace after a moment, her face full of sorrow. "A-Adaira, thank you. I—"

But Mistress Fairborn's emotions seemed to overpower her, and soon she was sobbing on Adaira's shoulder while the other woman softly rubbed her back.

Dr. Sherwin looked uncomfortable at the display, and he seemed to be about to say something when William asked,

"Mistress Briony, did he really do it? Did he try to kill the king?"

John grabbed his son in complete embarrassment. "William! You can' just say things like that!"

"But why na?" William asked with a perplexed frown. "That's what everybody wants to know, right? I'm just helping out by asking!"

"Aye, William, yer very helpful," Adaira said. "Except, there's one thing you did na think about."

"What's that?" the boy asked, turning to the innkeeper's daughter.

"Briony is very sad right now, so she may na be able to talk about it just yet. We have to be thoughtful about things like this."

The little boy's eyes lit up. "Oh, I see! I'd be upset, too, if I was in love with a murderer. Do you want me to go beat him up fer you, Mistress Briony?"

John winced and pulled his son behind him. "I'm deeply sorry, mistress," he said to the midwife. "Please excuse us."

The farmer sent William a withering glare that sent the boy careening out of the sitting room toward the hallway.

John tramped after him, pointing to their bedroom door when William turned to look back at him.

Once they were both in their room, John sighed and ran a hand down his face. *Well, that could have gone better.*

"Why did you do that, Da'?"

John pursed his lips and looked over at his son, so oblivious to how obnoxious he could be sometimes. "Because we need to start packing up our things."

William's brow furrowed. "Packing? What fer?"

John shut his eyes, wishing he didn't have to say his next sentence. "Because we're going to be leaving in the morneen."

"Leaving?" the boy squeaked. "What are you talking about? We're staying here with Mistress Adaira, aren' we? I thought we were all going to live here in Everton."

John's chest squeezed painfully. "Mistress *Stubbins* has changed her mind. We're . . . We're na getting married, after all. Therefore, we should be getting back to Hollandstoun."

"*What?!* Yer na getting married? Why na?" William asked in dismay.

"She decided she didn' want to," John said with a trace of bitterness. "I don' know the reason any more than that."

The farmer glanced over at William to make sure he wasn't losing control of himself. The last time that had happened, people had gotten hurt. And worse.

But rather than looking like he was about to explode, the lad's expression was thoughtful.

"William? What is it?"

"Were you mean to her? If that's what 'tis, maybe everything can be fixed by saying sorry."

A sad smile came onto John's face. "I'm afraid it isn' that simple."

The hope which had been sparkling in William's eyes only seconds before disintegrated, leaving behind a boy John wasn't sure he could control.

"But I don' want to go back to Hollandstoun!" William shouted. "Everyone there *hates* me."

"Na everyone hates you," John said gently. "Henry and Sonneta like you, don' they?"

"I want to stay with Mistress Adaira. She said she loved us. She said she was going to be my new stepmum!"

"I know, but like I said, she changed her mind. There's nothing we can do—"

"Nay, I don' believe that!" William asserted, crossing his arms. "You must have given up too easily. I'm going to go talk to her, and everything will be all right."

The lad pushed past his father and scurried out the door, leaving John to decide whether or not he should follow.

Ugh, this day just keeps getting better and better.

John started to turn to go after him, but as he did, something caught his eye: the sack he'd brought with him when he first came to Everton, the one he kept William's sealskin in—it wasn't in the place where he'd left it.

Where—

John spotted the bag on the dresser and went over to it. *Could William have moved this? Nay, he knows better than to touch my things.*

John stuck his hand in the sack, but when he did, all he could feel was the inside of the bag. He looked in and gasped.

William's sealskin was gone.

Who could have taken it? Why would someone take it? No one would know what 'tis, except fer—

John's eyes widened. *Where is Niall?*

***

Adaira flitted about the kitchen working on this and that as she tried not to worry about what her best friend was doing right then. Briony had left only a few minutes ago after making a very frightening comment to the doctor that she could handle herself better than he thought.

The spark in the midwife's eyes—so like the lightning a selkie could summon on command—made Adaira wonder if Briony had finally figured it out. *Could she know she's a selkie? That storm last night was terrible. . . .*

"Mistress Adaira?"

Adaira looked up, only then noticing she'd placed her hand over her heart. William stood in the kitchen doorway, his face puffy and red.

"William? What is it?" She waltzed over to him and touched his shoulder.

The boy's black eyes peered into Adaira's, searching for something. "Da' just told me we have to go back to Hollandstoun because you don' want to marry him anymore."

Adaira winced. She'd been so focused on how she was hurting John that she hadn't even considered what her refusal would mean for William.

"You told me you loved my da'," the boy continued. "Did you have a fight with him? Is that why you don' love him anymore?"

"Oh, dearie, I do love yer father. Very much."

"Then why don' you want to marry him?"

"I—'tis complicated," Adaira said, feeling more pathetic than she had in a long time. *He deserves more o' an explanation than that, and yet I can' give one to him.*

201

William wrinkled his nose and broke free of her grasp. "That's na an answer. . . . I've been practicing, you know."

"Practicing?"

The boy nodded. "At calling you 'Mum.' I was hoping 'twould be fine once you and Da' got married. Am I why you changed yer mind? You don' want me?"

Adaira's breath caught, as much from his heart-wrenching questions as from the fact that he'd called her Mum. She bent down to his level and said, "Nay, that's na it at all! 'Twould mean the world to me to be yer new . . . mum."

She hoped he could see her earnestness.

But William's lip quivered, and a tear slowly ran down his cheek. "Then why do we have to leave? What did we do wrong?"

The boy started sobbing, and Adaira gently wrapped him in her arms. "You didn' do anything, sweetheart. *I'm* the one who did something wrong. That's why I can' marry yer da'."

William drew back just far enough to look her in the eye. "You? I don't understand."

Adaira sighed and plopped her chin on top of the boy's head. "Like I said, 'tis complicated."

"It doesn' have to be."

The woman opened her mouth to tell him she was sorry—

But then a thought filled her mind, so intense it nearly knocked her over. *You've already lost one bairn, Adaira. Can yer heart handle losing another one?*

"M-Mistress Adaira? Are you all right?"

Adaira blinked a few times, realizing she was trembling. She quickly let go of the boy and gave him a shaky smile. "O' . . . course. You don' need to worry about me."

The genuine concern on William's face, the affection so evident in his eyes, made something in Adaira snap. *This has gone on long enough.*

Determination surged through the woman's veins. She loved this boy as if he was hers already. Nothing and no one was going to take him away from her. Not this time.

"In fact, William, you don' need to worry about leaving either."

The lad's mouth lifted. "You mean—"

Adaira nodded. "You were right. Why make things complicated? Yer da' and I love each other, so we should be together."

"Really?"

"Really. And I'm na going to let anything get in the way o' that. I promise."

William beamed with joy. "I'm going to go tell my da'!"

But Adaira grabbed the boy's arm as he started to run off. "Before you do that, there's something else I need to do first."

William tilted his head to the side. "What's that?"

Adaira steeled herself for the task ahead. "There's someone I have to find."

For there was only one person alive who could have written that note to her. Only one person who knew Adaira's secret.

And she wasn't going to let him threaten her anymore.

Priorities

Adaira marched through the market, her mind focused on one thing alone: finding Mr. McLaren. She didn't understand why he would care whether she married John Burgess or not—and he didn't seem like someone who would blackmail others—but he was the only person who knew about the babe she'd lost. When Adaira had gone to Bethany for help, the midwife had taken her straight to Mr. McLaren's house. And there, in the darkness of the mad fisherman's shack, Adaira had given birth.

Perhaps I can reason with him. There has to be a way to get him to stay quiet that doesn' involve letting go o' John. After all, the mad fisherman has been keeping my secret this long.

A few of her neighbors waved and greeted her, but Adaira kept her gaze straight ahead. She wanted to resolve this now, so she could go back to the inn and apologize to John.

But when she reached Mr. McLaren's stall, the mad fisherman was nowhere to be found.

"Mr. Buchanan!" she shouted toward the stall directly beside Mr. McLaren's.

A gray head poked out. "Eh? Oh, Adaira, what can I do fer you?"

"Have you seen Mr. McLaren?"

"I think he left to go fishing a few minutes ago. If you hurry, you might catch him!"

Adaira nodded her thanks and charged toward the dock. Mr. Buchanan had been right—Vincent McLaren was just leaving with his fishing gear.

"Mr. McLaren!" Adaira cried.

The middle-aged fisherman jumped and spun around in his boat. He was just a little ways off from the dock. "What are you doing here, lass?"

"I . . ." Now that she was looking at the man, her previous confidence dissipated. *He seems so harmless. . . .*

Don' let his appearance fool you, whispered her subconscious. *No one besides Bethany knew about the babe. It has to be him.*

"I need to talk to you. 'Tis very important."

The man moved to reattach his boat to the dock. "All right, then. Just be brief. I'm very busy right now."

"Mr. McLaren"—she cleared her throat—"I have to know why you wanted me to end my betrothal."

The mad fisherman cocked his head to the side. "Yer betrothal? Yer betrothed to someone?"

"Well, na since I broke it off," Adaira said, her anxiety starting to give way to puzzlement. "You already knew that."

Mr. McLaren slowly shook his head. "Nay, I'm afraid na. I'm sorry to hear it didn' work out, though. Who were you betrothed to?"

"John Burgess, o' course . . ." Adaira's brow furrowed. "Are you saying—"

"Ah, Mr. Burgess! I might have known," the fisherman interrupted with a chuckle. "A very kind fellow, that one. I've heard tell from many people how he has helped them in one way or another. And his son is quite unique, isn' he?"

"Wait, wait, wait. Then are you na the one who wrote this?" She pulled out the note.

Mr. McLaren's beady eyes scanned the paper. "My, that's some mighty fine handwriting there. Much nicer than anything I could write . . ." He trailed off, his cheerful countenance growing darker and darker until—

The man's eyes shot to hers, all levity gone from his expression. "Someone else knows about yer bairn?"

Adaira nodded, rubbing her hands against her arms as if that would curb the fear building within her. *If Mr. McLaren didn' write this, then who did?*

"Did you tell anyone what happened?" she asked.

"Na a soul. I would never share something so personal. 'Tis na my place," he said solemnly, placing a hand over his heart.

The man's tone, coupled with the way he looked her directly in the eye, suggested authenticity. *And he has never given me a reason na to trust him . . . But if he didn't tell anyone my secret, could Bethany—*

Adaira's stomach seized up at such a ludicrous thought. There was no way it had been Briony's mother.

But that means I have nothing to go on. Anyone could have written this note.

In the past, this would have been when Adaira's fear rose up and choked all the fight in her. She would have curled up in a corner and accepted whatever terrible consequences were to come, thinking she deserved them.

But I'm na going to do that anymore, she told herself as she felt fear rear its ugly head in her mind. She was done letting it control her.

"I need to find the author o' this note. Can you help me?" Adaira said, sounding much more confident than she felt.

The mad fisherman shook his head. "I'm sorry, lass, but I'm far too busy. You better go on now, so I can work on what I need to do. I'm going . . . fishing."

The man's voice was unsteady, making Adaira wonder if he was hiding something.

"You don' normally go fishing now. The best times are in the morneen and evening," she pointed out. His lie might have worked on someone else, but Adaira was a fisherman's daughter.

Mr. McLaren smirked, seeming to realize that very fact. "True, true. But sometimes I go just to clear my head. Drown out the noise in here," he said, tapping his temple.

Then he started untying his boat once more. "Have to be ready," he said under his breath. "As ready as I can be when facing such impossible odds."

Adaira's brow wrinkled at the funny statement. *This is the man Bethany trusted when I was in need. I wonder how far that trust went.*

"Mr. McLaren, what do you need to be ready fer?"

The man jumped as if he'd forgotten she was there. "Oh, nothing," he said, giving her a smile. "Nothing at all. Just talking to myself."

Adaira's nerves were jumping around her stomach like frogs, but before they could stop her, she blurted, "Bethany Fairborn trusted you a great deal. Did she also trust you with the truth about her family?"

Mr. McLaren's sharp intake of breath told her the answer. He immediately jumped out of the boat and grabbed her arm. "What do you know about that?!"

Adaira peeled her arm out of his grip and said evenly, "I know everything."

The fisherman's eyes narrowed. "Everything, meaning—"

She sighed. The time for skirting around the truth was over. She leaned toward him and whispered, "I know she was a selkie."

Mr. McLaren's defensive posture faded, and his eyes fell from hers. "How long have you known?"

"Since that day on the beach, sir. The day you killed Briony's . . ."

His gaze snapped back to hers, and Adaira thought he was angry until she saw the regret on his face. "Impossible," he whispered. "No one knew what happened aside from Bethany and me. Na even Briony until—"

The man slammed his mouth shut, but he'd already said more than he should have.

"Briony knows?!" Adaira shrieked, her heart racing in her chest. "She wasn't supposed to find out! Bethany made me promise she'd never find out."

Mr. McLaren's eyebrows rose. "She made me promise that, too."

"The day she . . ." Adaira's voice broke, but she pushed the final word out, "died . . ."

Adaira remembered everything about that day: the sounds, the smells, the pain. The pain she remembered all too well.

It was a grief she knew no one would understand, for no one had known how deeply she'd admired and loved Bethany. The older woman had not only been a second mother to her but also a confidante. And when she'd died, Adaira had lost the one person she could talk to about both Briony's secret and her own.

***

Adaira sat in the chair by Bethany's bed while the older woman slept. The midwife had influenza, and Dr. Sherwin had already said nothing more could be done. She would either get better on her own, or . . . she wouldn't. Briony had gone to buy some food from the market, and Adaira had offered to stay with her mother in the meantime.

"'Tis good to see you, Adaira," Bethany whispered, making the younger woman start in surprise.

"Oh, yer awake! How are you feeling?" Adaira asked, trying to look cheerier than she felt.

"I prayed you'd come, so I could see you one last time."

A sour taste filled Adaira's mouth, but she firmly said, "You mean, before you get better."

The midwife shook her head. "I'm na going to make it."

"Don' say that. Yer the strongest woman I know," Adaira argued, despite the tears that had escaped her eyes.

Bethany gave her a weak smile, one that told her she could hear the lack of conviction in Adaira's voice.

More tears spilled down the younger woman's cheeks. "You *can'* leave. I've already lost one mum. I can' lose you, too."

"Do you remember the first time you came here? How different things were between us then. You were just a wee bairn with a giant secret. One I was desperate to keep you from sharing."

Adaira let out a sad laugh. "I remember. I was so frightened you were going to call seals up from the sea that I had nightmares fer weeks."

Bethany's pale face grew paler still. "Only because you didn' know I had no power to do so. 'Twas lost long before you were born."

"What?" Adaira's tears instantly dried up. "You don' have any powers? Why would you . . ."

208

"When you came to me, I was sure you'd tell others what you knew. . . . So, I lied, knowing you'd be too scared to tell anyone if you thought the town was in danger. After getting to know you better, though, and seeing the joy yer friendship brought my daughter, I realized I'd made a mistake. But by that point, my shame kept me from telling you the truth. I don' expect yer forgiveness, but just know that I'm sorry."

Bethany broke down into a coughing fit, so pitiful that Adaira couldn't find it in her heart to be angry over the woman's deception.

Adaira let out a heavy breath. "I think I know why you did it. You didn' want Briony to get hurt. I don' want that either."

Bethany looked up at her in surprise. "You . . . you don' even seem upset."

"I'm far from perfect either. *You know that,*" Adaira explained with a solemn frown. "I just wish my mistakes had been fer something as noble as protecting my bairn."

The midwife's expression shifted from bafflement to compassion. "Yer hardly more than a bairn yerself. You didn' mean to—"

"You know that's na true! I knew what I was doing, and if it hadn' been fer you, I wouldn' still be here. Some days I wish that were the case."

Bethany didn't say anything more for a long time, and Adaira feared she'd spoken too sharply. But this feeling had been brewing in Adaira's chest ever since her miscarriage, ever since the night Bethany had saved her. And it felt incredibly freeing to finally say it aloud.

But then the midwife fixed her gaze on Adaira, her eyes so intense that the younger woman had to look away. "I gave you a second chance at life, something many people never get. You may na appreciate it, but 'tis yers nonetheless. And with that gift comes the responsibility o' using it well."

Adaira's shoulders fell. The woman's words had cut her to her core. *What's wrong with me? She's most likely going to die, and I choose now to tell her I wish she hadn' saved me?*

She opened her mouth, but Bethany spoke again. "I know. I know what yer going to say, but you don' need to apologize. Instead, I want you to make me one more promise."

When Adaira didn't object, the midwife continued, "After I'm gone, I need you to watch over Briony fer me. She has to stay away from the water. I may na have abilities anymore, but she does. And if she goes into the ocean or loses control o' herself, I fear what the consequences may be."

"Don' worry. I won' let anything happen to yer daughter. You can count on that."

"Thank you, Adaira. And just so know, you've been like a daughter to me fer a long time, too."

The younger woman grinned, genuinely this time, but before she could reply, she heard Briony opening the door. Adaira gave the dying woman a meaningful glance and rose to her feet.

"She's awake," Adaira said, turning to her friend. "I'll leave you two to talk on yer own."

***

But neither my secret nor Bethany's is nearly as confidential as I thought, Adaira admitted begrudgingly. *Someone knows about my bairn and used him to make me hurt the man I love.*

She refocused on Mr. McLaren. *And this man in front o' me—this overlooked, under-appreciated fisherman I've been avoiding because he reminds me o' my shame—he also knows the truth about the Fairborns.*

A truth Briony now knows, too.

Adaira ran her fingers through her curly brown ringlets as she tried to swallow this new information. *Briony knows she's a selkie. I don' have to hide this from her anymore?*

"When did Briony find out?" she demanded. "Did *you* tell her?"

Mr. McLaren crossed his arms. "Why do you keep assuming I'm the one who told? I'm very good at keeping secrets, you know."

"I'm sorry. I don' mean to accuse you."

The fisherman huffed and turned his head away. "Pardon me if I disagree."

"Mr. McLaren, please."

He slowly brought his eyes back to hers. "Mistress Fairborn came to my stall earlier today. I thought she wanted to talk to me because o' the storm last night."

"She must have been really upset. I've never seen her lose control like that before."

"See, that's what I thought too—that she'd caused the storm with that hot temper o' hers."

Adaira nodded. "I'm constantly having to calm her down. She really doesn'—"

Mr. McLaren held up his finger. "But, that's where we're both wrong. She wasn' the one who summoned the storm."

"What? But if she didn' do it, then who . . ." The young woman gasped. "Niall Moreland."

A shiver ran through her. She'd been so focused on protecting her own secret that Mr. Moreland had slipped her mind.

He was in the Burgesses' room, probably hunting fer William's sealskin—he may try to steal William away!

And John's na going to just let that happen, Adaira thought as she remembered John's conversation with Niall last night. *John already said he'd fight him if that's what it came down to. That's a fight John can' win. Niall would hurt him . . . or worse. And William could be lost forever.*

Adaira's fears of exposure didn't seem nearly as important anymore. All that mattered was protecting the people she loved.

The fisherman pressed his lips together. "It seems I'm the last one to find out we have another selkie in our midst."

Adaira held her tongue despite a strong urge to tell him there were actually three selkies in Everton. But William's secret wasn't hers to share.

Mr. McLaren continued, "He's also the one who told Mistress Fairborn about her heritage."

"What else did Briony say?" Adaira asked, her stomach tightening with dread.

"She said he's insisting she leave Everton with him."

"She can' do that!" Adaira erupted in an unusually passionate display. "She can' leave us like that! Her whole life is here."

Mr. McLaren raised an eyebrow, making the young woman blush in embarrassment.

"Indeed. But if she doesn', he may very well cut off her ties to the human world to make it easier for her to go."

"By 'cut off,' you don' mean . . ."

"What happened last night was only a taste o' Mr. Moreland's powers. If he wanted to, he could wipe out this entire town."

Adaira swallowed thickly. "But what about Briony? She could stand against him, couldn' she?"

Mr. McLaren sadly shook his head. "I fear she's na strong enough. She's na a pureblood selkie, fer one, and she doesn' know how to control her powers. Besides, Niall might bring other selkies with him—then we'd be outnumbered *and* outmatched."

"Other . . . selkies?" Adaira whispered.

What if—nay, I can' do that, she told herself, squelching the idea before it had even finished forming.

"Aye, 'tis highly likely others are involved. I couldn' find any fish this morneen, and that's rare fer me. Then, when I spoke to some o' the other fisherman, they said they didn' catch any either. One even said a seal tried to tip his boat over."

"If yer right, though, we could be slaughtered. What can we do? Is there any hope at all?"

"Well, I know what I'm going to do," the fisherman said, raising his knife in the air. "If they bring the fight to us, I'm going to do all I can to stop them. I'm going to go out right now and see if I spot any seals in the area. They can' use their powers while in seal form, so that's the time to strike."

As sunlight glinted off the knife in the man's hand, Adaira couldn't help but remember when he'd stabbed the seal that turned out to be Briony's father.

"You better get back to the inn," Mr. McLaren said. "There's na much you can do right now, but there's safety in numbers."

Adaira nodded, wishing they had a better plan. She turned to leave, but then that same thought from before returned to her mind.

And this time, she didn't dismiss it.

"Mr. McLaren," she said, interrupting the man's departure for what seemed like the hundredth time, "what if Briony wasn' the only selkie protecting Everton?"

"What do you mean?" he said with a frown.

"I mean, what if there was . . . someone else with selkie blood who could add his power to Briony's? Would that be enough to stop Mr. Moreland?"

"Perhaps, but who are you talking about?"

"I better go. Thank you, Mr. McLaren!" Adaira waved and hurried up the dock before the fisherman could ask more questions.

She had somewhere she needed to be.

The Price of Knowledge

John slowly made his way back to the inn, completely crestfallen. He'd searched through the town and along the beach, talking to everyone he saw, but there was no sign of Niall Moreland anywhere. Daniel Calhoun had told him the man never showed up for work today either.

What am I going to do? I can' leave without William's sealskin.

He pulled open the inn door and stepped inside, almost walking into someone before he realized a woman was standing right in front of him.

"John, I need to talk to you," Adaira insisted.

The farmer tried to brush past her with a terse "Na right now," but the woman grabbed his arm.

The warmth of her hand reminded him of how she'd pulled away when he'd tried to comfort her earlier. *Should I do the same thing?*

John wanted to, but his heart protested. He needed her too much right then to let his pride keep him from her touch. He longed to feel her arms around him as he told her his worries, his fears. Maybe they wouldn't seem as big if he had someone to share them with.

"Please," she said, her dark eyes peering up at him with a look he was powerless to resist. A look that told him she needed him just as much as he needed her.

"What is it?"

Adaira took a deep breath and then let out a weak laugh. "Where do I begin? There's so much you need to know. I . . . I know about William."

Alarm bells rang in the man's mind. "What about William?"

"I know he's—"

"Adaira!" shouted a voice, cutting off the rest of what she'd been about to say.

John and Adaira turned as Terrence hobbled into the foyer with a nasty expression. "I've been wondering when you were finally going to come back. This inn doesn' run itself, you know!"

The farmer rolled his eyes, ready to cut the fool down to size.

"I thought you said you didn' need anyone to help you," said Adaira, speaking up before John could.

The farmer looked over at the woman in shock, noting the stance she now stood in: hands on her hips, chin jutting outward, eyes staring her father down. This was not the same Adaira Stubbins he'd met weeks before.

And Terrence knew that, too. The fellow's knees started shaking so badly John almost felt sorry for him. If he hadn't been such a poor excuse for a father, that is.

"I-I need to speak with you. Privately," the man stuttered.

Adaira sighed and dropped her hands to her sides. "All right." She turned to the farmer and said with an almost-smile, "John, let's finish our talk later."

John's insides warmed even as Terrence's eyes nearly popped out of his head.

"I'm sure you don' have time fer that," Adaira's father muttered. "Too many things to—"

"Father, why don' we go to the sitting room?" Adaira said, cutting him off. She nodded at the farmer and ushered her father out of the room.

John stood motionless as he watched them depart, his mind replaying Adaira's words over and over: *"I know about William. . . . I know he's—"*

What was she about to say? William's what?

***

Adaira sat down in the seat next to her father, crossing and uncrossing her legs a few times. Her father never asked to talk to her like this. Something must be very wrong. "So, what was it you wanted to speak with me about?"

"Yer na really going to marry that fellow, are you?" he asked offhandedly, as if it was of little consequence.

But Adaira saw how he was gripping his cane so tightly his knuckles had turned white. She saw the anxiety shining in his eyes. That could mean only one thing: he cared about her answer.

"John told me you didn' approve," Adaira said, deliberately sidestepping his question.

"The man's no good fer you," Terrence shouted, slamming his hand against the arm of his chair.

Adaira didn't react; she simply studied the man before her as if she was seeing him for the first time. For all his bravado and sharp words, Terrence Stubbins seemed . . . smaller, somehow. As if he'd been wearing a mask all this time.

Smaller and full o' fear, she realized. *But what could he be afraid o'?*

"He's far too secretive," he continued. "Refuses to talk about his past . . ."

Adaira stopped paying attention to the man's words, instead thinking about what she was going to say to John when she met up with him.

"That can only mean he's trying to hide something bad, you know. He's trouble, that one. Maybe even worse trouble than Henry Milligan."

Adaira blinked a few times. "*What* did you just say? Did you—you knew about Henry?"

Terrence huffed. "O' course I knew about Henry. You only wrote to him a hundred times after he left."

Adaira took in a shaky breath. *He . . . he knows what happened?*

Her eyes widened as she remembered all the unsent letters she'd written after Henry left. They'd lain in crumpled balls in

216

her wastebasket for weeks before she could finally bring herself to burn them.

It would have been all too easy for Terrence to find them.

He knows I lost my babe. But that means—

Anger blazed through Adaira's blood as her mind reached a chilling conclusion. *He's the one who wrote that note.*

She shot up from her chair. "Father, how could you?! Were you that desperate to keep John and me apart that you'd resort to threatening me? Threatening to share my secret?"

Terrence leaned away from her, his gaze full of confusion. "What are you talking about?"

"Don' try to pretend you didn' write this," Adaira growled, pulling the note from her pocket and shoving it in his hands.

"This . . ." Terrence's face lost its color as he read over the note. "This wasn' me."

Adaira frowned, unable to comprehend what he'd just said.

"I didn' write this," the man insisted, his voice louder than before. "'Tis true I don' want you and Mr. Burgess together, but I would never stoop this low. What kind o' father do you take me fer?"

"Na much o' one," Adaira spat, not wanting to believe him.

It fits too perfectly.

Terrence shook his head as if he, too, was having trouble accepting what he was hearing. "You think I hate you that much?"

"Don' you? You, yourself, said you don' want John and me together."

"Because I don' want to lose you like I lost yer mother!" Terrence bellowed.

The room went dead silent for several seconds as Adaira took in the man's words.

Finally, she said, "'Tis just getting married, Father. You know how much Everton means to me, *how much this place means to me*"—she waved her hand around the room—"I wouldn' abandon it or you. Aye, there would be some changes, but that doesn' mean you'd lose me."

"O' course it does," he said gruffly, pursing his lips as if he wasn't going to explain further.

But, after a moment, he whispered, "Yer mother died giving birth to yer brother, and you've already had one miscarriage. If you were to be in the family way again . . ."

It was a possibility Adaira had never considered before, the idea that she might die as her mother had. *Could he be right? Would I die carrying John's child? My body has already failed me once; it could fail me again. And even if I didn' die, I might lose a second babe.*

I'm supposed to talk to John. I'm supposed to make things right with him. But what if that's the wrong thing to do? Should I burden him with a wife who can' carry a babe?

Adaira looked over at Terrence. "Father, I . . . I had no idea," she squeaked, emotions flooding out of her so powerfully she had to sit back down.

Amidst her tears, Adaira reached for her father's hand, desperate to feel someone's touch, desperate to make him understand she was sorry.

"Don'," the man snapped, his eyes as hard as flint. "I've clearly done a terrible job raising you. Otherwise, what daughter would believe her father capable o' such wicked things?"

"But, Father, I—"

Terrence rose to his feet and turned his back to her. "You don' need to say anything more. I'm going to the tavern."

With that, he teetered out of the room, leaving behind a great, swelling emptiness that seemed to swallow Adaira up in its wake.

After spending far too long in the silence, she remembered John was waiting for her. He was waiting for answers and, quite possibly, the chance to mend things between them.

But in light of her conversation with her father, Adaira knew that couldn't happen. It wasn't a matter of protecting her secret anymore: now she was choosing to forgo her dreams in order to spare John further heartache.

Even so, I still have to talk to him. He needs to know what Niall Moreland is planning. And William needs to know the truth.

Tempest Rising

Dinner at the inn that evening was especially quiet. Many of the people who were usually there were absent, and those present weren't in the mood for much chatter. Terrence still hadn't returned from the tavern, and while this meant no one had to listen to him grumble, Adaira worried for him. She also worried for Lucia, who was so forlorn over her brother's arrest that nothing Adaira said could bring a smile to her face.

Adaira wished the Burgesses would make some effort to lighten the room's atmosphere, but John was silent as he picked at his food, and William just kept giving her this wistful expression that Adaira couldn't bear to look at for long.

When Lucia finally pushed back from the table and rose to her feet to say she was turning in for the night, it was almost a relief. Adaira was normally very adept at displaying false cheer, but she didn't have much strength for it tonight. Not with everything going on.

John stood to excuse himself and William shortly after that, thanking Adaira for the good meal he'd barely eaten and ushering his son toward the hallway. William gave Adaira one last pleading look, but Adaira turned her head away.

I'm so sorry I can' follow through on my promise, William. But this is what's best fer you and yer da', she thought as she listened to their retreating footsteps.

Once they were gone, she quickly cleaned up the table before meandering outside. She wandered aimlessly down the road for several minutes, her heart in turmoil over the hurt she was causing William. *He wouldn' understand even if I tried to explain. He's just going to think I don' want him, and that's na the case at all.*

I wonder when I'll have the chance to talk to John. Maybe I should have asked him to stay behind after dinner. And what about Father? Should I get him from the tavern or should I let him have some time to himself? We have a long way to go if we're going to make things right between us. Or perhaps I should go find Briony, so I can talk to her. She probably feels so alone right now.

The innkeeper's daughter shut her eyes and took a deep breath of fresh air to calm herself. If she got too overwhelmed, she wasn't going to be of help to anyone.

"Adaira?" came a hesitant voice.

The woman's eyes flew open in alarm, adrenaline shooting through her as she realized someone was standing directly beside her.

After a split second, though, familiarity replaced her fear. "John! Yer here."

The farmer chuckled, his blue eyes sparkling. "I'm so sorry, Adaira. I didn' mean to frighten you."

Adaira felt a blush run up her cheeks, and she checked to see if anyone was watching them. It didn't take much for her neighbors' tongue to wag, and if someone saw the two of them together, Adaira feared the conclusions they'd come to.

It looks safe fer now, but if Father comes back anytime soon—

"I came to finish our discussion from earlier. I hope that's all right," John explained.

Adaira turned to the farmer, taking a step back and tilting her eyes toward the ground. "Aye, that would be good. Is . . . Is it true that yer leaving?"

"Well, there's na much reason to stay," John said, his voice so cold Adaira almost flinched.

Earlier, he seemed like he was hoping fer . . . She shook her head. *Maybe I was imagining it. But I've still got William's sealskin. He must have noticed it's missing by now, right? And even if he's na going to stay fer my sake, I wouldn' have thought he'd leave that behind.*

Adaira's eyes narrowed. "That's na quite true, though, is it? Isn' there something you'd like to get back first?"

The man's mouth dropped open. "What are you—"

BOOM!

The two of them looked toward a spot about five feet away—thin black scorch marks stretched across the ground, evidence of the lightning that had struck only seconds before.

Adaira trembled as her gaze rose higher, higher, higher, up to a sky filling with storm clouds. Soon, rain began descending upon them.

"Come on!" John shouted, grabbing Adaira's hand.

Stumbling, hurtling, charging in the direction of the inn, only then did Adaira realize how far she'd wandered off. They were almost to the gate when Adaira spotted a figure standing by the stones that marked—

"Father!" she screamed in recognition.

Terrence looked over, his face full of surprise. "Adaira, what are yoooou . . . d-doing?"

Adaira gritted her teeth. *O' all times to be drunk.*

Another bolt struck—just a few feet from Terrence this time—and Adaira called, "Father, get inside already!"

The old man lumbered forward, trying to get through the gate, but he tripped over himself and fell to the ground.

Adaira raced to his right side and yanked him up by the arm. "We have to go!"

John appeared on Terrence's other side to help, but before he could grab hold of the older man, Terrence jerked backward. Adaira, caught off guard by the sudden movement, lost her grip and almost toppled over herself.

"Father, what are you doing? 'Tis na safe out here." She reached out for him again, but Terrence shoved her away.

"Go on already!"

"I'm na leaving y—"

CRACK!

Adaira stared in horror as her father collapsed in front of her, struck full force by a lightning bolt.

"Da'!" Adaira fell upon him, pressing her ear against his chest. "Da'?"

She shifted position, ignoring the vacant stare in the man's eyes. *He's going to be fine. I just have to find his heartbeat and—*

A hand touched Adaira's shoulder. "Adaira . . ."

"Shh! I'm trying to listen."

"Adaira, he's gone. We have to get back to safety."

"Nay, I'm na leaving him!" she insisted, not looking up at John. "That's what he was so frightened o'. He thought I was going to leave him!"

She buried her face in her father's clothes, her nose filling with the smell of alcohol. But she didn't care. She wasn't leaving him.

John didn't say any more, and she thought she heard footsteps over the rain and thunder, but she was too hysterical to be sure.

"Da' . . ." she whimpered, her voice catching as she started to sob.

Rain mixed with her tears, drenching her skin and hair as she tried to make sense of something that was utter nonsense.

He's going to be fine. He's going to be fine. I didn' hear his heartbeat, but that's just because 'twas too soft. He's going to be fine.

Her father's body was so cold beneath her, making her shiver uncontrollably. But she wasn't going to leave him.

Unless someone made her.

Fingers dug into Adaira's clothes, slowly but surely prying her off of her father. "Stop! I can' leave him!"

But then there was warmth—a heartbeat!

Adaira's eyes shot open, her face lighting up in a smile—

Until she realized it was John's chest she was against; it was John's heart she was hearing.

A moan tore out of Adaira's throat. It was a broken sound, a weak sound, but a sound that quickly rose in strength, and before Adaira knew it, she was shrieking so loudly it made her ears throb.

For Terrence Stubbins was gone, and nothing was going to bring him back.

Hopes and wishes flashed through her mind, one after the next, faster and faster until everything went dark.

***

"Mistress Adaira?"

Adaira groaned as she woke, her head pounding like she'd been kicked by a horse. She blinked a few times as she took in her surroundings. No longer was she outside in such darkness she could barely see; instead, she lay in her bed, a candle on the table beside her. Someone stood next to her, eyes full of concern.

But it wasn't the right person. *Where's John?*

"William, where's yer da'?" Adaira asked, trying to smile despite the tears trickling down her cheeks.

For as much as she loved William, she needed John right then. She needed him if she was going to face a reality that her father was no longer part of.

"He went to help put out the fire at the tailor shop."

Adaira sat up instantly. "There's a fire?!"

William nodded. "Aye, Da' told me to stay with you and make sure you were safe. That I had to guard you like you were Mum." The boy leaned forward and whispered in her ear, "He's still in love with you, mistress."

Adaira wiped the tears from her face, glad to have the boy distracting her for a moment. "And what about Lucia?"

"She left with Captain Costa. I think they were going down to their ship."

They went out in this weather? She glanced out the window, hoping the storm had abated, but instead saw rain coming down in sheets.

"We have to bring them back," she announced, throwing off her blankets and springing out of the bed.

"They're long gone," William cried, racing after her as she went downstairs and threw open the front door.

Beyond the safety of the inn, the storm was even worse than before. A chilling wind blew rain into Adaira's face, nearly blinding her as she peered into the darkness.

She couldn't recall ever seeing a storm this bad, even the one on Johnsmas paled in comparison, and that storm had been—

The woman gasped. *Is Niall Moreland causing this storm too? Is what Mr. McLaren warned me about happening?*

As soon as she thought it, Adaira felt certain it was true. Everton was under attack.

Then that means we're all in danger.

At that moment, a figure caught Adaira's eye, someone running toward the inn—

"Briony! Come inside quickly! 'Tis too dangerous out there!" Adaira called, fresh tears forming in her eyes at the sight of her friend.

She grabbed the midwife and tugged her inside, drawing her into a wet, sobbing embrace.

"Adaira, where's Mr. Burgess?" Briony asked, but Adaira was too emotional to respond. She wasn't sure exactly what she was feeling—relief that her friend was all right, agony over her father's death, or maybe just fear for the fate of the town. The only thing she was sure of was that her legs were going to give out if she let Briony go.

"He's down at the tailor shop, trying to put out the fire," William commented.

"Then why . . . Adaira, what happened?" Briony asked, pulling away just enough to lock gazes with the innkeeper's daughter.

"M-My . . . father," Adaira sputtered. "He's gone. He's just gone."

Briony gaped. "What? How?"

Adaira's throat tightened, and the best response she could give was a head shake. Everything was still too raw, too recent, for her to voice it yet. Luckily for her, William was only too happy to share.

"I saw what happened, Mistress Briony!" the boy interjected. "'Twas the scariest thing I've ever seen! Mr. Stubbins was coming up to the inn, and this giant bolt o' lightning fell right on him! Da' and I got him to his bed, but he was already dead by the time we put him down. I did na realize how powerful someo—*something* could be!"

That's na how it went, Adaira thought, bawling more as the memory galloped across her mind. *You left out the part about how he wouldn' let me help him inside. If he hadn' pushed me away, I'd be the one dead right now instead o' him. He saved my life.*

Briony gently adjusted Adaira's position, pushing the younger woman upright before stepping back. The midwife's golden eyes shone with regret and some other emotion Adaira couldn't identify. "I'm so glad yer both all right. I'm really sorry about yer father, Adaira, and I know you'll hate me fer this, but I can' stay."

The sounds of the storm faded as Adaira's brain tried to make sense of what she'd just heard. "What?"

But Briony didn't repeat her words and instead turned to William. "Look after her until yer father gets back, aye?"

The boy lifted his chin as if he was trying to make himself look taller. "That's what I was doing! Da' told me na to let her out o' my sight. Right before he kissed her . . . blech!"

Adaira's eyes widened. *He kissed me?* Her initial response was anger at the man's brazen behavior. They weren't betrothed anymore, so he had no right to do that without her permission.

Rather like the first time you kissed him, her subconscious pointed out.

That was different, she argued. *Fer one, he was awake when I did that. And two . . .*

She sighed internally. *He left without giving me the chance to kiss him back. What if he doesn' make it? I can' lose him, too.*

" . . . Just keep at it, then," Briony said to William, just as Adaira's mind refocused on the current conversation.

The lad grasped Adaira's hand and smiled at her, making Adaira's heart swell with protectiveness and love. She squeezed his hand, promising herself she wasn't going to let anything happen to him. Or to anyone else she cared about.

Briony turned to leave, but Adaira grabbed her hand.

How can I make her stay? Adaira hadn't spoken to John about William yet, and she didn't want to give anything away with the boy right here, but she needed to do what she could to protect her friend. "Briony Fairborn, you better na be thinking o' going back out there in this. There's something *unnatural* about this storm. If you leave now, I may never see you again!"

Please, Briony. If Niall is the one behind this, I don' want you facing him alone.

But as the selkie-woman stared back at her, Adaira could see there would be no dissuading her. Come what may, Briony was determined to do this.

"Yer absolutely right," Briony eventually replied, "This storm is as far from natural as it could get, but if I don' go, more people are going to get hurt."

Adaira opened her mouth, eager to point out that most of the townsfolk couldn't care less about her and that she should think about herself for once, but Briony cut her off.

"I'll explain more later, but I have to go now."

I swore I would look after you. How can I—

But there was a new strength in Briony's face, one Adaira suspected came from finally knowing the truth about herself. And, as hard it was, seeing that strength gave Adaira the courage to let her go.

Maybe Mr. McLaren was wrong. Maybe Briony is powerful enough to beat Niall by herself.

Briony gave Adaira a soft grin before scurrying back out into the storm. *Please be careful, dearie,* the younger woman thought, sending up a silent prayer.

As soon as the other woman was gone, though, Adaira started having second thoughts. *Even if Briony is capable o' defeating Niall singlehandedly, I still shouldn' have let her go alone. I should have gone with her—*

What can I do against a selkie though? I'm na strong or fast, and I definitely don' have powers. Would I be any help at all?

Her head snapped over to the boy. *Maybe I should just tell William the truth myself. Then the two o' us can go help Briony. If nothing else, I can be a good distraction.*

She opened her mouth to do just that, but then something flashed back through Adaira's mind, something she hadn't noticed before. "William?"

"Hmm?" The lad seemed engrossed by the storm raging outside and not at all interested in what she had to say.

"When you were talking about the storm and what happened to my father, you said didn' realize how powerful someone could be. What did you mean by that?"

William turned to her, his eyes full of confusion and fear. "Nay, I said *something*. I didn' know how powerful *something* could be."

Adaira shook her head and bent down so the two of them were at eye level. The boy was visibly shaking and, if Adaira wasn't mistaken, holding back tears. "What is it, William? Is there something you need to tell me?"

The lad's face went white, and he clamped his eyes shut. "Nay, there's nothing," he cried.

But Adaira could feel William's hand growing warm against hers.

"This storm . . ." he whispered. "There's something wrong with it. I felt it before at the Johnsmas celebration. I didn' want to believe it then, but I'm feeling it again now."

"What are you feeling?"

William opened his black eyes and looked straight at Adaira. "Someone is controlling this storm."

The woman's breath hitched, as much from the boy's words as from the painful heat now coming off his palm. She let go, trying not to make it obvious that he'd burned her.

But William's eyes darted to her hand. "Did I . . ."

He held out his hands, staring at them in shock as tears rolled down his cheeks. "Just like before with Da'."

"What?"

William grabbed his head and started screaming.

Adaira was nervous to touch the boy again, but she put her hands on his shoulders over his clothes. "William, calm down! Tell me what's the matter."

The lad stopped screaming and shook his head, hands still against his temples. "I didn' slip in the mud the night Mr. Mendes's ship arrived."

Adaira frowned. "You didn'? But yer da' said—"

"He lied."

"Are you sure? Why would he do that?"

William sniffled, his face twitching as though it couldn't handle the tidal wave of emotions going through the boy's body. "He did it because . . . *I* started the storm that night. I don' know how I did it, but 'twas me. And Da'—somehow he knew 'twas me. He . . ."

William's face stopped twitching as he settled on a single emotion. And it wasn't one Adaira liked seeing.

Several lightning bolts struck just outside, and this time, she didn't think they were Niall's doing.

"Da' knocked me out that night," William continued, his voice cold and lifeless, "to keep me from finding out about my powers."

Adaira was so startled her hands fell from the boy's shoulders. *What? John . . . knocked him out?*

William turned to the open doorway. "I need to find who's causing this storm. Maybe that person can tell me the truth about who I am."

He raised his foot to take a step, but Adaira blurted, "You don' need to go out there to find the truth. I think I already know."

Betrayal

John charged up the hill, pushing his legs faster and faster. By the time he'd arrived at the tailor shop, several villagers had already been there. The building's thatched roof had been ablaze, but between John and about five other men, they'd been able to save most of it.

Now the farmer was on his way back to the inn, desperate to make sure Adaira was all right. She'd been deathly pale when he'd left her.

Rain pelted his skin, and the wind roared like an angry beast as John passed the churchyard. Everything was so dark he couldn't see the inn yet, but he knew he was getting close.

Just a wee bit farther. Then I'll see that all is well, he told himself, trying to temper the rapid beating of his heart. *William is taking care o' her. She's fine.*

But as the inn came into view, John realized Adaira wasn't the one he needed to be worried about, after all.

***

William spun around, his eyes wide. "What? You know why I have these powers? How I was able to burn you and start a storm?"

Adaira took a deep breath and nodded. *This isn' how I imagined you finding out, but I suppose it can' be helped now.*

"William, yer na like most people. Yer special."

The boy raised a suspicious eyebrow. "How so?"

Adaira cringed, for this was coming out all wrong. "Yer mum—she . . . she wasn' human."

"And how do you know that?" bellowed a voice that definitely wasn't William's.

Adaira started as John appeared in the doorway. She and William must have been so absorbed in their conversation that they hadn't even noticed him. Water dripped off the man's hair and clothes, but what stuck out the most was the blazing anger in his eyes.

He took two great steps and was in Adaira's face. "How do you know that?" he repeated, slowly drawing out each word.

Adaira gulped, her words stuck in her throat.

"Is it true, Da'? Is that why I have powers?"

The farmer whirled around to his son, a panicked look on his face. "Powers? What are you talking about?"

William scowled and crossed his arms. "Don' pretend like you don' know! I remember *everything* about the night Mr. Mendes came here. I know I started that storm. And I know you knocked me out to keep me from the truth."

John sputtered a bit, as though he was trying to think of an excuse but coming up short. "That's—that's na exactly right. I didn'—"

CRACK!

The bolt effectively cut off whatever the farmer had been about to say, for it had struck so close that it had almost hit the inn.

"William!" John called. "You need to get control o' yerself."

The lad's eyes narrowed. "I meant to do that. I'm tired o' you lying to me!"

"I'm na lying this time. Please, let me explain."

But the boy shook his head. "Nay, I want to hear it from Mistress Adaira." He turned to the woman, his gaze pleading.

Adaira hesitated, her eyes flickering from William to John. "William, I really think you should let yer father tell you. He knows better than I—"

William growled, and another lightning bolt hit the ground outside. "I just said I didn' want to. No one listens to me!" The boy turned his back on them but not before Adaira caught sight of the betrayal on his face.

"Dearie, please . . . we . . ." She trailed off and looked to John for help.

"I'm just going to have to find someone who will," William muttered under his breath.

His words were so low that it took the adults a few seconds to realize what he'd said, and that brief delay was all the time William needed to make a run for it. He dashed out the doorway, giving Adaira a distinct sense of déjà vu. It was altogether too much like the night Mr. Mendes's ship had arrived, wrecked and off-course, thanks to a storm.

A storm that Adaira now knew William had created.

And that was before he even knew he had powers, she realized. *What kind o' destruction might he cause now?*

"William, stop!" John chased after him in an instant, easily catching up before they'd even passed through the gate.

The lad spun around with a malicious glare. "Don' follow me, Da'!"

He lifted his hand to the sky, and a great deluge of rain descended upon his father. Except it wasn't just rain; it was—

John cried out, raising his arms over his head to protect himself from hailstones as big as Adaira's palm.

"John, get back inside!" Adaira shouted, hoping he could hear her over the wind.

Through the heavy downpour, she glimpsed William lowering his arm and scurrying off into the night. *Where's he going?*

But then she remembered the last thing he'd said, and she had an awful feeling she knew the answer.

Meanwhile, John fled toward the inn, hands still raised. Adaira could see him flinching under the hailstones' assault, and when he finally stepped over the threshold, he collapsed at the woman's feet.

"John?"

The man lay on his side, still conscious but breathing heavily. Red welts were forming on his face and hands, and Adaira suspected several more lay hidden beneath his clothes.

How could William do this to his own father? And hail? Where did that come from? I've never heard o' a selkie doing that before.

The farmer groaned and tried to get up, but Adaira held him down. "Don' move. Y-Yer hurt," the woman said shakily. Adaira's world seemed to be crumbling around her, and she had no idea how to fix it.

What do I do? I've never tended to someone hit by hail. What if he's injured internally? I need to find Dr. Sherwin. He'll know what to do.

"Let's get you to yer bed, and I'll fetch the doctor." Adaira moved her hands off of the man's arms and helped him into a sitting position, wincing when she heard his pained gasp.

"Is it yer chest? I hope the hail didn't hurt one o' yer ribs. When Gareth Peterson got attacked by one o' Matthew's rams, he got two broken ribs," she babbled.

The farmer didn't seem to hear her and coughed, "William . . . I have to get to him. I have to—"

"John, he's gone."

The man craned his neck and peered up at her. "What? Where did he go?"

Adaira didn't answer fast enough, for John grabbed her hands. "Adaira, where is he?"

The woman grimaced, hating what she had to tell him. "I think he went to find Mr. Moreland, but I don' know where Mr. Moreland is."

John's grip on Adaira's hands slipped. He shook his head. "Nay, he doesn' have any reason to go looking fer him. That can' be it."

"William sensed that the storm wasn' natural. He knows another selkie is behind it."

The farmer's mouth curled downward. "So, you know Niall Moreland and William are selkies, then."

"I've known since I overheard you and Mr. Moreland talking after the Johnsmas celebration."

"Then you know what a danger he is to William."

"And to the rest o' Everton."

John's brows knit together in confusion, so Adaira gestured to the storm outside. "All that is his doing. He's going to destroy the town."

"What? Are you certain?"

Adaira nodded. "'Tis what Mr. McLaren told me would happen if Briony didn' leave with him."

"Mr. McLaren? He knows about this? And Bri—Mistress Fairborn? What does she . . ." Understanding lit up the man's blue eyes. "She's a selkie, too."

Adaira didn't deny it. There was no point now. "She was here just a while ago. I think she's going to try to stop Mr. Moreland on her own. I don' know if she can do it, though."

"And you said William was on his way to find Niall Moreland right now? I have to get him somewhere safe. He could end up in the middle o' everything and get hurt. Or . . ." John's eyes glazed over as though he was remembering something. "If he chose the wrong side, something terrible could happen. Again."

"What do you mean?" Adaira asked, raising her left eyebrow.

John's expression fell, and he suddenly seemed as if he was carrying the whole world on his shoulders.

"The night Mr. Mendes's ship appeared, 'tis true that I knocked William out. But I didn' do it to keep him from finding out about his powers."

"Then why . . ."

The farmer's eyes met hers. "I did it because he killed someone."

To Take a Life

Two weeks ago

"Da', may I ask you something?" William said as he and his father made their way down the hall.

It had been a long day working on the Martins' crops, and John was worn out, but he looked over at his son with a grin.

"Aye, what is it?" John replied, thinking the boy was going to ask for a snack. They'd finished dinner a couple of hours ago, but William's appetite was pretty unpredictable these days.

The lad blinked up at him with his big black eyes and said, "May I go to the beach? Mr. Henry told me seals like to come up to the shore this time o' year. I want to see if there are any down there."

John stiffened, his senses sharpening as all his previous fatigue disappeared. "Nay, that's na going to happen."

The boy slowed to a halt and stuck out his lower lip, much like his mother used to when she was upset. "But, Da', I'm just going down to play with my friends!"

The farmer's anger flared up at William's disrespectful tone. "I don' care what the reason is. I already told you yer na to go anywhere near the water."

Tears welled up in the boy's eyes, but John knew better than to let them sway him. William had used that manipulation tactic on him one too many times.

"You don' let me do anything I want to do!" the boy screeched.

"That is na true, and you know it. 'Tis far too late to go out anyway even if you didn' want to go to the beach."

William huffed, but then a twinkle came into his eye. "Why don' you come with me, Da'?"

"You know that's na an option."

"But—"

"Just trust me," John said, giving his son a hopeful smile. "I'm doing this to protect you."

But William balked and replied, "I don' need you to protect me. That's what Mum needed. Why didn' you protect her?"

John gaped. *He thinks 'tis my fault she died?!*

Footsteps drew John's attention from his son. Someone had heard them.

Who could . . .

Then Adaira Stubbins was standing in front of him, almost like a shield—

"Stop," she stated, her voice direct and unwavering as she looked down at William.

The boy's anger instantly fizzled, and he looked away from her shame-faced.

John's eyebrows flew up to his forehead. *What am I seeing right now? When William gets into a mood like this, he barely listens to me. How is she—*

But then he realized she was stretching out her hand—

She can' touch him right now! The last time William got angry, his skin got so hot I almost had to let go o' it. I have to stop her!

John grabbed the woman's arm and pulled her away from the boy. "Don' touch him!"

His words came out more harshly than he'd intended, but the woman had scared him. *What if she'd gotten hurt? Ellie told me selkies can burn people with just a touch. William may na be a pureblood, but that doesn' mean he's na dangerous. Especially since he doesn' know what he is.*

John had always hoped William wouldn't inherit his mother's selkie powers. The boy was half-human, and he'd never shown signs of special abilities in all their time in Hollandstoun.

But his sealskin is still intact, John, said Ellie's voice in his head. *As much as you might wish it, William will never be fully human until you destroy it. Like you promised you would.*

John didn't have time to think about the promise right then, though, so he stowed it away in the back of his mind.

He glanced down, only then realizing he still had Mistress Stubbins's hand in his own. And she was staring up at him with terror in her eyes.

"Don' be mean to her," William cried before leaping forward and taking hold of John's arm.

A blaze of heat ran through him where the boy's fingers met his skin, and John jerked back instinctively, releasing Mistress Stubbins in the process. He quickly concealed his pain as best he could, tucking his arm behind him. The heat had been much stronger this time, and John was certain that when he looked at his arm in the morning, it would have bright-red burns.

Thank goodness Mistress Stubbins didn' touch him.

He looked over at her in relief, but the woman was still watching him suspiciously. Nervously. As if John was the dangerous one rather than William.

And while it made complete sense for her to react that way, the distrust in her eyes still hurt him more than he cared to admit. "Mistress Stubbins, I apologize fer disturbing you at this time o' night. Unfortunately, my son gets too excited sometimes and—"

"—Too excited? Da', that's na right at all!" William cried, stamping his foot to show how upset he was.

"And perhaps 'twould be best if he and I continued our conversation in our room."

But when John looked to his son, the boy wailed, "You always treat me like this!"

And before the farmer could react, William was off, charging past John and Mistress Stubbins—

SLAM!

John twisted around, his eyes bulging at the sight of his son barreling out the door. "William! Come back here!"

But the boy kept going, turning right and darting up the path. John moved forward to follow him, but then he heard Mistress Stubbins behind him.

I can' put her in harm's way, and I can' risk her finding out the truth about him.

He turned to the young woman, his tone pleading as he said, "Please, mistress. This is between me and my son."

The woman's brown eyes studied him for a moment, but then she nodded.

With that, John chased after his son, praying William wouldn't change direction and run to the water. *If he does, I may na be able to save him.*

Instead of going toward the ocean, though, William kept going farther and farther up the hill. Before long, John felt raindrops on his skin. The wind also picked up, bringing a terrible cold that made him shiver as it whipped through his hair.

He raised his face to the sky, a shot of terror going through him when he glimpsed black clouds above his head. *Nay, please. I'm na ready.*

He lowered his eyes back to his son's retreating form. *I have to calm him down before he hurts someone.*

The path William was on soon ended at a small cottage, but rather than stopping, the lad turned and continued running into the forest. John bolted after him, noting how they were drawing nearer and nearer to where the land ended in a steep drop. Everton was right on the tip of North Ronaldsay, Orkney's northernmost island. Beyond it lay miles and miles of ocean as far as the eye could see.

"William, stop!"

The boy came to a sliding halt just a few feet from the cliff's edge. But he didn't turn as his father ran up behind him, for his gaze was fixed on the beautiful sea stretching out before them.

And on the storm brewing in the sky.

John reached out to his son, but as soon as he touched the boy's shoulder, he drew his hand back with a hiss. William was burning up!

The sound caught the lad's attention, and he glanced back at John in surprise. "Da'? What—"

He broke off with a shriek, grabbing his head and falling to his knees—

CRACK!

Out on the water, bolts of lightning rained down from the heavens, striking the waves over and over with a deadly anger.

John's breath caught—there was a ship out in the middle of the storm!

The farmer went to grab his son's arm, but he stopped at the last second when he saw the red marks on his fingers. Burns.

"William," he shouted, kneeling down beside the boy, "you have to calm down!"

His son's cry faded to a whimper, and he looked up at his father. "I can feel it, Da'. I can feel the storm out there. Why can I feel it?"

"Because you made it. And now you have to make it stop."

William's eyes widened. "Da', what are you saying?"

John pointed at the ocean. "William, there's a ship out there full o' people, people could die!"

The boy turned, noticing the ship for the first time. He looked to his father helplessly. "Da', that's na—I can'—I don' know how to stop the storm!"

As he spoke, John felt the wind blow harder, and the waves on the sea seemed to rise even higher. The ship teetered back and forth, precariously close to capsizing. Several people were out on the deck, so small they were just specks in the farmer's vision.

But then one of them went overboard.

"William!"

"Da', I can' stop it! I don' know what to—"

One of the ship masts bent to the side, splintering as the top half collapsed onto the deck.

William threw his hands over his mouth, tears spilling down his cheeks. "Help me, please!"

The farmer scanned the ground until he found what he was looking for. With a heavy heart, he bent down and picked up a stone. "I'm sorry, son, but I don' know what else to do. This is going to hurt."

John took one more glance at the ship out on the water as it struggled to stay upright, and then he slammed the rock against the back of William's head.

***

And now that he remembers, he's gone headfirst into danger. I've failed him. A tear rolled down the farmer's cheek.

"'Twas the ship's first mate," John explained. "I don' think William saw the man go overboard, but I did. If I hadn' knocked William out, everyone on the ship might have been lost."

The man couldn't look at Adaira's face, for he was all too sure of what he would see: shock, judgment, and worst of all, fear.

But to his surprise, her small hand found its way to his cheek. "John, why did you never tell him he was a selkie?"

The woman's voice wasn't harsh or accusing; it was soft, sad, and so compelling he couldn't help but answer her.

"I . . . I promised Ellie I wouldn'. He'd never shown any signs o' powers before we came here. Ellie and I thought he could live without knowing."

Adaira slowly removed her hand and said flatly, "Well, you were both wrong, then."

John's gaze shot to hers, caught off guard by her change in tone. *Here comes the criticism, just like I knew 'twould.*

But there was no scorn in her eyes, only remorse. "I did the very same thing with Briony. Her mum made me swear na to tell her the truth, and I did everything I could to keep my word, but 'twas na enough. Briony still found out who she was anyway, and once she knows I've been lying to her all this time, my friendship with her will be over."

A great rumble of thunder sounded overhead.

The woman sniffed, her lips turning up into a pitiful smile. "That is, if we live long enough fer things like that. I do hope Briony can stop Mr. Moreland. Otherwise, we're all doomed."

John grasped her hand, not wanting her to give up hope. "Selkies aren' all-powerful. They can be killed by humans, too."

The farmer held back a wince, for he hadn't meant to reveal that much. But it was the truth. John knew the selkie wouldn't listen to reason. Therefore, the only way to ensure William's and the rest of Everton's safety was to eliminate the threat. Permanently.

John wondered if Adaira would see it that way though. *Will she be disgusted that I even suggested such a thing?*

He watched for her response, but rather than being taken aback by his words, Adaira's expression was pensive. "Even if we knew where Mr. Moreland was, do you really think you could . . . kill him?"

John set his mouth in a firm line and pushed himself to his feet, new strength flowing through him. "Aye, I do."

There was no question of it in the farmer's mind. That was something he was absolutely sure of. After all, it wouldn't be the first time he'd killed a selkie to save someone he loved.

John leaned over and placed a tender kiss on Adaira's lips. "Now stay here while I go find William."

A Family Matter

Adaira was completely dumbfounded as she stared at the redhead, her eyes homing in on the stiffness of his jaw and the way his hand clenched in a fist. He hid it well, but Adaira could tell John was in significant pain. He undoubtedly needed medical attention and shouldn't be moving. But the resolve in the man's eyes told a different story. He was going to find his son and save him, whatever the cost.

Just as John started to leave, though, Adaira grabbed his arm. "I'm coming with you," she said, tucking her fear into the darkest recesses of her mind.

The farmer frowned. "Adaira, I don' want to put you in more danger. You should—"

"What I should be doing is telling you yer na fit to go anywhere right now, so don' tell me what I 'should' be doing." She squared her shoulders defiantly. "I love William too, so let's na waste time arguing with each other, and go find him."

John opened his mouth as though he wanted to protest, but then he nodded.

"Good. There's just one thing I need to do first," Adaira said before bounding up to her room. Within a couple of minutes, she'd returned, and the two of them darted out into the rain.

Briony had gone down toward the main part of town, so Adaira figured that was the best place to start looking. She whirled to the left, but John put his hand on her shoulder.

"What is it?" she called over the howling wind.

The farmer pointed up the hill toward Drulea Cottage. The path was uneven, and many parts of it couldn't be seen from the inn, but the cottage was always plainly visible at the land's edge. It stood at the brink of a cliff, not far from Torin Woods.

And now, as Adaira and John peered up at the cottage, they saw someone standing beside it, hands raised in the air.

Niall Moreland, Adaira knew in an instant, her blood turning cold. But what was far more troubling was the second person going toward the cottage. A person far too short to be an adult.

"William," Adaira breathed, unconsciously breaking into a run. John kept pace next to her, his strong legs propelling him forward almost effortlessly.

Both of them knew they needed to get there fast, for there was no telling what Niall might do. Or what lies he might share.

***

When William reached the source of the storm's power, he gasped. He'd sensed the creator was someone like him, but he never would have guessed that someone was Mr. Moreland.

He always did seem like he was holding something back, the boy realized. The man's stories had held such detail, as if he was recounting real events.

What was the creature that could call down storms? William didn't remember, but perhaps it wasn't as mythical as he'd thought. Perhaps he was beholding such a creature even now.

Mistress Adaira said my mum wasn' human. Was she right?

Right then, William struggled to see much resemblance between his mother and the man before him. Mr. Moreland was standing with his hands outstretched, sending down torrents of rain and lightning. The clouds were darkest here, but they were nothing compared to the black fire in the man's eyes. William had never seen such anger. Such hatred. He could feel the rage billowing out from him, fueling the storm with energy.

Why is he so angry? Maybe I shouldn' have come here.

242

He was debating whether or not to turn around when Mr. Moreland's gaze shifted over to him. The murderous scowl on the man's face lifted, and his mouth spread into a frightening smile.

"William! I was wondering when you'd show up. Want me to teach you how to make some chaos, too?"

The lad quaked a bit. "I-I just want answers. I thought you could help me."

Niall laughed, sending shivers down William's spine. He lowered his arms, though the storm seemed no less bleak. "A quest to find yer true self, aye?"

William nodded.

"You and I are what the humans call selkies. Beautiful, powerful beings able to change our shape and take on the likeness o' seals."

The boy's eyes widened. "We can turn into seals? Really? How?"

"All we need do is don our sealskins, and selkie magic does the rest. Unfortunately fer you, I wasn' able to find yer pelt. It seems yer father hid it a wee bit too well in his efforts to keep you from being happy."

William's temper flickered. He'd often thought his father didn't want him to be happy, especially in these last months since Mum passed. The conversation that had led up to William's first storm zipped through the boy's mind:

"But, Da', I'm just going down to play with my friends!"

"I don' care what the reason is. I already told you yer na to go anywhere near the water."

William gritted his teeth. He was tired of being restricted, tired of being suffocated.

A flurry of lightning hit the ground near the lad's feet, at which Niall raised his eyebrows appreciatively. "Na bad. Just wait until I've had the chance to show you a few things. Then you'll really have fun."

The boy's lips lifted. He liked the sound of that.

"You can start by trying to aim yer lightning," Niall continued. "Why don' you send it down to Everton Inn? That's a nice, close target."

William drew back. *What? Everton Inn? But that's where Da' and Mistress Adaira are.*

Niall smirked. "What's the matter? Don' want to hurt yer precious Adaira Stubbins? If you knew what she was actually like, you'd be happy to see her dead."

"D-Dead?"

Is that what Mr. Moreland's trying to do? Kill people? William looked down at the village, thinking of all the people he'd met over these last few weeks. *They don' deserve to die. They're my friends. And my da' is down there, too.*

"Those people are murderers," Mr. Moreland explained. "They attacked me when I was a bairn. Might have killed me if I hadn' gotten away. They did manage to kill the leader o' my herd though, and fer that, they must suffer the consequences."

"But my da' didn' have anything to do with that!" William pointed out.

"Yer da'?" Mr. Moreland rolled his eyes, but then his face twisted into a wide smile. "Oh, dear lad, I almost wish I didn' have to tell you."

William frowned. Something in the man's tone was making his stomach feel quivery inside. "Tell me what?"

Niall's attention moved to something over William's right shoulder.

"Ah, just in time," the man called, his smile taking on a darker gleam. "I was just about to tell William the *rest* o' what you didn' want him to know."

William whirled around, only to see his father and Mistress Adaira hurtling toward them. They were breathing heavily, as if they'd run all the way here from the inn.

"William, are you all right?" Mistress Adaira asked once she reached him.

The boy's mouth started to crinkle up, joy shooting through him at the concern on her face. *She looks so worried. They both do.*

William turned to his father, who was eying him up and down as though checking to make sure he wasn't injured.

"I'm fine. I—"

"Remember what I told you before, William," Mr. Moreland cut in. "Remember yer da' just wants to control you and keep you from the one place where you can really be free."

John glared straight at the selkie and snarled, "Stop pretending you know anything about me or my family."

Mr. Moreland tilted his head back and let out a hollow laugh. "Oh, I know more about yer family than you realize. For instance, I know what really happened to yer wife."

Time seemed to slow down for a split second as William looked from Mr. Moreland to his father. "Da', what's he talking about?"

But John was standing stock-still, his face as white as a sheet. William turned to Mistress Adaira in confusion, but the innkeeper's daughter seemed just as confused as he was.

Mr. Moreland smirked. "Well? Don' you want to be the one to tell him?"

William's father muttered, "There's nothing to tell. She drowned at sea."

"Liar!" Mr. Moreland snapped, his face reddening with anger.

"And how would you know?" the farmer countered with a little more volume, though his voice was still shaky. "You weren' there when it happened!"

"But I know someone who was."

John Burgess shook his head. "Impossible. No one was there that night except . . ." He trailed off, leaving William to wonder what he'd been about to say.

Da' saw Mum die? He told me all he found were her shoes by the water.

Mr. Moreland didn't seem nearly as surprised. Instead, he seemed sad, like he was deeply troubled over something. *But what? What is he getting at?*

It didn't take long for William to get his answer, for Mr. Moreland soon opened his mouth and said in a slow, deliberate voice, "Except fer you and three selkies, right?"

"But I-I thought—" John sputtered.

"They died?" Mr. Moreland finished with a thin smile, unshed tears shining in his eyes. "All but one. My father survived. My mother and sister weren' so lucky."

Love Undying

"Yer sister?" John almost couldn't get the words out, for it felt knives had been shoved down his throat. *He can' be . . .*

But as the farmer scrutinized Niall, he couldn't help but feel like he was looking into his late wife's face. The pointed chin. The slender nose. The piercing black eyes William had also inherited. The resemblance was undeniable.

"Yer Ellie's brother."

The farmer was so shocked he didn't know what to do, what to feel, what to think. No longer was Niall simply an enemy threatening John's family. He was family.

"Elene was my sister," the selkie spat. Then his eyes took on a dreamy quality. "My parents were heartbroken when she told them she'd fallen in love with a human and wanted to leave the sea. They begged her na to do it, warned her o' the dangers o' humankind"—Niall threw John a pointed glance before continuing—"but their words fell on deaf ears. The next day, she disappeared without even telling me goodbye. My parents thought they could find her if we searched long enough, but as the years went on, I gave up hope. I knew she wasn' coming back to us.

"But then one morning, my mum told me she'd seen her in a small village. She and my father were going to bring her home, so we could be a family again. They asked me to come, too, but I refused. Elene had forsaken us, forsaken what it meant to be a selkie. I didn' want to see her."

Niall let out a sharp breath, seemingly overcome with emotion. "But I should have gone with them," he choked, tears streaming down his face. "If I'd gone, maybe things would have ended differently. Maybe she and my mum would be with me now."

The selkie's grief-stricken expression shifted, and his gaze homed in on John. "And you would be the one at the bottom o' the sea."

"Da', is what he's saying true?" William asked, pulling the farmer's attention away from Niall. "He's wrong, isn' he? You didn' kill Mum." The boy's eyes were wide, searching his father's for the truth.

"You didn' do it, Da'. You couldn' have," William whimpered. "Tell Mr. Moreland 'tis na true."

John touched his son's cheek, wishing he could tell William what he wanted to hear. But he'd lied to the boy so many times that he just couldn't do it again.

Not this time.

The farmer shut his eyes and shook his head. "I'm sorry, son. But he's telling the truth."

John felt William's skin warming beneath his palm, and he slowly moved his hand away before opening his eyes. The lad was staring at him as if he was seeing his father for the very first time.

And, perhaps in a way, he was. Every facade John had put up, every excuse he'd made to keep William from the truth, they'd all been stripped away, leaving behind only what was real. And the real John Burgess was a man who had killed his wife. The man who had killed William's mother.

John's shoulders slumped at the disillusionment on his son's face. He'd been running from the truth for so long it was almost a relief for everything to come out now.

But William doesn' know everything yet, whispered a small voice in the farmer's mind. *He deserves to hear how it happened.*

He's never going to believe another word that comes out o' my mouth, John argued. He could see it in the boy's eyes. He'd lost him. He'd—

Lightning crashed down from the sky, scorching the ground between John and his son.

"Murderer!" William roared, lifting his hands in the air. The clouds above them seem to grow darker still, fueled by the boy's rage.

Before when William had summoned the hail, it had merely been an obstacle to keep his father from following him. This time, William wasn't holding back.

"John, run!" Adaira cried, pointing at the danger overhead.

But the farmer was done running. If this was the consequence of his actions, John was going to face it.

There was just one thing he had to tell his son first.

John sky-blue eyes met his son's fiery black ones, and in a gentle voice, he said, "I love you, son. Always."

William scowled, the words seeming to only infuriate him more. He lifted his gaze toward the clouds. "I'm na yer son. Na anymore."

But before the boy's wrath came down as deadly lightning, someone stepped directly into William's path.

"Wait, lad!" Niall called, raising his hand to the air. The clouds lightened a bit, though the storm continued to churn over the rest of the town. "There's something you still need from him."

The older selkie turned to John and placed a burning hand on the farmer's arm. "Where is William's sealskin?"

John hissed at the searing heat but didn't answer. He wasn't about to help Niall kidnap his son. If William had that sealskin, there would be no hope of seeing him again.

What's the use though? asked a broken voice inside him. *He hates you now. He would have killed you if Niall hadn' stepped in. Why bother trying to keep William from leaving?*

He glanced once more at his son, wondering if the happy, playful bairn he'd raised was still in there. *Has the sea taken you?*

Ellie had spoken once of how the ocean's power was a double-edged sword. One side was calm and restorative, but the other was turbulent and cruel. And if a selkie chose to let his anger control him, the sea's penchant for violence could overwhelm him. Sometimes to the point of death.

William never would have tried to kill me o' his own volition, John told himself. *It must be the ocean's influence over him.*

But then again, I've never given him reason to be this angry before.

William still looked furious, but John thought he saw a twinkle of fear in the boy's eyes—

The heat from Niall's hand intensified, drawing John's attention away from his son.

"Ahhh!" John couldn't hold back a groan this time, which made his assailant's face light up with glee.

"Na nearly so arrogant anymore, are you?" Niall's mouth flattened, and he leaned in close. "Now, I'll ask you again: Where is William's sealskin?"

"I know where 'tis!" squeaked Adaira.

Niall looked over to her, but John cried, "She doesn'! Don' listen to her."

The selkie shoved John away and slithered over to Adaira. "And where would that be?"

"I . . ." The woman reminded John of a frightened rabbit, her eyes darting about for a means of escape.

"You said you knew where William's sealskin is. Was that na true?" Niall snarled, his face getting dangerously close to hers.

"Leave her alone," John shouted, rising to his feet. "She has nothing to do with this."

"Well?" Niall said, ignoring the farmer and grabbing Adaira's chin.

"I found it after I caught you searching the Burgesses' room," the woman mumbled, keeping her eyes on the ground. "Then I took it somewhere safe."

John's breath caught in his throat. *Adaira had the skin? She said I needed to get something back when we were talking before the storm. That must have been what she meant.*

"And that place is?" Niall snapped, his patience clearly growing thin.

But at that moment, Adaira lifted her gaze, her eyes boring into the selkie's with surprising audacity. "I'll only take William and John to it."

Niall's eyes narrowed. "You don' get to make the rules. I decide where—"

The selkie cut off, his gaze moving to the town below them.

Nay, na to the town, John realized. *To the sky.*

A small circle of blue sky had appeared out of nowhere above the church. As the farmer watched, it stretched in all directions, reaching all the way to Everton Inn before it stopped.

Niall growled. "Briony." He released Adaira's chin and turned to William. "I'll take care o' her. You go get yer sealskin, understand?"

The lad nodded, his mouth still an angry line.

Or is it? John wasn't so sure anymore. The boy was stiff as he moved, making the farmer wonder if his son was in full agreement with everything Niall was doing.

Even so, William marched over to Adaira and said with authority, "Let's go."

***

Adaira guided the Burgesses through Torin Woods, praying her plan would work. Thunder rumbled as they wove between trees, reminding Adaira of the looming danger.

If I can' get William to forgive his father, he might join Niall in his attack on the town. And even if Briony can stop Niall on her own, I doubt she can stop two selkies.

An insidious thought slipped into her mind: *But what if John doesn' have an explanation fer killing his wife? What if he really is just a murderer?*

Adaira's heart clenched, and she immediately dismissed the notion. This was John, not some random person she'd just met. She knew him. He wasn't a killer. If he was responsible for his wife's death, there had to be something important he hadn't shared.

"Is it much farther?" William called from a few steps behind her.

"Na much farther."

She tried to meet John's eye, hoping she could silently encourage him, but the farmer wouldn't glance her way as he walked beside his son. He seemed so broken he could barely bring himself to walk at all, his feet dragging in the sodden earth.

250

Torin Woods was a relatively small group of trees that fringed Drulea Cottage on one side and wrapped around Mary's Hill on the other. Most people stayed out of the forest because of the rumors of trows and fairies, but Adaira and Briony had spent many hours playing here as bairns. Adaira's current route led the trio southwest of the Fairborn residence, and before long, the trees opened up to reveal their destination.

"My sealskin is *here*?" William asked, looking very perplexed as he came up next to Adaira. John, too, was rubbing his forehead as if he didn't understand.

For they'd reached none other than Loch Isla.

How different the circumstances are this time from when I last brought William here, Adaira thought bitterly. But she was hoping the familiar setting would help with the next stage of her plan.

The lad scurried through the rain to the shelter of a few trees by the loch's edge. Here lay the log where the two of them had sat when Adaira taught William how to fish. It hadn't been long so ago, yet it felt like a lifetime had passed.

Until Adaira saw William hesitate before starting his search, making her realize he was remembering that day, too.

I can reach him, she told herself.

The lad looked all around the log, but when he didn't find the skin, he turned back to Adaira with a glare. "'Tis na here. Did you lie to me too?"

"Yer pelt *is* here, but before I show it to you, I want you to do something fer me."

William curled his lip. "Why would I do something fer you? I don' owe you anything."

His menacing words tore at Adaira's heart, but she tried to see past the venom to the boy she loved. "I know you've been hurt, but please, don' shut me out." William crossed his arms but didn't say anything, so she continued, "All I'm asking is fer you to listen. Surely you can give me that much."

"Fine," he grumbled. "What is it?"

Adaira gathered her courage and declared, "I want to tell you a story."

The boy furrowed his brow. "What? Why would you want to do that now?"

Rather than answering him, she said, "When 'tis over, if yer willing, I want you to hear what yer father has to say about yer mum's death."

Adaira heard John let out a soft gasp, but she kept her focus on William. The boy started to shake his head, so Adaira added, "You can choose to just walk away after I'm done if you want. I'll still give you the sealskin. Agreed?"

The lad chewed on his lower lip for a long moment and shot a glance at his father, who still appeared confused.

"All right. But tell it quickly," William finally said.

The woman gave him a light smile before she shifted her thoughts to the task at hand. "I'm going to tell you a story o' regret. A story o' loss and heartbreak."

William sat down on the log, eyes wide with fascination. The anger seemed to fall off of him, and he was again the carefree boy she'd met in the market.

The innkeeper's daughter swallowed, trying to ignore the tremor in her hands. "The story o' a lost bairn and the woman who would do *anything* to get him back."

Adaira shut her eyes as chills ran over her skin. She rubbed her arms in an effort to warm them, but the cold was already settling into her bones.

It had been so cold that night. The night it had happened.

A Cold Winter Night

"The young woman lived in a small village," Adaira began. "'Twas winter, the coldest one the people had ever been through. And 'twas dark. So dark almost all the time, making everyone gloomier than usual."

"Including the bairn and woman?" William interrupted.

Adaira coughed a bit. "The woman, aye. Which was very unusual since she always tried her hardest to be cheerful. Her father noticed that she seemed ill, but she just told him she was tired.

"The truth, though, was that the young woman wasn' feeling like herself at all."

"But what about the bairn?" William asked again.

John shushed his son as he would if this were any other time. As if the previous few hours had never happened. But there was a look of comprehension in the farmer's eyes, one that made Adaira suspect he knew all too well that she was speaking of herself.

She blushed and whispered, "The b-bairn wasn' born yet. That was why the woman was feeling so strange. She was . . ." Adaira let out a soft breath. ". . . with child."

She kept her eyes firmly planted on the ground by her feet, unwilling to look her companions in the eye. If the three of them made it out of this, John would never want to be with her now. She'd just destroyed any chance she had of a future with them.

But what kind o' future would it be if 'twas based on lies? said a small voice inside her.

Na a future I want, she realized. *Na anymore.*

"Mistress Adaira?" William asked. "Aren' you going to keep going? What happened to the woman next? Did she tell her husband?"

Adaira turned to the lad, staring into his eager face. It was clear he hadn't made the connection between Adaira and the woman in her tale, which she was glad of.

Maybe one day I'll explain everything to you, but fer now, I hope the lesson is enough.

She gave William a tender smile. "Well, the young woman hadn' told anyone yet because 'twas still very early, and you know what they say about fairies stealing away unborn children. But on a particularly chilly night in January, the woman was just about to blow out the candle in her room when she felt her stomach grow tight."

William gasped. "She was going to have the babe!"

Adaira nodded. "The feeling went away at first, so she shut her eyes and went to sleep. But a few hours later, she woke up feeling it again. And this time, 'twas much worse. She knew then what was happening.

"It had been snowing the day before, and when she opened the door o' her house, she almost couldn' get out. But she had to. She had to get to the midwife, so she pushed her way outside and marched up to the midwife's house—"

"Through the snow?" William asked, his mouth hanging open.

"That's right."

"When she was about to have a babe?" The boy's eyebrows furrowed, and he cocked his head to the side. "Mistress Adaira, is this a real story?"

Adaira almost laughed, but she knew if she did, she might cry, too. "Aye, William, 'tis a real story. And aye, she did go up a hill through the snow all the way to the midwife's house. She was just about to knock on the door when the midwife opened it.

"'Is it the babe?' the midwife asked, looking down at the woman's stomach.

"'How did you know?' the young woman said. Remember, she hadn' told anyone yet."

"But couldn' everyone just look at her stomach and know?" William pointed out.

"Na yet. But somehow, the midwife knew anyway. She took the young woman to a safe place and helped her have her babe, but . . ."

Adaira choked up, unable to continue.

"But what?" William asked.

She took a deep breath, willing herself to finish what she'd started. "The midwife put a small bundle in the young woman's arms, smaller than a loaf o' bread. Smaller than you when you were born.

"The midwife looked at her and said, ''Tis a boy.' But there was no smile on the midwife's face, no joy o' bringing a new life into the world. The young woman stared at the tiny face and realized he wasn' breathing. He'd come too early. Too soon." Adaira's mouth trembled as she struggled to maintain her composure. "The babe didn' make it."

"Oh," William mumbled, his expression an odd mixture of sadness and confusion. "He was already gone?"

Adaira slowly nodded, her ears ringing as she thought back to the dreadful silence as Bethany had lain the baby in her arms. Silence that should have been full of infant cries.

"And his mum? Did she ever forget him?" There was a hint of desperation in the boy's voice, and at first, Adaira wondered at its presence. But she soon discerned that he was relating to the lost bairn, hoping the babe's brief life had made a difference.

Adaira peered deeply into William's eyes and said, "Nay, na once."

The boy shuffled his feet in the soft grass. "'Tis a sad story, but I don' understand why you told it to me. What does it have to do with me or Da'?"

"I told you because I want to remind you that loss leaves a scar. Na one that you can see but in here,"—she pointed to her heart—"and losing a bairn may leave the biggest scar o' all."

She gestured to John, trying not to look at the farmer too closely for fear of judgment in his eyes. "William, if you leave yer father and go with Niall Moreland, you won' just be putting a scar on yer heart—you'll be putting one on yer father's." Adaira reached out and cupped the boy's cheek in her hand. "And also on mine. Please, William. I love you too much to lose you."

The confusion melted from the boy's face as he contemplated her words. No one spoke for a long moment, though internally, Adaira was praying harder than she ever had.

Then, before she knew what was happening, the boy launched himself into her arms and buried his face in her neck. Adaira quickly returned the embrace, squeezing William's small body with as much love as she would her own son. For that was how she saw him, even if he never would be in the eyes of the law. Even if no one else understood it.

William slowly pulled away and swiped at the tears dripping down his face. "I love you too," he whispered.

Adaira put a hand on his shoulder. "Then, fer my sake, give yer da' one more chance."

The lad's eyes darted toward his father, his lips pressing together in a slight grimace. "All right, Da'. Tell me what happened to Mum."

***

John blinked a few times, unsure if he'd heard William correctly. *He's . . . He's giving me the chance to tell him?*

The farmer licked his lips, not wanting to share this secret, horrible truth that had haunted his dreams almost every night since it happened.

Don' be stubborn, John, his subconscious said, practically kicking him. *This is the only way left fer you to protect him.*

The farmer let out a sharp breath at the irony. Protecting William by explaining his failure to protect Ellie didn't make much sense in John's mind.

He turned to Adaira, who nodded encouragingly. She seemed to be saying, "Please, only the truth this time."

John gritted his teeth. After she'd been so vulnerable with the story she'd just shared—for he had known from the moment she'd started that it had been her own—it would be downright shameful for him not to tell the truth now.

And if it meant protecting William from Niall, John was willing to do anything.

Hope's Fragile Flower

Seven months ago

One cold November morning, John woke with a start. He shot up into a sitting position and scanned the dark room for intruders. His gaze landed on his young son, sleeping soundly in his bed, perfectly safe. But the uneasiness in his gut didn't subside, so the farmer's eyes continued their sweep while his ears listened for any unusual sounds.

He turned to his wife's side of the bed, not surprised to see it empty, save a light impression on the sheet. Elene always woke before John did and tended to use that time to get started on breakfast.

But then John noticed how thick the darkness was over everything and realized it wasn't time for cooking yet. Ellie should have still been sleeping at his side.

Perhaps she went out to look at the ocean. She hadn't done that as much since William was born, but sometimes she would still go out before sunrise and watch the waves break over the sand near their home. John had placed a rocking chair beside the garden for this very purpose, for he knew how important the water was to her. And there she'd sit for anywhere from a few minutes to an hour, singing a magical, grief-stricken song that ebbed and flowed like the sea itself.

She'd told him many times that she was happy here, that she didn't regret the choice she'd made. But John knew part of her heart still belonged beneath the waves. Maybe it always would. The thought had bothered John when they'd first wed, knowing her heart would never fully be his, but over time, he'd come to accept it and love Elene as she was.

The farmer never interrupted her while she sat in her chair, giving her solitude to mourn over the life she'd given up. It was just one small way to respect the sacrifice she'd made to be with him.

But today, John didn't hesitate to go outside, for the warning in his heart was too great to ignore. "Ellie," he called, stepping out and shutting the door behind him. It wouldn't do for William to catch his mother weeping while staring at the sea. They hadn't told the boy of Ellie's heritage yet. They were waiting until he showed signs of selkie magic himself.

There was no answer as he rounded the house.

"Ellie," John said again, more urgently this time. She wasn't one to play games with him, not when she knew how important it was to be cautious.

Elene's parents had been outraged when she'd told them she wanted to marry a human, calling her a traitor for even considering such a thing. Selkies didn't take desertion lightly. It was only through a great deal of deception and cunning that Ellie had misled them into thinking John lived in the Shetland Islands, a place the herd regularly traveled to during the year.

"Sweetheart, are you—" John broke off when he reached the garden, his eyes homing in on the empty rocking chair.

In an instant, John spun around and darted back into the house. He knelt beside his bed and pulled out a dusty trunk from under it. William was still asleep, and John didn't want to wake him, so he gingerly undid the latch.

The trunk had sat undisturbed for years, and John had nearly convinced himself he was being ridiculous as he slowly lifted the lid.

John pressed a hand against his mouth to hold back a gasp.

Elene's sealskin was gone.

The farmer leaned back as he tried to think of a valid reason why the pelt would be missing. *Perhaps she just wanted to hold it fer a moment.*

John shook his head. *That doesn' explain where she is. She wouldn' have taken it somewhere that one o' our neighbors could have seen it. And why now? She hasn' touched it since before William was born.*

Maybe she decided to destroy it. Ellie had talked about that a few times, of ridding herself of the temptation to go back to the ocean, of truly becoming a human for good.

But that answer didn't satisfy him either; she would never have done something like that without telling John first.

Did she . . . leave us? The farmer peeked out the window to the sea beyond his small home. He didn't want to entertain such a notion, but—

Movement caught his eye. He squinted, trying to make out what was in the water. It was so far away—

John's mouth fell open. *Ellie.* He clambered to his feet, grabbed his knife, and dashed outside, his gaze on a group of seals near the beach. There were three of them, all roughly the same size, all completely ordinary at first glance.

But when one took a moment to really watch them, it became obvious that something strange was happening. Two of the seals held the third's flippers in their mouths, almost as if they were dragging it away from the shore. And the third was desperately trying to escape.

"Ellie!" John cried, scrambling down to the beach.

The third seal's head immediately turned in his direction, and it gave a pained yelp.

John knew they were too far out for him to swim, so he headed to the nearest fishing boat and jumped in. Within seconds, he'd untied it and grabbed the oars. He gave no thought to the fact that his neighbor, Adam Thomson, wouldn't appreciate him borrowing the boat without permission. John had more important things to think about right then.

"Ellie, hold on!" he called.

The third seal, the one he was certain was his beloved wife, cried out again, sounding more distressed than before. John's arms strained against the oars, rowing as fast as he could.

When he looked over his shoulder, he saw Ellie fighting harder against her attackers, snapping at their heads with her teeth. Finally, she managed to wrest herself out of their grip as a wave broke over them, diving out of sight before John could reach her. The other two seals swiftly followed her, leaving John unsure which way he should go.

A few moments later, a seal head bobbed up from the water and turned to John.

"Ellie?"

He couldn't tell one seal from the other, but it seemed to be looking at him with recognition. It swam toward him, and John held out his hand to help it get into the boat—

"Ahhh!" John careened forward as the boat tipped. He tried to steady himself, but the boat continued to lean.

He gasped in a breath of air just before he slammed into the cold water, sinking like a stone.

John tried to swim toward what he hoped was the surface, but his head was so disoriented he couldn't be sure. *Hold on a wee bit longer, Ellie. I—*

The farmer let out an involuntary moan, his mouth filling with water. One of the seals had seized his leg!

He tried to shake the seal off, kicking at it with his other foot. When he landed a good hit, the seal released him, and he swam with all his might until he broke through to the surface.

"Ellie!" John cried, his head swiveling in all directions. He was shivering uncontrollably, his body unused to such low water temperature. He had to get back in the boat. If he didn't, he'd get so cold he'd lose consciousness and drown.

But then he spotted a dark shadow zooming toward him. He tried to swim out of the way, but he wasn't quick enough—

The seal rammed into his stomach, knocking the breath out of him as his head went back underwater. John thrashed in all directions at the shock of cold, his forearm unintentionally connecting with the seal's skull.

John lifted his head above water and paddled back to the boat. He'd put his knife in the bottom of it when he'd started rowing. *Maybe it didn' fall out when the seals tipped the boat.* John prayed that was so as he pulled himself out of the water.

His eyes scanned the—

There 'tis. He picked up the dagger in his right hand and spun around, ready to defend himself.

He didn't have to wait long, for within seconds, the boat started leaning again. But this time, he had a weapon.

The farmer leaped back into the sea without hesitation and swam under the boat to meet his adversary head-on. The water was murky, but he swiped at the large shape in front of him, his knife connecting with flesh.

The seal drew back, a large slash across its chest, but John wasn't about to let it escape. He moved forward, but a second seal bit down on his left arm.

John held back a wail, his whole body trembling at the sudden pain. He turned and stabbed the second seal in the back, driving the dagger in to its hilt before wrenching it out again.

The seal released him, giving John the opportunity to swim back up. As soon as he'd crested the surface, he called his wife's name once more. *What if the others hurt her?*

A gray head appeared next to John, and relief flooded over him—

Until the seal's face morphed into a snarl.

The farmer's eyes narrowed. *'Tis time to finish this.* He lifted his knife and thrust it forward.

But just before the dagger reached its target, another seal broke through to the surface, directly in the knife's path.

A bloodcurdling cry burst from the seal's mouth as the dagger pierced its belly, so anguished that John was certain he'd seriously wounded it. Maybe even mortally so.

When John pulled the knife out, it was slick with blood.

A third seal head emerged next to the others, and John lowered his dagger. "Ellie?"

But the seal that turned to him wasn't the one that had just resurfaced; it was the one he'd stabbed in the stomach.

Time slowed as John looked into its big black eyes. They looked so frightened, so sad.

The farmer dropped the knife in his hand, instead grabbing the seal before him. When it didn't lurch away and instead melted into his arms, John's worst fears were confirmed. *Ellie, how could I have done this to you?*

The other seals became invisible to his eyes, for they no longer mattered. All that mattered to him lay in his arms. Dying.

Na if I can help it. John frantically pulled the selkie back to the boat, dropping her into it as carefully as he could before heaving himself in beside her.

"Ellie? Is it you?" John whimpered, even though he knew the answer.

The seal was breathing heavily as blood flowed from her wound. John was so horrified at the sight, at what he'd done to her, that he felt almost paralyzed. But he had to get her back to town. He had to get her to the doctor, or she'd be lost.

"Lie still. 'Tis going to be all right."

The farmer's mind was in a daze as he rowed, rowed, rowed, praying for a miracle.

They'd almost gotten to the shore when his wife wheezed, "John . . ."

The farmer whirled around to see that his wife had shifted back into human form and now lay on her back on the boat's floor.

"Ellie!" John leaned toward her and brushed her hair away from her face. The woman's pelt covered her midsection, but John could still see blood pooling onto the boat's floor. Her skin was paler than usual, and her dark eyes seemed distant.

As if she'd already left him.

"I-I'm so sorry, Ellie," John stuttered, eyes brimming with tears. "I didn' mean to—"

The selkie-woman put her fingers to his lips, silencing him with her gentle touch. She smiled weakly. "Shh, 'tis all right."

John kissed her fingers before pressing them over his heart. "Nay, 'tis na all right. Yer hurt. And 'tis my fault."

Ellie shook her head. "I know you were trying to save me."

"I'm going to get you to Dr. Brown," John said, trying to sound reassuring despite how hopeless he felt. There was so much blood. "He'll know what to do."

Ellie's lower lip trembled, her gaze fearful but determined. "You can' take me there."

The farmer's brows pulled together, for he couldn't believe what he was hearing. "What are you—What are you saying?"

"Please, John. No one can know what I am. Think o' what would happen to William."

"But you'll die if I don'! By my own hand. You can' ask me to do that," the farmer replied, his breath coming in pained bursts.

She can' be asking me to just . . . let her die. She can'. I can' lose her.

"No one can know," Ellie repeated, her eyelids drooping.

John grabbed her face in his hands. "Stay with me, Ellie. I'm right here. Stay with me."

The woman blinked a few times, and her eyes refocused on him.

"Why did you do it, Ellie? Why did you get in the way?"

"I had to," she whispered, her voice so faint John could barely hear it. "They're . . . my parents."

John went slack-jawed, suddenly feeling like he had been the one stabbed. "Y-Yer parents?"

Ellie nodded. "Did they make it? Are they all right?"

The farmer glanced back at the water. Nothing stirred nearby. The sea seemed as still as dea—

Wait. What's that over there?

In the distance, a pair of seals moved through the mist. They were slow, clumsy, and—

John's heart clenched. A fin was moving toward them in the water. Even if the selkies could recover from the wounds John had given them, they stood little chance against sharks.

The farmer shut his eyes, wishing he could turn back time. Wishing he'd woken when his wife had risen from the bed. Wishing he'd insisted they leave Orkney, make a life for themselves somewhere safer. Wishing . . .

"John?"

He looked down at his wife, so weak, so beautiful. He took in all her features: her thick brown hair, her black eyes, the light sprinkling of freckles across the bridge of her nose.

"Aye, Ellie. They're going to be fine."

A gorgeous smile lit up her face, so bright it was like the sun after a rainstorm. "I'm glad. Then there's just one more thing."

"What is it, sweetheart?"

"William doesn' know anything about selkies. Please let it stay that way. 'Tis too dangerous o' a life fer him."

"But, Ellie, what if his abilities come? You told me they could come any day now. He's the right age."

"Or they may na come at all. Maybe he'll take more after you," she said, gazing up at him with adoration. "But if they do come, I want you to burn his sealskin."

John drew back, his blood ice-cold. "Burn it? Ellie, that's something that connects him to you. I could never—"

His wife's mouth curled downward. "You have to, John. Trust me."

John's tongue felt as heavy as lead, but he forced himself to say, "All right. I will."

"Thank you. I . . ." Ellie's voice faded away, her eyes drifting shut.

And then her chest stopped moving.

John froze, waiting second upon gut-wrenching second for her chest to rise once more. For the sound of her breath to reach his ears.

But it wasn't to be.

"E-Ellie? Ellie!"

The farmer grabbed her shoulders, trying to compel her eyes to open, but there was no response. Her body lay limp in his arms, an empty vessel, drained of the lovely spirit which had housed it only moments before.

John released a bitter, ugly groan as everything crashed around him. Nothing made sense anymore. Nothing mattered. He wept against her neck, unable to breathe, to think, to do anything as rivers fell from his eyes. Almost as if his body was trying to empty itself, too.

But his stubborn spirit refused to depart as Ellie's had, and while he wished with everything in him to go with her, something unseen held him back.

Something he couldn't quite rememb—

William!

John's eyes snapped open as he came to himself. He didn't know how long he'd been there, but the seals were no longer in sight. He glanced about, realizing the sun would be rising soon.

And that meant he had to get the boat back to the dock before its owner found it missing.

***

John shared as much as he could, though he spared his son the worst details of the pain Ellie had endured. Even so, by the time he'd finished, he was practically blubbering. Saying it aloud brought his guilt and grief to the surface, but it was also cathartic.

He looked up at William and Adaira, nervous about their reaction. Both of them had tears on their cheeks, too, but John wasn't sure if that was a good sign or a bad one.

"What about Mum's body?" William asked, his words dripping with sorrow.

"I buried her next to the garden, just under where her rocking chair used to sit."

William's face lit up with understanding. "So, that's why you go out there so often. You wanted to be near her."

John nodded, staring down at his hands. "I'm sorry I didn' tell you all this from the beginning. I thought I was protecting you by na telling you the truth, but I see now that I was only protecting myself. If you give me another chance, though, I promise I'll try to be the father you deserve."

He felt a timid touch on his shoulder and looked up into his son's red-rimmed eyes.

"Son?"

William sniffled and leaned his head against John's arm, whimpering. The farmer rubbed the boy's back, his heart swelling as hope bloomed in his chest. Hope for forgiveness. Hope for a new start.

And 'tis all thanks to one person, John thought, his gaze darting to the innkeeper's daughter.

The Aftermath

The Burgesses' tender reconciliation was so beautiful it made Adaira feel like she was intruding. She started to wander away to give them some privacy, but then she remembered the deal she'd made.

She pulled William's sealskin out from under her clothes, glad she'd thought to retrieve it before she'd left the inn. She waltzed over to the Burgesses and tapped William on the shoulder.

"I believe I owe you this," she said when the boy turned to her.

William's eyes bulged as Adaira placed the pelt in his hands. He stood shocked for several seconds as he stared at it. "This . . ."

"Belongs to you."

The lad smiled as if she'd just given him the whole world. And in a way, maybe she had. Now he had access to a new world beneath the waves.

A world neither she nor John could ever be a part of.

"You had it with you all along?" John asked. "Why did you bring us all the way out here, then?"

Adaira shrugged. "I wanted to give you the chance to talk to William on yer own."

The farmer stepped toward her, his face glowing with gratitude. *What's he doing? Why is he lifting his hand?*

For the man was reaching out as if he was going to touch her cheek—

But just before his fingers grazed her skin, he stopped, his hand suspended in the air.

"What's wro—" Adaira started to ask, but then she noticed the same thing John must have noticed: it wasn't raining anymore.

Adaira glanced up, her mouth dropping when she saw patches of blue sky above them. The clouds weren't as dark now either, and they were definitely thinning out. "Is it . . . is it over?"

"I don' know," the farmer said. "William, what do you think?" The two adults turned to the boy, who was peering up at the sky with a frown.

"William?" John pressed.

The lad looked at his father, his entire body tense. "I need to go back. Now."

John opened his mouth to speak, but William glared and added, "Da', I have to stop him. What if he's hurting Mistress Briony?"

The farmer hesitated but then sighed. "Fine. But I'm coming, too. No more running off on yer own."

"What about you, Mistress Adaira?" William asked. "You may want to stay—"

"We go *together*," Adaira said firmly. She wasn't about to let the people she loved run headfirst into danger without her, especially when they were going to help Briony.

William's lips curled up at the corners, and he nodded. "Together."

With that decided upon, the three of them bounded back into Torin Woods, Adaira leading the way. *Briony, dearie, I hope yer all right. And if yer na, hold on a wee bit longer. We're coming fer you.*

The heavy wind and rain had damaged much of the forest, uprooting some of the smaller trees and breaking large branches off several of the larger ones. The trio had to watch their step as they went, otherwise they'd end up tripping and falling flat on their faces. Still, they moved quickly, not wanting to waste a precious minute. Not when Briony's life was on the line.

Every so often as they ran, Adaira glanced up, noting how the clouds were steadily disappearing. *That means she beat him, right? She stopped him from attacking Everton. Maybe everything will be under control by the time we get there. I probably don' even need to worry.*

Adaira swallowed several times, her throat incredibly dry despite her attempts at optimism.

And when the three of them arrived, the scene that met their eyes was anything but under control.

***

John gaped at the scorch marks scattered around Drulea Cottage. Spindly black tendrils wove in and out along the otherwise green earth, haunting evidence of the supernatural fight that must have ensued. A single strike could kill someone, and it looked like over thirty lightning bolts had struck the area. *If one o' those bolts hit Mistress Fairborn . . .*

The farmer's eyes scanned for signs of the midwife. He prayed he wouldn't find any.

"Stay close," John told Adaira and William. The area appeared deserted, but Niall might still be nearby.

Adaira gasped and tore off to the right.

"Adaira, 'tis na safe! You can' just—" But John broke off when he saw where she was going. There, at the road's edge, just before the path dipped out of sight, lay a body.

John and William dashed after Adaira, reaching her side as she bent down to Mr. McLaren's body.

"Is he . . ." William started to ask, but he couldn't finish.

"Mr. McLaren, 'tis me, Adaira," the young woman cried, touching the man's arm. When there was no response, she pressed her ear to the fisherman's chest.

As if there was a chance he was still alive.

"He's gone, Adaira," John whispered, rubbing the woman's shoulder.

A dark stain covered the lower half of the fisherman's shirt as well as the ground Mr. McLaren lay on. Blood.

John swallowed thickly, the sight reminding him of Ellie's death. *But why was he stabbed? Couldn' Niall have just killed him with a bolt o' lightning? What was Mr. McLaren doing here, anyway?*

269

Adaira softly wept for a few minutes while John and William stood silently over her. John hadn't realized the mad fisherman meant so much to her. He'd have to ask her more about him later.

"He didn' deserve this," the woman whispered. "He was a good man."

John started to offer some words of solace, but then he noticed that William was no longer next to him. Fear gripped the farmer's heart, and he swung his head around.

He breathed more easily when he spotted the boy a short distance away, examining some scorch marks closer to Drulea Cottage. "William?"

The lad turned and called out, "Come over here. There's something you should see." He pointed to the cottage's entrance.

Is Mistress Fairborn in there? John wondered as he and Adaira hurried over. *Maybe I should go in first in case Mistress Fairborn didn' make it.*

But what William had found wasn't another body. It was a pile of ashes just over the cottage threshold.

"What in the world? Was there a fire in here?" Adaira muttered.

William shrugged and kicked at the ashes, his shoe unearthing a small piece of material. He squatted down to get a closer look. "I think"—The boy turned to John, his expression grave—"'tis a sealskin."

Adaira put a hand over her mouth, her eyes wide with anguish. "'Tis Briony's, isn' it?"

"We don' know that yet," John assured her. "We need to keep looking around."

Adaira slowly nodded. "Aye, yer right. She may be fine."

John smiled encouragingly, wishing he could give her something concrete. He did a quick scan inside the cottage, but the house was empty.

He stepped back outside. *If only there was something here that could tell us more.*

But then John glimpsed something out of the corner of his eye. *Are those . . . clothes?*

The farmer marched over to the edge of the cliff, William and Adaira trailing behind him. As he drew closer, he realized he'd been right: a woman's clothing indeed lay abandoned on the rocky precipice. *Why would Mistress Fairborn take off—*

"Look, down there!" William shouted, gesturing to the sea beneath them.

Something was swimming just below the water's surface!

"We have to get down there," Adaira stated, her hands clenched into fists. Gone was the distraught woman John had comforted earlier; now she looked ready to conquer the world.

"We don' know what's going on," John argued. "We can' just rush into things. 'Tis foolhardy."

Adaira crossed her arms and glared. "Briony's down there. She must have needed to turn into a seal. That's why her dress is here."

"What about the burned sealskin we found? It could be hers."

"Then why would she undress? Besides, she isn' anywhere up here. We've looked. She has to be down there," Adaira said, her voice as hard as steel.

"That's na true at all. What if—"

But all John's assertions evaporated when movement caught his eye. In the heat of the moment, he hadn't noticed something hobble past Adaira. A large, dappled creature with short, smooth fur and strangely intelligent eyes.

And it was heading toward the edge of the cliff.

"William, don'!" John cried, pushing past Adaira to grab the seal before it leaped over the side.

But the farmer's fingers only snatched at the air, for William was already diving toward the dark sea below.

Rescue

William hit the water with a small splash, vanishing from sight before John could stop him.

But the farmer wasn't giving up that easily.

John took a deep breath. He wasn't a strong swimmer, and he hadn't stepped foot in the sea since Ellie's. His skills might not be enough to save his son. *What if I don' get to him in time?*

Something—or someone—was still moving below the water's surface. If it was Niall, there was a strong chance he'd try to drag William off with him.

And beyond that, Ellie had warned John the ocean would try to lure the boy away, try to make him forget his humanity if it could.

John was about to jump when Adaira gripped his arm. "You can' go that way. Look!"

She pointed to several sharp rocks jutting up from the water. If John miscalculated even the slightest bit, he could get impaled.

Adaira tugged him away from the edge before handing him a small pile of clothes. William's clothes. "Let's get Mr. McLaren's boat. I'm sure he won'—*wouldn'* have minded."

John grimaced but nodded in agreement. *If I get hurt, I may na be able to help William.*

Adaira smiled, and the two of them shot down the hill, their feet moving so fast it seemed like they were barely touching the ground.

But it still was too slow. *We need to be there now! William could be—*

John cut the thought short as he and Adaira flew past the inn, through the market, and onto the town pier. A few boats were tied up along it, mostly small fishing boats, but there was a conspicuous gap toward the end. A gap where Mr. Mendes's ship should have been.

Where did it—who would be mad enough to go out in a—Mr. Mendes was arrested, wasn' he?

John shook his head and refocused his mind. That wasn't important right now. All that mattered was rescuing his son.

Adaira bounded past the farmer and stepped into one of the larger vessels. John helped her untie it from the dock and jumped in. He grabbed the boat's oars and rowed with all his strength while Adaira kept a sharp lookout for any sign of seals.

The clouds had all but disappeared from the now-bright sky, for sunrise had come and gone without John realizing. That was good, though, for that would make it easier to find William now. He hoped.

***

When William opened his eyes, he was surprised at how far his vision spanned. The world had been dark when he'd first transformed into a seal, but here in the ocean, everything seemed clear. Sharp. Dazzling. William's seal eyes seemed to pick up even the smallest ray of light as it refracted upon entering the water.

Which meant it took almost no time to discover what was going on down here: a battle.

William stared in shock as Niall and Mr. Mendes grappled with each other a few feet away from him. *How did Mr. Mendes get here?*

The merchant was wielding a knife, but Niall soon knocked it out of the other man's hand. It floated down to the sea floor, a short drop since they were still close to land.

Is Mr. Mendes attacking my uncle, or is it the other way around? William wasn't certain, and he didn't want to go after the

273

wrong person, but if Niall and Mr. Mendes didn't rise to the surface soon, they were going to run out of air. William, on the other hand, felt quite comfortable and got the sense he wouldn't need another breath for a long time.

Before the selkie-boy could decide who to help, though, another seal appeared, seemingly out of nowhere, and bit down on Niall's leg.

William darted behind a large rock on the sea floor, hoping the other seal hadn't seen him. He tried to make himself as small as possible, now wishing he hadn't been so impulsive. If the other seal came after him, William doubted he could out-swim it. And he definitely couldn't outfight it. *I wish Da' was here. . . .*

A shriek filled William's ears, so piercing it sent shudders through his body. *That was Uncle Niall. The seal must be killing him!*

Then Niall cried out in a distorted voice, "Nay! Don'!"

William peeked out from his hiding place just in time to see his uncle sinking while the other seal pulled Mr. Mendes toward the surface. Without hesitation, William surged forward and seized Niall's arm in his mouth.

I have to get him out o' here! The selkie-boy undulated his tail back and forth, propelling them upward. Niall's eyes were closed, and he didn't struggle as William dragged him along. *He must have fainted from being underwater too long. He needs air, or he's going to die!*

William gritted his teeth. *I'm na losing any more family. Na now, na ever!* He zoomed up the rest of the way to the surface, sighing in relief when Niall let out a choked gasp.

He's alive! William started to drift toward shore, but then he paused.

A short distance away, the other seal was hauling Mr. Mendes onto the beach. William didn't want to risk the other seal attacking him, so he swam farther down the coastline until he reached a spot behind some boulders. He heaved Niall out of the water and flopped down in the sand beside him. *Why don' selkies have supernatural strength? That would have been so much nicer.*

William panted, trying desperately to catch his breath, for he knew they couldn't stay here long. Once Everton started waking up, they couldn't afford to be seen.

Questions peppered the boy's mind, questions he had no answers for. *Was that Niall's sealskin we found before? Does that mean he can' turn into a seal anymore? Where will he go? And that other seal in the water—why was it trying to save Mr. Mendes? How did Mr. Mendes get there, anyway?*

William groaned, wishing he could simply sleep away his troubles. *Perhaps I can, just fer a wee bit. . . .*

***

"John, there!" Adaira called, pointing to a small seal on a strip of beach between some rocks. It was lying on its belly near something—

John turned back around before getting a good look and started rowing over. The seal had to be William. It was too small to be an adult. *It has to be him.*

When they reached the shore, John jumped out of the boat with a giant smile that quickly turned sour. A pale body lay on the beach next to his son. Niall Moreland's body.

"What in the world . . ." Adaira mumbled, her face just as disgusted as John's. "Is he . . ."

But it soon became evident that the man was still alive, for his torso was rising and falling. *Is he wounded?*

Niall was lying on his side with his back to William and didn't seem to hear John and Adaira approach. John glanced at the man's face and noticed his eyes were closed. *He's unconscious? Why is he here instead o' trying to steal William away?*

Then John spotted some bright-red gashes on Niall's hand and leg. Gashes that looked a lot like bite marks. *Did William do that to him? Did Niall hurt William?*

The farmer hurried to his son's side, making the seal yelp in surprise. It blinked a few times as if it was just waking up. "Sorry, I didn' mean to frighten you. Are you hurt?"

John didn't know how much William could understand in this form. *Does he even recognize me? Maybe I shouldn' be so close.* He

275

eyed his son warily, staying completely still in case William viewed him as a threat.

But then the seal's mouth curled up in what could only be a smile and rubbed its head against John's shoulder.

The farmer smiled in return, and Adaira, who'd gotten out of the boat just after he had, reached out to stroke William's back.

"We were so worried. Are you all right?" she asked.

The seal nodded before moving over to Niall and extending its flipper toward the man's chest. John's eyes widened as he took a second look at his brother-in-law. The man was bleeding from a deep cut dangerously near his heart.

The wound was a little over two inches wide, straight on one side but rounded on the other. It wasn't bleeding profusely, but the sickly pallor to the man's skin suggested he'd already lost a great deal of blood.

A wave of nausea wracked the farmer's body, and he had to look away to keep himself from hurling. John didn't normally have such visceral reactions to injuries, but this particular sight was a bit too familiar. *That's na a bite mark.*

"What could have made that?" Adaira whispered, her voice shaky.

"A knife," John replied.

The seal barked once and nodded. It tilted its head and stared at John expectantly.

"What is it, son?"

William leaned his head toward Niall, and this time, John understood the message as well as if the seal had spoken aloud: "Save him. Save my uncle."

"Absolutely na! He tried to destroy the whole town. I'm na going to—"

William glared, and John got the distinct sense the seal was trying to tell him it was still the right thing to do.

John sighed in defeat. "Fine." He tore off a piece of his shirt to press against Niall's wound, but when he got close, the man's hand wrapped around his wrist.

"Don' touch me," Niall snarled. Then he opened his eyes, and his expression shifted from anger to confusion. "What are you doing? Did you . . . save me?"

"William did," John said, nodding to his son. "But I need to put pressure on yer wound. Yer losing too much blood."

Niall released John's wrist and closed his eyes once more as the farmer pressed the cloth over the cut. *He seems like he's only barely hanging on. Am I wasting my time trying to save him?*

"Why are you doing this?" Niall coughed. "Why aren' you just leaving me to die?"

Why indeed, John said to himself.

"Because yer family," he growled, "whether I like it or na."

Niall's eyes shot open in surprise, but then he winced as if he was almost ashamed. "I . . . I don' know what to say."

Adaira bent down and practically shoved John out of the way, so she could lock eyes with Niall. "I know what you can say. You can tell us what happened to Briony," she demanded, jabbing the man in the shoulder.

Niall flinched at her touch but didn't look away. "I can only assume she got her dear Mr. Mendes to safety." A smirk came over his face. "If he didn' drown first."

Adaira's face reddened with anger, but before she could reply, William let out a sharp bark.

"What is it, son?" John asked.

The seal shuffled frantically, jerking its head to the left as if it was trying to tell them something.

"Do you know where Briony and Mr. Mendes are?" Adaira asked, clasping her hands together.

William nodded and glanced in the same direction: back to the left, closer to the cliff where Drulea Cottage sat.

"We have to go find them," Adaira insisted, looking to John for support.

The farmer lifted the cloth off Niall's chest and was glad to see the cut had stopped bleeding. *Maybe he's going to be all right, after all. He still needs to see Dr. Sherwin though.*

"I can' leave Niall here by himself," John pointed out.

"But Briony might be hurt even worse than he is. Mr. Mendes, too."

John scowled, for she was right. But he'd already agreed to do what he could for Niall. He turned away from Adaira and tried to think, to piece together some sort of solution that would be best for everyone.

That was when his eyes landed on the small seal beside him. "William, I'm going to need yer help."

In the Eye of the Beholder

"Briony," Adaira called, her ears straining to hear a response. She'd lost track of how many times she'd shouted her friend's name, though, and was no longer surprised when there was no answer.

The woman sighed and continued trekking across the coastline, John at her side. She didn't want to lose hope, but they'd been searching for Briony and Mr. Mendes for what felt like hours.

If Briony was strong enough to get Mr. Mendes to shore, surely she's fine . . . right?

After William had returned to human form, he'd told them of the seal that had helped Mr. Mendes get to safety. *He said he saw them over this way, but maybe he was wrong. If only he hadn' stayed behind with Niall, perhaps we would have found them by now.*

It was still hard for Adaira to believe Niall and William were related. A large part of her wished they hadn't discovered that connection. Then they could have just left Niall behind without feeling guilty about it. Maybe.

Adaira didn't have time to think about it much, though, for her heart was pulsing with fear. Every step they took might be putting closer or farther away from her dear friend.

What if we're na even looking in the right place? There were many islets around Everton. It would be easy for William to get confused. Even the locals could barely keep track of them all.

"John, we're na making any progress. Perhaps they're na even on the beach anymore. Let's go back to the cliff by Drulea Cottage and see if we can spot them from up there." Even though returning meant passing Mr. McLaren's body again, the cliff offered one of the best vantage points in all of Everton. *We should be able to see them from there. . . .*

The farmer readily agreed, and the two of them made their way back up the hill, Adaira trying her best not to wheeze from all the exertion. The village was still quiet as they walked through it, telling Adaira they hadn't been searching for nearly as long as she'd thought.

"Briony!" Adaira cried once they'd gotten to the cliff. She stumbled as she moved toward the edge, her energy all but depleted.

"Adaira, be careful," John warned, grabbing her arms to steady her.

Adaira looked up at the redhead with an exhausted smile. "Thank you. I—" She broke off and spun away from the man, her attention focused outward. She could have sworn she'd just heard something rise over the wind.

". . . Please . . . I'm here," called a voice.

Briony!

Adaira stepped out as far as she dared, her eyes sweeping along the shoreline until they landed on a lone figure. She waved her arms over her head. "Briony, I see you!"

She shouted to John, eagerly pointing to the woman lying on the sand. *She's alive! She's—* Adaira did a double take. *Where's Mr. Mendes? And why isn' she getting up? Is she too wounded to move?*

Adaira bounded down the hill, nearly losing her footing in her haste. She ran like her life depended on it, her previous fatigue completely forgotten. For even though Adaira's life didn't depend on her speed, Briony's might.

But when she'd almost reached her friend, who lay on her back with only a sealskin as a covering, the innkeeper stopped in her tracks. *What if she's already . . . already . . . I don' want to find out.*

Heavy footsteps sounded behind Adaira just before John plowed past her to Briony's side. He fell to his knees and shook the woman's shoulders. "Wake up, mistress. You have to wake up."

The words jogged Adaira from her state of shock, and she went to her friend's other side. She leaned in close to Briony's face, smiling when she heard breathing. *Thank goodness.*

"Let's get her inside. We don' want anyone to see her like this and start asking questions," John said, moving his hand toward her back. He'd only just started lifting the unconscious woman when his expression froze.

"What is it?" Adaira asked, a fluttery feeling building in her stomach.

John frowned and pulled back his hand. It was covered in blood.

Adaira gasped. "H-How did she—I-Is that . . ." But she couldn't find the words she wanted to ask.

"Help me roll her to her side, so we can see how bad 'tis," the farmer told her, and the two of them gently turned Briony over. A pool of blood lay under the midwife, but her only visible injury was a small, round—

"John, is that what I think 'tis?"

The farmer grimaced and moved Briony back to her original position. He peered down at her before pointing to the sealskin. It was still wrapped around the woman's torso, preserving her dignity, but it also had a telltale hole. Right where it touched Briony's upper chest. "That's where the bullet went in. It must have passed all the way through."

"But who would shoot Briony? Niall doesn' have a gun. And where's Mr. Mendes? I thought William said she saved him." Adaira's vision started to go hazy. *Briony's strong, but can she survive a gunshot? Who would do this to her? Briony, you can' leave me like this!*

John grasped her hand in his. "Breathe, Adaira. Those are questions we can ask later. Fer now, let's get her to the inn."

Adaira nodded, her salty tears dripping onto her lips. John placed one hand on Briony's back and the other beneath her knees before rising to his feet. The movement evoked a low groan from the midwife, and Adaira immediately scolded John for not being more careful.

The farmer said nothing, seeming to understand Adaira's worry well enough that he didn't take her rebuke personally. Instead, he took slow, purposeful steps all the way back up the beach to the inn, waiting patiently as Adaira hurried ahead of him to open the front door.

"You can put her in here," the innkeeper said, gesturing to an empty guest room on her left. John lowered Briony onto the bed, his arms quivering as he released her.

"I better go find Dr. Sherwin. I don' think she's bleeding anymore, but that doesn' mean the danger has passed. I need to get back to William and Niall, too." He started to turn away, but then Adaira clutched his hand.

"John, wait."

The farmer stared down at their joined hands, his expression curious and uncertain. Adaira let go and looked away, heat rushing to her cheeks. *I can' just hold his hand like that. John knows about my past now. He doesn' want to be with me anymore. Aye, he's helping me with Briony, but he's na doing it fer my sake. He's doing it because he's a good person.*

"I wanted to say thank you." She peeked up at him from beneath her lashes, hoping she'd see a hint of a smile, but the farmer just nodded and went on his way.

Giving her further validation that the love they'd shared truly was gone.

***

When John ducked out of the inn, he was in such a rush he almost didn't see the person marching directly toward him. "Oh, I'm sorry!" He jumped out of the way at the last second, balancing on his right foot as the other man tried not crash into him.

"Watch where yer going," Matthew Levins grumbled before turning to go inside.

"Wait," John called. "Do you know where Dr. Sherwin is?"

282

The tacksman threw a dirty look at him over his shoulder. "If you hadn' been such a coward and had been around when Everton needed you, you'd already know he's dead."

"Dead?"

Matthew sighed and whirled around. "Aye, a stray bolt o' lightning hit him while he was tending to people at the church. That's where everyone gathers if there's a town emergency. Because the rest o' us care enough to check on each other."

John huffed. "'Tis na like I would know that. And I wasn' being a coward when I helped put out the fire at the tailor shop. I didn' see you there. Are you sure I shouldn' be calling you the coward?"

"Did you at least keep Adaira safe?" Matthew asked, ignoring the farmer's challenge.

"She's fine, but Mistress Fairborn is hurt. Is there anyone else in town who could help her?"

"That commodore brought a surgeon with him. He's over at the church still."

"Can you go get him?"

"What?" Matthew bristled. "Go find him yerself. I don' care what happens to that wench."

John's eyes narrowed, and he took a step toward the tacksman. "Well, you *should* care because she happens to be Adaira's best friend. And if you love Adaira like you seem to, you'll do all you can to help Mistress Fairborn."

Mr. Levins blinked a few times, so flustered he couldn't speak. Whether that was thanks to John's hostility or his bold claim, though, the farmer couldn't tell.

Not that it was an inaccurate claim. John had seen the way the tacksman softened around Adaira. And the way he watched her when he thought no one was looking.

Matthew's expression shifted several times, first displaying shock, then fear, then denial, before eventually settling on bitter defeat. "Fine. I'll get him just so I can be the one who gets the credit fer it."

Enmity gurgled in the farmer's belly, but all he said was, "All right. I have another patient to bring to him." John turned away and darted off. He'd left his brother-in-law in a weak state on the beach. *Is Niall still all right, or were his injuries too severe? If he is still alive and the surgeon helps him, I don' know what I'm going to do. He's too dangerous to go free, but no one would believe me if I said he was responsible fer the storm. And the deaths.*

John swallowed and ran faster, unsure what he hoped to find.

Building Something Better

A while later, the inn's front door opened. Adaira had been restless ever since John left, wishing she knew what to do for Briony beyond hiding her sealskin and covering her with blankets. The midwife seemed to be resting comfortably for now, but Adaira was certain she'd be in agony when she regained consciousness.

If she woke up at all.

"Ah, Dr. Sherwin, I'm so glad yer—" Adaira broke off when she realized an unfamiliar dark-haired man was entering the room. "Who are you?"

"I'm Salvador Vela, surgeon aboard Comodoro Cardoso's ship," the man explained, looking down his nose at her like she was barely worth an introduction.

"Is this the patient?" He shoved past her to examine Briony without waiting for Adaira to answer.

The innkeeper was flabbergasted by the surgeon's rude attitude, but then a second man entered the room. "Matthew, what are you doing here?"

The tacksman smirked. "When I heard Mistress Fairborn was in trouble, I rushed to get the surgeon. I wasn' about to let anything happen to Everton's midwife."

Adaira furrowed her brow, not believing his sudden act of chivalry. "You hate Briony. John was going to find Dr. Sherwin."

Matthew rolled his eyes. "He asked me to help him out. Said something about bringing another patient."

"But where is Dr. Sherwin?" Adaira demanded.

The tacksman's face fell. "Oh, that. Well, he . . . I'm sorry to say he didn' make it."

Adaira took in a sharp breath and put her hand on the wall to steady herself. *Dr. Sherwin is dead?* She wasn't sure how much more loss she could take.

"I'm sorry, Adaira," Matthew said, patting her shoulder a few times. "This storm really hurt the whole town."

Even more than you know, Adaira thought as she swallowed a lump in her throat. She glanced back at the surgeon, who was starting to lift Briony's blankets.

"Stop!" Adaira cried, hurrying over and returning the blankets to their place before the surgeon saw more of Briony than was necessary. "She only has the one injury here." She pointed to the gunshot wound at the top of Briony's chest.

The surgeon's lips pinched together in irritation, as if he couldn't believe she thought she could interrupt him. "I am just examining my patient, senhorita. Unless you think you'd do a better job?"

But Adaira held firm. She wasn't about to let this man— doctor or not—rob Briony of her dignity. Or see the skin between her toes. In a syrupy sweet tone, she replied, "O' course na, sir. But there must be many other people who need yer expertise as well. I know Briony wouldn' want you to neglect them."

Dr. Vela huffed. "I've never neglected a patient in my life, but don't worry, senhorita. Comodoro Cardoso told us we'd be leaving as soon as possible, so I won't spend any more time here than I have to. If your friend has any other injuries besides the one you mentioned, it will be your fault for not allowing me to complete my examination."

Adaira held her palms up. "That's fair. Is there anything I can help you with?"

"Who shot her?"

The innkeeper grimaced and shook her head. "I wish I knew."

***

After the surgeon departed, Adaira stayed close to Briony's side. Dr. Vela had said the midwife could wake at any time, but Adaira didn't quite believe him. Not when Briony was just lying there, looking so much like Bethany had the day she'd died. *You have so much life left to live, Briony. Please fight.*

Townsfolk wandered in and out as the hours rolled by. A few expressed concern for the village midwife, but most just wanted to tell Adaira about all she'd missed in the chaos of the storm. She learned that the tavern's roof was severely damaged and that the Buchanans had lost over half of their crops. She was glad to hear that there hadn't been any other casualties than the ones she already knew of.

"What about Mr. Mendes and Lucia?" she asked after Penelope McGuff told her how Briony had rescued her when her house caught fire. The two of them sat in Briony's room beside the bed. It was nearing lunchtime now, and the midwife still hadn't stirred aside from an occasional groan.

Penelope scrunched up her nose as if she smelled something bad. "That commodore fellow— unpleasant brute—is saying they jumped on their ship as soon as the storm eased up and disappeared."

Adaira's eyes widened. "They're gone? Just like that?"

Penelope nodded. "And now he's running around, demanding someone tell him where they went." She put a hand on her chest. "Gracious. Why he thinks any o' us would know where those fugitives are heading is beyond me. He even went so far as to claim Briony tried to help them escape! When I heard that, I told him how she would never do something so unseemly. . . ."

Adaira stopped listening at that point, for her head was spinning. *I thought he loved Briony. He certainly seemed to. Why would he leave her in such a state?*

He couldn' have been the one who did this, could he?

After Penelope jabbered on for a few more seconds, she realized Adaira was no longer paying attention and was just staring at Briony with a forlorn expression. The older woman patted Adaira's hand. "There, there. I'm sure she'll wake up soon. I better take my leave, but I'll come back morn."

Adaira slowly nodded, not looking up as Penelope saw herself out.

John and William poked their heads into the guest room soon after that.

"How is she?" the farmer asked, waltzing over and placing his hand on Adaira's shoulder.

The woman shook her head, wishing she had something good to share. "There's been no change since you left her. The doctor did all he could, but 'tis up to Briony now."

William walked over to the midwife and stared at her so hard it was like he was trying to look through her.

"William?" Adaira asked. "What is it?"

"'Tis just . . ." The boy turned to the innkeeper with a grin. "Da' told me she's a selkie like me. I have so many questions to ask her when she wakes up!"

Adaira sent John a deadly glare. "That wasn' yer secret to tell."

The farmer held up his hands, his expression sheepish. "I'm sorry. But when Niall left, William was beside himself, thinking he had no one to talk to about selkies. I didn' want him to feel alone."

"Niall what?!" Adaira jumped to her feet. "You let him leave?"

John frowned, immediately on the defensive. "O' course I didn' *let* him! He knocked William out while we were searching fer Mistress Fairborn, and by the time the lad had woken up, Niall was gone. We looked fer him fer hours, but there's no trace o' him."

Adaira growled, hating that that villain had slipped through their fingers. She plopped back into her chair and pressed her fingers to her forehead as she tried to calm down.

"I'm sorry, Adaira," John said, his voice timid and remorseful.

"'Tis na yer fault. I think the last few days have just worn me out," she explained, looking up at the farmer with a weak smile.

John nodded. "In that case, let me take care o' lunch. I'll put something together and bring it to you."

"I better help you," William said. "Yer still a terrible cook."

John rolled his eyes but laughed. "All right, if you insist."

Adaira's lips turned up as she watched them scurry out. She was glad to see them getting along with each other again. *Nay, 'tis more than that. They look like a family again. And even if bringing them back together cost me my chance at happiness, 'twas worth it.*

She glanced back over at her friend, squealing when she saw the woman's eyes open. "Briony! I feared you'd never wake!"

The midwife blinked a few times as she got her bearings, but then her gaze landed on Adaira, and she grinned. She reached out to clutch the innkeeper's hand. "Adaira, you can' know how glad I am to see you."

But the joy on Briony's face was short-lived, for a shadow soon crossed over her countenance as she remembered something. "Santiago, is he . . . Did he leave?"

Adaira winced, hating to be the bearer of bad news. She nodded. "His ship vanished shortly after the storm. Lucia, the captain, they're all gone. I'm sorry, Briony."

She attempted to squeeze Briony's hand as a comforting gesture, but the other woman pulled her hand away and tried to sit up. "Nay, I have to get to him! How long was I out? When did the ship leave?"

"Slow down! Yer in no condition to move, let alone get to the ship. Besides, there's more we need to discuss."

Briony inhaled as if she was about to protest, but Adaira narrowed her eyes. Briony closed her mouth, and Adaira continued, "After the storm passed, John and I went to look fer you. We . . . we found Mr. McLaren. Briony, what happened?"

When the midwife didn't respond, Adaira internally sighed. *You may na want to talk about it, but 'tis time to get everything out in the open.* "You told me the storm was na natural and that you had to leave or more people would get hurt. As yer friend fer over half yer life, I think I deserve an explanation."

Briony shifted uncomfortably in the bed and refused to make eye contact with the innkeeper.

Adaira bent down to the locked chest beneath the bed. She pulled it out and inserted the key she'd been carrying in her pocket. Inside was Briony's sealskin.

"Does it have something to do with this?" she asked, lifting the pelt and holding it out to the midwife.

Briony's gaze darted over, but the moment she saw what Adaira had, she gasped. "Nay, it can' be!" She grabbed the sealskin and inspected it, her hands pausing when they grazed the bullet holes.

"I'm sorry, dearie. I'm so sorry."

The midwife frowned, as if she didn't understand Adaira's words. "This is—"

"—Yers. I know."

"What? How do you know that?" Briony's mouth fell open.

Adaira gave her a miserable smile. "You've always been a wee bit different, haven' you? After that day on the beach when I saw yer webbed toes and then the seals came . . ."

This is it. This is my moment to tell her what Bethany said, to tell her I've been protecting her secret all these years.

But a bolt of fear shot through her, and instead, she said, "I started to wonder if calling you a changeling was na that far off. I thought maybe you'd summoned the seals to rescue you, and if I was mean to you again, you might set them on me. That's the real reason I became yer friend. Na because I felt bad fer what I'd done, but because I feared what you might do to me."

Why did I do that? I should have told her everything. My promise to Bethany doesn' apply anymore.

Adaira gathered her courage to reveal the rest of the truth, but before she could, Briony snapped, "Are you saying this friendship has been a lie?"

The innkeeper went pale. "Nay! Nay, that's na it at all!"

This is na how I wanted this to go. I need to fix it!

"Aye, the friendship started under false pretenses, but it did na take long before I realized how good o' a person you are. A far better person than I am," she finished pitifully.

"Because you thought I would hurt you if we weren' friends."

Adaira dropped her head, overwhelmed with shame. *How awful I sound when you say it that way.*

"Adaira, that does na make sense! Think o' all the times I've been bullied, and I've never hurt anyone fer it."

Adaira's stomach twisted. *Aye, that's true, except . . .*

She wrung her hands, for she had to ask the question that was plaguing her. She looked up into her friend's hurt-filled amber eyes. "What o' Alastair then?"

Briony shook her head. "You really think I could do something like that?! I had nothing to do with his death!"

"We were only bairns then . . ." Adaira babbled. "I would na blame you fer it. He was horrible to everyone, but he always treated you the worst. If I had that kind o' power and he'd gone after me, I might have done the same thing just to protect myself."

The midwife's eyes clenched shut as if she was only barely keeping her temper in check. Adaira glanced out the window, but the sky seemed didn't look any darker. Yet.

"'Twas na I who killed him! 'Twas Niall."

Adaira froze. "What? Niall?" She looked at the heartbroken woman before her, the one she'd dared to call her friend.

How could I have thought her capable o' killing Alastair? O' course 'twas Niall. Why didn' I realize that before? And now I've accused her o' murder.

"Briony, I-I'm sorry," Adaira stuttered. "I suppose I should have known 'twas na you."

"Do you know what helped me get through all the abuse over the years? What kept me from losing my mind?" Briony's voice grew louder. "'Twas having you as my friend!"

Finally, the midwife opened her eyes, and Adaira could clearly see all the hurt she'd just caused shining back at her. *She hates me.*

"I—"

"Leave, Adaira. I . . . I need to be alone."

The innkeeper ran from the room, tears rolling down her face. She didn't stop until she reached the kitchen, where she pressed her face against the wall. *Now I've done it. Good job, Adaira. I've lost the only family I had left.*

Breathe. Just breathe. I can figure this out, right?

"Adaira?"

The woman broke down in sobs and fell into John's arms, bawling just as much as she had when her father had died. For this felt like yet another death, one that deserved proper mourning.

John said nothing for a long time and simply rubbed her back. "I'm so sorry, Adaira. Did Mistress Fairborn na make it?"

Adaira stepped out of the man's embrace and shook her head. "'Tis na that. Briony is all right, but . . . I've been keeping the truth from her fer a long time. I knew she was a selkie before she did, but her mother made me promise na to tell her. I didn' want to lie to her anymore, so I tried to be honest."

"Her mother made you promise na to tell her? What?" John waved his hands. "Wait, you can tell me about that later. What did Mistress Fairborn say after you told her the truth?"

"She got so upset that I couldn' even finish before she sent me away. I don' think she wants to ever see me again."

"I'm sure that's na true," the farmer said, wiping a tear from her eye.

"But 'tis!" Adaira insisted, turning away from him. "You didn' see her face. I shouldn' have told her anything. I should have just kept the truth bottled up like I always have. 'Twould have been better."

John tapped her cheek to get her to look at him once more. "You and I both know the toll that can take. Even though she didn' receive it well, you did the right thing."

Adaira stared into his sky-blue eyes, wondering how he could be so sure. "The price o' telling the truth feels too high this time."

She's my best friend, the one who has always been there fer me. She was there when my mum died. She was there when Henry left. And I want her to be here fer me when you leave, too.

"Sometimes being honest costs us dearly, but 'tis still our responsibility na to lie to those we love. And if we work hard at it, perhaps we can build something better than what was there before."

The farmer's gaze trailed down to her lips, making Adaira's breath catch. *Am I imagining it?* She leaned slightly forward, waiting for him to kiss her.

But instead of bridging the gap between them, the farmer stepped back. "You said you didn' finish explaining everything to her. I believe the best thing you can do now is go back and try again."

If only she'd gotten the chance.

Frozen

A short while later, John glimpsed Adaira out of the corner of his eye. He smiled and placed a bowl of soup on the kitchen counter. "William and I just finished. Be careful, though, because 'tis very hot." He turned and quickly filled two more bowls, one for William and one for himself.

"He means *I* just finished," William corrected as he grabbed some spoons. "I did almost all o' it. Da' only—What's wrong?"

John spun around, his eyes immediately going to Adaira's face. He hadn't noticed before, but the flush she'd had earlier from crying had been replaced by such a wan countenance she looked like she might faint. He hurried around the counter and grasped her arms. "Do you need to sit down?"

Her only response was a hesitant nod, so John helped her to the nearest chair. She took a few shallow breaths, clenching and unclenching her fingers several times.

"Mistress Adaira?" William asked. "What is it?"

"They're taking her away," she whispered.

John's protective instincts flared. "Who? Who's taking her away?"

But Adaira didn't need to answer, for a great clatter of footsteps came from the hall. John strode over to see who was causing all the commotion, his jaw dropping when he saw the commodore and two of his men carrying Mistress Fairborn out of her room on a stretcher.

"What are you doing? You can' move her! How did you even get in here?" John hadn't heard anyone come through the front door.

They must have come in through the door at the back o' the hallway. Well, they're na getting out that way if I can help it. John shuffled past them and made a point of standing directly between them and the door. William and Adaira, who'd followed John, appeared on the other side of the corridor, effectively blocking the sailors in.

Comodoro Cardoso barked orders at his men in Portuguese. The two men stopped and slowly eased the stretcher to the floor. He turned to John with a sneer. "If I'm to retrieve Senhor Mendes, I need her with me. That means you're in my way."

John pushed his shoulders back, saying nothing.

"Ah, so you're aware. Then I assume you also know the consequences of opposing the Portuguese government?"

"John, you better let them go," Adaira urged.

"But, Adaira, Mistress Fairborn needs to rest until she recovers."

Briony, who had been silently watching the exchange, inclined her head toward the farmer. "Mr. Burgess, don' worry about me. I'll be all right." She twisted her lips up into a half-smile.

"My surgeon will take excellent care of her, I assure you," Cardoso added in a condescending tone.

John huffed but stepped aside. "If yer sure, Mistress Fairborn."

"Aye, thank you, Mr. Burgess."

The farmer scowled as Cardoso and his men went by, not liking this one bit. *She may be a selkie, but she's very weak right now. And I don' trust the commodore one bit.*

Once Briony and the sailors were gone, John turned to Adaira. "I don' understand why we're letting her go."

The woman sighed. "I hate it, too, but Briony thinks she can handle it, so I'm going to trust her. After how much I've let her down, 'tis the least I can do."

The following days flew by as townsfolk did their best to forget the terrible storm that had ravaged their home. Buildings were repaired, market stalls were rebuilt, crops were resown. But not everything could go back to the way it had been before. Not when lives had been lost.

Vicar Peterson presided over a joint funeral for Terrence Stubbins, Vincent McLaren, and Dr. Ewan Sherwin once eight days had passed[28]. The whole town showed up—probably more for the doctor than for Terrence or Vincent—but the vicar was kind, giving each man equal praise as he recounted their deeds. Adaira hadn't even been aware of several of the things he said about Terrence, and by the end of the funeral, she wondered if she'd really known her father at all.

She received many heartfelt condolences as the villagers began to disperse, but the emptiness within her was difficult to bear. She'd lost far more people than was fair, and without Briony here, she felt more alone than ever.

John and William hadn't stood with her during the ceremony, and Adaira knew everyone was secretly wondering about it. She didn't know why John hadn't plainly stated that they weren't betrothed anymore, but she knew someone would ask her soon.

Once everyone had left the churchyard, Adaira drifted back toward the inn. Rather than going straight inside, though, her feet took her to the pile of stones by the gate. Her mother and father's bodies were next to each other now, but her son had been buried alone. Her thoughts drifted as she stood in front of the unmarked grave. Perhaps her father had known what this place was all along, and that was why he'd never removed the stones.

Adaira lifted her gaze to the sky and whispered, "I miss you, Da'. I hope yer finally happy now that yer back with Mum." She knew Vicar Peterson vehemently believed any child who died without being christened was destined for eternal

---

[28] Orcadian tradition required corpses to remain in their homes for eight days before burial.

suffering, but Adaira's heart told her differently. "Give my peedie[29] boy a hug fer me, Da'. And tell him I'm sorry. I'm sorry to both o' you."

A rustle caught her attention, and she turned to see John a few feet away. He held a bouquet of wildflowers in his hand. His eyebrows were drawn together in a sad, pensive expression. "Is this it?"

The woman tilted her head to the side. "Is this what?"

"Is this where he's buried? Yer son, I mean."

Adaira sucked in a sharp breath. *He knows.* She wasn't surprised exactly; she'd been too emotional as she'd told William her story. But it was still jarring to hear him say it aloud.

The farmer's face was unreadable as he stepped forward. *Are the flowers fer me?* She almost held out her hand, but then John walked past her and laid the bouquet in front of the stones.

After all the tears Adaira had shed at her father's funeral, she hadn't thought she could cry anymore today. The abrupt tightening in her throat told her otherwise. *Why is he doing this? He should want nothing to do with me now that he knows what I did.*

Unless he—

Stop, Adaira. You were wrong before. He could never want to be with someone like you.

"Thank you," she said, coughing to hide the tremor in her voice. "When are you and William planning to go back to Hollandstoun?"

It hurt to ask the question, for part of her was still wishing they would stay, but Adaira knew she was going to have to accept it sometime. The sooner she did, the sooner her heart could heal.

The farmer kept his back to her, but his shoulders stiffened as if her words had injured him, too. "What was his name?"

"What? I asked when you and William were leaving."

John whirled around, his eyes locking onto hers. "I know that," he said coldly. "But I wanted to know yer son's name."

---

[29] Small.

The tears she'd been holding back sprang to her eyes. "He doesn't have one, all right? Why do you want to know, anyway? To mock me? To tell the whole town Briony isn' the one they should have been shunning?" She let out a bitter laugh before continuing, her voice growing louder and louder. "I know what I did was wrong. And I know I can' take it back, but I've spent all my time since then trying to make up fer it. Even though I know 'twill never be enough!"

She threw her face in her hands, letting herself feel the full weight of her shame. This was the truth she'd been hiding from, the reality she hadn't wanted to face. Nothing she did would be enough. Nothing. She'd always be the woman who had done the unthinkable, the woman who wasn't worthy of love or friendship or forgiveness.

A calloused hand on her arm interrupted her wailing, and she reluctantly looked up. Condemnation, judgment, disgust— those were the emotions she was fully prepared to see as she met the farmer's gaze.

But John's face held none of them. His eyes were soft as they beheld her. Almost as if he was sad for her. "Adaira, we've all done things we regret. You know I've done more than my fair share."

"Then why are you punishing me?"

The farmer shook his head. "I'm na trying to. I only asked because I care. Because I wanted you to have someone you could talk to about—" He gestured toward the stones. "I wasn' trying to make you feel worse fer it."

"But you did. I can' think o' him without remembering what a horrible person I am."

"Yer na a horrible person, Adaira."

The woman scoffed. "I'm na someone you could marry, though, am I? Na someone you could be proud o' or trust to help raise yer son."

John grabbed her hands, his eyes burning with such intensity Adaira flinched. "Stop putting words in my mouth. I never said any o' those things. Yer the one who ended our betrothal, and yer the one keeping us apart now."

What? Adaira couldn't have heard that right.

The farmer's grip loosened, and he lowered his head. "'Tis up to you what happens from here. You can stay frozen, afraid to love, afraid to move forward. Or you can forgive yerself." John's gaze flicked back to her, and she thought she saw a hint of a smile. "I know what I hope you choose."

Without waiting for her to respond, John released her hands and stepped back.

Undeniably Worthy

Adaira remained at the stones for a long time as she mulled over John's words. *He still wants me even after knowing everything. Being honest didn' ruin my chances with him.*

She grinned until his final words came back to her: "You can stay frozen . . . or you can forgive yerself."

Forgive myself? Adaira could hardly believe she was considering such a thought. Not after what she'd done.

But if I could let go o' my past, a beautiful future could be waiting fer me.

Heavy footsteps approached from behind her. Figuring John must have returned, she said, "I don' know if I can do it."

"Don' know if you can do what?" asked a deep voice. One that definitely wasn't John's.

Adaira grimaced. *Why do I do this to myself?*

"Matthew." She turned to the tacksman with a tight smile. "I thought you were someone else."

"I guess I'm just na someone on yer mind very much." There was palpable distress in the blond man's tone, but before Adaira could ask him about it, he continued, "You didn' answer my question though. What is it you don' know if you can do?"

"Oh, that . . ." Adaira touched her face, feeling the telltale blush on her cheek. She was tempted to lie, but he'd always been so kind to her that instead she said, "Have you ever done something so bad you'd do anything to keep people from finding out about it?"

"Aye, I have," he said firmly.

Adaira frowned, the man's earnestness piquing her curiosity. *What could he have possibly done?*

She cleared her throat when she realized he was waiting for her to go on. "What if yer guilt made it impossible to find happiness? Should you let it go, or should you keep holding onto it since you can never fix what you've done?"

The man's expression darkened, and he didn't speak for a long moment. "I think yer looking at this all wrong. Yer na the same person you were before. The Adaira who made the mistake is long gone, and a new Adaira stands in her place. A wiser, kinder, more compassionate one. And she is undeniably worthy o' happiness."

Adaira stared at the tacksman in amazement. "You . . . you really believe that?"

Matthew stepped forward until there was only a small distance between them. "I do."

The woman beamed from ear to ear, for it was like his words had opened a locked door in Adaira's heart, and now she could step through to the other side. Maybe forgiving herself wasn't so impossible, after all. "Thank you, Matthew."

The tacksman broke eye contact and turned away, seemingly uncomfortable with her praise. *Or maybe he doesn' want to stand so close to me. We are almost closer than is appropriate.* Adaira took a step back.

"I better get going now," he muttered. The pain she'd heard in his voice before was back again.

"Matthew? Are you all right?"

He chuckled, but didn't look in her direction. "You know, I think that's the first time you've ever asked me that, but the truth is nay, I'm na all right."

"What—What's wrong?"

But Matthew didn't respond or even glance at her; instead, he started brushing off his pants leg like she hadn't spoken.

She touched his shoulder. "Matthew?"

The man looked up, shifted slightly away from her, and smiled. "'Tis nothing."

"Are you sure?" Adaira asked, moving closer, so she could gauge whether or not he was being honest with her.

Matthew again appeared nervous at her proximity, but he kept the smile on his face. "Truly! You don' need to concern yerself with me. I'm fine. I'm always fine."

"Well, thank you fer what you said," Adaira replied, choosing not to press him further. "You've given me a lot to think about."

"I'm glad I could be o' help. I really do need to be going now."

"I'll see you later, then," Adaira said with a nod.

Her eyes followed Matthew as he ambled away, grateful for the man's friendship despite his flaws. She didn't know what she'd done that he treated her so differently, but she appreciated the wisdom he had to offer. *He could stand to be kinder to his neighbors though*, she thought with a frown.

But after all he said, where does that leave me?

The innkeeper's gaze drifted to the ocean beyond Everton Inn. She'd been watching the waves ever since Briony left on the commodore's ship, but so far, the only boats she'd seen belonged to her neighbors. *Are you even going to come back, dearie?*

Adaira wouldn't blame her if Briony didn't. Everton had always mistreated the lovely midwife. And now that she knew Adaira wasn't the friend she'd pretended to be, there wasn't much to come back to.

That's na true, she argued with herself. *I may na have been completely honest with her over the years, but my love fer her is real. She has to know that.*

A dark speck just below the horizon caught Adaira's eye. It was so small she could barely see it, but it was moving toward Everton. Fast.

The woman squinted against the rays of sunlight reflecting on the water. *What is that?*

Adaira gasped and made a mad dash for the beach. She didn't bother following the road but instead cut through the churchyard, over the path to the vicarage, behind the tailor shop, and down to the shore. Vicar Peterson happened to be walking toward his home as she went by, but she barely heard his shouts of disapproval. Not when she was positive that she'd just seen a seal.

No wonder I couldn' find Briony's sealskin. Adaira had searched for it for days after the midwife's departure. When she hadn't been able to find it, she'd feared one of her neighbors must have stolen it. *But Briony had it with her all along!*

The innkeeper skidded to a stop when she reached the sand. She pushed her curly ringlets out of her face and scanned the shoreline. *I thought this was where the seal went, but maybe I was wro—*

A bark interrupted her thoughts, and the woman's head swiveled around. A grey seal was peeking out from behind a large rock on the beach, its black eyes trained on Adaira.

"Briony? Is that you?"

The seal's head went up and down in a distinct nod.

"Oh, I'm so glad to see you! But why are you still a seal? Why don' you—" Adaira broke off, her mouth forming an "O" as understanding hit her. "You need clothes, don' you?"

Another nod.

Adaira held out her hand. "Wait right there. I'll go get some." She rushed back to the inn and snatched up a pink dress from her room. When she returned, the seal was waiting there anxiously, its nose sniffing the air as if checking for predators. "This should fit," Adaira said as she placed the dress on the ground. She turned away to give the selkie some privacy.

"Thank you," Briony murmured a few minutes later.

Adaira spun around, her heart both overjoyed and anxious at the sight of her dear friend. Briony's long black hair was matted, and her skin was paler than usual. Bruises and cuts lined her arms, and there was a haunted look in her eyes as if she'd seen far more than anyone should.

"Briony, what happened?"

A choked whimper rose from the selkie's throat, and Adaira instantly held out her arms. Briony fell into them willingly, weeping against Adaira's shoulder for several minutes. Their positions reminded Adaira very much of how Briony had embraced Adaira as she'd wept over her father's death.

That's na why Briony's crying, is it? Did someone pass away?

"Is Mr. Mendes . . . ?" Adaira trailed off when she felt Briony flinch. Whatever had transpired while the midwife was gone, she wasn't ready to talk about it yet. *That's all right, Briony. Take all the time you need. But I've got a lot I need to say to you, so I hope yer ready to listen.*

The innkeeper stepped out of her friend's embrace and grabbed her hands. "Let's get you inside. You look like you could use a cup o' tea."

Briony nodded, her mouth quivering with emotion. "I'm so glad I got back to you."

Adaira smiled and pressed their foreheads together. "So am I, dearie. So am I."

***

John sat in a rocking chair out behind Everton Inn. He'd been there for a while now, peering at the skyline. William was out playing with friends, taking some time to enjoy normal activities after the life-altering events of the past few days. John was glad of it, too, for the farmer was nearly worn out from all the questions his son had been asking him. They'd spoken of Elene often, laughing and crying over shared memories they hadn't thought about in ages. William had also asked several questions about selkies that John hadn't been able to answer, but he'd told his son they could think on those mysteries later. Together.

He still wanted to be cautious about William using his gifts, but the farmer now realized suppressing them wasn't the solution. They were part of William's identity and, as such, deserved to be understood. And enjoyed.

What that would look like, though, John hadn't a clue.

The farmer took a deep breath. The sky was calm today, peaceful. Or perhaps it was just John's heart that was calm, for the anxiety that had been squeezing it for the past six months was finally gone. William knew the truth now, and miraculously, John hadn't lost him.

But that's all thanks to Adaira. Her bravery created that miracle. He craned his neck back toward the inn, wondering what the innkeeper was doing. He hadn't seen her since he'd told her he still wanted to be with her. He was tempted to seek her out and declare his love once more in the hopes it would convince her to accept it. To accept him, flaws and all.

But he needed to give her some space. She'd been through so much, far more than he'd realized when he'd first proposed. If he pushed too hard, she might agree to marry him out of obligation instead of desire. And John would never want that.

The man's stomach rumbled, reminding him that he hadn't eaten all day. *I'll just grab something from the kitchen and eat in my room. Adaira may na be ready to talk to me yet.*

He rose and marched toward the inn, but before he'd reached the door, it opened. There stood Adaira, her face lighting up at the sight of John. "I was looking fer you."

The farmer's eyebrows rose, hope kindling in his chest. He slowly approached her. "You were?"

"Briony's come home," the woman declared, giggling with joy.

John stumbled mid-stride. "Oh, that's . . . wonderful. Is she all right?"

Adaira's face sagged a bit, but she nodded. "I just sent her back to Drulea Cottage. She—she hasn' told me what happened yet, but 'tis weighing heavily on her. I'm going to give her some time to sort through it all before I ask her."

John rubbed the back of his neck. "And did you tell her the rest o' what you needed to say?" In the last few days, Adaira had explained to him how Briony's mother had forced Adaira to keep Briony's heritage a secret all these years. John had been so angry to hear what Bethany Fairborn had done, but when he'd voiced his displeasure, Adaira had asserted that the deceased midwife had simply been trying to protect her child. Much like John had.

"I did," the woman confirmed, her gaze trailing away from his. "She didn' say much, but she listened." Her eyes found his again, and she said firmly, "Thank you fer encouraging me to tell her. Even though 'twas hard to do, I believe Briony and I can start over now. And I think our friendship will be even stronger fer it."

John smiled. "I'm very glad to hear that. After all the loss you've experienced, 'tis time you gained something instead."

Adaira's mouth twisted into a funny shape, almost as if she was trying not to laugh. "I hope that's na all I am to gain."

The farmer's stomach tensed. "What do you mean?"

The innkeeper leaned forward in a very deliberate manner, her thin lips curling into a smirk as she brought her face close to his. "I mean, I was thinking 'twas about time I got married."

John mirrored her smirk, warmth growing in his chest. "Oh, you were thinking that, were you? I take it you've made yer decision, then?"

Adaira nodded and rocked back on her heels, her playful expression turning shy as she awaited his response.

John held back a chuckle, for the woman had no idea how adorable she looked. "In that case—"

"Just kiss her already!" shouted a voice.

The farmer's eyes widened, and he and Adaira whirled around, both their faces as red as John's hair.

"Well?" William said, his hands on his hips. The lad stood a few feet away in the grass, his face impish. "Are you going to or na?"

John rolled his eyes. "You know better than to tell me what to do," he scolded, his lips threatening to lift at the corners.

The boy shrugged. "I'm just helping."

"Mhmm." The farmer tapped Adaira on the shoulder, and as soon as she'd turned, he said, "You heard him."

And before she could utter a word, John pressed his mouth to hers.

Epilogue

Five weeks later

"Stop worrying," Briony ordered as she adjusted the garland on Adaira's head. "If that person was going to tell, 'twould have already happened. 'Tis yer wedding day! Whoever 'tis is a wee bit late."

Adaira scratched at her shoulder; ever since she'd put on this beautiful dress, she'd felt terribly itchy all over. She wasn't used to such finery, and she knew she didn't deserve to wear white. But it had been her mother's dress, and Briony had told her she would stick pins in her if Adaira tried to take it off. "Aye, but—"

"Besides, even if the whole town did find out, would that change what yer going to do today? John knows the truth and still loves you. Are you going to walk away from him because yer frightened?"

Adaira shrugged. "I suppose na."

"Good," Briony stated, lifting the younger woman's chin. "People are going to be arriving fer the wedding walk[30] soon. Are you ready?"

---

[30] Before a traditional Orcadian wedding, all those attending the ceremony would arrive at the bride's house. From there, they would embark on a formal march to the church.

Adaira nodded, but her heart was fluttering in her chest. "Thank you, Briony. If you weren' here, I don' think I could make it through this."

Briony scoffed. "Nonsense. You'd be fine."

A knock sounded at the door, and both women started. "That'll be Mr. McGuff with his fiddle. I'll go let him in and give him his pudding[31]." She spun Adaira toward the mirror. "While I do that, you just marvel at how gorgeous you are."

Adaira winced, for she'd managed not to look up to this point. She'd barely been able to keep down her breakfast, and the sight of herself in wedding attire might be more than she could handle.

But one quick peek wouldn' be too bad, right?

The innkeeper's eyes darted to her reflection, and she stopped dead at the breathtaking woman in the glass. Red, yellow, and pink wildflowers sat atop her brown hair, which flowed in curly tresses down to her shoulders. Her mother's simple yet elegant white dress fit almost perfectly, accentuating Adaira's natural curves. Briony had done a splendid job on her makeup as well, highlighting Adaira's warm brown eyes and making her lips appear fuller than they ever had.

But what made Adaira the most surprised wasn't the grandeur of her clothes or makeup or hair. It was her smile. She hadn't realized before that she was smiling, but now that she had, the effect was so powerful that she almost seemed to glow.

And this was a genuine smile. Not one she'd put on to pretend she was happy. She *was* happy. Happier than she'd been in a long time. For she was about to marry the man she loved. The man who loved her. The real her.

And that knowledge gave Adaira the courage to walk out the door.

***

---

[31] It was customary for the fiddler to receive a special pudding prior to the wedding march.

The celebration lasted long into the night, complete with music, dancing, and merriment. Everton weddings were always festive occasions, but Adaira's neighbors seemed particularly jolly for this one. Perhaps it was because the town's last ceremony had been her father's funeral. Or perhaps it was because everyone agreed that she and John were such a perfect match for each other.

And indeed, they were a perfect match. Not just because their personalities fit well but also because they both understood loss in a way many people didn't. They both understood the power of a deception, even one done with good intentions. And they both knew the importance of moving forward and not letting their pasts define them.

Adaira danced from partner to partner, laughing so hard she could barely breathe. Nothing could steal her joy tonight. Nothing. She didn't even mind that Henry had brought his betrothed, Mistress Wood, who didn't seem to care for Adaira in the slightest.

By the time guests had started drifting off to their own homes, Adaira was utterly worn out. But before she and John turned in for the evening, there was one more thing they needed to do.

Adaira grabbed her husband's hand and led him down Mary's Hill. They didn't speak as they walked, but she could tell John was confused when she didn't take him into the inn. Instead, she strolled over to a small pile of weathered stones. Her son's grave.

"I wanted to change the answer I gave you before," she explained, leaning into John's side. "My son's name is Hugh."

"Why did you choose that name? Is there someone in yer family named Hugh?" the farmer asked.

Adaira shook her head. "It means heart, and I chose it because he shall always be a part o' mine."

"I wish I could have met you, Hugh," John whispered, bending down on one knee to touch the stones. "I wish I could have been part o' yer life. But more than that, I wish you could have gotten to know yer mum. She's an amazing woman."

Tears glittered in Adaira's eyes, her heart simultaneously tearing apart and knitting back together as she watched the exchange. Even though she'd lost so much of her family, today, she and John and William had started a new family. One Adaira would fight for with all her strength.

"Did I miss it?" asked a smooth voice.

John and Adaira turned, their eyes widening when they saw the figure behind them.

"I was trying so hard to make it on time," Niall sneered. "After all, 'tis frightfully inconsiderate to miss a family wedding."

Author's Note

Thank you for coming along with me on this exciting ride! I hope you enjoyed reading this as much as I enjoyed writing it. For those of you wondering, yes, there is a new book coming. I love cliffhangers, but I'm not so mean as to add one here without also having plans for a third book. For news on that and other upcoming releases, visit www.clairekohlerbooks.com and become a website member. You'll then have access to inside information, my author newsletter, and exclusive content, such as character profiles and backstories.

And be sure to leave an Amazon review to let everyone know what you thought of the book.

www.ingramcontent.com/pod-product-compliance
Lightning Source LLC
Chambersburg PA
CBHW021224310726

48971CB00006B/1674